Our Lady of the Dunes

a novel by

Jeannette de Beauvoir

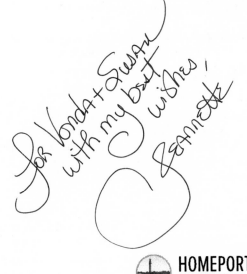

HOMEPORT
PRESS

OUR LADY OF THE DUNES

Copyright © 2016 by Jeannette de Beauvoir

Published by HomePort Press
PO Box 1508
Provincetown, MA 02657
www.HomePortPress.com

ISBN   978-0-9974327-5-6
eISBN   978-0-9974327-4-9

Cover Design by Kyre Song

Our Lady of the Dunes is a work of fiction. Names, characters, places, situations, and incidents are the products of the author's imagination and used fictitiously. Any resemblance to actual events, locales, or persons, living or dead, is purely coincidental.

For Cherry, with love

Other Books by Jeannette de Beauvoir

In Dark Woods
Deadly Jewels
Asylum
Murder Most Academic (as Alicia Stone)

Prologue

I wish you could see the dunes as I saw them that year, traveling out from Boston for the first time, young and impulsive and more than a little frightened. They were the last thing on our journey out to the lower Cape, the outer Cape, stretching out for miles; and all that was beyond them was the sea.

There were the dunes, and in them there were the dune shacks.

The shacks surprised you, appearing where nothing had been at first glance, clinging organically to the sand or standing oddly and majestically separate from it on stilts; some of them barely noticeable, others obvious, silhouetted against the sea. They were all baking under the hot sun that June, pressed down into the sand until they seemed to be part of it.

Later, when I saw them in bad weather, they seemed as grotesque and gnarled and crippled as the trees that still manage to live in this apparent desert, wind-swept and frightening. Then, the dune shacks seem to grow out of the sand, not be pressed into it; growing like gnomes—or something else, something mysterious, something with an ulterior motive.

They were my world for so short a time, yet it was the only time, I've often thought since, that really mattered. It was the time when I was the most alive, the most myself: Jessica Stanford, Girl Growing Up. In a very real way, everything that has happened to me since that summer has been postscript.

And in that time, during that real time, the time I spent in the dune shack, I wrote my narrative of myself. We're all doing that, all the time, aren't we? Inventing and reinventing ourselves, writing the story of our lives even as we're living them, reworking a scene here and an episode there, reliving some memories and putting others away... and all so that we can make sense of who we are. There are so many conflicts inside every one of us that we need to keep the fiction alive somehow that we are rational, coherent individuals. We're such a kaleidoscope of selves: to capture any one of them is nothing more than a temporary explanation, an ongoing work.

Most of us keep doing it, every day, every moment; but I think that my own narrative was written in its final form during that summer and the book has, since then, gone out of print. Been closed up, gathering dust, the final words written, even though the final years haven't yet been lived.

I shake the thought, twitching my shoulders as though to shrug it off. I'm not here to be morbid. I'm here... well, I'm not really sure why I'm here. I'm hoping that the dunes will tell me.

Who was I, then? The proper young Bostonian with the touch of rebellion, or the seaweedy wild woman at the brink of civilization and the edge of her own life? The lady... or part of the dunes themselves? Maybe that's what I've come to find out, too.

Things have changed since I lived here. Even the people out in the Province Lands are different now; they're almost respectable, or at least they aspire to be. Folks may still be living out here, but they're less eccentric, less marginalized, than the people who lived on the backshore in my time. No crazies with piles of newspaper filling their shacks, or mementoes of more bohemian times, or pictures of sparrows. There are coyotes living in the dunes these days instead of foxes; their raw cry, I am told, fills the night,

And the National Seashore forbids nudity, now.

There's a poet in the dunes, I hear, who talks to the birds just as Sophie once did, and an artist or two (for what is an artist without some eccentricity?); but most of the shacks serve as summer homes, now, for those who want peace and simplicity on their vacations. It's not the same.

I knew I was wrong to come back.

***

Louis' shack, our dune shack, is still there.

Am I surprised? I must be, I suppose, or I wouldn't have said that. Perhaps in some childish way I still believe that if I'm not looking at something, it ceases to exist.

And I turned my back on the dune shack and everything that happened there a long time ago.

I walk out to see it, though I could have taken the dune taxi, which now, I understand, takes tourists out into the dunes to gawk and sigh. But I am walking: it's my first time back in Provincetown, the first time I've dared come. In the year since my husband died I've been taking stock of who I am, and that includes who I once was. It was that thought that drove me out here, finally.

The dunes are more difficult to walk in than I remember, though their windswept hollows and graceful lines haven't changed; the memory of those hills is etched permanently in my heart, their climbs and descents part of my muscle memory... but I nearly give up after the first hard climb, the high dune off Snail Road, when you emerge from the cool green corridor of beech trees and a veritable cliff of sand stands facing you—how had it seemed so easy for me when I was sixteen? I can hardly breathe, now, but I press on.

I know that I'm not going to have any more chances to come here.

I see the dune shack as it always first appeared, long before I reach it, silhouetted against an impossibly sharp blue sky, and I want to be there now, the sudden desperate urgency of the need taking me by surprise.

I cannot respond to it: the sand makes you take life one step at a time.

And I am frightened, too, of being there again. Can I still run my fingers over its weathered wood, will it give me slivers again if I'm not careful? Is there still that loose board on the back porch where the sand-frogs like to hide, and where Sophie and I left notes for each other?

What about the blood—can you still see the blood?

Infuriatingly, the dune shack remains out of reach: hills of sand come up and eclipse it as soon as I have the thought, and I must be content with trudging on, catching the occasional glimpse as the path twists around the pale mountains of sand.

It's hot, today, and I can feel sweat tricking down my neck, between my breasts. My body is betraying me; my muscles no longer take the sand in their stride, my eyes shy away from the brilliance of the sun reflecting off ocean and sand. In the years that have come between me and that girl, I've gotten older, my body aged by time and childbirth and the worries of all the lives I live: a mother, a widow, a grandmother, a college professor.

That girl... I once ran over these dunes, lithe and strong, scrambling and falling and laughing, long brown hair pulled back in a ponytail, limbs tanned dark by the sun despite the remonstrances of the adults around me.

I keep my eyes on my goal, plodding along, every step draining energy.

I don't waste any of it. I don't look to the other places, the places of violence and tears. I don't consider the man from Dresden who never lived to see what my country did to his beautiful city. I don't think about the dark blue eyes laughing at me over the old photo albums. That place is long gone. So are those people.

Including, perhaps, me.

Chapter One

All that anybody can talk about, lately, is the war.

There have been long meetings, tiresome meetings, people closeted for hours in Daddy's study. They argue at night, their voices raised: argue about patriotism, about duty, about God, even. There's a contingency that thinks the American government staged the attack last year on Pearl Harbor just to get America off the fence and into the struggle, to get us rationing our food and growing victory gardens and keeping us frightened. And then there are others, their voices more strident, who insist that the only road to peace is through war, which seems a funny concept to me.

I'm supposed to be in bed, but instead I sit on the stairs, breathing in the deep rich tobacco smell coming from the room below me, twisting a lock of my brown hair around my finger, listening to the voices raised in anger, watching as Anna goes yet again to the front door, summoned by the bell, to admit still another participant into the fray.

It is 1942, and I am sixteen years old.

Mother talks about the war, too, but she her approach is more practical than my father's. "He's a dreamer, that one," she'll say whenever anyone says something about Daddy; it's not in her to criticize him.

It's Mother who is practical; it's she who stands, thin and willowy and elegant, in the basement of our brownstone with Anna and counts cans. The Depression didn't end very long ago, and Mother—who didn't suffer all that much during it, to tell the truth—vows that the war isn't going to do what the Depression couldn't. I think she's starting to be afraid that that vow will be put to the test, and sooner rather than later.

And so they count cans, their faces and voices anxious, and later I go with Anna on extravagant shopping trips to DeLuca's, consulting Mother's lengthy lists, buying up tins of smoked salmon and containers of some sort of milk that doesn't need to be refrigerated, and big jugs of water. We take a taxi home—Mother might be vigilant, but she has a practical eye as well—and when we're back, they arrange all the new provisions in the basement and start counting again.

The door to the study opens abruptly and Daddy comes out. He sees me right away, sitting there on the staircase, so he can't be *that* much of a dreamer. "What's the matter, you couldn't sleep?" He is frowning, but that doesn't mean anything; everyone seems to be frowning, these days. "Come on up, I'll tuck you back in."

I give him a practiced exaggerated sigh. Daddy hasn't tucked me into bed in years. "I'm not *three* anymore, you know."

He looks at me oddly, as if for the first time considering this fact. "No, you aren't, are you?" he asks. A thought strikes him. "You want to come in and listen?"

This is amazing. *Important* things happen in Daddy's study, things that even Mother is not privy to. I've never been invited in, not when there are people there, so I don't allow him enough time to change his mind. "Yes, please."

He reaches out a hand and takes mine. "Just be very, very quiet," he admonishes. I nod.

The study is filled with smoke. There are a lot of men in there, two of them with pipes, one with a cigar. There are two women there also, something I hadn't anticipated, and one of *them* is smoking, too. Good for her, I think. Mother caught me smoking under the stairs at Christmastime and I thought she was going to have a heart attack. Or give me one.

Which was, of course, the point: both hers and mine.

We do this most of the time, my mother and me, this odd little dance whose steps we've memorized and enter into, again and again. I transgress; she is shocked; she is hurt; I feel guilty; she feels better. There's no need for punishment: it's an economical way to raise children. Sometimes I wonder why my parents didn't have more of us, since they'd obviously given a great deal of thought to proper parenting.

It leaves me singing about the wicked witch being dead every time I feel that I've won, and muttering unintelligibly when she does; but that's an ongoing part of life *chez* Stanfield, too.

Speaking of what happens *chez* Stanfield, Daddy doesn't do any of the discipline in our house. He doesn't think about the Depression, either; like Mother—and me, for that matter—he was shielded from its extreme hardships by Family Money. He grew up in this same brownstone, cushioned by the same comfortable investments in Swiss bank accounts that will always take care of me, too. He is consequently easygoing—not in the sense of having been *spoiled*, exactly, just in the sense of never having had to worry.

Which is, in its own way, being spoiled, I suppose.

What I like most about my father is that he has always acted like I'm a person. Not his child, to be molded and taught and influenced; but like a real person, with my own opinions and talents and mistakes. Mother would never permit me to participate in a discussion with her friends—assuming that she in fact *has* discussions with her friends, which I somehow rather doubt—but I've been permitted to voice my thoughts once or twice at dinner parties, so I go with confidence into Daddy's study now.

"Listen, my cousin Bernie is a correspondent for *Life*," somebody is saying. "He's over there now. London. They're saying that Britain's next to go."

"It'll be over by Christmas," offers the cigar-smoker comfortably, a portly man wearing a red vest. He gestures knowingly with the cigar. "Anyone can see that."

"That's exactly what they kept saying about the last war!" interjects the youngest man present, someone not much older than me, one of my father's students perhaps. I look at him with interest. Someone who knows his history, I think, and without a thought for my promise to Daddy, I blurt out, "Exactly! The first Christmas, the German soldiers and the British soldiers called a truce, and they even shared their food and played games. They all thought it would be the only Christmas they'd ever spend at war…" My voice trails off as the room is suddenly silent, everybody looking at me.

I think that Daddy might be about to send me away, but then the young man nods and says, vigorously, "Precisely! No one ever thinks it's going to last, but history proves us wrong, every time."

"So what do you want to do?" demands another. "Christ, remember Pearl Harbor! Look at what the Japs are capable of! They'll be all over California next. Little suicide bombers, they don't give a damn about life, they don't give a damn about civilization."

"And look at Hitler! The world needs us!"

"Since when did we decide to fight everybody else's battles for them?"

"Since they bombed us! Your country needs you, you can't deny that."

"Yeah? Then why aren't *you* enlisting?"

I tune them out. My cheeks are still flushed. I'm not sure whether I'm exhilarated or embarrassed. That image stays with me, has stayed with me since I read about it, the horrible wet frigid weather, the soldiers—boys, really, not much older than me—cold and scared and lonely. Looking out through the barbed wire of No Man's Land. Who had the idea first? Did some German boy raise a flag, or was it an English voice that called out to the other side? They played soccer, I think I remember, an improvised game, and shared plum pudding and schnitzel.

And the next day they went back to shooting at each other again.

A loud voice brings me back to the present. "He wouldn't dare!"

"You don't think so, Wayne? How many countries do you think he needs? When it's world domination that's on the table?"

"That's not the point. The point is that the Treaty of Versailles left them with precious little. Understandable that they'd overreact. Pure logic. Pure psychology. He'll prove his point and —"

"And what happens in the meantime?" It is Daddy's voice, calm and quiet. Funny how his voice is always the quietest, but everyone stops and listens to him anyway. Maybe it's *because* he's so quiet. Maybe it's because he always has something to say. "What happens in the meantime?" he repeats. "Putting aside the question of occupation—which is, by the way, rather a big issue to just put aside—you have to ask how long someone can stand aside and watch suffering and do nothing about it."

"It isn't our fight, Walter," says one of the pipe-smokers, someone I recognize from other late-night arguments in my father's study. "It has nothing to do with us."

"It's our war now," says one of the women, shaking her head. "This is all useless, it's mental games you're playing. We're in it and we're in it for good, even if Hitler never invades America. It's the right thing to do. Sometimes you just have to do something because it's the right thing to do."

Daddy hasn't taken his eyes off the pipe-smoker. "Common humanity argues that it has everything to do with us," he says, his voice low and curiously steady.

The door opens and Mother comes in, her expression forbidding. Bed check, I diagnose instantly, and me found to be missing. "Walter, what is she doing here?"

"Listening," says my father calmly. He looks unperturbed.

Mother glares at him, then at me. "Time for bed," she says repressively, and I feel rather than hear the argument being taken up around me again as I leave the room. She looks beautiful tonight, my mother, in a flowered dress that brings out the violet in her eyes. She has the most extraordinary eyes. This probably isn't the best time to tell her so; she'll suspect an ulterior motive. I try a frontal assault instead. "There's no school tomorrow," I observe.

"I don't want you listening to them," she says irritably, climbing the stairs ahead of me.

I take a deep breath. "Do you think we were right to go to war, Mother?"

She turns and looks down on me. Unfair spatial advantage, and she uses it. "I think," she says, "that you're supposed to be studying French this summer. Monday, at the *Alliance Française*. I think that's what *you* should be thinking about."

I shiver. "But…"

She's already turned away and climbed the rest of the stairs. Standing by my door, she turns back to face me. "Now go to bed, Jessica," she says, her voice unexpectedly gentle. "Don't think about the war, it'll ruin your complexion."

And on that extraordinary note she is gone.

I think about it anyway. I think about the *Alliance Française* and wonder if there's going to be such a thing as the French language a hundred years from now.

Not if the Germans have anything to say about it.

***

Anna waits until Mother is gone for her morning round comprised of volunteer work and gossip, and then she brews the coffee. Two cups: one for her, one for me. I'm not supposed to be drinking it yet, but Anna likes the midmorning break and encourages me in my rule breaking.

The sun streams down through the high kitchen window and creates a halo around her head; Anna's hair is blonde, streaked in places with something darker, always in a loose coil at the back that's constantly coming undone. She's forever sticking hairpins in.

The halo, I think, may be a little exaggerated.

"Are you worried about the war?" I ask her, still thinking about last night's discussion. It's a reasonable question: Anna is German. From a place called Osnabrück. I should be ashamed to report that I have no idea where that is. But I can find Germany on a map, at least; *that* was drilled into us all last spring in class. Germany and its ever-expanding borders, which now include France; but we were told not to change our textbooks. "Wait and see," said Miss Whittaker.

I wonder what it feels like to be part of an imperial power.

"Of course I am worried," Anna says in her accented English, stirring rationed sugar into her coffee. I take mine black—excessive as usual, as Mother points out every chance she has. Anna shrugs. "But it does nothing to worry, does it? It does not change nothing."

Her words are practical. Anna and my mother have a great deal in common: no-nonsense, both of them. It's probably why Mother chose her to be our housekeeper in the first place.

I look at her more closely. "You mean that you don't think about it, ever? Don't you have family there, in—um—Osnabrück?" I pronounce it differently than she does.

She nods, sips her coffee, puts the cup down and adds more sugar. She has a liberal hand with it, which is fine with me: I've practically grown up on her Bavarian apple cake and *Lineerschnitten* and *Ananastoertchen*. The only difference between us is that I don't put on weight. "Yet," says Anna, darkly, when I point this out.

"I cannot help them, can I?" Irritation in her voice, now; I'll have to step carefully through this conversation. "There is not nothing I can do."

"That's what somebody was saying last night at Daddy's meeting," I say inoffensively. "That there's nothing we can do."

She snorts and shakes her head; two hairpins go flying. "Ach, your father and his meetings!" She sips at her coffee; this time, it meets with her approval. "Ach. He thinks that talking will change the world, that one."

I think that there's a good chance that it will, eventually, but it's not an opinion that Anna wants to hear. "Have you heard anything from your family?" I ask instead, incautiously. Perhaps if I'm allowed into the study again, I'll have something to say, some news to share; I could become important. "Do you know that they're all right?"

I think for a moment that she's going to be angry, but then her features relax as she decides to answer. It's what she always ends up doing—I can be very perseverant, and it's sometimes easier for her to just give me what I want. That happens a lot with people, I find: you can wear them down until they just give in. I've often used it to my advantage. "My brother is in the army," Anna says at last. "His wife–Gertrude her name is, you remember, *mein Engel*, I showed you her picture last summer? –she writes to me every week, she tells me he is still good, still alive, in the Channel Islands I think."

There is a moment of quiet as we both contemplate her statement, the shadows behind it, the German occupation of Guernsey and the other islands just off the coast of France. I just heard about it in school the week before we got let out for the summer. Close to France, but belonging to England: a stepping-stone. I shiver even in the warm kitchen.

"Come along, then," says Anna, seeing my expression. "We'll go to the market. Go comb your hair, *liebchen*; put it in a braid."

It's not *my* hair that needs capturing, but I do it anyway, out of long habit of obedience, and watch her as she checks the contents of her cupboards, shaking an almost-empty box of Lux, peeking into the box of M & M doughnuts, opening the drawer where she keeps the rationing tickets and counting them carefully. "We'll do the shopping," she says, nodding, busy, comfortable in her domain. "It will do us both good, I am thinking."

***

In the event, we don't make it.

Boston is changing with the war. After last night, I look at my city with new eyes, narrowed eyes, eyes that ask questions. There's a poster up in front of the Arlington Street Church that urges passers-by to "pray for peace," but that seems overly optimistic to me. Peace means the end of the war, and I'm not sure I see God reaching down and handing the victory to anybody anytime soon. Mother thinks he's on our side; but Father Andrewes, the assistant at Holy Trinity, says that nothing is that simple, and for once religion and psychology are in perfect agreement, because that's what Daddy says, too.

There are other posters as well, ones that aren't as optimistic. One at the entrance to the Common shows an airplane flying over a burning city, and it says, "O.K., Tojo, You Asked For It: Air Mail from Boston!" Anna just thins her lips when she sees that and shakes her head, a couple of errant hairpins flying. "Don't pay no notice to that, *liebchen*," she says, touching my arm, pulling me away from it. Right next to it is another, somewhat more useful in content: "Save Your Cans: Help Pass the Ammunition—Prepare Your Tin Cans For War."

There's a kiosk on Charles Street with something even darker, though: "This Is The Enemy," says one, showing a German thrusting a dagger into the Holy Bible, while another has a picture of a man tied to a chair with a bag over his head and informs us that "This Is Nazi Brutality."

I glance at Anna out of the corner of my eye. I'm trying to imagine how I'd feel if I lived in Berlin or Koblenz or even her own Osnabrück and saw posters that showing Americans as executioners. Not sure how I'd feel. Not sure how she does, either: Anna can be inscrutable when she chooses.

The posters are new; I was on Charles Street three days ago and the ones up then were less strident, exhorting us to think about whether our trips were necessary and reminding that needless travel interferes with the war effort.

"Hey! You, Kraut!" The voice is male and close by and I turn to stare, wondering who he's yelling at.

"You! Kraut bitch!" Anna's grip on my arm tightens and it hurts and I'm about to snap at her when it's as if the world slowed down and I'm seeing what's really happening and it's at that moment that I realize he's shouting at *us*.

Well, at Anna, anyway. Which might as well be me.

"Who are you talking to?" I demand, putting as much of the generations of Old Boston as I can in my voice. Anna pulls on my arm again. "Leave it, *liebchen*," she says softly, urgently, but I'm not in a mood to listen.

They're standing just a few feet away from us, boys just reaching toward adulthood, the dangerous age if Daddy is to be believed. Three of them. Two of us. Not sure that Old Boston is going to help me here. "Leave us alone!"

"Nazi spy!"

Anna gasps at the words, as though the wind has been pulled out of her body, and I'm ready to do something, though I'm not really sure what that is. They see my hesitation, and they've won. The tallest of the three reaches into the string bag he's carrying and a tomato whizzes right at us, catching me squarely on the cheek. It hurts more than I'd have expected, and tears spring to my eyes.

Anna is dragging at me. "We go now," she says, firmly. "We don't want no trouble here."

Another tomato catches her on the shoulder and bursts, running blood-red down her white blouse. "Come quickly now," she hisses at me, and because I don't know what else to do, I obey.

Chapter Two

The house is silent.

That's not a good sign, I think. Anna has pushed me into a chair in the kitchen and has gone to find my father, and the door to his study has been closed for a very long time. I get up, once, to see if there's any applecake in the breadbox, but there isn't, and I return to my seat, not sure what is the right thing to do. My cheek is burning.

She comes back into the kitchen, uncharacteristically silent, and motions for me to follow her. "What is it, Anna? What's going on?" I know I'm whining, but I can't help it: is Daddy mad at me? Did I do something wrong? Should I have protected Anna?

"Let me see it," is all he says when I reach the study, and there's nothing but pain in his voice. He touches my cheek, briefly, then looks at Anna, standing in the doorway. "Get cleaned up, both of you," he says. "And Anna, when Mrs. Stanfield gets home, ask her to come and see me right away, will you?"

"Of course, Doctor."

In the kitchen, she dabs at my cheek, and it hurts even more. "What did they put in those tomatoes?" I demand, cranky, and she shakes her head. "It is such a waste," she says. "Come, *liebchen*, there's coffee, and applecake."

"Where did you hide it?" But even to my own ears, my protests aren't as strident as usual. I won't admit it, of course, but what happened has me thoroughly frightened.

I sit back at the table as though the last two hours hadn't happened, and Anna fusses around me, even giving me two pieces of cake without being asked. That's a first. At some point she leaves and I hear her voice, low, my mother's higher-pitched and querulous, and then a door slamming, but I sit and eat with determination. Maybe I can pretend it didn't happen. I remember, belatedly, that we'd been talking about Anna's family. "What happened to your brother's wife? You were going to tell me before."

She sighs. "They've sent their children away, to the countryside, where they'll be safe."

"Safe from what?" I feel a sudden spurt of resentment: last I heard, it wasn't Germany that was being invaded. And after this morning it's easy to blame Anna for my lacerated cheek.

"The bombings." She looks at me as if I'm mentally retarded. "The bombings, from England. They drop their bombs on the cities, not in the farmland. Gerta and Heinz will be safe in the countryside."

I have a mental picture of Anna's niece and nephew, tents pitched in a field, romping through the tall grass while British planes fly overhead. "I'm glad your family is okay," I say politely.

"It's important to think of these things," Anna says primly. "Important for children to be made safe. Like your *papa* thinks now of making you safe."

I put down my coffee. This is something new. "What do you mean?"

Her eyes grow wide and she fumbles wildly with the hairpins. I've stumbled onto something important, something she isn't supposed to talk about. I press my advantage. "What do you mean, he wants to make me safe? Anna, you have to tell me!"

She pushes the last pin into her rebellious hair, stands up, gathers our cups, takes them over to the sink. Our kitchen is at the back of the brownstone, and there's a greenhouse-conservatory beyond it; it's catching all the morning sun, sharp and beautiful and achingly peaceful. It should be a tranquil moment. "Anna!"

She turns from the sink, wiping her hands on her apron. "Miss Jessica, you know I cannot be telling you this. Your *mutti* will have my job!"

"You know that's not true." My mind is racing. "Are my parents sending me away, too? To the country?" And where the hell is "the country" anyway?

The farthest Mother will go is out to visit Walden Pond in Concord, and that's only because she has some sort of unhealthy obsession with Thoreau. My father considers a walk across Boston Common to be roughing it. "Anna …"

She shrugs, as though the matter were out of her hands now. "He now thinks it might be better for you to not be in the city," she says.

That's a surprise. Daddy must be more upset than he seemed. Mother, yes, maybe; Mother's always talking about the evils of the city, white-slave trafficking and the perils of drinking at an early age "that can only lead to the gutter"; I can see her sending me away for safety's sake. But Daddy?

And then there's the whole question of… "Anna!" I say again, abruptly, as the thought dawns on me. "What about *school*?"

She stares at me. "It is the summer holiday," she says. "There is not no school now."

"If I'm supposed to be in danger now, it's not going away in September," I say pointedly. But this isn't a conversation for her; I'm already plotting how to confront my parents with my illicit knowledge. "Did they say when?"

She shrugs again. "Soon, Miss Jessica. That is all I know. Everything. Except ..."

"Yes?"

She turns back to the sink. "Except that I'm going with you."

***

My parents are arguing. In Daddy's study, again; maybe it's something about that room, it brings out bad passions in people.

I don't bother listening at the door to wait for the right cue to interrupt them; my entrance is going to be dramatic, all by itself. I open the door and step inside.

Mother turns and glares at me. "Civilized people," she says acidly, "knock before entering a room."

Daddy looks tired. He doesn't say anything.

It's my moment, and I milk it for all its worth. "When, exactly," I say, and pause, "were you planning on telling me?"

Mother says, "tell you what?" automatically, but Daddy waves a hand at her, the gesture one of defeat. "Let's not play any more games, Alice," he says. "Anna told her."

"How do you know?"

"How else would she know?" There are lines on his face that I could swear weren't there a month ago. He sits down on the big leather sofa. "It's not because of you, Jessica," he says to me. "Or at least not just because of you."

I haven't finished playing my cards yet. "So who is it because of?" I inquire, my voice as sarcastic as I can make it. "Herr Hitler?"

My mother gasps. "How…?

"It's because of Anna," my father says. "Come all the way in, Jessica. You should learn to make a commitment: in or out, but close the door. And sit down."

He so rarely gives me orders that I obey him immediately, perching on the edge of the big armchair that matches the sofa. The leather is cool and smooth under my bare thighs. "What is it?" I ask, quietly. There's a time to be dramatic, and this clearly isn't it.

Mother is hovering by the window. "We didn't want to have to tell you," she says, fretfully, looking out onto Commonwealth Avenue as though expecting to see someone there, listening in. "It didn't seem fair to burden you, but–"

Again my father cuts right to the point. "What happened to you this morning, that's only the beginning," he says quietly. "Life here is getting more and more difficult for Anna. And we think that it won't be long before it becomes dangerous." He gestures toward a newspaper on the hassock in front of him. "A German-American man was killed in South Boston last week. People stood by and watched, and they applauded when it happened. It's only a matter of time."

My eyes are round as saucers. "What? What's only a matter of time?"

"It's already started," Daddy says. "Even before today. Anna's been followed, enough to make her afraid, and she doesn't scare easily. People are spitting at her in the street when they see her. They refused to wait on her yesterday at the greengrocer's on Charles Street. And then today—well, that's the last straw. It can only get much worse from here on out… You could have been hurt, pumpkin, and that's as serious as I want it to get." He exchanges unhappy glances with my mother and takes a deep breath.

I ignore his concerns about me. "Refused service?" When I used to go with Anna to DeLuca's, when I was little, they gave me cream caramels and laughed with her about how fast I was growing. They refused to let her do her marketing at *DeLuca's*?

Mother has had enough. "They wouldn't wait on her, Jessica," she says impatiently. "They told her to take her business elsewhere. They said they don't want Germans for customers."

I stare at her. "But she was buying food for us. *We're* not German."

"Hatred isn't logical, pumpkin," Daddy says. When did he start sounding so tired? "And it's only going to get worse. You've seen the posters they're putting up: they're painting all Germans with the same brush. They're saying that they're all evil, they're all spies, and Anna is very vulnerable to it. It's dangerous and it's going to get more dangerous, and Anna—well, she's part of our family, isn't she?" I nod dumbly. "And I don't know how to protect her." He takes a deep breath, sounding defeated. "And I don't know how to protect you, pumpkin, either. Not here, anyway. We want Anna someplace safe, and we want you to go with her."

"Why? Why me?" I'm imagining life without Anna at the brownstone, and how I might exploit it for more freedom. Probably not.

"Because she shouldn't be alone, and neither should you." He catches my eyes. "We want you someplace safe, pumpkin, someplace where you can stay and be hidden. Both of you. Your mother and I have discussed it, and despite some reservations on her part"—he flashes her a look—"we've found a place where we think you'll be all right. I know I can count on you, Jessica. You can take care of each other out there."

"Out where?"

Mother makes a fluttering sort of movement by the window, her diamonds catching the light, sharp and bright. My father frowns at her, then looks at me again. "We're sending you to Cape Cod," he says.

"They don't hate Germans on Cape Cod?"

"Jessica, don't be impertinent." My mother has found her composure, as she invariably does when the issue is important, usually something having to do with manners. "That's *quite* enough. You'll do as we tell you."

My father shakes his head. "It's a reasonable question," he says; I don't know if he's talking to her or to me. "But where you'll be going, I don't think you need to worry very much."

My eyes widen. "What do you mean?"

"My cousin Louis," says Daddy, and gets no further. "You've never met Louis," Mother interjects fretfully. "He's the black sheep of your father's family."

Black sheep may be irresistible, but I have no intention of leaving Boston. "*You* can go with Anna," I say to my mother. "I don't want to go away."

Mother flutters. "Jessica, you're not being—"

"I'm not going," I say again, firmly.

Daddy is smiling, now, and that irritates me more. "You can't make me," I say to him, menacingly. I really don't like that smile.

"Louis," Daddy says to no one in particular, "is an artist. Or he was, when he was younger. Very avant-garde."

"I'm not going," I say again, but even to my own ears the protest sounds halfhearted. I'm an artist, too. At least I paint. At least I try to.

He doesn't seem to have heard me. "He never sold very much, though, come to think of it."

"No one likes his paintings," Mother assures me. "They're all too ..." She shivers, the description eluding her. "Too something," she finishes, firm if vague to the end.

Daddy looks at her as if she's carrying on a completely different conversation from him. As, perhaps, she is. "Alice, just let me finish," he says. "You may annotate it as much as you'd like afterwards."

That shuts her up. Maybe she doesn't know what annotate means, I think meanly.

"Louis is in San Francisco now," my father tells me. "But he has a place on the Cape where you can stay. It's small, but you and Anna should be comfortable there. And quite safe. It's the cities that will be targets, if it ever comes to that." He glances at my mother, but she's still working out whether annotating is a good or a bad thing.

He reaches for his pipe and starts the ritual, scooping out rich-smelling tobacco from the can by his chair. He does it automatically; his cool gray eyes never leave me. He's about, I realize belatedly, to hook his little fish. "It's pretty much in the middle of nowhere," my father says. "It will be a change for you, pumpkin. I can make arrangements for you to get groceries delivered and trash picked up, or you can do that if you want. Once every two weeks should be fine." He waves a hand, as though to make it so: such arrangements are not his forte. "You'll bring along your schoolbooks, of course. I'm not having you get behind in class." No war is going to interfere with his daughter's education, I think, with a sudden surge of affection for him.

He's got me intrigued, as he knew he would. "Will I have a curfew?" I ask. "Can I come and go as I please?"

"There's nowhere to —" my mother starts, but Daddy holds up a hand. "You can do whatever you want, Jessica," he says. "We just want you and Anna to be safe. It's hard for your mother to let go of you, but I think it's the right thing to do."

Mother sniffs her disapproval. It's clear that this argument has been going on between them for some time, maybe even before this morning's episode. "There are people out there –" she starts, but Daddy cuts her off. "It's safer than Boston, Alice," he says, and I can hear in his voice that he's already said it before. "It's the safest place for Jessica to be. And she's going."

Mother sniffs again, but says nothing. Her disapproval has a rearguard-action flavor to it: she knows she's lost.

Daddy sighs and turns to me. "You'll need to grow up a little faster than we wanted, pumpkin," he says. "You'll have to be in charge out there."

I wonder if Anna knows I'm to be in charge; but the thought is seductive. Definite possibilities are already showing themselves. I shouldn't give in too easily, but … I get up and walk across the room, sitting on the fat arm of his chair and taking his hand in mine. "I'll take care of her, Daddy," I say solemnly, feeling older than my years, the childhood name for him feeling, for the first time ever, awkward. I feel that I've crossed some invisible line, that I've somehow left a bit of the childish me behind. "I'll see to it that no one hurts Anna."

Mother turns from the window. "You might as well tell her the rest," she says waspishly.

Daddy squeezes my hand and winks. "Oh, yes, I forgot to mention," he says, and the tired lines are almost all gone from his face now. "Louis' place? It's about fifty yards from the Atlantic Ocean."

Chapter Three

There are no landmarks at the beach.

The sand stretches on and on, uninterrupted, the waves lapping at it on one side, the high dune cliffs rising above it on the other. This sand is the dividing-line between two worlds, the active living world of the ocean and the less apparent but equally alive world of the dunes.

It is here that I have come to live, in a ramshackle cottage a stone's throw away from the dune cliff, surrounded by sand and with the ever-changing vista of the sea spread out before me. I go to bed and wake up to the sound of the waves lapping on the shore, and I haven't yet missed the sound of traffic that filtered up to my bedroom in our brownstone on Commonwealth Avenue.

Louis' former home is a one-room affair, built – as far as I can see – of mostly debris: pieces of wood bleached and smoothed by the salt water, timbers so massive they could have only come from one of the numerous shipwrecks off the Cape; plywood patches here and there. It's ugly as sin.

I love it.

It's mostly windows anyway, Louis' shack, two big windows facing the water, where a door leads out to the equally ramshackle porch where Anna and I spend some of our time and take all of our meals; smaller windows in back, facing the sand and the mosses and the odd crippled trees that are all that grow in this windswept place. There is neither electricity nor running water *chez* Louis, and I can appreciate my mother's disdain for the place as I make my furtive sorties to the privy at night. I call out to the dune frogs when

I go, and move my flashlight energetically; they all come out at night, and I'm afraid to step on one in my bare feet. It would feel awful, and the frog would no doubt appreciate the experience even less.

We sleep in bunk beds, Anna on the bottom, me on the top; and every morning after the sun sets the ocean alight in flames of orange and red, I take our buckets and hike down a hill of sand to the pump, then bring the water (who knew that water is so heavy?) back up to the shack for Anna to use, heating it on the woodstove, then pouring it through the filter for our morning coffee.

I have been here five days, now, and already it feels that life in Boston is a memory, a lifetime away, my parents, the brownstone, school – as if *that* life had been unreal, an illusion, and all that matters now is here, this, the immediacy of this moment.

The moment has included very few people, though even the eccentrics of the dunes have curiosity, and more than once I've felt eyes on me, only to turn and see movement, a blur of color, nothing more. I saw a man walking on the beach one morning, his pants legs rolled up to his knees and his feet in the surf; I hear a woman singing, sometimes, when the wind is just right, her voice as beautiful as the sea, as plaintive as the cry of the gulls.

At night, before Anna puts out the lamp, I pose my ritual request. "Anna?"

"*Ja?*"

"Tell me something good."

"Something good, *liebchen*, is that we are safe in the sands."

I like the way she phrased that. The sands, the dunes, they are our world now. Our protectors. Safety may be illusory, but it feels like if it's anywhere, it's here.

"You cannot take nothing for granted," Anna says, and for once, we are in perfect agreement.

Mother was, predictably, unhappy about it all. "The people who live out there," she hissed at me, "are different." She still waged a halfhearted campaign to keep me in Boston; Daddy had clearly made this decision, and she was unhappy about it. Conflict between my parents is something I'm unwilling to explore.

I like different. "How?"

She sniffed. "Only eccentrics live in the dunes."

Better and better. "Be fair, Alice," Daddy remonstrated with her, the gray eyes oddly gentle as he looked at her, her beauty tempering his responses. "Some of them are artists," he says to me.

"I'm an artist," I said boldly. No one in my family thinks much of my canvases, but I don't ever let them forget they exist.

Daddy ignored me. "People out there are artists," he repeated, "they're writers ..."

"And which of those is Louis?" Mother's voice was low, dangerous, but Daddy didn't take the bait. "Louis is a character," he said, easily.

She sniffed again, and relented slightly. "He certainly is that."

Now that I'm here, though, I can see what Mother means. It is a place of extremes, these dunes that stand between the town of Provincetown, which curves back on itself, sheltering a bay and a protected little harbor, and the sea – the real sea, the Atlantic Ocean. In the mornings the dunes are cool and inviting, but by afternoon they're hot, burning my feet with their intensity. I learn quickly to put socks over my bare feet after the sun's been up a while.

When I stand with my back to the sea, all that there is, stretching out to the horizon, is sand, smooth and undulating, mountains and valleys and caverns of sand. They are a hundred feet high, some of them: mountains of sand. Rising above the dunes is a single stark reminder of humanity's existence: the Pilgrim Monument, two hundred and twenty feet tall, standing watch over Provincetown and its harbor.

There's no monument to stand watch out in the dunes.

We've arrived in the aftermath of disaster, it seems: only two weeks ago, the dune taxi driver tells us, on June sixteenth, the town was filled with casualties from the sea. Two ships – an American freighter and a British one – were torpedoed off the back shore, which is where we live, and the Civilian Defense Units responded, setting up shop in a hotel-cum-hospital, treating the survivors. I look at Mother's face and am glad that she didn't know about it until now, or I'd probably still be in the brownstone on Commonwealth Avenue.

Locked in.

Mother's fears notwithstanding, it's a reminder that the war is closer than it seemed in Daddy's study, closer than all the discussions over which he presides. Here, there's nothing between us and the war, no comfortable buffer zone. I think about that sometimes, staring out at the place where the sea and the sky meet; but I'm still unable to really comprehend what is happening out there.

Mother latched on to that, too, of course. She might have initially missed the part about the freighters being torpedoed, but she's very good at collecting gossip of all three varieties: untrue, possibly true, and I-heard-it-from-Angela true. She reports it all faithfully back to Daddy, and then they argue. There was some dark battle going on between them, I saw that before I left Boston, Daddy wanting to send Anna and me to the dunes, Mother resisting. I still don't know what it's about—I'm smart enough and old enough to know it's not really about me, even though they say it is—and I tried to stay away from the crossfire before I left the city.

She pounced on him one morning at breakfast about a week before we left. "Provincetown," she said darkly, "is under martial law."

"What's martial law?" I asked.

"What kind of nonsense is that?" asked Daddy rhetorically, not even looking up from his morning copy of the Boston *Globe*. He seemed amused, which always infuriates Mother.

"What's martial law?" I asked again.

"I heard it on the wireless," she said smoothly, ignoring me. Mother doesn't read much, and spends much of her time either gossiping (though she doesn't call it that) or listening to the wireless for her news. The household schedule moves around her chosen programs. "Martial law in Provincetown, and now it seems I'm the last to know that some ships have sunk off the Cape. I have to say, Walter, that I fail to understand how you can consider placing your daughter under martial law." She made it sound like a hard-labor camp.

Daddy sighed. "It's a rumor," he said, and turned to me. "Martial law is when civilians need to obey the military. It's instituted in a time of emergency." He looked at Mother. "Don't you think I looked into it? There's no martial law, Alice, it's just a rumor. And there are always ships sinking off the Cape. Jessica will be quite safe. They're even encouraging tourists to come for the season. Specials at the boarding houses, two-for-one dinners at the restaurants. Couldn't be safer."

She arched her carefully plucked eyebrows. "Couldn't be safer? With vessels being torpedoed?"

"They're not torpedoing the dunes, Alice."

I thought that with all that going on I'd feel closer to the war, and maybe I do, a little; and yet at the same time I feel miles away from *everything* now that I'm here.

They're constantly shifting, the dunes, constantly on the move. Out by Route Six there is still forest, but the sands are encroaching on it; you can see trees half-buried at the point where dunes and forest meet, and you know that ten years from now the trees will be gone.

There's an odd sort of unity, actually, in the ocean waves on one side and the waves of sand on the other. It's almost as if they were mirror-images of each other, and I wonder if there's an analogy with my life somewhere in there.

What they really have in common, though, is their vastness. If I look straight out to sea, the next land my eye would encounter is Greenland – or is it Halifax? I should have paid more attention to my geography classes; but, either way, it's hard to imagine that kind of scale. The dunes aren't as vast as the Atlantic Ocean, of course;

but they, too, stretch out for miles in three directions. If it weren't for the Pilgrim Monument, a lone sentinel on the horizon, I'd believe that they too would go on forever.

And difficult, now that I am here, to imagine a life outside of them.

The beach, I am told, stretches forty miles to the south: we're close to where it ends, here at the tip of land called the Provincetown Spit. And as happens in most starting-points – and at all endings – the area does seem to have collected an odd assortment of inhabitants; I wouldn't begin to call it a community. They are the sort of people who gather at the end of something, at the end of a forty-mile beach, at the tip of the Cape, at the end of the world.

Louis, for example. As we packed up my things to leave, I asked my mother about him. Specifics, I specified.

Mother was taking underwear from a drawer and stopped in mid-action, taking my question seriously. "Louis' father had plans for his life," she said. "He wanted him to take over the shipping line after he graduated from Harvard." She resumed motion, like a marionette, her arms depositing their load of frilly underthings into the suitcase that lay open on my bed.

Anna could have packed for me, but Mother wanted to do it. I think it was supposed to be a gesture.

"What did he do instead?" I asked, swinging my feet, impatient to be off. I was fascinated by this shadowy character whose home would soon be mine. Maybe some day I'd have a reputation like Louis', I thought. Jessica Stanfield, Girl Eccentric.

She shrugged. She didn't want me knowing about Louis. He's too much like me, too excessive. What he did, it transpires, is take his family's shipping business a little too much to heart and in fact shipped *himself* out, on a merchant steamer a semester before he was due to graduate college. "How long was he gone?"

"Years," my mother responded. She clearly wished that he had stayed gone. "He was involved with the theater after that," she pronounced distastefully. Involved with more than just the theater, though she herself never ever gossips about anything like that, she said, then proceeded to do so anyway. There was an actress. Well, several actresses, though not quite all of them at once, my mother hastened to add. She is judgmental but fair. "There were a number of affairs," she said. "They all ended badly."

How many affairs end well, I wondered, but I said nothing.

Louis had been in New York City, then, but had returned to Boston, penniless and still without a career goal in sight. He was sleeping in the subway tunnels when his family, scandalized, plucked him back above ground and set him as firmly as they could on his feet. "They made him a very generous offer," said Mother, holding a dress up in front of me. "Does this still fit you?"

"It never fit me," I said, taking the dress from her and stuffing it back into the closet.

She sighed and sat down on the edge of my bed. "They told Louis he could finish college and go on as planned. He'd work part-time in the shipping clerk's office and start learning on the job. It was very generous," she repeated, in case I'd missed it before, the tale of the family's great generosity, "but Louis said no. Just like that! Said he wasn't interested."

She stopped yet again, amazed by Louis' obtuseness, and again I prodded her. "So what happened?"

She stood up. "Henry took over instead. Your Uncle Henry. And perhaps it all worked out for the best, because Henry really *does* have a head for figures, which Louis never did."

"Why didn't I ever hear about any of this before?"

She looked at me, her gaze cool. "You never showed the remotest interest in family matters," she said, and I left it at that, because she was of course right.

Daddy was more forthcoming. There's a twinkle in his eye when he talks about Louis; I love that twinkle and what it says about both Louis and Daddy. "He's a character, all right," he said. "He collected things – let's see, what was it, exactly?" He searched the recesses of his memory. "Matchbooks, that's it! Matchbooks, and matchboxes too. Had some from all over the world. He lives out of a steamer trunk – or at least he did, then – and those matches took up a fair part of it. Your grandmother was always convinced he was going to set something on fire; she hated it when he stayed with us. But he never did."

Only the world, I thought dramatically and enviously. "When did he go to the Cape?" I asked.

"Oh, years ago, pumpkin." Daddy settled back in his chair and began filling his pipe with tobacco, the smell rich and loamy and sweet. I breathed it in deeply: it is the scent of my father. "He built that shack by himself," he said, tamping down the tobacco in the bowl of the pipe. I waited as he applied one match after another; it usually takes him about five of them. Three, today: a new record. I smiled as he drew in, deeply, and released the fragrant smoke into the air. "Let's see: where were we? Louis's house out there ... you know, pumpkin, the whole family had written him off, but I'll tell you, when I went out there and saw that shack, I was impressed. Don't think *I* could do that, build something out there, live with that kind of isolation."

I didn't think he could, either, but I didn't say so. Daddy needs his audience, his disciples, his books.

He had the pipe firmly under control now. "The place was perfect for Louis," he said between puffs. "It's just a wasteland out there. You can only drive on the sand on special tires, so no one drives in. There's a taxi with the tires that goes round and delivers groceries, some of the folks out there aren't able walk out of the dunes and into town." He stopped and considered. "Some elderly people, seems to me. And there's a beach, sure, but who wants to make that much effort to go to the beach? When there are beaches all around that are easier to get to? No: the only people who live out there are Louis' kindred spirits, wild people. Unconventional people. People who don't much care what the rest of the world thinks about them."

Without thinking, I said, "People who collect matchbooks."

He twinkled at me and nodded. "People who collect matchbooks," he affirmed, and we smiled at each other. There was a moment of friendly silence, and I wondered if he was comparing Louis' life to his own far more conventional one. Though it has to be said that even Daddy is unconventional by his family's standards, with his meetings and his philosophy club and his talk about politics. Not to mention his occupation: being a psychiatrist isn't everybody's idea of the Thing To Do.

"But now he's in San Francisco," I said at length, wanting to get back to the point, to learn more about my black-sheep family member.

Daddy nodded, more briskly this time. "I wonder how he's managing in the city," he said, as though considering the question for the first time. "Since he likes his solitude so much, and all."

"You can be alone in a city," I pronounced wisely, having read it only that week in a book.

He glanced at me and didn't answer, probably realizing that the thought was not my own, so I took another tack. "*Why* did he leave, then?" I was already thinking about how and when I would be able to travel to California, to meet this fascinating second cousin of mine.

Daddy pulled in meditatively on the pipe, releasing a long fragrant plume of smoke before responding. "It was a woman," he said at length. "With Louis, it's always a woman."

And that, it seems, was that.

Anna has no information on Louis, and even less interest than she has information. "Thank *Gott* he built dat cabin," she says grimly, her hands going automatically to her head, to rearrange her hairpins, "and thank *Gott, mein Engel*, that we have a place to stay."

"The only people who live in the dunes are eccentrics," I tell her. "They won't care that you're German."

"As for that, we will see, *liebchen*, we will see."

We've been here five days now, and I am, it has to be said, disappointed that I have yet to meet any of these famous eccentrics. Mother was right: they're here because they want to be left alone.

They're certainly leaving *us* alone.

I try to imagine what they must think, whether they are wondering about the two women living in Louis' shack. Is there a dunes gossip-line? Do the tree swallows tell the marsh hawks that someone has moved in? Do the toads, colored to match exactly the sand in which they live, hop along the dune trails with the news?

I leave the shack early every morning, before Anna is stirring in her narrow bed beneath mine. I slide down from my perch on the upper bunk and slip into my clothes and am out the door while her snores still fill the room we share. And I explore our world, which feels new and exciting every morning.

We are at the northernmost tip of the Cape: from our vantage point, the sun rises from the water ... and sets back into it. Mornings are best, a crisp wind coming in off the ocean, the sands of the beach untouched. Every morning I begin the day the same way: I take off all my clothes and run into the ocean, whooping, because the water is frigid, cold even in the shallows where I splash for a few minutes before getting out again. The Labrador Current sweeps by, and I imagine ice cubes in the water.

But it is a test, and every morning I want to pass it.

The beach is endless, stretching out on either side of me as far as I can see, the sand undisturbed, smooth and glowing gold in the rising sun. I walk down beside the water, my clothes wet and sticking to my skin, and when I turn to walk back to the dune shack, my footprints are already gone, washed away – covered, really – by waves or the incoming tide.

Anna wakes slowly and crankily. She sits with her coffee, staring into space, answering my attempts at conversation with monosyllables, her hair shedding more hairpins than usual. I've learned to leave her alone as she passes through the liminality of awakening, the threshold between one world and the other, and so I linger on the beach, picking up bits of shell and stones and the occasional piece of sea glass. I have already amassed a fearsome collection of beach detritus that Anna has decreed must be kept outside, so I created a kind of sandbox, bordered with lengths of abandoned timbers I've scrounged, where I arrange and rearrange my treasures. It's art, I tell Anna.

By the time I return to the shack, the sun has started climbing in earnest, and Anna has her hair more or less under control and is ready to face her day.

And there is a lot to do in a day out here. It is not, as I remind myself with some amusement, just another day at the beach. "*Liebchen*, come now, there's work" is a phrase I begin to hear with monotonous regularity. Anna—and my parents, through her—has apparently decided that I'm no longer too delicate for rigorous work. I don't know whether I'm pleased or disappointed.

The shack has to be swept out continuously – we live on sand, we're surrounded by sand, and it is everywhere: in our clothing, beneath our feet, almost in the air we breathe. I am forever bursting in through the shack's screen door, sweeping prodigious amounts of sand along with me, without thinking; and Anna, for her part, has gotten used to scolding me for it. A lot.

I think I might be starting to get on her nerves.

Then there's the question of water. That's my responsibility, and I fulfill it with considerably less graciousness than Anna would like. Down the hill, over a small rise, bucket in hand. Prime the pump. Pump the water, fill the bucket. Back up the rise, up the hill, the water sloshing all over. And remember that these aren't just any hills: they are sand dunes. For every step you take, you slide back at least half a step, and sometimes more. You must attack the sand with your toes, forcing them to find a grip, to hold it and your weight as your other foot does the same thing.

My first day out here, I'd spilled all the water before I made it to the top of the first rise.

I am developing muscles that I never knew I had from all this walking in the sand. The scramble from the beach up the bluff where the dune shack sits is steep and long; I am still panting at the top ... but less so, already, than I was when I started.

As soon as I have fetched the water, it seems that Anna has already used it. I've never given indoor plumbing a second thought, and I make the mistake of saying so to Mother the first time that she and Daddy make the trek out to see if we are still alive. "Indoor plumbing!" she snorts, and I know that I'm in for a lecture about How Difficult Things Were During The Depression.

Don't get me wrong: for most people, they were. But not for people like us. I resent how Mother wears an experience that she never *really* experienced as if it were a badge of courage.

My parents have walked out to see us, and Mother is exhausted from the hike; I can see that. They left their car out where Snail Road intersects Route Six and followed the dune ridges—I think that my father has some mental map of the dunes from the days he used to come out to see Louis, though he never speaks of those days in front of my mother—but even so, it is rough going, and walking in the sand is always difficult. Mother is pale and perspiring when they arrive; Anna sits her down in the shade of the shack and sends me, predictably, for more water.

To my surprise, Daddy offers to help. He picks up another bucket, takes off his jacket, and sets off with me. His leather city shoes make deep impressions in the sand; he has loosened his collar and removed his tie, unheard of in the company of those he still like to refer to as "ladies." I have pointed out how Edwardian this sounds, but he just tousles my hair when I do. "A little respect never hurt anybody, pumpkin," he says.

He pumps the water while I hold the buckets steady, and I am oddly pleased that he is getting more out of breath than I am. "So, you doing all right out here?" he asks between gasps for air, his voice carefully casual.

I am not fooled. "Why, are you worried about us?"

He straightens up from the pump, his hand in the small of his back. I recognize the action and the accompanying grimace. "It's wild country," he says obliquely by way of response.

"We're fine," I tell him. Jessica Stanfield, Frontier Girl. "It's perfect out here. I don't ever want to go back." From being stubborn about not coming out, I've gone full circle to being stubborn about ever leaving.

His expression clouds. "Best you stay here for a while," he says in apparent agreement. "It's not so good these days out there. There's a lot of hatred, a lot of irrationality. Even in Boston. I'd never have believed it, but I'm seeing it now. They're whipping up people's fear, and fear does ugly things to the human mind." He pauses. "And to the human heart, too."

I'm not interested in a philosophical discussion, no matter how compelling. "What about school?"

"We'll deal with that when it's time," he says with a slight shrug, and I wonder if school will be put on hold for the duration. I wouldn't mind that at all. "It's safer here," Daddy concludes, and I think he's surprised that his own prediction turned out to be true.

"For Anna?"

"For anyone."

Mother is worried. "What about the other people out here?" she asks, and is relieved when we say that we haven't met anybody yet. She is convinced that they are all thieves or murderers or people who don't know which fork to use at dinner. "I saw a man on the beach one morning," I offer, but have to admit that by the time I had scrambled down the sand from the bluff, he was gone. Just as well: Mother would have demanded his genealogy.

"What about provisions?" asks Daddy, more practically. For all that Mother says he's not very down-to-earth, he really is. He is sitting in the shade of the shack now, a rickety chair on a makeshift porch, wiping his brow with his handkerchief.

"All is well," Anna tells him solemnly. She has taken pains for their visit, wearing a dress that the sun hasn't faded too much yet, proper shoes instead of sandals, a bit of lipstick. Her hair came undone altogether before they arrived, and she let me brush it out, shining fine and light and blonde in the sunlight, before gathering it back into a knot and sticking in the hairpins that will no doubt be lost before the day is over.

Daddy arranged for the dune taxi to stop by once a month with food and batteries and kerosene for the lamps and the small refrigerator, and already Anna has our ration tickets neatly divided into the appropriate piles: red for meats and cheese, blue for canned goods.

The taxi's only stopped by once since we got here; it is my task to deal with Sebastian, the driver, so that no one in Provincetown can start talking about a German woman living out in the dunes. Anna's accent is not heavy, but we cannot take risks: the threat is too real. At night before I go to sleep I imagine lynch mobs pouring out into the dunes and surrounding the shack.

The wind is shifting now, coming from the north, off the ocean, and we feel the chill in spite of the sun. I love every mood of the dunes, but this is perhaps the one I love the best: the sun hot, the breeze tipped with ice, the sands alive and moving with wind and salt. Mother is unimpressed, ready to leave. The dune taxi is coming for them, which is good: I don't think that either of them could make it back out, tired as they are; the cold wind lasts only as far as the first high ridge.

Mother tugs fussily at my blouse before she leaves; Daddy envelops me in a hug, then brushes a lock of brown hair from my face. It's always blowing into my eyes; I'm seriously considering cutting it short. Mother would *die*. "Take good care of yourself, pumpkin."

I grin. "I am," I say.

Anna watches the dune taxi until it has disappeared from sight; there's longing I can read in her eyes along with something else that I don't quite understand.

I don't wait to find out what it is. I'm already heading down to the beach.

Who knows what the tide is bringing in?

Chapter Four

Anna tells me that I must go into town.

"The taxi-man, Sebastian, he has told them about you," she says, her arms up as she straightens her hairpins, jabbing them in with excessive energy, "and about your aunt, *ja*? I am supposed to be your aunt, remember? Your aunt who feels so poorly? We cannot have people coming out here to see if I am well. You must go to town, *mein Engel*, so that they are not curious."

I don't want to. "What do I do, wear a signboard?" I ask her sarcastically. "Jessica and her aunt are fine, don't worry?"

To my surprise, she smiles, showing straight white teeth and just the tip of her tongue. "It is an idea," she says, chuckling. "Go, now."

Anna with a sense of humor? This is something new.

It's a long walk. A very long walk. Across the dunes—already a good distance—to Route Six, cross the highway, then down Snail Road as far as you can go until you reach the harbor. There are trees on either side of me as I walk, the grotesque stunted trees of the Cape, twisted by generations of wind; but they're their own kind of woods, and the shade is wonderful after the dunes.

There isn't a whole lot of shade in the dunes.

Turn right on Commercial Street and the trees change almost at once: protected here, they are taller, less twisted, elms like the ones I see all the time on Boston Common. I walk and walk and walk… The muscles I am developing in the dunes don't help me on the pavement, and it feels hard and unyielding beneath my feet.

It's on Commercial Street that the magic of the town starts to take over.

I am walking past houses with neat groomed lawns, tiny gardens with profusions of flowers of every color imaginable, tidy houses with shutters to close them off to the weather, a large yellow clapboard house with the figurehead from some long-ago whaling ship attached above the front door. There are smells here, honeysuckle, cloying and thick, and roses, tame and tight, not like the beach roses of the dunes. The lilac is everywhere, spilling over walls, sidling up beside houses, and its scent is deep and rich; I stop and breathe it in deeply, deliberately; it reminds me, suddenly, of home and the lilac bushes in the Public Gardens, and I feel an odd stab of loss that I don't want to analyze.

A dog barks furiously at me from its tether in one yard; farther down, a screen door slams and a woman's voice is raised in a question. There's a sense of harmony, of slowness, of life lived at a comfortable pace, something I've never experienced before on a city street: Boston teems with energy, with a sense of being driven, the minutes ticking away, no time to lose. Here there is energy, it hums all along the street, but it doesn't outpace the life lived in these houses.

I peer unabashedly through windows into brick-warmed kitchens, rooms filled with chintz and cats, an occasional easel with a half-finished canvas upon it, and my pulse quickens. The roses entwine themselves along fences and they smell like I imagine drugs would smell, opium and hashish, mysterious and heady.

At one corner, a fence runs along the sidewalk, and beyond it a lodging house. In the front yard, two women — dwarfs, they are

— are rooting about the bushes, gardening. One of them straightens and smiles at me. I return the smile uneasily, embarrassed by her deformity as she herself is not, embarrassed by my own reaction to her. I say "good morning," but my words sound a little too hearty. I wonder if other people respond to them that way, too.

The street runs parallel to the harbor, I can smell it, the fish and seaweed, and I am intrigued by the tameness of the waves, accustomed as I am to the pounding taken by the backshore. Here they float in, daintily almost, kissing the stones before withdrawing with a ladylike hiss; farther down the street, the stones disappear and it is sand punctuated by jetties where the gulls drop clams and oysters to break them open. Some of the jetties are deserted, and I wonder if it's because of the war, whether pleasure boats once pulled in there, and I remember Daddy telling me about racing his sailboat somewhere on the Cape.

I can't remember, now, where that was.

The sun is glinting on the water and I turn back to the street again. The neat little houses of the East End have given way now to shopfronts: there's a tea salon and a bookshop, an art gallery and a hatter, all of them side-by-side with hardware and ship's stores and a woodworker's shop, and I am delighted by the informality of it, how it's so hodge-podge, as if some hand had just scattered them all, willy-nilly, down Commercial Street. Mother would be appalled, accustomed as she is to the rarefied air of Newbury Street and Boylston Street, where only the latest in fashion, accessories, and (that most important accessory of all) hairdressers can be found. I see my own reflection in a shop window, and my current coiffure— long brown hair that I forgot to pull back, wild and tangled—would give any of those hairdressers nightmares. I shrug it off and walk on and giggle at the mannequins standing in the next window. They're naked. Mother would be beyond appalled; she'd have fainted (or at least pretended to) by now.

I'm loving every moment of it.

When I finally get to the center of town I find it focused, still reeling from the recent encounter with the enemy. There's a big sign announcing that awards will be given to the Civilian Defense Unit a few days from now — if I have the date today right, which is doubtful — with speeches recognizing everyone in the town for their quick work and bravery in rescuing so many of the unfortunate sailors whose ships were torpedoed. The signs are up all around the Town Hall and there's a brass band practicing on the front lawn, so it must be soon; people passing by stop to watch, and in minutes there's a small crowd gathered.

I stand in front of the signs, frowning. Two freighters, I am thinking, and close enough in to shore for there to be survivors to rescue. Good thing Mother didn't realize how close that was … and don't I wish I'd been here when it happened! I know, I know: yet another incarnation of my inability to see what my future looks like. Jessica Stanford, Emergency-Worker Girl.

"Isn't it thrilling?" trills a girl standing next to me, and I transfer my frown to her. "What's thrilling about it?"

She smiles, her ordinary face lit from somewhere inside, transformed into beauty in the moment. Her eyes are cornflower-blue, and they sparkle. "It makes the war seem *real*," she says.

"And this is a *good* thing?"

She blinks at me. "Of course it is," she says. "All our boys are out there–" her gesture appears to include the sky "– and here at home we did something to help them! We helped the war effort! It's better than a victory garden! It's better than saving cans or… or anything! Isn't it grand, to be able to help?"

"Grand," I repeat, nodding, my eyes drawn back to the poster. I'm resenting her, I know, because I missed the excitement, all the smaller boats of the fishing fleet out there, pulling men from the water, that same Commercial Street I just walked down alive and bustling with purpose, with stretchers and shouted commands, the serious business of saving lives. The hotels, I read in the Province-town *Advocate,* the newspaper the dune taxi delivers, served as temporary shelters and makeshift hospitals for those who couldn't be transported, and even the tourists were pitching in to help. The Crown and Anchor is right down the street: I'll have to go inside and try to imagine what it was like. "Were you here when it happened?" I ask her.

The cornflower blue eyes are alight. "I was," she says, the recent memory dancing in her words. "There were ever so many of them, and they were all of them hurt—some of them badly hurt. I didn't look too much at that part," she confesses, a shadow crossing her face. "But I helped at the hotel, I did! Ran and got bandages from Doctor Barrow, and he came up, too, and we all pitched in to help." She smiles sunnily again. "And they say the town's divided, but it wasn't so at all, we were all working together, the Portugee along with us, like there weren't any differences at all."

"What differences are there supposed to be?" I ask involuntarily, and she frowns, her eyes narrowing. "Where're you from, anyway?"

"Boston," I say, then I add dutifully, thinking of my mission for Anna, "but I'm here on the Cape for the summer with my aunt. She's not well, she needs the salt air." Just a couple more tourists, my tone implies. Nothing to see here. Move along.

She looks at my dress, which, while perhaps the worse for wear since we've been in the dunes (everything fades in the sun when we hang clothing out to dry on the line), is still one of which Mother approves—meaning, of course, that it was expensive. The cornflower eyes take it in, assessingly, then travel back up to my face. She's decided where I fit in her world. "Well, here in Provincetown," she says, confidingly, "there's people like us, and then there's the Portugee. They're fishermen and people who work on the docks–you know, they cut fish and prepare it to go off on the train to Boston and New York. Things like that. And some of them work as help, too. And everyone says they're different from us."

Help. The word echoes in my mind. When did it start being a noun instead of a verb? And what does that make *Anna*?

Rebelliously, I start liking these "Portugee" already.

I turn back to the sign, dismissing the girl with the cornflower eyes and the ignorant attitude. I stare at it until I feel rather than see her move away, and I let out a long breath that I didn't even know I'd been holding in.

The ceremonies are scheduled for later this week. I think I'll give them a pass. Tell me to dislike someone or something, and out of sheer perversity I'll seek it out. It's gotten me in trouble before.

I expect that it will get me in trouble again.

The street beckons, and I forget Cornflower Girl as soon as I turn away from the Town Hall. Behind Commercial Street lies the harbor, with a series of piers jutting off into it, and down in this section of town all of them are filled with activity, all of them foreign and scary and wonderful.

Boston has a harbor, too; but I've never been there, it's not part of my prescribed life of private school and church and carefully selected friends and activities. I don't venture down the piers today, but I look at them with longing, watching people moving with purpose and assurance, brown muscled arms lifting weighted boxes in the sunlight.

The Boston Boat, as it's called, is in, down at the steamboat landing, discharging a dozen or so passengers, none of them looking any too happy. I wonder if that's why Daddy and Mother take the train: Daddy loves the water, but now that I think of it, I can't remember Mother ever being near it. Perhaps she, too, would have that inward-looking preoccupied expression on her face, the sure sign of queasiness.

I stop at the Portuguese bakery on my way back and, dipping into my pocket for the ration tickets Anna gave me and some coins to accompany them, I buy a bag of sweet rolls. The owner himself rings me up, curiosity glinting in his eyes, and I again remember my mission. "I'm Jessica Stanfield," I say, and reach across the counter to shake his hand, a gesture that appears to both surprise and embarrass him. Mother would have out-embarrassed him for sure, I think with satisfaction. "My aunt and I are staying out at my uncle Louis' cottage for the summer," I report dutifully.

Something behind the dark eyes relaxes: he has me pegged, now. Summer people. We smile at each other in perfect understanding. I eat half the sweet rolls on the long walk back to the dune shack, and Anna is so relieved to see me that she forgets to scold me for eating them.

This is *nothing*, this living out on the backshore, I decide. Sun and sea and endless sky, and a walk into town when I need to see new faces.

I could stay out here forever.

***

There is a new wind plucking at me when I head down to pump the water for the evening washing-up; it's coming from a new direction, strange and disorienting, and there's a sharpness in it that cuts at my skin.

The wind brings with it a sense of foreboding; I feel a sudden presence at my back, dark and close. I stop and spin around, my hands automatically out in front of me to ward off whoever it is, whatever it is—but there's no one there. I can't shake the sense of being watched, and I scan the horizon, but it's that indeterminate twilight after the sun has set when inanimate things come alive and whispers are carried in the air, and I see nothing, I see everything.

I can't remember feeling this—Daddy would call it an "irrational fear"—before. Panic, the ancients called it, after the god Pan, the god of wild untamed nature, who inspired sudden fear in lonely places. Well, here I am, Jessica Stanfield, Frightened Girl, alone with Pan himself; and I can feel his breath at my back. My feet stumble on the path to the dune shack, and when one of the dune-grasses wraps around my ankle, I fancy it's grabbing at me, and I cry out.

It's a reminder, I think when, relieved, I'm back in the shack, watching Anna arrange and rearrange the hairpins in her beautiful streaked hair, grateful for the light and the company.

It's a reminder that nothing is completely safe, not ever.

Chapter Five

I am walking farther and farther afield all the time. The dunes are endless, and so is their fascination. No two are alike, even if you think they are; each has a shape and a feeling that is all its own.

Tiny beings live in the sand; you have to step carefully when you go on the paths—in the evenings, the sand-toads appear out of nowhere, from right under your feet, hopping away in quick consternation.

There are birds everywhere, tree swallows that dart and dip to catch insects on the fly; arctic terns, knifing quickly into the ocean on their daily fishing expeditions; the shearwater with its distinctive cry, soaring and dipping over the dunes; the many variants of gulls, wheeling and screaming over the water, arguing noisily over a fish or crab, then flying back into the dunes at night to sleep.

I see the other dune shacks, but I am careful to skirt around them, mindful to give them a wide berth. Mother would be proud of both my analogies and of my caution, though it is not because I am afraid; if people come out here for solitude, there's a good chance they won't be pleased at having it interrupted. It's out of respect, not fear, that I don't approach the other shacks.

They're an odd group, these shacks, eclectic in design–some on stilts, while others nestle into the very side of a dune, with only the roof visible–and yet they all have one thing in common: in their desire for privacy, they have been built so that none of them looks directly into another. The hills created by the dunes are used here to great advantage; one can be close to a shack and yet barely able to tell if it is inhabited or not.

As I find out.

I bump into one of them, literally, coming round a dune and there the shack is, rising abruptly out of the lee of the hill, and a wizened man peering crossly out at me from its shadows. The shack is surrounded by little square boxes on poles, and the air is humming with the flight of tree swallows, flitting in and out of them. I gasp in delight, and his expression lightens. "They're beautiful!" I exclaim.

His face creases into a smile.

"What are they?" I ask, curious and delighted to at last be near one of the famous eccentrics of the backshore.

"Tree swallows," he says, and his voice sounds old, decrepit, unaccustomed to much use.

We have some swallows near Louis' shack, too, but not as many as are here, whizzing around and diving into the small holes cut into the birdhouses. I watch them for a moment, then watch him, too, the face creased with a permanent smile of affection. Impulsively, I speak again. "I'm Jessica Stanfield," I say politely, but don't offer my hand: I do have some sense, after all. "I'm living in my uncle Louis' shack."

"Don't have much use for people," he answers obliquely. There is a long pause as he gives the matter some thought, and I'm about to leave when he speaks again, finally, his voice creaky with disuse. "The birds, them? I got all the time in the world for 'em."

I don't know how to respond to that. *Yeah, they're more interesting? Maybe people would be nicer to you if you were nicer to them?* Hardly. So I stand there for a moment gaping at him: Jessica Stanfield, Socially Inept Girl. But I'm smiling as I walk away.

Mother would just *hate* the people out here.

I am at the beach mornings and evenings, watching the sun rise and later watching it slip back into the sea, seeming to accelerate as it goes. I love the mornings best. The light falls at a longer angle over the shack, washing it with warm light, light that's full of promise, and the ocean is sharp, well defined; everything is lively and fresh. By afternoon, with the sun high, the colors seem to fade. A haze appears over the water. Evening is slow to arrive and quick to leave; afternoons, I have found, last forever. Insects become frantic in their attempts to enter the shack, and even the birds seem subdued, colorless, their chirping desultory.

It is afternoon and I have nothing special to do. Anna is sitting in the shade of the front shack wall, repairing the mosquito netting that we have cocooned around our bunkbeds. The air is still, hushed, expectant. The tide is high, abnormally so, following the full moon; and I can hear the surf, the waves coming and going every seven seconds (or so my father maintains), their sound amplified by the cliff of sand a dozen yards away.

The sound calls me, draws me out, down the crumbling path with the sand hot under my bare feet, down to the beach, the empty beautiful beach that I already think of as my own.

Today it's not empty.

Off to my right, just before the beach curves away behind the bluff, someone is attempting to put a rowboat to sea.

I am gaping, I know. The sun is shining on dark hair, a checked shirt, trousers. It's a boy, perhaps from one of the shacks; but where did the *boat* come from?

I am thinking as I am walking, my curiosity aroused (well, what would you expect, I haven't seen anyone my own age in weeks!), automatically moving closer to him. He's still struggling to get the boat past the first set of breakers, up to his waist in the water when, for some reason, he looks back and sees me.

It's not a boy, it's a girl, long crinkled black hair in a thick braid down her back, wearing pants and a short-sleeved shirt that's open at the neck, skin darkened by the sun. She seems annoyed. "Well?" she shouts at me.

"What?" I shout back, stupidly. The conversation is picking up nicely.

"Are you gonna watch me, or are you gonna help?"

I think of my dress, laboriously washed by Anna up at the shack. I think of what my mother would say. I wade in after her.

The stones in the surf are sharp under my bare feet, but I'm not going to stop now. She's chest-high in water by the time I get to her and grasp the side of the wooden dinghy, gasping. She's a little breathless too. "Steady it, will ya?" she yells, and before I realize what she's doing, she's heaved herself up into it. The boat rocks dangerously, and I grab onto it to steady myself; I can feel a slight undertow snatching at my legs, and I'm grateful to the muscles the sand has given me.

I cling to the side of the boat. She's sitting in it now, picking up the oars from the bottom. "Thanks!" she calls as she fits them into the oarlocks.

"No!" I manage to shout. I just realized that she intends to row off on her own, and I am *not* going to have ruined a perfectly good dress without getting *some* fun out of it. "Help me in!"

For a moment it looks like she won't; then she pushes an oar aside, leans forward, and hauls me—nearly effortlessly—up into the boat where I sprawl, short of breath and my heart hammering. "Thanks," I manage to gasp.

She picks up the oars again and begins to row, long gliding strokes; we're skimming the water's surface like the seabirds I watch from Louis' shack. Out here, paradoxically, the sea is calmer: the waves that throw themselves with such wild abandon on the beach are only swells farther out, and the dory rides them gently and gracefully. The girl handles the boat easily, offhandedly almost, with the economy of movement I always associate with people who are very good at what they do.

Seen closer up, she seems to be about my age, perhaps only slightly older. Both of us are soaking wet. Her hair is black and wiry, trying to escape from the braid in tendrils of tight curls. She's wearing men's clothes, work-clothes, and I can't stop staring at them. I want to dress like that. But what does it mean? Mother would die if she saw a girl dressing like that. Even Anna... well, I'm not sure how Anna would react anymore, Anna's been showing me sides to her that I never imagined. Maybe Anna would want to wear men's pants, too. Denims, like this girl is wearing.

I think Daddy wouldn't mind, but I also think he'd analyze it to death, and that would take all the fun out of it. I'm still staring at the girl and she feels my gaze on her and looks my way; her eyes are bluer than any sky I've ever seen. "Well?" she asks, her voice aggressive.

Fair enough. I did invite myself on board, after all. "Do you live in the dunes?" I ask. She must; her very persona defines eccentricity. I wonder if it's her voice I've heard sometimes in the evenings, singing plaintively, sadness carried on the night air.

She almost smiles, then, but I don't know what I said that was funny. "No. I live in town."

There is a moment of silence as I try to decide which question to ask next. I have so many: If you live in town, why were you launching your boat by the dunes? What are you doing in the dunes, anyway? Why does your mother let you dress in men's clothes? Who *are* you?

She isn't in the mood to chat, in any case. "Best I can do is leave you to Race Point beach," she says, the words coming in spurts between her breaths as she pulls at the oars. "I gotta get this boat back before my brother knows it's missing."

"Can I walk back here from there?"

She stops rowing for a moment and studies my face. "Only if you have a couple of hours," she says.

My mother is always saying that my impulsiveness is going to get me in trouble someday. I *hate* it when my mother is right.

I try another tack. "Can I get to Provincetown from Race Point?" I ask, thinking I can get a ride back out on the dune taxi.

She shakes her head, resting her arms on the oars, tanned and strong. "You really don't know what you're doing, do you?"

I'm about to say something smart, but I can't think what that is, and I smile instead. "No, I don't."

She starts laughing. "Well, at least you know what you don't know." She stows an oar and sticks out her hand. "I'm Sophie."

I take it. "My name's Jessica."

"Jessica? What kind of stuck-up name is that?" She starts rowing again. I can see her muscles under the sleeves of the shirt. "And what's somebody named Jessica doing out all alone in the dunes?"

I think for a minute, looking at her position at the oars. "What kind of stupid transportation keeps you looking where you've been instead of where you're going?"

She starts laughing again, and I join in. "I live out here," I tell her.

"In one of the dune shacks?" She is impressed in spite of herself.

I preen myself, spreading my skirt out daintily–and wetly–on either side of me. "Yes," I say primly.

There is nothing for a while but the creaking of the oars, the slapping of the waves on the sides of the boat, Sophie's breathing and grunts as she moves us through the water. I run my tongue over my lips and taste salt.

We round another bluff and Sophie changes direction, pulling us closer to the shore. "I know who you are," she says, suddenly. "You're in Louis' old place. I heard somebody was there. They were all talking about it in town."

"You know Louis?"

She shrugs, pulls at the oars. "Nobody knows Louis. He likes it that way." A mischievous look from under her lashes. "From what I hear, I think my aunt Tania must've known him *real* well, though."

I am shocked, though the last thing I want to do is show it, so I giggle instead, then get mad at myself for giggling. It's such a little-girl reaction. It's stupid. I need to find better ways to deal with embarrassment. Maybe I'll put it on one of the to-do lists that Mother is forever making.

But, really: Sophie's aunt and my uncle? And… what did they do together? The thought of real actual sex takes my breath away for a moment.

After a few minutes Sophie apparently realizes that nothing else scintillating is going to come out of my mouth. She sighs and puts the oars down into the boat and shifts around so she is, in fact, facing forward. She starts the motor at the back, and after that there's no talking at all, just the sharp taste of salt and the sharper wind in my face.

We're nearing the shore now, and I can see some low buildings sitting on the sand. We pull up to a makeshift dock, and Sophie scrambles out, tying the boat before giving me her hand to help me out. I grab her and feel a line of electricity shoot up my arm. "I'll get the dune taxi," says Sophie. She smiles; she knows she's reading my mind. "They'll take you on out t'Louis' place."

She heads up the dock to the low buildings squatting beyond the beach. People there, more people than I've seen together in one place for a long time, and I realize how much the dunes have changed my perceptions of things. "Wait!" I call.

Sophie turns back.

"Come see me again?" I ask, and hate myself for the eagerness in my voice. I didn't realize until this moment that I miss having people my age around. Or maybe just people around. Jessica Stanfield, Society Girl.

"Maybe," she concedes, and is gone.

It's a tedious trip back, bouncing in the back of the dune taxi with the provisions he's bringing out to the other shacks, and it seems to take forever. We make the regular rounds first, Sebastian making it clear that I'm taking him out of his way—not that he won't be paid for it, I think sourly—and I'm interested to see that few of the shack people come out to greet him. He lifts provisions onto porches and into doorways, tooting his horn each time, once calling out to somebody named Estelle, and I hear an answering voice from inside, but Estelle never appears. The man with the bird-houses pokes a hand out a window with a gesture that could be a wave and could be something rude; I can't tell, and Sebastian isn't talkative today.

I find myself instead rubbing my forearm and thinking about how strange it felt when Sophie touched me there.

By the time Sebastian drops me off I'm not thinking about much of anything at all. The somnolence of the dunes, the heaviness of the day, the heat and tiredness all seem oppressive, weighty. Even the air itself is heavy, filled with moisture, pushing me down.

Anna scolds me when I tell her the story, and there is fear in her eyes as she does, fear I haven't seen there before. The hairpins seem to agree, slipping out of her fine hair in a veritable deluge. "You're not supposed to be talking to no one," she says. "You're not supposed to tell no one we're here."

What? And this from the person who—albeit jokingly—wanted me to wear a sandwich board downtown? "She says that everyone in town knows someone is living here, anyway," I say. "You *told* me to go in and talk to people, Anna. You can't have it both ways."

I'm bristling because she's being unfair, and that's not like her, and I suddenly, passionately want Anna to stop acting in ways that aren't like her. I want the old Anna back. I want my peace and security back. I wonder where her fear is coming from, and what possible harm she thinks that Sophie–a girl my own age–can bring us.

The only thing I really know is that Anna's fear, from whatever source it derives, grows daily. She has started pacing the shack at night, four steps in either direction, while I lie on my top bunk balancing a kerosene lamp or a flashlight as I try to read. From time to time, she peers out the door or a window into the darkness, then resumes her pacing. Sometimes she goes out onto the porch in the dark, as though to sniff the wind; but the mosquitoes always drive her back inside. They're voracious, the mosquitoes.

She watches the sweep of light from the lighthouse as though mesmerized by it.

We can't see the Race Point Light from Louis' shack, but we can see Highland Light away to the southeast, and she fixates on the lighthouse as though it were a searchlight, coming ever closer, ready to swallow her whole. I find her fears ridiculous, and I tell her so with all the arrogance of my sixteen years.

The lighthouses are impervious to the war. I know that in England they have blackouts, that people cover their windows so that no one can see them; Daddy's said he thinks it's a terrific idea, but it's not catching on very well here. The Provincetown monument is, amazingly, still lit at night, and the lighthouses–there are several of them around, Highland and Race Point and Long Point and

Woods End–both illuminate the night and punctuate it with soft bellows, regular puffs of sound.

They're necessary, the lighthouses, of course. The Germans aren't the only enemy, here on the coast: there's something far more immediate (and to most people's minds, far more dangerous). The fog is a daily companion, often encasing us in soft white dampness; at times I cannot even see the ocean. It moves in gradually, insidiously, and suddenly the world has gotten smaller. Sounds are amplified in the mist, and distances distorted; it's a little like being in an odd kind of funhouse where up is down and nothing is quite as it seems.

Perhaps that's what life is like, too, I find myself thinking: nothing, in the end, is what it first seemed to be.

On clear days, you can look straight out toward Stellwagen Bank, where the ocean bottom swells up and a rich feeding ground for fish and birds alike beckons. There are whales offshore at Stellwagen, but many come in closer, and Daddy has left me a pair of binoculars at the shack: on fine days, I go out on the porch and scan the horizon, and more days than not I can see the blow of a whale, sometimes even a flash of tail or fin, the water trailing off it, sparkling in the sun. It never fails to amaze me, like I'm looking at something prehistoric, something that's been there since the beginning of time. Jessica Stanfield, Nature Girl.

I am close to touching magic, out here.

The dune taxi brings us mail, too, and I finally figure out that that's where Anna's fears are coming from. I know this now from Daddy. "You need to be strong for her," he writes to me. "She's going to need you to be strong. Bad things are happening in Germany."

"What things?" I ask Anna, and she turns away from me, tears glinting in her eyes, oblivious to the hairpins she's shedding. She doesn't want to talk about it, and even though I scribble furious notes to Daddy, he doesn't say anything else about it, either. I am frustrated beyond belief. How can I help if I don't know what I'm doing? Why don't people trust me enough to tell me what is really going on? I'm not a child anymore, but they all act as though I were. I'm fed morsels of the truth, pieces of it that I'm left to assemble like some demented jigsaw puzzle, but never getting the whole picture because everyone's holding back their pieces. Either tell me or don't tell me, but don't give me cryptic messages that tell me to protect Anna from something I don't even know exists!

It's all very maddening.

I go down to the beach every day and look for Sophie, and of course she's never there. On the really hot days, when there is shimmering light hovering just over the dunes and sprites seem to dance in the shadows, I wonder if I dreamed her, imagined her, whether I'd had one of Mother's so-called episodes.

If this is where she comes, why doesn't she come back?

I walk out at night, too, to escape from Anna, to get away from the fear in the shack that's so thick you could slice it, to feel that I'm part of the dunes, of something bigger than the war or Anna or Daddy or Sophie. Everything seems more primal at night, somehow, and the hissing of the waves below me as I walk the headland is reassuring.

There's one of those fogs moving in tonight, thick and damp. I can't hear the waves anymore, all there is are the mournful blasts of the foghorns that replaced the Coast Guard lifesaving station they closed twenty years ago.

They're the ghosts of the dunes, the guardsmen. They were the ones who built the first shacks, so their wives and girlfriends could live close by when they were on duty. Some nights when I'm down on the beach alone I can see their ghosts, walking two by two, patrolling up and down the beach, day and night, summer and winter. Was it a horrible job? Or did they enjoy the peace of the night, the hiss of the ocean, the moon spreading liquid silver over the sea?

Nights and nights and nights with nothing to do but walk and talk, walk and talk... and then finally the night where they stumble on a ship, one that didn't know about the sandbars here, that lost its way in the dark on a night without stars. Then they set up a flare, attracting as many people who wanted to pillage the wreck as those who wanted to help.

The whole of the Cape is littered with wrecks, a thousand or more of them in all, many of them recent.

Daddy's been sending me what wisdom he can glean about my new home, writing down everything that he reads and hears. "There've been so many shipwrecks on the back shore," he writes me, "that it's called an ocean graveyard. More than a thousand wrecks just between Truro and Wellfleet!"

I think of the guardsmen now as I watch the fog and wonder if the horns will keep the ships safely off the shoals tonight; but the reality is that I'm wondering about it so I don't have to think about

Anna, about what is happening to Anna, who has always been the strongest woman I know.

Seeing her afraid scares me more than anything else I can imagine.

She has dragged the rocking chair into the shack from the porch and she is sitting in it, the lamplight etching creases in her face I don't remember seeing before. She is old by my standards, Anna, but I know that she is not really old: in her early forties somewhere, no gray in the fine blonde hair yet, slightly plump and still very pretty.

I do know enough to know that those worry-lines don't belong on the face of anyone that young.

Now she sits there, rocking back and forth, her hands smoothing the flimsy airmail letter that they delivered for her today—encased safely in a letter addressed to me from Mother so that no one would see Anna's name—over and over again, the movement of her hands matching the rocking of the chair. She isn't worried about her hairpins, which are all sticking out at off angles. Anna *always* worries about her hairpins.

Suddenly the room feels too small, the smell of the kerosene oily and stifling. "I'm going for a walk," I announce, pulling a sweater on over my dress.

Anna doesn't say anything.

I snap on my flashlight and follow the ridge out along toward where I know a grouping of dune shacks lie: I don't care anymore if the inhabitants are eccentric, or if they want their privacy. If I don't see another person besides Anna soon, I'm going to go mad.

If she doesn't beat me there first, that is.

I think I hear howling somewhere off in the distance, muffled by the fog, and I shiver. Are there wolves on Cape Cod? I don't know, but there's no reason to think that there aren't any. And bears, too, probably, I say to mock myself, to snap out of the sudden claw of fear I'm feeling at the base of my spine. Sure, Jessica, there are all sorts of creatures out here, just waiting to jump on you. Lions, perhaps. Goodness, if you're thinking along those lines…

A dune shack looms up suddenly in the mist; I nearly bump into it. Unlike ours, there is no porch running all around this cottage: my hand reaches out and touches shingle. It is damp with the ocean and the fog. I feel my way along it, groping in the dark, and drop my flashlight.

There is a tinkling of shattering glass and the light goes out.

I take a deep breath. I will not be afraid. I will not be afraid. I grope along the wall in the darkness, the mist wet up against my face; I am a blind woman, reading Braille for survival.

I round the corner and feel along the side facing the ocean. Slowly, one step at a time, the sand, too, is cold and clammy against my bare feet. I find myself thinking, absurdly, I should have put on shoes tonight.

On the other side of the wall, something moves.

I hear the bump as something heavy is shifted, followed by complete silence, and in that moment I know that I am listening to someone listening to me.

The foghorn from Highland Point bellows a warning.

And I, who just a few minutes ago had craved company, now find myself fearing it. I haven't any choices: whoever is there has heard me, and in any case, I'm not at all sure that I can find my way back along the ridge in the dark. One misstep, and I could fall over the bluff overlooking the beach …

I take a deep breath. I feel along the wall until my fingers find a doorframe. I move further, locate the latch. If there's a murderer inside, I think, it can be worse than this horrid anticipation.

My hands are shaking. I lift the latch. The door swings open, and suddenly there is a bright light shining full into my face, blinding me.

I put up a hand to shield myself from it, and then Sophie's voice comes at me out of the darkness behind it.

"Not," she says crossly, "you again!"

Chapter Six

"Would you put that damned light out?" I demand. My hand is still up in front of my face, shielding my eyes. My heart is hammering uncomfortably. "You gave me a fright."

"Oh, and what do you think you did t' me? Creeping up on me like that?" But she lowers the flashlight beam. "What are you doing here?" Sharp.

"I went for a walk," I say, defensively.

A mocking tone creeps into her voice. "On a night like this? Without a flashlight?"

I start to tell her how I broke it, and then decide to take a different tack. "Okay," I say, giving up. My heart rate still isn't normal: for a moment, I was really scared out there. "Have it your way." I sound sullen and I don't mean to. "You still scared me," I add, softening my voice. I take a deep breath. I need to stop feeling so defensive. "Whose shack is this, anyway? I thought you said you didn't live in the dunes."

I sense rather than see or hear her movement. There is the hiss of a match, and the wick of a kerosene lamp catches, spilling a pool of yellow light around it. The familiar acrid greasy smell. "No one owns it," says Sophie, settling the glass carefully over the flame. "Not anymore," she adds, and there's a sadness in her voice that I don't know how to touch, I don't know why it's there.

I feel cold at my back, and close the door behind me. This shack is smaller even than ours, with no sink or cooker or refrigerator. Just a double bed with a quilt pulled up on it, two chairs, a table.

And books. The books are everywhere, shoved into makeshift shelves on the wall, piled on the table, spilling onto the floor. There's a braided rug here and more books on it, so many that I can't even tell what color the rug is. Or maybe that's the effect of the light. Hardcovers, the little paperbacks you get for twenty-five cents, notebooks … my eyes rise to meet Sophie's. "Yours?"

She doesn't pretend to misunderstand me. She puts her flashlight on the table and curls into one of the armchairs, automatically pulling a blanket down around her shoulders. "Mostly, yes." She pauses, then adds, "Sort of." There's a book open by her elbow; she must have put it down, turned out the lamp, when she heard me outside.

I sit down, uninvited, in the second armchair. "Whose shack is this?" I ask again, my eyes scanning the titles with an almost voracious interest. Doctor Zhivago. A collection of plays by Molière. Schopenhauer. Rudyard Kipling. Dante. I look at her again, wondering.

Sophie shrugs. "No one lives here," she repeats. "Not now, anyway. The old lady who lived here, it just got too hard for her to stay." She clears her throat. "Life out in the dunes, I mean. It's not for everybody, and especially not when you get old, even though there are a lot of really ancient people here, now that I think of it." She pauses and catches up with her own thoughts. "I mean, you don't get to meet them, much, but I've been coming out here for years, so they trust me." A speculative look. "You meet anybody, yet?"

"Besides you, you mean?"

She frowns; I'm not following her agenda for the conversation, apparently. "There's a man with birdhouses around his shack," I say, still looking around the room. The lamp casts grotesque shadows on the walls, flitting over the books, making them seem to move, take on the lives of all the characters they're holding inside. I shiver involuntarily. "And sometimes we hear singing."

Sophie knows who I'm talking about. "Her," she says, dismissively. "Crazy Edna."

Crazy Edna? "Who's that?"

Sophie's not interested. "Lady who lives in the house on the stilts," she says, diffidently. "She sings all the time."

"I'd *noticed* that," I say. Wasn't that what I'd just said?

Sophie shakes her head. "Crazy Edna," she says again, then embarks on a rapid-fire tour of the dunes. "There's her up on the ridge, then Louis—that's you, now—and this place in the hollow. If you went back up to the ridge and followed it, you'd get t' Max's shack, he's an artist but he's in New York now and I think he's going t' go away t' the war but I can't be sure." She is silent for a moment, and I don't say anything. "Anyway. After Max it's the two old ladies, I don't know their names, nobody knows their names, they're sisters and they're always yelling at each other. They don't talk t' anybody else, not even Sebastian, and they're always blaming each other for all the things that go wrong."

"Like what?"

A quick shrug. "Anything. I lay in the dunes one day and listened t' them, but it got boring after a while so I left. The only interesting things were when they both were yelling that Mamma liked me better than you. They went on with that one forever. Oh, an' one of 'em is always telling the other that she's the one does all the work, and the other says, no, it's *her.*"

I have an image of Sophie lurking outside dune shack after dune shack, and she suddenly seems much younger than she really is, a child uninvited to the party who still listens in the doorways.

A little like me.

"Tell me about this place," I say, gesturing. The shadows around me grow and jump in response, and I wish I hadn't moved so abruptly. How can she stay here alone at night? I'd never get to sleep: I'd be seeing things slithering around the spines of the books. Like I'm doing now.

Sophie is more prosaic. "The lady who lived here, she moved back t' her house in town. She'd already taken t' staying there winters, anyway." She looks at me, her gaze considering in the flickering light. "What are *you* going t' do in the winter?" she asks, a certain challenge mixed with something like satisfaction in her voice.

I shake my head. I don't know. Perhaps Daddy and Mother have plans, but somehow, I don't think that any of us have looked that far ahead, yet. Louis' shack is no place to winter, I've already figured that one out.

"Anyway," says Sophie, "I look after it for her. I patch up what I can, and get someone in t' repair what I can't."

"And in return," I say, "you get a place to escape to."

The dark eyes grow very wide in the lamplight. "Yes." It's a whisper, and I laugh out loud. "It's okay. You don't need to worry about me telling anybody," I point out. "Who would I tell?"

I think again of the dunes, of the imaginary whisperings from herring gull to marsh hawk, from sand toad to rabbit; but there's probably another communication system here, too, following the route of Sebastian's deliveries: Max, the old arguing sisters, the man with the tree swallows …

Sophie places a protective hand over the book that is open, pages down, next to her. I wonder if she feels threatened by my presence here, another girl her own age. A thought occurs to me. "Why does it matter, anyway, that you come out here? You said you take care of the place for somebody. If you have her permission, then what's the problem?"

"No one would understand," she says, her voice low.

"That you come out here?"

"That I come out here t' *read.*"

I stare blankly at her, and she turns angry again. "No one would understand," she snaps. "Not in my family. They don't—they'd think I was lazy. Trying t' get out of work. Everyone thinks that way: reading's not for working people."

There is a long silence after her revelation. I'm trying to come to grips with the concept of reading as luxury—at my house, we read as naturally as we breathe. Well, Daddy and I do, anyway. I realize suddenly that I have no idea what Mother does when she's alone. "What's your family like?" I ask, curious.

Her hair is down, tonight, and she takes a lock of it and twirls it around her finger, a nervous gesture. A habitual one? Daddy says that people all have gestures they make when they're stressed. "My dad's got his own boat," she says, and then stops, as if that explained everything.

It explains nothing. We have a boat, too, a Lawley with immense sails that Daddy keeps at the Boston Yacht Club. We don't go out in it very often, of course, because of all his meetings, and Mother's flat refusal to set foot on it; but we do have a boat. What that has to do with reading – or not reading – is a mystery to me.

Sophie sees my incomprehension. "His own boat," she repeats, and her voice takes on that same aggressive edge it had when we first met down on the beach. "You don't understand anything, do you? What do they teach you up there in Boston, anyway? It's a *fishing* boat, a dragger. Well," she amends her thought, striving for accuracy, "he owns it with someone else, but it's mostly his, and he's got four men working for him." There is some pride in her voice, now, too. "My ma works over t' – over *at* – the fish market down the wharf. She cuts fish, cleans them." A sharp bright glance in the lamplight to see if I'd caught the self-correction. "My brothers, too, they're on boats. One of 'em works for Dad, and two of 'em goes out on the *Mary Frances*, and they're out for a month or more, most of the time."

I don't say anything. I've never seen a fishing boat, not before I went into Provincetown, there aren't too many at the Boston Yacht Club. I have no idea what she's talking about.

Sophie takes my silence– well, okay, never mind, I don't know *how* she's taking my silence. She looks uncomfortable and I feel bad about that, too. I have no idea how to tell her that I'm not judging her, that I'm not like the other people who live and move in our circles in Boston. Like my mother.

Or maybe by being so careful not to judge, I'm judging?

"My dad and my ma," she says, finally, "didn't go past eighth grade. Well, my dad, anyway. My ma, probably less: she came over from Portugal—well, the Azores—t' marry my dad, it was set up for them before they were even born, and who knows how much schooling they'd think a girl needs, back there." She shrugs, dismissing it. "Two of my brothers didn't finish high school – didn't seem like there was much need, seein' as they were just joining the fleet anyways. My brother Tony just graduated, but he was already on Dad's boat part-time while he was in school, and there's nothing else t' do around here, at least nothing that makes that kind of money, anyways, so it didn't really matter." She straightens, unconsciously I think, in her chair. "Me, I'm different," she declares. "I'm finishing high school, and goin' on t' college if I can get a scholarship. Three hundred dollars, that's what I'll need. I'll do it, too."

"That's why you read so much?"

"I read so much 'cause I love t' read," she says crossly. "No one in my family loves t' read. I told you, they all think it's just for rich people. Or 'cause you're trying to get out of work. Ma doesn't even know how."

I look around myself again at the library filling the small room. "But where did you get–" Her eyes meet mine and I stop. "The lady who owns the house?" I guess.

"Yeah," Sophie concedes. "I've been coming out here for a long time. Helen's a nice lady. We can talk about all sorts of things. She tells me I can dream. When she moved back in town, she said I could use her shack. She gave me most of these books, anyway." She sighs. "Don't know what's gonna happen when she dies, though."

I've pulled some of the books closer to me and to the lamp so I can read more of the titles. I look up, startled. "Is she going to die?"

"Everyone's gonna die, Jessica." It's the first time she uses my full name, and I like how it sounds—it has a different flavor on her lips: exotic, foreign. I wish she would say it again, it makes me feel like *I'm* exotic, somehow.

Maybe to her, I am.

Sophie's miles away. "She wouldn't have moved back into town if she hadn't been poorly," she says, and sniffs, her hand brushing something off her face. "She loved her dunes, Helen did."

"And you," I say, not knowing where the words are coming from. "She loves you, too."

She looks at me, startled, and I see the tears shimmering in her eyes. "She is amazing," she says, and there's suddenly energy in her voice, the drive of the storyteller. "She had this dream… She lived in New York City, see, and it was summertime, and hot, and she had a dream—a vision is what she called it—of a sand bank with a shack nestled into the side of it, and a stunted tree beside the shack." Sophie is telling the story as if it's her own. "This sand bank was right next t' the ocean. And it seemed cooler there, cooler than in the city. She saw it like it was a photograph." She looks at me quizzically. "So she went looking for it."

I smile politely, completely disbelieving. "She went looking for something she saw in a *dream?*"

Sophie nods. "She believed it was real," she says. "So she started looking for it. And when she came t' Provincetown, somebody told her about the houses in the dunes, the shacks. She walked out here and saw this one, nestled into the bank like her dream told her it would be, with the little stunted tree beside it, and she knew that she wanted t' stay here forever."

There is silence. I imagine the courage that it takes to have a vision and then follow it–literally–all the way out here, out to the edge of the world. If that had happened to me, Daddy would have commented that Messrs. Freud and Jung might have something to say about my dreams.

Belief is a tricky thing.

"She bought this house for fifty dollars," Sophie says in a voice filled with wonder. "I don't know what will happen when she dies."

"Do you visit her? Now, I mean; in town."

She nods "Every day."

"Every *day*?"

She doesn't say anything. There's nothing more that can be said, really. I imagine a life that's so entwined in other lives: the busy family, fishing-boats coming back into the harbor after weeks at sea; the love for something you also can't wait to leave behind; the daily visits to a lonely woman who at last has had to give up on her dream. There's a richness in Sophie's life that people like me, people from brownstones on Commonwealth Avenue, can only imagine. That's real wealth, I think; our money is nothing. I feel very small, suddenly, my life and concerns petty and ridiculous.

I stand up, my shadow looming large in the lamplight. "I should go."

Sophie doesn't protest, doesn't ask me to stay, and there's an odd stab of disappointment in my stomach. "Have you got a flashlight?"

I shake my head, feeling stupid again. "I broke mine. I didn't bring another."

She takes my unpreparedness for granted. "I didn't think so. I'll walk you back. You can hurt yourself in the dark—or step on the frogs."

I wait by the door while she carefully extinguishes the flame in the kerosene lamp; it leaves a heavy, oily scent in the air. Outside, the moon has risen, fat and bright and yellow, lighting the dunes, casting shadows and humps of movement all over the sand.

I shiver. The dunes are a reflection of the moon, a pockmarked lunar landscape. The sea is growling in echoes to our right.

Sophie snaps me out of it. "This way," she says briskly, the flashlight beam bright and wide. The path lights up as if by magic, focused into flashes of light, while the landscape recedes, disappears. We are walking alone in a vast darkness, only our trail illuminated, the blackness always a presence at our backs. We could be in a forest; we could be in a moonscape arctic tundra; we could be anywhere. Sophie takes the lead and I stumble behind her, not wanting to admit my fear of looking around, of peering behind, of seeing what might be following us.

Louis' shack is bright and inviting and shining in the darkness like a lighthouse, like a beacon, the windows glowing with imagined warmth.

We stop at the bottom of the path that leads up the ridge to the house. Anna's silhouette appears at one of the windows, briefly, then is gone. "That your mother?" Sophie asks, curious.

"No. It's our housekeeper," I say, my answer automatic, prethought. Probably shouldn't have said that. I want to tell her more, to return the gift of trust that she gave to me in telling me about her family, about Helen; but Anna's secret isn't mine to give. "She's staying with me out here."

In Sophie's world, I realize belatedly, people don't have house-keepers. I can feel her eyes on me, but I don't know how to respond. "Thank you," I say finally, inadequately.

"Be seeing you 'round," she says, and turns to go back down the path. I don't want her to go; I want to stay curled up in Helen's shack, I want to read and drink coffee and talk with Sophie forever. I feel curiously bereft as she walks away from me, lightly, casually, the encounter one of many in her world, meaningless. There's an emptiness I feel in my chest, and I want her to stay. I don't want her to go. I watch and wait as her light grows smaller and smaller, bobbing along the path, a lone firefly in the night; and then the fog encloses her, and she is gone. I'm suddenly afraid that I'll never see her again.

I shake off the feeling and go in to face Anna's questions.

Chapter Seven

Anna cannot keep a secret.

She is waiting for me, anxious, but she has no interest in where I've been or what I've been doing. It's a nice change.

She is waiting for me; she wants to talk.

She is still holding the airmail letter, the one that came carefully enclosed in one of Mother's letters; she is holding it like a talisman, like an icon, something concrete she can clutch in a sea of insecurity. The flimsy paper is her lifeline and her terror. I wish we'd never seen it.

Her eyes are glinting with tears, her hair wild and unfettered and shining in the lamplight. I snap myself back into the room, putting thoughts of Sophie out of my mind. Okay, Jessica, time to decide which you want to be. The whining child who wants everything the way it used to be, who needs Anna to always be the same? Or the person Daddy believes you can be, who can let other people lean on her?

I know the answer even as part of me says a nostalgic goodbye to the tantrums and the stamped feet.

I take a deep breath and will myself to be transformed into the calming adult, even as Anna is the desperate child. I feel curiously empowered by that knowledge, older and wiser than my years, as I put my arms around her. "What is it, Anna? *Was ist geschehen?* What does the letter say?"

She clings to me and starts sobbing.

We stand there, awkwardly, in the lamplight. She's still shedding hairpins and one of them is sticking into my arm, uncomfortable, but I don't want to move and disturb whatever is happening here. I've never seen her like this; I've never felt that I needed to take care of anybody. I'm used to being the one that other people take care of, and I'm not sure I like the role reversal. I don't know what to feel, how to react. I don't know how to do this.

I stop thinking about what I'm doing and just do it, rocking her in my arms as best I can. "Shh," I croon softly, the way that Anna herself used to do when I was smaller. "Shh, shh. It's all right. It's going to be all right," I say. That's what my mother says to me when I'm in some sort of crisis, and it never works. The very fact of needing to say that everything's all right gives the lie to the words.

The reality is that we only tell someone that it's all right when it clearly isn't.

Anna knows the hollowness of the expression—she's used it enough herself in the past—and her grip tightens on me. I am afraid, suddenly: if Anna is in distress, then the world is surely changing. It's not just me changing, but everything: the earth shifts, dramatically, dangerously. Anna doesn't give in to emotion; she doesn't feel terror or ecstasy or any of the radical emotions that buffet the rest of humanity. Anna is unflappable. All my life, she has been the personification of calm. Joy and distress come and go; Anna stays the same.

Feeling her losing control suddenly doesn't make me feel like a wise adult anymore; it makes me feel very, very small and very, very scared. I want to tell her to stop it, to pull herself together, to take care of me like she's always done, like she's supposed to do.

But I've chosen not to do that. Not this time, anyway.

I take a deep breath and say the lie again. "It's all right, Anna. It will really be all right. But you have to tell me. I can't help you if you don't. Tell me what's happened. Tell me what's wrong."

She pulls away from me, finally, wiping her eyes on a corner of her apron, sniffing and hiccupping. She holds the letter—it's damp, now—out to me.

I take it hesitantly, as though it might burn me, and I unfold it, moving closer as I do to the kerosene lamp on the table; but it's no use, the words have been blurred by the damp of night by the sea, the ink smudged by her hands and her tears.

Besides, it's written in German. Which just goes to show how she's really not paying attention. And Anna *always* pays attention.

I take her hand and ease her into one of the chairs—high-backed wooden ones, we have, not like the soft encircling armchairs at Helen's shack—and I pull another one next to it, at a right angle. Still holding her hand, I sit and put the letter on the table. "You have to tell me, Anna. I can't read it."

"What?" She looks at me, blinking, her eyes focusing. They're grey-blue, like the sea on a stormy day, a window on the storm inside her raging out of control. I nod encouragingly. "Tell me."

She gestures, weakly, toward the flimsy offending packet of papers. "It is from my sister," she says, and stops.

We'll be at this all night at this rate. I wish Daddy were here: he'd know what to do, how to calm Anna, make her feel safe. He's always known how to do that for me.

Anna takes a deep, shuddering breath and lets go of my hand. I put it on her shoulder, instead; I don't know if she needs the contact, or if I do. "*Ja,*" she says, suddenly, and straightens her back, squares her shoulders. "I get hold of myself. I will tell you now."

I let my hand drop away. She's gone someplace else in her head, someplace that's giving her something that I can't, whatever strength I was trying so inadequately to share. She doesn't need me, now.

But she still needs to tell it, to say the words. Perhaps speaking them is what will make them real for her. Perhaps that's not such a good idea.

"My sister, she says things are very bad at home–in Germany– right now." Another deep breath. "My father, they made him lose his shop."

Anna has a father? I've never given her age any thought; now I narrow my eyes, looking at her face. I forget that she had a life in Germany before she came to America. She's been around for as long as I can remember.

"The soldiers came and took away his shop," Anna is saying. "That happens before. It is closed, it is over." She takes a deep breath. "And then they came and took away my father."

I frown. "I don't understand."

"It is because he is Jewish," Anna says, her voice absent, almost disinterested. "It is very bad to be Jewish in Germany right now." She looks at me and sees that I'm not understanding. "Imagine how it is, *liebchen,* someone walks into your house and says, now you must go. Pack what you can and leave. Leave everything behind, all your furniture, your liddle things, your books, you may never see any of it again but it's not your choice to make. Go away, find another place to live. These things, they now are all ours. Imagine yourself what they feels like, somebody saying that to you, you can take with you only what you can carry, you not know where you can go. That's very bad, and it is what is happening now." She takes a deep breath. "Sometimes, before they take away the house, they take away the people. And so it is with my father. He is gone."

I pat her hand uselessly and think about what she's saying. It's not the first time that we've heard about how the government feels about Jews; it's been in the newsreels at the cinemas for months, and it seems to me that half the people who sit in Daddy's study at his impromptu soirées are Jewish, so there've been a lot of passionate discussions about it, voices raised, expressions of fear and anger.

We're officially Episcopalian, of course; but that only covers Sundays and holidays and relatives. We are the family of a psychiatrist: the real household gods are Freud and Jung.

"I didn't know you're Jewish," I say to Anna. "You never go to… temple." Or is it synagogue? I have no idea. Jessica Stanfield, Religious Education Girl.

I'm embarrassed, suddenly, by my ignorance.

I don't have to be, apparently. "Bah!" she says, with a wave of her hand, coming back to my presence with a click that's nearly audible. "Silliness, all this religion. It always ends in tears. Does it help you to live a better life? *Nein.* Does it help you to earn a living? *Nein.* I see you go off to your church on Sundays and I think, it is good, if it makes them happy, then religion is fine. What you want to believe, you can believe. Me, I don't believe in nothing. I tell you, this religion, it always ends in tears."

I'm confused. "But if you don't go to temple..."

She looks at me and there's a glimmer of a smile, but it's sadder than anything I've ever seen. "Being a Jew, it is not something one does, *mein Engel*. Being a Jew, it is what one *is.*"

I don't really understand what she's talking about, but with wisdom that I don't usually exhibit in such circumstances, I manage to remain quiet. There is a space of silence, and I am aware of the kerosene lamps flickering, of the light and shadows they cast out the window, of the hissing of the waves down at the beach. I'm still no closer to knowing what to say to her. Her father has been imprisoned, or worse; what does one say? How can such inadequate things as words touch that kind of event?

Finally, desperate to find something to say, I ask, "What about the rest of your family?" I am thinking quickly, nervously, trying to remember what she has said about her family. I'm ashamed to admit that I rarely have really paid attention. Anna is a fixture of my life, not a real person, not in any real way. "Your sister?"

She shakes her head. "My sister, she is married to a Lutheran," she says quietly. "A good man, Bernd is. She is safe. For now, she is safe. But people talk; you know how people talk. It will be best for her to go away."

"Where can she go?" I have a sudden idea. "Here? To America?"

"To America, yes, if they can find the money. But not here." She shrugs. "Our *mutti*, she is in Dayton, Ohio. Gerta will go to her, and her children with her."

Dayton, Ohio? "Won't people there turn against them, too?" I ask. "I mean, Anna, look what happened to you in Boston! People were mean to you, and worse, Daddy says it was going to get a lot worse." I leave the thought unfinished: if urbane, educated, cultured Boston can blame a German woman for the war, then how much worse will things be in Dayton, Ohio, which as far as I am concerned is absolutely in the middle of nowhere?

Anna is unperturbed. "*Mutti* has been there for such a long time," she says. "Since Gerta was very small, and me also." She looks at me and smiles, a ghost of her old smile. "You think that it is a modern thing, the divorce, *ja*? But it is not. My father, all he loves is his shop. *Mutti*, she wanted someone to love her, too."

And she found her joy in Dayton, Ohio? I'm still a little stuck on that one. Not to mention the mother who left her two daughters with a man whose work is his life. I smile encouragingly. "So Gerta will be all right?"

"If she comes to America, yes. But what has happened to Pap, what has happened to our home... I cannot understand."

The lamp is making a hissing sound, and Anna gets up, brusquely, to see to it. "It is time to sleep now," she announces abruptly, suddenly quite her old self.

I'm not finished yet. "But why should they take ..."

"That is enough talk of that!" she snaps. "It was not right to tell you. We will not talk of it again. Come along, do your teeth, get undressed. It is time for bed. No more talk tonight."

"Anna?"

"Yes?"

"Tell me something good." I need it more than you know.

"No more talk tonight," she repeats instead, crossly, and I sigh and give up. Not tonight, maybe, I think as I go mechanically through the motions of my evening ritual, brushing my teeth and spitting into the sink, scurrying out to the privy. But soon, Anna: soon you need to tell me what's happening in Germany.

And why.

***

The next day turns cold, as New England sometimes does in the summertime, when the waves come in on long rollers of white foam and the air feels like it's taken its last breath off an iceberg.

The wind whips the sand and howls around the shack. When I get out of bed, sliding down from my upper bunk, it's cold enough for me to see my breath in the air.

Behind me, Anna is coaxing the woodstove to life. I wrap myself in my blanket and peer out the front windows. The end of the bluff looks like the edge of the world. There's nothing beyond it— no sea, no air, nothing. There are voices in the wind, sounding eerily human. I shiver and turn to help with breakfast.

By midmorning, a little of the ocean is visible. It's still coming in on long rollers of white foam, as I've seen before when the weather turns, and the gulls return; two of them are screaming at each other right above the shack. The wind hasn't let up, though, and farther out, the water is a boiling churning mass of whitecaps and frothy waves. There's rain now, too, and the wind is driving it with such force that it sounds like sleet on the windows and roof.

Anna clearly feels that our shared True Confessions time is over. She is brusque with me, occupied with a hundred small tasks that suddenly need to be done at exactly this moment. I try to talk to her, I mention Germany and Ohio and the philosophy of the Third Reich; but I'm rebuffed sharply; she clearly feels she has already said too much. Finally she tells me to leave her alone. I watch her and watch the blurry ocean horizon and wish the rain would let up.

When it does, I'm out of the dune shack like a shot.

The sand is wet on top, hard-packed, easier to walk on. I retrace last night's steps automatically, without thinking much about what I'm doing, without allowing myself to remember the feeling of loss as I watched Sophie walk away last night.

Helen's shack appears suddenly, surprising me as much today as it did the first time: you're alone in the dunes, then suddenly there's this little cottage, weathered and shingled, with a long sloping roof coming almost to the ground, nestled organically into the side of the dune. It looks like a fairytale house, like there should be roses climbing its sides, as if a mythical small creature ought to live inside.

Actually, there *are* roses climbing its side, I note.

I knock on the door, tentatively, but I know that Sophie isn't there: it would have been insane to walk in from the highway in this morning's storm. It still looks threatening: the sky slate-gray, the ocean the same, only darker.

I knock, anyway, and as if in response to my knock, a flock of gulls suddenly comes wheeling up over the headland from the beach, calling and crying together. They come down over me, flying low, their big magnificent wings carrying them effortlessly in the wind, making constant minute adjustments for airflow. Somewhere in their crying I can hear a child's voice calling.

I shake myself and turn again to the door, opening it cautiously, tiptoeing in, as though someone might be there in the room, waiting for me. It is empty, but not deserted: I can still sense the echoes of Sophie's voice, of her presence, and behind that some deeper one, an older presence, the spirit of a woman in a hot New York apartment who had a dream of a house by the sea.

I know that I don't belong here, and still I stay, running my hand over the spines of the books, picking up one after the other to read the inscriptions inside, a page or two of text chosen at random. I'm not sure why I'm here.

Behind me, the door slams shut.

I whirl around, the book in my hand falling to the floor. I approach the closed door slowly, half-expecting it to be locked, part of me thinking I'll be trapped here where I shouldn't be. But it opens easily to my touch. I shake myself: it is the wind, and there is no lock on the door. I am quite safe.

All the same, I go outside, look all around me, as though expecting shapes to rise up from the dunes themselves, unable to shake the sense that someone somewhere is watching me. I'm being silly, and I'm scaring myself, not the brightest thing to do when you live in a place as isolated as this. "Get a hold of yourself," I mutter, and go back into the shack.

This time, I close the door behind me.

The book I dropped is halfway under the bed. I kneel on the faded braided rug and feel sand gritting under my knees; there is no escaping the sand, even in this magical room where time seems to have stopped. Reaching in to retrieve the book, my fingers touch wood, and what I draw out, instead, is a picture frame.

The image in it is faded, printed in sepia tones, but quite clear and recognizable: a man standing in front of a dune shack, one I haven't seen before. He is dressed formally for the dunes, trousers and a suspender and a proper shirt. Beside him is a table, with a meal laid on, tablecloth and everything. A woman is sitting at the table, about to pour tea, her hand holding the teapot suspended in the air forever over the cups. There is a child sitting there, too.

I pass my fingers over the images of the people, slowly, but feel nothing. Disappointing. Turning the picture over, I can read the inscription on the back: Gene and Agnes O'Neill, 1916.

I turn it back over and look at the man with more interest. That's Eugene O'Neill? I pass my fingers over it again, aching for contact, for communication. Look-East-to-Cardiff Eugene O'Neill? Here?

I am on my knees again in an instant, groping below the bed. And now there are more photographs, all of them framed, all of them in the same sepia tones, and my eyes meet eyes that have written the English curriculum of my school, the wilder curriculum of the books I've stolen and read under my covers at night in my staid Boston brownstone. John Dos Passos. Edna St. Vincent Millay. Eugene O'Neill. Tennessee Williams. Others whose names I don't recognize, but vow now to find out about: Susan Glaspell. Jig Cook. Clare Leighton. Mary Heaton Vorse.

I look at them all and wonder what they are doing here in Helen's shack – and what they *were* doing here, in Provincetown, for that is clearly where all of the pictures have been taken, either or in town or in the dunes. Pictures of plays being staged by the people who wrote them. Pictures of couples who never were officially couples. Pictures of gaiety, of anger, of inebriation, of joy. What was going on? Why were so many talented people drawn here?

And who, oh who, is Helen?

I am suddenly afraid of being discovered with these secret riches spread out around me. I bundle them together and push them back under the bed, their serious and laughing eyes alike entrusted to its shelter once again.

And that's when I find the journals.

Chapter Eight

When I get back to Louis' shack, Sophie is waiting for me.

My stomach does a minor somersault. She and Anna are sitting together at the table inside, and the air is fragrant with the smell of apple cake. Anna only makes it when she is particularly pleased about something, on account of the rationing.

I have a feeling I'm not the reason for this particular batch.

They have similar accusations waiting for me. "Why didn't you tell me you have a liddle friend?" demands Anna, while Sophie has a similar issue: "Why didn't you tell me Anna's German? That *that's* why you're out here?"

I sit down on the lower bunk, Anna's bed; they're taking up the only two chairs we have. "Looks like the two of you don't need me to tell you anything." I can't help but sound resentful. Maybe even petulant.

Anna shakes her head sorrowfully, as though she's gone astray somewhere in raising me. A few hairpins take the opportunity to escape and skip to the floor; I'll be picking those up later, no doubt. Anna ignores them and turns back to Sophie, putting a hand on her knee (Sophie is, I note, wearing a dress today; heaven knows what Anna would say about her slacks and men's shirts) and patting it. "Just another minute, *liebchen*, and you'll be tasting the best applecake in the world!"

Sophie looks delighted. "I'll vouch for that," I put in, trying to get back into the conversation… *and* Anna's good graces. I'll do next to anything for her applecake.

It doesn't work: Anna glares at me. "Sophie brings news from the town," she announces. "It's good to have news, *nicht wahr?*"

She always sounds more German when there's company.

I ignore her. "What news?" I ask Sophie.

She glances at Anna before answering. "Well, it's all so far away," she says doubtfully. "And I'm not sure I understand what's happening... but... There was an announcement at Town Hall yesterday, they said German troops are in Egypt." Her voice is small, controlled, careful. "They're close t' Cairo. That's the capital. There was a battle near some place called–um–El Alamein." Her voice hesitates, stumbles over the foreign name. "The *Advocate* says they're going t' have all of North Africa by fall."

I think of that night when Daddy let me into his study to listen to his students arguing, I remember the earnest voices, the predictions. Not much of a war, they said. Not in Europe, anyway: all of America stands transfixed, looking west, looking to Japan. The European war can't last. Over by Christmas, they said.

Over by Christmas? I look at Anna, but she has gotten up, is busying herself at the kerosene oven, the one she only uses for baking, taking the steaming applecake out. She is suddenly disinterested in news. My mouth feels like I've swallowed sand.

Sophie is watching me, expressionless. She doesn't know what strange unspoken conversation just took place between me and Anna, and I am equally baffled myself, I just know that something did. What is Anna thinking? What should I be thinking? I have to say something, so I try and remember what Sophie just said. "Why is North Africa important?" I ask, finally.

"It is part of the world, isn't it?" she asks crossly, impatient with me, with the secrets that I'm not sharing with her. A moment ago she would have agreed, shrugged over why North Africa should be important. "They're heading toward Stalingrad. That's in *Russia*," she adds, looking at me, making it obvious it's for my benefit. "And they're bombing Britain. London. How much longer can it all last?" She sighs, and there's a long moment of silence before she speaks again. I wonder what she's trying to get her courage up to say. "There's more," she adds in a small voice.

A snake that's been sitting quietly in my stomach uncoils suddenly, cold and heavy and scary. I know without asking that this is going to be worse than any news from the Soviet Union or Egypt. I look to Anna for comfort, for sympathy, but she's somewhere else, she's ignoring us altogether. She puts the cake on the table, fetches plates and forks. I stare at her, unsure how to respond.

It's all a little surreal.

I wet my lips and look at Sophie again. "What?" I ask.

Anna is pretending our conversation is not taking place. "You taste dat applecake," she says to Sophie, brandishing a knife, cutting into the cake. The smell is overwhelming: sweet and almost sickly. Or maybe the sickness is just in my mind. "You tell me it is not the best you have never tasted."

Sophie looks from me to Anna, distressed. She doesn't know if Anna isn't hearing her or is ignoring her. "It may be just rumors," she says, slowly, "but it was in the newspaper, in the *Advocate*, this morning. They're building workcamps in Germany and in Poland."

"We have workcamps here," I point out, relieved. Is that all? I'm glad, now, for the long discussions in Daddy's study on which

I've eavesdropped, glad that I know enough to not sound completely out of touch. For some reason I haven't stopped to analyze, I want to impress Sophie. I want her to like me. I want her to think highly of me. I'm scared when she ignores me in ways I'm not scared about anything else.

She glances at Anna. "They're not the same," she says, her voice low. Why is she being so careful of Anna? What does she know? "They're special ones, especially for Jewish people."

Anna is pouring the chicory coffee. "Do you want sugar?" she asks Sophie. She never offers me sugar: we've all learned to drink this awful stuff black; now here she is, being polite, being the perfect hostess. I don't get it. We might as well be back in the drawing room of the brownstone on Commonwealth Avenue, for all she seems perturbed. "We still have some from our tickets, for the coffee and the applecake." She finishes slicing the cake and starts passing plates around, as though nothing were happening, as though we were discussing the weather. It's wrong, it's wrong on so many levels, Anna never avoids *anything*.

I turn to Sophie, baffled. "Why?" I ask her. I am genuinely naive. "Why are they making special camps for Jewish people?"

"I think," she says in a very small, very scared voice, "t' kill them."

The knife clatters to the floor. There's a long silence after it falls, and then both Anna and Sophie bend to pick it up at the same time. There's sulphur in the air, not the scent of the dunes, the scent of death.

The snake is twisting inside me again, and I don't want to know, I don't want to know if the Germans are building workcamps to kill Jewish people, I don't want to know anything bad that could touch Anna. Desperate to find something else to say, I remember Daddy's letter. I look at Sophie. "Portugal?" I ask her. "The Azores? What's happening there?" Sophie's mother came from the Azores, islands off Portugal's mainland, I remember, and I know from Daddy's letters that the Provincetown "Portugee," as Cornflower Girl called them, come from the Azores. Daddy must have wondered why I was asking; or maybe he was just pleased that I have intellectual curiosity about my temporary home.

Sophie shrugs. "It's safe, for now. That's what my father says, anyway. Portugal is neutral. A lot of Jewish people are coming there, and others, people involved in resistance movements who are in danger and have to leave. They're arriving in Lisbon, and then they go on to the United States from there. Or staying in Portugal. It's the safest place in Europe." She sighs again. "My father got a telegram from my uncle Alvaro. They knew we'd be worried."

"The whole world," says Anna unexpectedly. "It is the whole world that should be worried."

Chapter Nine

After we eat the cake, Sophie and I walk down to the beach, scrambling down the headland and arriving in a spray of sand. "She's sweet," says Sophie. "Are you really sixteen? When's your birthday?"

I pick up a stone and try skipping it. No luck. "November thirtieth," I say. "How old are you?"

"Older than you," she says, grinning. "My birthday's September second."

"Coming up soon," I observe casually, my heart racing. I can do something for her birthday… but what? We walk for a few minutes without speaking. The wind is fresh, now, not as biting as it was before, though the surf is still loud. Gulls wheel over us, screaming.

Sophie grabs my arm. Urgently. "Look over there!"

I follow her pointing finger. Just a few feet offshore, a seal has poked its head out of the water and is regarding us with benign curiosity.

To my astonishment, Sophie starts talking to it. "Hello, there, *querido,*" she coos. The seal rolls with the swell of the waves, but it is Sophie I'm watching, her look of perfect joy and perfect amazement, her one-sided conversation. "Aren't you the handsome one? Yes, you are!… Oh, *look* at him Jessica, he's gorgeous!"

I feel bemused. It's just a seal. "You must see them all the time."

The seal doesn't like the turn the conversation is taking. With what looks like very little effort on his part, he rolls over and into a wave, leaving a flipper out of the water just long enough to convince me it was a statement. Sophie sighs deeply, the breath seeming to come from somewhere secret and ecstatic inside her, and she turns to me. "Of course I do," she says. "Whales, too, you know? It's magic. It's always magic!"

I am smiling now, too. She's like a child: her joy is infectious. "What else do you love?" As soon as the words are out of my mouth, I want to call them back.

Sophie doesn't seem to notice anything wrong. "Out here?" she asks. "Everything. Simply everything." She starts talking very fast, breathless: "The hawks... they find an air current and follow it round and round, hardly moving, and they can see so far–miles, they say. That's better than any human can see! They're amazing."

She starts walking backward in front of me, the words tumbling out. "And the tree swallows, they sing with this gurgling sound, it sounds like they're underwater. Have you heard them? The beetles, and the clams, and–oh, the whole ocean, you know? It's like this whole other world, out here." I look at her and try to imagine Daddy–the only person whose opinion has really mattered to me in the past–talking with such love about nature. It doesn't work. Maybe there's something special, a connection, between women and the earth, something that men can't access. Some kind of sacred feminine thing. I file it away in my mind to examine later.

Sophie's enthusiasm is boundless. She takes a deep breath and falls back into step next to me. "It's so extraordinary, in the dunes," she says. "I wish I could be out here all the time, like you are. I wish I didn't *ever* have to go back to town."

"What's wrong with Provincetown?" From what I've seen, it's nice enough, maybe even better than nice enough, and I remember my walks into town, the flowers and peace of the East End, the bustling activity down on the piers. And the tourists, too: people with cameras, picnic-hampers that they lug down to the town beaches and set up with umbrellas for shade. This year, they're on bicycles, the tourists, instead of cars; but they're still here. *Time* magazine published a scare article that said the beaches were closed, the roads were closed, Provincetown was under martial law. I remember Mother screeching something about it. From what I've seen, she was the only one who paid attention: the tourists, them, are all here in droves.

Sophie shrugs. "It's not the same," she says quietly. "Everybody knows what everybody's about—at least, that's the way it is, over in our part of town. Over t' the East End, maybe, there it's different. There are all those people there who aren't from here, people from off-Cape, the artists and the writers, that's the only place in Provincetown where you're allowed t' be yourself, and the rest of us don't live there. Can't afford t', not anymore." Her expression and voice both grow dreamy. "But the East End... it's a magical place, Jessica, you go walking there, you can feel it in the air, you can taste it."

I'm lost. "Taste what?" I've walked in the east end, and I'm disappointed to think there was something there I missed. I saw lodging houses, cottages. I saw artists at work, yes, and I smelled flowers and thought about the merger between the harbor and the art; but I didn't *taste* anything. Not even metaphorically.

"People making things that weren't there before." She shakes her head, her eyes on the sand, and then she takes a deep breath and gives me a gift, the knowledge of her own tension, the contradictions inside her heart—which are, it transpires, the same as the ones in the town. "Seems they all liked Provincetown 'cause it was a fishing village... and then the first thing that they did when they got there was spoil it, change it from being a fishing village. Mary Heaton Vorse—and she's still around, can you believe it, she had a reading over t' the Provincetown Bookshop on Commercial Street last week—she's the one who started it all. Loved Provincetown, so the first thing she wants t' do is change it. Explain *that* t' me." A quick glance from under her lashes. "And still... they're the only people in town worth knowing."

I say, thinking of the journals in Helen's shack that I stayed far too long reading, "They fell as much in love with the romance of the place as with the place itself."

Sophie nods. She knows I've read them, the journals, the outpouring of Helen's words that describe living among the bohemians in Provincetown, the words that describe the forging of another world. "But that's not so bad, is it?"

I shrug. I don't know the answer to that, not for the artists of today, of 1942. I've acquired a romantic befuddlement of my own with the earlier part of the century. "Those journals, Sophie—Helen lived all that. I read about it. The plays, and the parties, and the times when—" it's hard to put this into words "—when the excitement of doing something significant together just bubbled over, I can feel it, the way she describes it. I can feel their passion." It's a word I love, having come only recently to feel it myself. "She did it all. With those people."

"Yes," she says, and there's sadness in her voice, now. "It always comes back to those people."

Her conflict is clear. I don't know what to say.

"But out here," she says, and the freedom, the relief, the sense of expansion is in her voice, the sudden letting-out of worries, of cares, of fear, "out here, it doesn't matter, *nothing* matters. You can be poor as dirt and have a place here. You can be crazy as a bat and have a place here. You can drop your past, leave it behind like an old shirt, when you come out here. You can be anybody you want, and no one cares." She laughs, her voice a sliver of sunlight. "It's the only place in the world worth living. 'Course, you have t' work for it. It's not easy, living in the dunes."

"I," I say carefully, "have figured that part out."

Sophie bursts into laughter. "I'll bet you have! Boston, and all. I'll bet you never used a privy before in your life!"

This is, of course, true. Nor, for that matter, have I ever shared a room before, either–especially when said room constitutes the whole of the house. That was a new one, too. Or primed a pump and pumped water. Or... "But *you* manage," I point out, deciding not to continue cataloguing my woeful lack of experience. It's too depressing. "You dress how you please, you go where you please–Sophie, you said you'd be the first person in your family to go to college!"

"Yes," she acknowledges. "There's that."

We've drifted far down the beach; other dune shacks are silhouetted above us on the headland, odd-shaped, misshapen, the product of shipwrecks, with stories of life and death carved into their very beings. "Let's sit down," she suggests.

I flop down next to her, then sit up, scrunching my toes down in the sand, still damp from the rain. It's been getting imperceptibly brighter for a while and now, as if on cue, the sun comes out, sparkling bright on the surface of the water. "Isn't it just perfect?" Sophie sighs. Her hand finds mine and our fingers intertwine, the response automatic, natural. "A day like this—it's hard to believe what's happening over there."

Over there. Of course. Look out to sea from Race Point, and your first stop is Portugal. Look farther north, and it's England... France. I shiver. "Will the war ever end?" I ask, rhetorically.

"Of course it will," says Sophie immediately, absolute certainty in her voice. "It has t'. They always do, somehow."

I sigh. "Anna says that they've closed businesses that belonged to Jews. Her father was sent off... maybe even to one of those workcamps you told us about." My voice is tentative. Her hand feels warm in mine.

"Is Anna Jewish?"

I nod. "Yeah. I never knew."

There's a pause, then Sophie says, in a small voice, "I am, too."

I look at her in astonishment. Here I was thinking that I didn't know anybody Jewish; now it's turning out that everybody I know is. "I thought everybody in Portugal was Catholic."

"Most are, I suppose. And they chased the Jews out—oh, ages ago. Fifteenth century, I think." She sighs. "But a lot stayed. They're called *Cristaos Novos*–new Christians. But they never were." She laughs, a little uncertainly. "Christian, that is. Anyway it was way far back, and I'm probably as much Catholic as I'm Jewish, now. It never seemed t' matter much. We always go t' St. Peter's with everybody else. But when I hear about these things, I feel more Jewish. Isn't that weird?"

"I don't know." Frankly, I cannot fathom what I'm trying to take in. Jews killed in Germany. Anna's family moving to Ohio. Sophie's ancestors hiding, pretending, frightened. Nothing seems to change. And is *everyone* I know Jewish?

She decides to rescue me. "How come you don't know that much about Anna?" she asks.

I take a deep breath. "I guess I never cared," I say, ashamed of the truth. Ashamed that I never realized, until this moment, that I hadn't cared. "I never thought about it, I mean. About her as a person."

"Because she's your servant?"

Anna, a servant? I suppose she is. I always think of her just as Anna. I remember Cornflower Girl calling her the *help*. "Because," I say, sadly, with a burst of sudden distressing insight, "I'm usually too busy thinking about myself."

She squeezes my hand. "Wow. I don't think I've ever heard anyone say that before. It must have been hard t' realize that about yourself."

"Don't do that!" I involuntarily pull away from her, my words sharp, and I hear them and laugh to take the edge off. "You sound just like my father!"

"Why? He's insightful too?" She pokes at me, mischief in her voice.

This is something I can't joke about. "No. Well, maybe. He's a psychologist. He teaches it, too. Teaches people to be psychologists. Insightful is one of his favorite words."

Sophie is giggling now; she seems to find it all irresistibly funny. She flops back in the sand, her eyes on the sky. "Favorite words should sound like something," she says. "Something serious. Like bathysphere."

I lie down, too, missing her hand, propping myself on one elbow so I can see her, relieved at the subject change. "Surreptitious?" I suggest.

She squeals in delight. "Perfect! And irrefragable."

"Not fair! That's not a word!"

"Is, too! There's a dictionary over at Helen's. Want t' make a bet?"

I shake my head. "Not a chance. I'd lose. You've probably read half the dictionary."

"Probably," she agrees.

We stay in place, still, for a long moment, as the laughter dies and the silliness dissipates all around us. But we're still looking at each other, still looking in each other's eyes.

The moment stretches out, long and shimmering, too long, too bright, and I decide that it's time to stand up. Only instead of standing up, I bend over instead.

Just a little distance. Just the distance between her lips and mine.

***

Anna is perfectly composed when I return to Louis' shack, which is far more than I can say for myself. "Nice girl," she comments, and I feel myself blush. "Yes," I agree dutifully. "She's nice."

My hands, some remote part of myself observes, are shaking. Anna sends me down to the pump to fetch water, and I go silently, mechanically. My heart is still pounding, and there's a curious warmth spreading through my stomach that I usually associate with Christmas, or birthdays, or other occasions of similar anticipation and delight. My body seems to be fine with what just happened; it's my brain that's whirling.

I just kissed a *girl!*

It was, I argue to myself as I pump the water, my muscles working automatically, the coldness of it tingling on my skin, it was just a kiss. A kiss isn't bad. A kiss doesn't mean anything. Doesn't *have to* mean anything, I amend the thought slightly.

I'm finding that I rather hope that it does.

I'm still wondering exactly what I think about it all by the time night falls. I want to think about it, and don't want to think about it. There's a feeling in the pit of my stomach, the feeling I used to get on Christmas Eve, hardly able to wait for morning, anticipation and excitement and a little nausea. It's like all my Christmases, all my birthdays, every wonderful thing that's ever happened to me, all rolled into one.

Mother would *die* if she knew.

I slip back down to the beach after dinner to watch the sunset; the tide's already washed away the hollows where Sophie and I were lying, the place where our bodies had been. With the ocean, the past is always the past. The beach is bare, smooth, waiting for to-morrow's imprints.

Maybe it didn't happen. Maybe I imagined the whole thing.

The tingling in my stomach when I think of Sophie, when I think of that kiss, tells me that I didn't imagine anything. I close my eyes and can feel it again, the softness of her lips, the little gasp of surprise, her arms coming around me and pulling me in closer. Her mouth tasted of something sweet, it felt just like my own.

Anna puts out the lamps, one by one, and the smell of kerosene fills the room, swirls around us in the air, thick and cloying. I climb into my upper bunk, wiggling down into the covers, as she arranges the mosquito netting over the bed. "*Guten nacht, liebchen,*" Anna says, her voice oddly gentle, a little distracted; she has a lot on her mind as well.

"*Guten nacht,*" I respond, and the last of the lamps goes out. There is a pause. "Tell me something good, Anna," I say, automatically, but I already know something good. Something very, very good.

"Tomorrow," she answers, grunting softly as she settles into her bunk bed beneath mine, "you will take a bath."

"Not fair!" I protest. "That's not something good."

"It is good for me," she says stolidly, and that is that.

I stare at the ceiling, what I can make out of it in the darkness. It's made of cheap wood, and there are cracks running through it here and there. When I go to bed before Anna, and the lamps are still lit, I trace the patterns, find maps in it, try to decipher coastline and mountain, island and bridge.

Now I see the outline of a building, Trinity Church, Copley Square, Boston. There's a Morning Prayer service going on, and I've slipped away; I told Mother that I needed the ladies' room, but what I really need is to avoid the sermon. It is a beautiful day, early fall, with the air crisp and clean and the sun still bright and warm. I slip outside and lean against the side of the church; the stone soaks and absorbs the heat, and I feel it warm on my back.

I'm not, it transpires, the only one who doesn't want to hear the sermon.

Evan Winters approaches me lazily. He's a year ahead of me away at a prep school somewhere. I wonder what he's doing in town in September. He leans one shoulder against the stone and regards me with amusement. "The psychiatrist's daughter," he observes, probably thinking how very cool he sounds.

"The lawyer's son," I say, trying to look as indifferent as possible.

He grins, tosses a coin in the air, fields it deftly. "Not overly religious, are we?" he asks.

"I'm smarter than the rector," I say, boldly and no doubt inaccurately. "His sermons bore me to tears." I try to look bored to tears—without actually crying, of course.

"The Episcopal Church," Evan says, as though in response to my remark. "Anglo-Saxon America at prayer." The coin goes up again, sparkling in the sun. He catches it and stretches his hand out to me, coin face-up. "For luck," he suggests.

I reach to take it and he seizes my hand, drawing me closer to him. "There's a price," he adds, and before I can react, his arms are around me and he's kissing me.

They're not like the kisses Daddy gives me; this is open-mouthed, wet, and to my consternation I feel his tongue inside my mouth. For a panic-stricken moment I wonder if he's having a seizure.

Evan pulls away, the smile still on his face. He doesn't refer to the kiss; neither do I. All I can think of is how strange he is and how quickly I want to get away from him. The coin is warm and bright in my hand; I slip it into my pocket. "They've got another good five minutes to go in there," Evan observes diffidently. "Want to go downstairs?" Downstairs is the crypt, where no one will be while Morning Prayer is going on.

I am blushing, though I don't know why. "No," I say with some confusion. "I have to get back in. Mother will be furious."

"Suit yourself," Evan says, and as I open the big, heavy, iron-studded door, I see him sauntering off in the direction of the public library. He's tossing another coin in the air, and it catches the sun, a flash of brilliance that I can still see minutes later as I dutifully take my place in the pew next to my parents.

Later, when I'm alone, I look at the coin: it's a silver dollar. I put it under my pillow, though I don't know why.

It was my first, my only kiss; and now there is another, a memory to go over and over again in the night, to polish and touch and relive. To keep under my pillow, far more precious than Evan's silver dollar.

I still don't know what I think about what I did down there on the beach. But I know how I feel.

I'm in love with Sophie Costa.

Chapter Ten

I am awake early and out into the dunes before Anna is even up and about. I walk with an energy I didn't know I possess, my legs strong and confident in the sand. The world is bright and polished and pretty and new, and I could be the first, the only human in it. Except for the joy I'm feeling, the joy that comes from the magic of someone else...

The sounds of the surf on the sandbar and the beach fade behind me; in minutes there is a high dune between me and the ocean, and I could be miles away from it, anywhere, in the desert or on the moon. I skirt the mosses and odd little pink growth that cluster around the misshapen trees that insist on living here despite the inhospitable ground.

A hawk glides above me, intent on finding its breakfast. I am irrelevant to it; it is focused, intense, prepared for the sudden drop to earth that will allow it to live another day, the steep dive that will bring death to one creature and life to another.

Birds are everywhere; the shorebird migration that will take them from the arctic to South America has, extraordinarily, begun already, and the terns are gathering on the sand, over the ocean, in the dunes, stocking up. I've seen them in the evenings massing on the beach, thousands of them, and the jaegers harassing them for the fish they've just caught. There are ospreys, too, hunting small mammals along the high-tide line, eating the meadow voles they find there. It was Daddy who tucked the birding books into my suitcase, and I read them in bed at night, the flashlight illuminating first one familiar form and then another.

I've never been very interested before in nature as a concept, as an abstract. Nature, for my family, is an afternoon on the swan boats in the Public Gardens, or a walk over Boston Common; nature is the ritual summer foray up into the White Mountains of New Hampshire, with Mother fretting about getting bitten by bugs and getting her dress soiled, and Daddy looking longingly for a quiet place to read a book in peace.

I'm a city girl, born and bred. And, it has to be said, feeling slightly superior to anybody who isn't.

Out here, though, I begin to realize how limiting and narcissistic that existence ultimately can become. It's starting to occur to me that I've been missing out on something important, something essential in a magical mystical real way. Cities are all about people: what they do, who they meet, what they wear, what they create, how they can leave something of themselves behind, a mark, a child, anything so that other people will know that they were there.

And people have been around for such a small amount of time! The dunes are prehistoric, taking me back to an age that thought only of survival, the immediacy of every day, of every moment. All the things that seem so important are diminished by the timelessness of the backshore.

Here glaciers moved slowly and grandly over the landscape, scraping the bedrock, depositing boulders where it would; here glacial kettle holes show up in unexpected places, creating small ponds of tranquil surfaces and unplumbed depths; here the ice age carved an oddly-shaped bay, nearly encircled by land, a sandbar that would shift with still more climatic changes, move as it is buffeted by hurricanes and snowstorms.

Here, for hundreds of years, nature has played with humanity, daring it to construct something permanent, laughing at people's limited ideas of permanence. Here the ocean gives life and takes it away just as quickly. Here storms throw ships up against the coast, pounding them onto rocks, stranding them on sand, creating a graveyard of merchants and pirates and adventurers alike.

And yet, in all the important ways, nothing changes.

There is no mark to leave behind here; everything is transient, impermanent. My footsteps, washed away by the tide. The dune shacks that have succumbed to storms, to the wind and rain that have lashed this sandbar for the past thousand years and that will, no doubt, continue to do so long after we're all gone: they'll go, too, as they already are, one by one.

We think that we make our mark, but we pass on and leave no impression of our passage here, and that is what is right. Death here in the dunes is as natural as birth, it is a cycle that repeats and renews the shifting sands. All creatures are pulled into the cycle; all play their role. As I walk I pass the carcasses of dead beetles in the sand and dune grasses, dozens of them there, as though their lifespan had come to an end all at once, today.

Here, too, is magic. The dunes are swept with stardust, filled with shapeshifters, with fairies, with strange and powerful creatures of the night that are wilder than our wildest fantasies. You feel them, rather than see them; you sense their eyes watching you, their laughter trailing after you, their whispers in the dark, in the tall dunes grasses, marking your passage and dancing merrily in your wake. The shapeshifters are trees, they are mist, they dissolve into the very sand beneath your feet when you try and look at them. But the magic is there, just beyond reach, visible only – as are all of the important things in life – just out of the corner of your eye.

Boston is bereft of this energy, bereft of this mystery, bereft of this magic. To live in the city, I conclude, is to lose a fundamental part of your soul.

***

I've gone back to the shack with the tree swallow nests, but the door has been closed and the man inside invisible. I wrote about him to Daddy (Mother would be shocked speechless, and for reasons I don't understand, I'm not taking as much pleasure in baiting her these days as I used to), and he wrote back that he's a poet, and a well-known one at that; he said he'll send me some of his books, but he hasn't, yet.

There's a couple that lives in the shack closest to us, up on the ridge, and I don't dare tell Anna, but the smells coming from that shack rival even her applecake. I see the woman pumping water in the mornings if I'm out very early; I don't see the man, but I can hear their voices, sometimes, talking together, carried on the wind, and in the night there's a faint glow from their kerosene lamps. She's an artist, I discover one morning when I wander over that way and see her standing before an easel, painting–well, painting her dune shack, which seems odd when there's the vastness of the ocean spread out before her.

Perhaps that's the point. Perhaps vastness cannot be captured on canvas. I think about it sometimes and I long to try, and sometimes I take paper and pencil out with me to the beach; but I think that in the end my neighbor is right. You cannot imitate that kind of art.

Chapter Eleven

When I get to the top of the highest ridge, Sophie is there. What is the most surprising is that I'm not even surprised.

She is wearing shorts and a sleeveless plaid shirt, her arms tanned and smooth, her curly black hair more or less caught back in a hairband. She is crouching by the side of the path, concentrating on something. "What is it?" I ask, making my voice as casual as I can, as though nothing happened between us yesterday. My thoughts about nature flee; all I see is her.

"Something's growing here," she says, and her voice is full of wonder. "In the sand." I look, and she is right: small bits of lichen, dry and brittle, some of them shaped like starfish. "It's like a miracle," she says reverently.

I don't know what to say. I want to touch her again. I stop myself, unsure of how she might respond.

"There are voles in the dunes," Sophie announces briskly, standing up in one long fluid motion. She brushes off her knees, even though there is no sand on them. I wonder if she's feeling as awkward as I am. "And mice, too."

"I know," I answer. "One of them lives in the shack with us. I hear Anna arguing with it in the night."

Her eyes meet mine, and she smiles broadly. She really likes Anna. "Arguing?"

"Well," I admit, "it's a little one-sided, but it makes her feel like she's doing something. She says that if she catches it, she'll drown it. Him, actually: she's sure it's a he. She tells him in the night how she's going to kill him. Lots of different ways." I shiver, despite the hot sun, aware that I am babbling. "I hope she never catches him."

"She won't," says Sophie confidently. "Mice are smarter than we are. In their own way, of course."

"Of course," I agree, straight-faced, before the silliness of the statement gets the better of me and I start laughing. She smiles at me, mischievous. Casually, naturally, as if we'd been doing it forever, Sophie slips her hand into mine. "Come on," she says. "We've got things t' do."

"What things?" I ask, as the warmth from her hand spreads up my arm. I hope my voice sounds all right; I'm scared of what I'm feeling, and scared of losing the feeling, all at the same time.

"I promised Anna," she says lightly. "We have t' take her fishing today. Come on," and she tugs me, lightly, her hand still in mine. We walk down the path together. My hand is starting to sweat; I worry that she'll take her hand away, wipe it on her shorts, disgusted. "Fishing?" I echo. "In your boat?"

"Of course in my boat, silly. You only get the little fish if you do it from the beach. Anna said she wants something for supper."

"You and Anna say a lot to each other lately," I say sourly. There's a cold feeling in the pit of my stomach. Surely I can't be jealous? Of *Anna*?

Sophie giggles, pulls me toward her, hugs me briefly, and then we set off again. "You must be tired of all that tinned beef, admit it!"

I have no problems admitting it. "What kind of fish?" I ask instead, not wanting to give in too easily. I don't like Anna and Sophie having conversations that don't include me.

"All sorts," she says confidently, unaware of my thoughts. "Bluefish, stripers, mackerel, haddock, cod, sometimes even a tuna. Well," she adds, doubtfully, in an apparent effort to be totally truthful, "probably not tuna. My dad gets them sometimes, though he's really a dragger. It's been an extraordinary good summer, the fish don't know there's a war on, don't you know. Six draggers did 87,000 pounds last Monday." She comes back to the topic. "Anyway, we won't go out very far–not like he does."

I am glad to hear it. I'm trying to picture the three of us in that tiny boat and can't remember whether or not Anna can swim.

As it turns out, not only can Anna not swim, Anna has no intention of setting foot in a boat. "Not me," she declares roundly, wiping her hands on her apron, shaking her head so hard that the hairpins scatter. "I tell you, *liebchen*, I get off the boat in New York harbor, I say not never again. I am being sick all the way from Germany." She punctuates her comment with a knife, slicing through the air to emphasize her point. "No. More. Boats."

She is making sandwiches, packing us a lunch to take with us. "You be good girl, you take good care of my *liebchen, nicht wahr?*" she asks Sophie, with a concern that should have been touching, except that I'm too busy panicking. Me and Sophie, alone in a boat for hours together.

What if we kiss each other again?

What if we *don't* kiss each other again?

There's a warmth spreading up through my stomach, with a hollowness behind it, a happy excited feeling. It's too wonderful. It's too scary. Oh, God: what if we actually *talk* about what is going on between us?

Anna packs us some applecake. "You come in when you want some more, yes?"

"Yes, Anna," we say in unison, and dissolve into giggles together. "Out! Out! Away with you!" she cries, making shooing gestures with her hands. I can imagine what she'll write in her next letter to my parents. "Jessica has found herself a little friend, they're so sweet together…"

Sophie's drawn the boat up to the high-tide mark, and I wonder again at how strong she must be. We push it down to the water together, our feet sinking deep into the sand, scrabbling for balance. I remember my last, less-than-graceful entry into the boat, and I look up to meet Sophie's eyes, dark blue and filled with a light that seems to encompass the sky. "You can get in first, this time," she says, and I know that she's been following my thoughts. She shrugs, a gesture I'm coming to see as characteristic. "I'm not being polite," she adds. "Otherwise you'll probably capsize us both."

I climb in with as much grace and dignity as I can muster while it's still in the shallows, and Sophie pushes it further, wading up to her waist before lifting herself up with her arms, sliding in, graceful as an eel. We wait until we're just past the Peaked Hill bar to lower the outboard motor, and Sophie starts it with little fuss and an economy of movement that reminds me she's been on the sea for her whole life. I feel clumsy and helpless, bereft of useful skills, in an unfamiliar element. She seems not to notice.

The sound of the motor precludes conversation, so I relax and watch the water skimming by under us. It's a bumpy ride, as we jump from wave to wave, and I tighten my grip on the edge of the dory. The spray hits me in the face and I lick my lips and taste salt.

My hair is blowing all around me. It's a little scary, too, this speed, the loud *thunk* as the bow hits the waves, and I wonder about all the shipwrecks that have happened on this coast. I wonder if we will die, and I find that I don't really care. I've let go of everything.

It's the most wonderful thing I've ever experienced.

We slow down presently, and then Sophie cuts the engine and the world falls silent around us. From here, you can't hear the ever-present background sound of the dunes, the wind moving swiftly over sand and grass, the waves washing up on sand and rock. Just the gulls screaming overhead, and the cormorants and the gannets diving close to us, hitting the water and knifing in with grace.

The sea makes a soft slapping sound against the sides of the boat, and there are gulls floating nearby, looking contented and a little bored. The sky today is slate blue and flat; there's haze on the horizon. Far out to sea, a steamer is slowly making its way east, probably out of Boston and heading to Europe. I watch it with a kind of hypnotized fascination.

Sophie sets out fishing rods swiftly, deftly, and doesn't ask me if I want to help. I keep my eyes fixed on the steamship so I don't have to look at what she's using for bait; I'm pretty sure I won't like it, whatever it is. That's the other side to nature, the cruelty of it. One creature has to die so that another can live, the eternal cycle of being on the planet. Death is as much a part of the cycle as is life, and often that death is violent. More often than not, actually.

That's something else that you forget, in the city.

She sits back, finally, satisfied. "That should do the trick," she says, nodding, and than, without looking at me and in a matter-of-fact voice, she asks, "Do you have a boyfriend?"

I feel my stomach contract. Reluctantly I take my eyes off the steamer. "No," I say, as evenly as I can manage. "Do you?"

"Don't have much use for boys," she says, and now she turns and studies my face. "They don't seem t' spend an awful lot of time thinking."

"They spend an awful lot of time thinking about the wrong things," I say tartly, remembering Evan Winters and his invitation to slip downstairs for a few minutes.

"I guess," she concedes, considering my words. I decide that with three brothers, she has more experience with boys than I do.

But I'm not particularly interested in talking about boys.

Sophie's a lot braver than I am. "I was just wondering," she says, her voice still casual, "about what's happening."

I am a coward. "What's happening?" I repeat stupidly. "What do you mean?" She knows that I know what she means.

She leans forward. "Between us," she says.

Now or never. I take a deep breath. Never mind her not respecting my lack of courage; I'm rapidly coming to the point of despising myself. I lean toward her, take both her hands in mine. We sit there for a moment, facing each other in a little rowboat that's bobbing gently in the swells, looking at each other, saying nothing. I am suddenly aware that out to the east, beyond that line of haze, there's a war going on. It makes what I have to say even more necessary, even more urgent. "I think I love you," I say.

Worst thing that can happen is she'll kick me out of the boat and I'll drown or get eaten by a shark or something. No, that's a lie, of course: the worst thing that can happen is for her to laugh at me, to say that she was just making fun of me, to say that she doesn't care. My stomach twists in fear. That's what's going to happen, I decide; that's the truth, and she's trying to find a way to let me down gently, to tell me the truth without hurting me too much, that she was just amusing herself and that it was altogether meaningless. I hold my breath and shut my eyes. Let's get it over with quickly, I pray. Just let it happen quickly, so I can get over it and start healing. Just tell me that it was all a mistake. Just tell me that it's meaningless. Just tell me that I don't matter to you, that you were mocking the girl from the city, seeing how far you could go to be cruel to her. Just go on, just get it over with. I'm still holding my breath when she speaks.

"I love you, too," says Sophie.

***

I am trailing my fingers in the water, languid, self-assured. "You'll freeze your hand off if you go on like that," says my love, prosaically.

"Do you ever go swimming?" I ask, secure in our declarations. We can talk of inconsequential things now.

"Here? Of course not," she says, her voice showing that she finds the question insane beyond remark. Her eyes are on the fishing lines. "Water's always too cold on the back shore," she says. "Even in August. Daft people go in. Not me. Over to the harbor—" she catches herself "—over *at* the harbor, sometimes, in the summer. It's more protected there. Here, it's straight off to the North Atlantic."

I shiver. "I thought this *was* the North Atlantic," I say, and she laughs. "The Labrador Current," she says, and the words themselves sound frigid.

The line twitches again, and Sophie is on it in a heartbeat. "What should I do?" I ask, alarmed, and she responds quickly. "Stay out of my way."

She has the pole in her hands and she seems to be playing with the line, pulling it in and letting it out a little. It starts to irritate me. "Are you playing with it?" I ask crossly. "You don't have to torture it, just because we're going to eat it."

She doesn't spare me a glance, or bother to respond to my lame remark. "It's the way to catch 'em," she says, and then saves her breath. She pulls it in, finally, shimmering silver and green and blue in the sunlight, dancing all over the bottom of the boat. I pull back suddenly, instinctively, sharply, and nearly capsize us then and there. "Stop, Jessica!" Sophie shouts, and I hear the steel in her voice. I seize the sides of the boat and pull my legs up under me. She grabs the fish and pulls the hook out of its mouth, turning to put it in the box behind my seat.

I am appalled. "You're just going to let it die there alone?" I demand. "Isn't that cruel?"

She looks at me as though I had just revealed my alien ancestry. Alien as in off the planet. "Jessica, it's a *fish.*"

"And fish don't feel pain?" I'm sounding petulant, and I don't care. Unaccountably I feel as if I'm going to cry, the tears pressing hard and hot against the backs of my eyes.

"Oh, for heaven's *sake*," Sophie exclaims. She reaches behind her and comes up with a mallet. She flings the fish back to the bottom of the boat, whacks its head, and puts it back in the metal box. "Is that better?" she demands. "A quick death?"

I uncoil my legs and put them back down, slowly and gingerly. "Thank you," I mumble. I'm feeling both vindicated and silly.

Sophie clearly has an idea about what I should be feeling. "So now you're happy," she says, shaking her head. "Where do you think your chicken comes from, anyway? Your meatloaf? You think they grow like that, out on the farm? You really think every butcher is humane?"

I am defeated and know it. "Probably not," I concede.

"Probably not," she repeats in agreement. "Try: never. You want to eat this stuff, but you don't want to know how it got to your table. You want to be protected from all that. Do you really think the beef is *born* wrapped in paper?"

"I never thought about it," I admit. I'm starting to seriously toy with the idea of eating nothing but lettuce for the rest of my life.

Sophie takes care of that one. "And don't go thinking that you'll be more pure if you give up eating meat," she says. There are flames in her eyes, I'd swear there are. Her passion is both endearing and exciting. "They harvest wheat with combines. Combines and tractors, they kill all the wildlife in the fields, and the farmers poison the rest. Mice and rabbits and everything else in their paths."

Maybe I'll never eat anything again, I think. No one, nothing can live without killing something else. It seems supremely unfair.

It's time to make peace. I swallow, hard. "What kind of fish is it?" I ask finally, and she grabs a quick breath as though to continue the argument that I just abandoned. She just looks at me instead, and a slow smile smoothes out the anger. "*Fish*," she says, relenting. "Don't they teach you *anything* at that expensive private school you go to?"

"Nothing useful," I say. "And how do you know that I go to an expensive private school, anyway?" Our gazes meet and we answer, in unison, "Anna."

Sophie laughs and begins pulling up the lines. "That should do for supper," she says. "Don't want to make you commit too many murders in one day." She catches my look and grins. "Just joking."

"Was that our first fight?" I ask her.

"Think we did it before," she says cheerfully. She stows the fishing gear but makes no move to start the motor. "I wish I could go to a good school, the way you do."

I don't know how to respond without sounding shallow. Her world is far away from mine... much farther than the miles between Provincetown and Boston. "They don't teach you much that's useful, as you just demonstrated," I say, trying to make light of it.

She is looking out at the haze on the horizon. "I want to be a writer," she says. "I write a lot, now, but I know I could be better." She glances at me. "You know? With more education?" A quick shrug. "That's why I'm going t' college. I have to go t' college."

"What do you want to write?" I'm fascinated by her passion. The only thing I know for sure that I want out of my future is to not be like Mother.

She smiles, a quicksilver thing, there and gone again. "Novels," she says. "I've got so many stories in me, I just need to find a way to get them out. In good English, not what we speak around here."

I think of how she corrects herself. "Those are the mechanics," I say, knowing my words to be heresy in the mind of my English teacher. And my parents, too, come to think of that. "If you have the stories, that's what counts."

"Then I count," she says lightly, and picks up the oars. "Do you want to row?"

"Only if you get tired and want me to take a turn." You don't have to row the swan boats in the Public Garden, and I have no illusion that my strength—even with my daily water pumping—is up to the task here.

"Never mind," she says, and pulls at the oars, seemingly effortlessly. I can see the muscles moving just under the skin, beneath the roundness of her arms. "What do you want to do, Jess? With your life, I mean?"

"You mean, what do I want to be when I grow up?" I counter, half-mockingly, and then I sigh. "I don't know. I was just listening to you and wishing I had that kind of passion. I wish I could be an artist, a painter, that seems to be the only thing I'm good at, but Mother says it's fine for a hobby, not a career."

So much so that she didn't allow me to bring any paints out to the dunes, out where the sky and the water and the sand scream out to be painted. "And there aren't any careers that really interest me." I shrug. It may not be the best time to tell her that Family Money will always take care of me anyway, career or no career. Anna's probably told her, anyway. "Besides, with the war on…"

Sophie stops rowing, pulling the oars in so they don't slip through the oarlocks. She leans forward, her eyes alight. There's excitement in her voice. "But what about if we could? Do exactly what we want?"

"We can't," I say automatically. "Daddy says that people need to focus on reality. Doing what you want with your whole life, that's just a fantasy. Daddy spends a lot of his time separating people from their fantasies."

"I am starting," says Sophie roundly, "to get very tired of Daddy." She reaches across and takes my hand as if to lessen the sting of the words. "Just imagine it, Jess! We could live in Provincetown, or even in the dunes. My father says that half the people in town these days are artists or writers, anyway. We'll live together, and you'll paint, and I'll write, and I'll even catch fish for our supper! We'll be happy, won't we?"

Her dreams stretch out as far as the horizon.

A thousand reasons to say no are on the tip of my tongue. I squeeze her hands in mine, and say, "Let's do it."

Chapter Twelve

Anna is fearless with the fish.

"You'll stay to help us eat it, *nicht wahr*?" she asks Sophie, even as she's chopping off the head and tail with swift economical movements of her knife. I try not to flinch.

Sophie gives me a shy smile. "Thank you. I will."

"Your *mutti* and *papa*, they will not worry for you if you stay?"

"My father's been out two weeks now," Sophie says. She sees Anna's raised eyebrows. "Out at sea. Out t' Georges Bank, or Stellwagen Bank, it depends on the reports. Of fish, I mean." She's struggling for the words; it's hard for her to explain something that's been a given for her entire life. "They stay away for a long time if there's nothing there. Sometimes they stay out a long time even when the catch is good, and salt the fish while they're out there." She shrugs. "We're used to it. I think my mother's relieved when she doesn't have to feed so many at supper."

Anna shakes her head in commiseration, and a few errant hairpins get loose. "Poor child. Do you know when he'll be back?"

"Next week, maybe." Sophie looks as though she doesn't care, one way or the other.

It's been at least that long since I last saw my parents. Maybe it's not such a bad thing, this protracted absence. "Is it dangerous?" I ask, to make conversation. Anna is sizzling some butter substitute in her big cast-iron pan on top of the wood stove. It smells delicious. My mind flashes, unbidden, to our conversation in the boat, and I wonder how many woodland animals die to bring us butter–

or whatever passes for it, these days. I eye Sophie sourly; no doubt she knows.

And, given half a chance, would be more than willing to share.

She's not privy to my thoughts, and answers my question instead. "It's the most dangerous occupation in the world," Sophie, fisherman's daughter and sister, says seriously and matter-of-factly. "Men get caught in the nets, get blood poisoning from hooks, are hurt by the equipment, get washed overboard. Almost every year, there's one boat in the fleet doesn't come back." She has a faraway look in her eyes, and I feel the gulf between us, our experiences, widen. "It's not for nothing they call each other the finest kind."

The finest kind. I think about the expression as we eat dinner, the respect that they must have for each other to earn that name, the horrible weather and uncertainty and danger. The finest kind. I'm starting to look at Sophie in an entirely new light: she's strong in ways that I never dreamed people had to be strong. Which is, of course, exciting all by itself: there's something very attractive, very alluring, about strength and competence, and Sophie's got both. I want to reach over and touch her hand, but I don't dare, not in the light of this new strength I'm seeing, it's intimidating as well as exciting.

The long summer evening stretches out ahead of us, fair and warm and filled with promise. Summer may be short, but its days are wide, unending. After dinner I walk with Sophie back to the highway, to Route Six. She's stowed the boat above the high-tide mark; it will be safe overnight.

The sun's lit up the ocean to the west as we set out, and it's already below the horizon when we reach the road. I have to go back right away; I don't want to be caught in the dunes after dark. I've seen the tracks, and while I'm far more likely to scare the fox than the fox is to scare me, I'm not taking any chances.

I brush Sophie's fingertips with my own, and there's a movement in my stomach as I do. "I'll see you tomorrow," I say.

Her eyes are wide. "Tomorrow," she agrees, and puts her arms around me. We're nearly exactly the same height; I'd thought she was taller. Her lips are soft against mine, gentle, yielding. She tastes of honeysuckle and sun. "Tomorrow," she says at last, a little breathlessly.

Behind us, a herring gull screams in the dunes. I turn and head for home.

***

Sophie does not come the next day. Or the one after that.

I walk the beach alone, finding little joy in the treasures at the water's edge, the cries of the black-backed gulls and the cormorants wheeling above … not even in the magic of the dark shape offshore that suddenly breaks the surface, blows, and is down again with the grace of a dancer.

I feel sick with worry. Did she change her mind? Has she realized, suddenly, that what's happening between us is real? Does it scare her too much?

Does it disgust her?

Finally I walk over the tallest dune, the wall of sand that separates my world from the other one, the everyday world of other people. I toy with the idea of walking into town – it's not as if I haven't been there already, and I even know a few people to say hello to, Mr. Nelson at the grocer's, the woman who sits outside her house and paints. I start to walk, my muscles charged with purpose, the woods on either side of Snail Road deep and cool and inviting after weeks in the sun of the dunes, and even surprise a deer feeding by the roadside; but I stop myself. Do I know where Sophie lives? Do I know how to begin to find here there? We live together in my world, not hers. And if she *has* decided that she wants nothing more to do with me, then how would she feel about seeing me in Provincetown, even assuming that I *could* find her? It could be the most embarrassing moment of my life. The worst moment of my life.

I retrace my steps to Louis' shack, disconsolate. What on earth was I thinking? Of *course* she's decided to have nothing more to do with me. I know what Daddy's profession says about people like us—I dare not even think the word, the label, the illness—and it stands to reason that she'd had second thoughts.

But when I think about never seeing her again, never touching her again, all I can feel is despair. I don't care if she's a girl or a boy or an octopus: I love her.

The shacks are landmarks: the poet's shack, Helen's shack, finally our own, where I fling off all my clothes and crawl, miserable, into my upper bunk.

Anna comes into the dune shack, squinting, her eyes readjusting after the glare outside. She puts a hand to her hair and a few hairpins come out, as though shedding. "Why are you in bed, *liebchen*? Are you sick?"

"I don't feel good," I say. It's my heart that's being torn out, but I cannot say that to Anna, and what I say is true, anyway: I've never felt worse. It's breaking apart in my chest.

She reaches up into the top bunk, feels my forehead. "No fever," she says, assessingly, running down in her mind, no doubt, a list of possible symptoms and corresponding remedies. "Have you eaten much today?"

I roll over on my side, my back to her. "I just want to be left alone," I say. I know I'm being rude, and I don't care: my world has fallen apart. What use is courtesy at a time like this?

Anna clucks with concern and busies herself at the stove; the odor of kerosene fills the room. I feel nauseated.

She is making me soup, as she always does when people are sick, no matter that we're in the middle of a blazing hot New England summer, no matter that it's not even mealtime. She coaxes me and I don't have the heart to refuse. I eat the black bread and half of the soup, obediently, wondering of there are any cliffs in the vicinity from which I can cast myself. What is the sense of living without Sophie? I've known her for just a few weeks, and already I can't imagine my life without her.

I crawl back into bed, miserable. A mosquito buzzes by my ear and I look at it hopefully. Maybe it will give me malaria. Maybe I'll just lie here in my bunk until I die.

The misery makes way for anger as the sun sets. How dare she? Didn't she say we'd be together forever? Didn't she just want to live with me, here, beside the ocean, and shut the rest of the world out? How can she betray that? How could she betray me?

And the least she could have done was tell me. To my face. Be honest with me and with herself. What kind of person is she, anyway?

And then the misery sets in again as I tell myself, wretchedly, that she's the person with whom I'm in love, the only one I'll ever love, and the world is cold and empty without her.

I bury my face in my pillow to muffle my tears.

Anna is worried. On the third day, she is talking about putting out the flag, the sign to the dune taxi that Sebastien should stop by the shack. I tell her it's a girl problem and her face clears, understanding. "Ah, *mein Engel*. For you I will make my own special tea."

Why is everything that's supposed to be good for you *hot*?

By the fourth day, I have unhappily reached the conclusion that just lying in bed is not going to make things better. Despite my ardent attempts to do so, nobody has died, apparently, of just lying in bed; and if I eat any more of Anna's soup and black bread I will die not of passion but of boredom. Not a very dramatic way to go.

Besides, I'm starting to smell.

If Anna is relieved at seeing me out of bed, she doesn't say so. "Soap and water," she diagnoses quickly, and puts the kettle on to boil. Half an hour later I am scrubbed and scoured, dressed in fresh clothes, and drinking cool lemonade – my reward for having rejoined the land of the living.

The dune taxi comes by in the early afternoon when the sun has just started its slow crawl to down to the horizon, and I help Sebastian unload, take the new provisions up the rise to the shack, bring our rubbish back down. I have no idea what Daddy is paying for these weekly trips–not that my family ever needs to wonder whether we can afford anything–but I expect it's rather a lot, since Sebastian is always in a good mood, eager to help, quick with suggestions for improving our lives.

He knows that I live with Anna, but Daddy's told him that she's an elderly aunt, fragile and perhaps not in control of her faculties. Sebastian always asks after my aunt, polite and obsequious concern in his voice; and I always tell him that she's doing as well as can be expected.

"Ah, well, the sea air's probably doing her good, the dear old thing," he says today, humping a wooden box of vegetables up to the porch. That's as far as he's ever gone. On really hot days I offer him a glass of lemonade–Anna makes it with fresh lemons and hardly any sugar, not that there is any to be had because of rationing, so it's tart and wonderful in the heat–but we always sit together on the porch while he drinks it.

If he is at all curious about my aunt, he doesn't betray his curiosity.

Today he's scanning his list. "Think I've got everything you asked for, miss. Or at least what there was to be had down to Nelson's."

"Thanks, Sebastian." I hand him the new list, dictated by Anna, scribed in my handwriting. We're not taking any chances.

He takes it, glances at it, and folds and stuffs it in his pocket. "See what I can do, miss. Not everything's available, you know." He glances around. "Too much sand here, or I'd tell you to plant a victory garden. Or maybe you won't be here long enough for that?" The curiosity is there, even masked by casual conversation, and I shrug lightly. "No telling," I say noncommittally, and he nods, as though I'd just confirmed something for him. He pats the pocket where he put the list and says again, "See what I can do." The action appears to remind him of something. "Almost forgot, miss. Letter for you."

Mother writes, dutifully, every week. Daddy occasionally adds a note, but only when he has something to say.

Mother can take five pages to say nothing at all.

"Thanks, Sebastian." I take the envelopes from him, one for me, one addressed to me but which is really for Anna–my mother does not trust me to relay messages–and a third that has neither stamp nor postmark. "What's this?"

He glances at it. "Came for you by hand," he says. "Manny's girl, I think, was brought it in. Few days ago. No, I lie: mebbe yesterday."

My name is written across the envelope, the penmanship careful. Manny's girl? My heart starts to beat uncomfortably fast. "Thanks, Sebastian," I say again, and he touches his hat, briefly, before he turns to go.

There is no question of reading it right away: I'm expected to help Anna sort the marketing. I'd never done that, before coming out to the dune shack; never even knew what foods, precisely, went into the menus and meals that ended up on our table. One of the many things I never questioned, living a life of ease: the "staff" took care of everything.

Now I wonder how much of life I've missed.

"Here, Anna, let me help you, that's too heavy."

She glares at me. "And now I'm supposed to be as frail as your imaginary aunt, *nicht wahr?* I'm not on my deathbed yet, *ja?*"

"Of course not." I laugh, suddenly, inspired by the sudden surge of hope in my heart. Manny's girl. It has to be Sophie. It has to be.

I'm putting the tins of peas on the shelf when the sudden thought creeps, unwelcome, into my mind, and my stomach responds immediately to the thought, a cold hollow feeling grabbing at my insides. What if she's written to say goodbye? Sent me a letter because she can't face me in person?

Mother sent a letter like that, once. She told me the story with a smile, a reflection of some past pleasure. "We really weren't meant for each other," she said, her eyes far away. "I knew that if I told him in person, he'd have a thousand reasons why it would work. But I knew it wouldn't."

"Had you already met Daddy then?"

"Good heavens! Of course not! I dated *quite* a lot before I met your father, you know." For some reason it was important to her that I understand, that I see how attractive she once was, how fortunate Daddy is that he is the one she chose. "This was a nice boy, a fellow named Prentiss. I just knew it wasn't going to be—splendid—between us. So I wrote him a letter instead. I thought that it would break it to him gently."

"And did it work?" I was still a little stuck on her vocabulary, wondering what a "splendid" relationship would look like. Had she gotten what she wanted with my father? Was my parents' marriage splendid like that?

She lifted her shoulders slightly, daintily; my mother never shrugs. "I'm quite sure it broke his heart," she said, as though recounting something that had happened to someone she had never met, scarcely caring. "He didn't marry until—oh, years afterwards. Or so I heard," she added quickly, as though it might be unseemly for her to have knowledge of an old boyfriend's life.

"What did the letter say?" I asked, only half interested, I was waiting to finish the conversation so that I could go paint. I was wondering, actually, if I could paint her face the way I was seeing it then, half in light and half in shadow, with lots of room for allegory, for the implication that people live in both worlds. I wanted to paint her then, but she'd never let me, and besides, she hadn't finished her story yet.

"Oh, I don't remember," she said airily, dismissively, then gave the lie to the statement with perfect recall. "Dear Prentiss–his name was Prentiss, you see."

"I did figure that out, Mother."

She ignored me. She closed her eyes, and to my amazement, came up with the entire text verbatim. "Dear Prentiss, I wrote, I know that this will come as a terrible shock to you, but you must promise me to be brave. I have decided that we cannot go on any longer like this. It's no use, really. Please remember me as someone who was fond of you, and above all, don't do anything foolish."

It was almost a dare. I couldn't resist. "And did he?"

"Did he what, dear?"

"Do anything foolish."

"Well," she said with some asperity, "he married Gabrielle Duchesne, didn't he?"

Now I touch the pocket where Sophie's letter sits, the physical contact reassuring, both eager to get away from Anna so I can read it and petrified of what it might say. At last I can't wait any longer. "Anna, I'm just going around to the privy."

She has finished sorting the rest of the groceries and is trying to tame her hair, sitting at the table, moving hairpins about. She looks up at me, surprised. "But I was going to read you the letter from your parents, *ja*?"

This is one of Anna's ploys to be sure that no gossip gets by her. I think she feels terribly cut off from Boston, from a life there that she loved. That's a new thought to me, too: that Anna could have a life, likes and dislikes, friends I've never even met. All I knew was when it was her day off, and that only because on those days she was absent from *my* world; I never even thought about what was going on in hers, or if she *had* a world. She was just Anna.

It only occurred to me to question how coming to the dunes would change my life, not how it would change hers. And it makes me think about things that aren't easy to think about.

I wonder, now, what it was like for her, when they refused to serve her at DeLuca's.

She reads her letters aloud, with a pause here and there as she decides whether or not to either edit or editorialize; and then courtesy requires that I do the same, read her my letter from my parents. It's a ritual, one she looks forward to all week. We drink lemonade and eat applecake and read what she longingly calls letters from home.

Letters from civilization, is what she means.

I feel sorry for her, but I can't wait. "I'll only be a few minutes, Anna, I really have to go. Really. I'll be back before you're ready." I make sure that my letter from my mother is out on the table, in plain sight, so she doesn't suspect me of scurrying off to read it in private. "I'll be right back."

"*Ja, ja.*" She is back to sorting things. Anna loves sorting things. Maybe it's her natural Teutonic sense of order coming to the fore. It's pleasant for those of us who benefit from her tidiness.

I escape with both relief and trepidation. It's still light – I haven't yet figured out why days out here are longer than days elsewhere – and I close and latch the privy door with some relief. It doesn't smell as awful as you would think: Anna has a neat trick of putting popcorn down for the bacteria to feed on, so it composts itself quite nicely. I have no idea where she learned to do that.

Leaning against the door, aware that my hands are shaking, I pull the envelope from my pocket. I stare at it for a few moments, following the neat schoolgirl cursive, as if willing it to not be a letter such as the one that my mother had written to the unfortunate Prentiss; then, taking a deep breath, I rip it open.

Jess, my honey,

I know that you wonder where I've been, and I'm sorry that I couldn't get word to you earlier. It's not anything to do with you and me, so put that idea out of your head right now, don't think that I don't know what you've been thinking! I love you and that's that.

I am grinning like a fool. She loves me, she loves me, she loves me! And she's a mind reader, to boot: otherwise why would she have gotten straight to the point like that?

I'm not able to come out and see you—or even go out to Helen's place, for that matter. It's very bad here, you have to understand. There's been an accident… My father's boat is gone, and everyone on it, too—my dad, my two brothers, and my dad's partner. It's not just overdue; Coast Guard found some life-preservers, it's clear to everybody that it's gone down, though no one is saying the words, not yet, anyway. They might as well, that would make it easier. My mother is desolated. I look at her and I feel so distant, you know? These things happen—these things are supposed to happen. Is it me? Am I wrong? Am I really cold? I just feel—removed—as if it had all happened to somebody else. Fishing boats go down, fishermen die, it's been that way since the first person put bait on a line. She knew it would probably happen back when she married my father—her people, in the Azores, they live off the sea, too. So it's a tragedy, but it shouldn't be a surprise.

What is *surprising is that the Coast Guard has kept the bits of the boat they found, and won't return any of it to my mother. That's not happened before, not that anybody has ever heard of, they always give everything back to the families. I've been up the station at Race Point and been arguing with them for her—we don't even know if any bodies've been found—but there's way too many military types up there suddenly, it's not normal, and they've got better things to do than talk to a girl. I can't figure it out, Jess. No one cares that much when a boat is lost, leastways not them, even though they sometimes say that they do. The only ones who care are the finest kind—the other fishermen. But this one, they care about, and there's something wrong about that.*

I'm trying to find out what's wrong, and before you go quoting your father to me again, yes, I know that it's easier to do that than to grieve my loss. Don't worry: we'll do that and we'll do it proud, if you've not been to a Portuguese funeral you've not seen grieving at all.

Helen is being wonderful and letting me stamp my foot and get angry and I think she wants me to cry, but I can't, not yet. And I'm neglecting her. If you have the time, Jess, can you stop by and see her for me? Just make sure she's okay? I told her you might come by and there are directions at the end of the letter. It would take such a load off my mind. My mother is driving me crazy, and I think she's a little jealous of the time I spend with Helen. And this kind of needs to be her time, you know?

Anyway, I'm going to try and get this sorted as soon as I can, and even if I can't, I'll be out there soon to see you. Tell Anna I miss her applecake and for you—well, it aches in my side when I think about you and miss you, you know? Such a physical thing, love. I didn't know that about it before.

love, Sophie

I need to go to her, I think; but I immediately realize that I wouldn't know where to go, or what to say. Sophie's said it all.

And the fact that she still hasn't told me where she lives says it all, too.

I tuck the paper into my shorts pocket—the days have turned hot again, with a blazing hot sun and afternoons that seem to last forever, and I've decided to hell with convention, I'll take a page from Sophie's book and dress as I please. I took a pair of slacks that I'm not supposed to wear anyway and cut them before Anna could tell me not to, and now, *voilà!* Shorts.

Anna isn't happy about me wearing them, but I don't care.

I hurry back into the dune shack, slamming the screen door behind me, away from the mosquitoes.

Anna's made lemonade, and the applecake is cold from the tiny kerosene refrigerator. It is clearly an event. We open our letters in companionable silence, scan them, a comfortable ritual, part of our lives in the dunes. But my mind is out at sea with Sophie's father, and she's right: I'm wondering if she's spending all her energy wondering about the Coast Guard so she doesn't need to feel her loss.

I think about Daddy dying and my throat closes up.

Anna is the first to speak; her letters always come from my mother and are filled with sensible information along with a healthy dose of what amounts to gossip, though neither Mother nor Anna would ever characterize it that way. "There's been a shortage of eggs," Anna observes.

I'm deciphering Daddy's cramped handwriting. "Everyone's talking about the camps in Europe," I say, my counterpunctal response. Our eyes meet, disturbed.

Anna starts to speak, then stops herself, and goes back to reading her letter instead.

I clear my throat. "I got a note from Sophie," I say. There's no reason to keep it from her.

She's still half-immersed in Mother's words. "Oh, *ja?*"

"Anna—" I wait until she looks up. "It's awful." I swallow. "Her father's dead. Her father, and her brothers, and everyone else on the fishing boat."

That gets her attention. "*Ach*, it's terrible for her," she says, compassion in her voice. Every time I feel so frustrated with Anna that I could scream at her, she shows me this side, this caring. "The poor little one. What happened?"

I feel the note in my pocket, my beloved's handwriting, my touchstone, and a wave of guilt washes over me. Sophie lost half her family, and all I can do is be glad she still loves me. "She doesn't know," I say. "They're not saying."

"Who is not saying, *mein Engel?*"

"The Coast Guard." I shiver after I say the words, and then suddenly it happens, like a kaleidoscope twisting until the right pattern falls into place. The pattern is there, and I get it, suddenly I understand what Sophie's talking about: I feel the shadow of something big and evil just beyond my sight, glimpsed in a split-second out of the corner of my eye, something dark and slithering turning over, flexing its muscles, readying itself...

The Guard is back, now, or will be by the end of the summer: the station at Peaked Hill Bars, less than half a mile from our dune shack, is re-opening in August, with men from Boston coming down to fill out its complement, to keep watch on the shoreline. Or so I read in the *Advocate* last time I was in Provincetown.

But it's not the Coast Guard that I'm afraid of. That dark shadow I'm sensing is something else.

I clear my throat against the tears that are pressing against the backs of my eyeballs, against the fear that's suddenly all around me. "They said they found some parts of the boat, but they won't say more, and Sophie says that never happens."

"*Ach*, well," she says comfortably, "they're in charge, this Coast Guard, *nicht wahr?* They'll know what to do."

"Yes," I agree. "But will it be the right thing?"

***

Of all the places favored by the creatures of the dunes, shimmering shapeshifters and illusionists, magicians and will o'the wisps alike, the sand is one of the most alive; I can imagine it moving beneath my feet.

It's not just the sand-toads, though I've come to watch for them, blending perfectly in with the sticks and the sand and the stark shadows of the noonday sun; I've taken to humming to myself, just as Anna does, as though the sound might warn the toads of my approach.

Neither of us wants me to step on them.

I walk in the surf and know that I'm not alone. Mole crabs are beneath my feet, buried in the sand. Sand hoppers feed on the tideline. I pick up the spent shells of crabs that have abandoned them, big horseshoe crabs still filled with eggs, the promise of life that will never be; the shells of clams and scallops that have died. Holes in the sand may point to clams or mussels or the sea worm called the feather duster. I know all of this because Sophie taught me, her knowledge of the sea and its creatures better, more thorough and more intimate, than any book.

I am constantly amazed by the myriad creatures that live here, in the dunes, in the ocean—even here, its very edge—and I feel both humbled and excited to be a part of it all, to be connected to it. This morning I leave Anna and take my coffee out to the top of the bluff and stand there, feeling the sun and the breeze, looking out over the water.

The tide is high and two seals swim by, side by side, paddling along lazily and rolling over to sun themselves. If I were in the water right now, even just up to my waist, I could touch them. I watch them and am oddly reminded of me and Sophie, and I smile.

Everything about Sophie makes me smile.

Tonight as I curl into my upper bunk, the one with the window next to it, the one with the only breeze in the still little shack, for the first time in years, Anna reaches up and smoothes my hair back from my forehead. "Don't worry, *liebchen*," she says. "It probably will end soon."

But as I drift off to sleep, I know in my heart that something has started that has no end. And I don't have the courage, anymore, to ask her to tell me something good.

Chapter Thirteen

I go to Helen's shack, first.

Maybe it's not such a good idea; the Helen I'm about to meet isn't the Helen in these pictures, but I run my fingers over them just the same, scan the titles of the books that surround me, breathe in what I imagine to be the same air she breathed, when living the hard life of the dunes was her chosen life. Sophie's voice echos all around me. "She saw this place in a dream, in New York City…"

All the long walk into Provincetown I remember those words, that story, I think about the city, shimmering in the heat, and the vision of the cottage by the sea, and the woman who talked and laughed and ate and slept with more literary giants than I'll probably ever even read. She was beautiful, Helen was, with her crimped hair and her daring bathing-dresses.

And that light in her eyes that nothing, I'm willing to bet, would ever extinguish.

I'm right about that part, as it turns out.

The house is on Pearl Street, set right up against the pavement with a small white fence encircling it. The fence needs paint and the house is oddly familiar; I can't place it at first, but I think I saw it in those pictures, with all those people posing in front of it, hands shielding eyes from the glare of the sun, smiles recorded for forever through the lens of a camera. The enormity of the past is weighing on me and I have to take a deep breath before I have the courage, finally, to knock on the door.

It's flung open with the force of a whirlwind. I squint as I look into the darkness beyond the screen door; it seems that no one is there. There's a moment of silence, then a voice, sounding not unlike Sophie when she's cross, demands: "Yes? Are you going to say anything or are you going to just stand there?"

I swallow. I still haven't seen who's speaking. "I'll say something." It sounds impossibly inane and I try again. "Sophie sent me. To talk to you." I'm irritated, as much with her as I am with myself. The manners I've been taught don't stand up well to the people I've been meeting lately; there's a whole set of rules here I need to learn. Or maybe it's just about unlearning the ones I know. In any case, she could make this a little easier, or so it seems to me.

And I can't shake the feeling that perhaps Sophie sent me here with more in mind than just "looking in" on Helen.

"Talk to me about what?" There's movement beyond the screen door and I catch a glimpse of someone slightly shorter than I am, a flower pattern on a dress, loose long gray hair. I still can't see her face. And the irritation is growing. Don't want to play by the rules? Fine: I don't have to, either. I feel incredibly bold. "I'm sorry," I say, as politely as I can. "I must have the wrong house. Sophie told me that you are her mentor and her inspiration, and I know that you wouldn't treat one of her friends like this. Sorry to have disturbed you."

I turn away, fully prepared (or so I tell myself) to walk away from the house on Pearl Street; but that seems to be what Helen was waiting for. Her sudden hoot of laughter rocks the street and sends birds flashing up and out of nests half-hidden below the eaves. The sound of their beating wings hangs in the air. "Come in, then," she says, and the screen door opens. "You can't be all bad, with an attitude like that."

"I trust," I say primly, grasping the doorframe and stepping through it, "that I'm not bad at all."

"Huh. Remains to be seen. Come in, then, come in."

She is hobbling ahead of me down a short dusty corridor, and I latch the door behind me and follow her.

We end up in a crowded room filled with chintz, pictures, and books. The pictures aren't framed, as though the room's inhabitant hasn't taken the time or the patience for proper framing, has eschewed propriety in favor of quantity, spending her time instead tacking or taping them up on every available space: walls, the sides of bookcases, even some on the ceiling, photographs jostling each other for space, sometimes overlapping even—faces and landscapes and abstracts, some of them oddly familiar and I feel as though this room is, somehow, an extension of her shack in the dunes, of the persona she became out there. Above our heads, a ceiling fan turns lazily round and round.

Helen—for it can only be she, though she hasn't bothered to say so, and perhaps that would have been redundant—has settled herself in one of the chintz-covered chairs, her cane placed between her knees, her posture rigidly straight. She keeps both hands on the cane, as though ready to use it at any moment, though whether for escape or attack isn't immediately clear.

I sit on the small loveseat—covered in a different chintz—nearby. I've decided that standing on ceremony, observing the rules I've been taught, doing the odd little dance that Mother and her friends do when they visit each other, is neither expected nor respected

here, so I don't wait to be invited to sit. It's an odd feeling of freedom, of release; there may be more to all this free living than meets
the eye. I promise myself to analyze it later.

I have enough on my hands right here.

Helen is looking at me grimly, and I feel even bolder as I return
her stare. Mother would absolutely have the *vapors* at my behavior.

I can't help it, though: Helen's eyes are mismatched, one blue
and one brown, I've never seen anything like that in my life. It's
strangely disconcerting.

She gives me time to take her in, the lined skin, the thick beautiful gray hair framing her face in long wavy tendrils (what would
Mother say?), the sweater she has on over her dress even on this
hot day. She's wearing earrings, long and silver and bright, and her
feet are bare. I finish my inspection and raise my eyes to her face
again. "Well?" she challenges me. "Do I pass muster?"

"You're older," I say diffidently. "But you wore the same earrings when you were twenty." The age part is obvious; but I recognize the smooth quicksilver at her ears from some of the
photographs in the shack.

Helen smiles, and the eyes suddenly seem to be just right, as
though of course anyone interesting would have mismatched eyes,
reflections of moods past and yet to come. "Older isn't so bad,"
she says, but her voice sounds wistful.

Older sounds pretty good to me; I'm impatient to be there, impatient to explore all the options opening up in front of me, impatient to see what will happen with me and Sophie, impatient to say
things that people will remember. I look around the room again. "I
love your pictures," I say, not feeling that it's as much of a non

sequitur as it sounds. "I saw the ones out in your shack, pictures of you with all those..." My voice trails off: I was about to say "famous people" and then I realize how fatuous that will sound.

Helen's mismatched eyes twinkle. "Famous people?" she guesses, and I raise my chin to look at her. "Yes," I agree, and it's suddenly all right.

"I knew some interesting people. We believed in believing," she says, and that sounds right, too. I dare ask a question I wouldn't have dreamed of asking five minutes ago. "Who was your favorite? I mean, Eugene O'Neill, Edna St. Vincent Millay..."

The eyes are still on me but she's off somewhere else. "Emma Goldman had the best hats," she says in a dreamy voice, then snaps back to the present with an almost audible click. "Best hats on the best head," she says briskly. "But we were all intellectuals then, weren't we, even those who didn't have as much to work with as the rest of us did."

I laugh; I can't help it: she's smart and funny and I can see why people are drawn to her like moths to light. Then... and now. She looks at me, assessing. "I should offer you tea," she says.

I shake my head. "Never touch the stuff," I say cheerfully. Mother would melt into the earth if she heard me: simply dying wouldn't ease her embarrassment enough. I smile impishly. This is a lot of fun: an adult who's as aware of flouting the rules as I am. "Sophie loves you," I tell Helen, another non sequitur that just seems to fit.

She nods; she knows. "We've been good for each other," she acknowledges. "She's quite fond of you, too, don't you know."

I narrow my eyes: does she *know*? "I love her," I say, frankly, leaving Helen to make what she will of it.

She nods again. "You should follow your heart," she says, as though it were the most natural thing in the world. Most adults I know spend their time telling me not to follow my heart. "The things you do? It's all part of learning, isn't it?" She smiles. "It's the things you didn't do that you end up regretting."

"What do you regret?" I ask her, without thinking.

The response is immediate. "Oh, that's easy. Not being in the Olympics."

I'm startled. "Was that an option?"

Helen looks at me, her eyes twinkling. "Everything's an option," she says. I want to pursue it, but she hasn't finished talking about Sophie. "She was born at the wrong time, Sophie was."

"Too late?" I ask, thinking of the photographs surrounding us, the echoes of laughter from the past, the community that put on plays together and wrote poetry together and celebrated free love together. I can see Sophie there, standing a little to the side, commenting on what she was seeing, not caring what other people thought of her.

Helen shakes her head. "Too soon," she says, cryptically. "Far too soon." She studies me. "So you're here. She told you to look in on me?"

I don't lie: odd as it seems, there's something about her that makes me feel I could never lie to her. "She's worried about you," I say. "She – loves you. A lot. And she's got to take care of her family right now, she can't be here every day the way she wants to be."

A shadow crosses her face: she knows about Sophie's father. But when she says something, it's oddly unrelated. "Tell me," she says, and the dreaminess is back in her voice, "how the ocean looked this morning when you left the dunes."

***

Sophie is back.

Sophie is back! My soul is singing.

Not that I've been watching (or so I tell myself), but I see her from way off through Daddy's binoculars, just after she crosses the first dune, and I'm out the door like a shot, Anna calling remonstrations after me. "*Liebchen*! Put socks on your feet!" I didn't put them on, my first really hot day out in the dunes, and burned the soles of my feet on my way down to the pump to draw some water. That isn't happening to me again, and I'm putting them on even as I run.

I have wings on my feet, but the sands still have a life of their own: they force you to slow down, to move at their speed, when all I want to do is fly.

I keep the binoculars with me as I run, stopping every time I reach high ground to scan the dunes anxiously for a glimpse of her. The sun is still on the rise, off behind me, to the left, and it casts a rosy glow over the sand and the scrub grass and the stunted trees and the running girl.

Sophie! Sophie is home!

She sees me now, too, and she is running as well. I wave energetically; we're still too far from each other to hear a shout. She's wearing shorts today, and sandals, and the wind whips at her scarf when she reaches the summits of the dunes.

And then we are together, suddenly, hands clasping each other automatically, hard, then I throw my arms around her and hug her to me, tightly, so tightly that for a moment it feels like I can't breathe. I feel her body trembling through the thin cotton of her shirt. "Jessica," she gasps, and I let her go, and she pulls me back toward her and starts kissing me, my face, my neck, and I find that I can't breathe again. "Sophie," I manage to blurt out. "I thought I'd never see you again."

She pulls away, cupping my chin in her hand, looking straight into my eyes. "I will never leave you, Jess," she says, softly and intensely. "Never, never, never!"

I am swimming in delight. I laugh and throw my arms around her again and my voice is a shout of joy. "I love you!" The moment is perfect, and like all perfect moments, it vanishes too quickly. The shadow passes over, like a cloud covering the sun. The beast has shifted, and the earth along with it. "Oh, Sophie," I say, pulling back, remembering. "I'm so sorry about your father." I am sincere if belated in my condolences. Daddy would have been ashamed of my priorities. "Your father, and your brothers. I'm awfully sorry, Sophie."

There are tears welling in her eyes. "Something is happening," she says, and her voice has changed, it's small and scared and it's scaring me now, too. "Something is going on out there."

"Out where?" But I know already. I've felt the thing that's there, felt it holding its breath, felt it waiting. I wonder how much Sophie knows.

Jeannette de Beauvoir

"It was no accident," she whispers, and then stiffens, as if waking up from a trance. "Come on, Jess. Let's not talk about it."

Anna has seen us coming and already has the ersatz coffee ready. "You two, up so early in the morning," she grumbles, but she is smiling. My Anna is lonely out in the dunes. "Miss Sophie, so sad about your family, *ja*," she says. The dune taxi brought the official news of the Costa boat. "It's terrible to lose father and brothers, and you so young. And your poor *mutti*, I cannot think of how hard this must be for her." That's Anna's real frustration, that she has to stay in hiding, that she cannot go and comfort Sophie's mother, make her applecake, hold her as she weeps.

"Thanks, Anna," says Sophie, slipping easily into one of the chairs at the table and sipping the coffee that Anna automatically puts in front of her, like she is already a member of the family. Sophie seems to always drink it black and very hot. I'd burn my tongue if I ever tried that.

There's something in her voice, though, the same shadow that was there when she told me to stop talking about her loss, and I wonder if Anna can hear it.

Anna bustles around her: she shows love, concern, sympathy by cooking, by baking, by offering food. I suppose that it works; as a child, I always found it harder to cry with a piece of Anna's applecake in my hand – and mouth. Smart Anna.

Sophie is being polite. She sips at her ersatz coffee, she nibbles at her pastry; she answers all of Anna's questions, giving her the news she craves, the contact with others, the opportunity to participate, if only from a distance, in someone else's tragedy. If Anna glimpses the shadow moving behind Sophie's account, feels its breath weaving through her words, she is ignoring it. She latches on to other concerns. "But surely they will give you the bodies!" she exclaims, her distress more important in the moment than her hostessing duties. "They must give them to you! To be buried! It is not natural!"

Sophie responds, and there is a catch in her voice. "They won't even tell us which ones they've found," she says, and I can see that she's close to tears. "We don't know—we don't even know..." Her voice trails off, and I get up and put a hand around her shoulders, protectively. "Anna, talk about something else."

But Anna is looking frightened now, too. She is thinking of things that she shouldn't think about, any more than Sophie should be thinking about her loss; and I know what they are, the shadow that follows her every day now, the knowledge of the camps.

She spreads her hands out flat on the table; they are calloused but shapely, I see with some surprise, and am once again reminded that Anna is still young, a real person apart from me and my needs, and beautiful in ways I've never thought to notice. "*Mein Gott*," she says bleakly.

"What is it, Anna? What's the matter?"

"It is just," she says simply, "that I realize I am a Jew, after all."

Chapter Fourteen

We head out to the dunes as though drawn–toward the sea, away from Anna, I'm not sure which it is.

Sophie has more news from town that she didn't want to share in front of Anna, news about Helen. "I'm stayin' in her shack for a bit now. Can't go see her in town anymore. She has someone there with her all the time, a nurse, she can't stay alone," Sophie says, not looking at me.

I'm shocked: I was there only days ago. "She seemed fine…" I stammer, feeling at fault, as though I should have stayed with Helen, made sure that she would be all right, protected her from whatever it was menacing her, menacing all of us. "She was tired, but fine, really fine!"

I'm trying to convince myself, and Sophie knows it. "You don't have t' go see her anymore," she says, gruffly. "I can take care of things."

I start to say something automatic, and then stop. I'm thinking about how I've been jealous of her growing relationship with Anna, and I wonder if she feels the same about me. Perhaps she'd never meant for me to meet Helen in the first place.

There's no time for that kind of thought, though: I'm supposed to be taking care of Sophie, not Helen. Her father and brothers gone, and now the woman who is her mentor and friend is slipping away, too.

There is darkness, and it is spreading… moving forward, closer, slithering as though it has a life of its own. I feel uneasy, as wild things do when a storm is coming. There *is* a storm coming,

I'm sure of it, or perhaps something even worse, and it's creeping closer all the time.

Sophie is still talking about Helen. "She just can't be by herself anymore, and that's that. She fell yesterday, and she was ten hours on the floor before anyone found her."

"Oh, no!" The guilt tightens around my throat like a noose. "Was she badly hurt?"

"She was sick. She was cold. She broke some bone in her wrist, had t' go t' doctor's." Sophie sounds close to tears.

"Who found her?" I ask.

"I did."

There seems little to respond to that, and so I stay silent. We walk along, hand in hand, with one of us occasionally stumbling, or taking a misstep; the sand is like that.

"I called the priest, too," Sophie says suddenly. "T' come see her. Just in case."

Helen didn't strike me as being particularly religious. "Is she Catholic?"

"Wasn't for a long time," Sophie says, looking straight out to sea, her eyes on the horizon, the place where ocean and sky meet, the place where her father died. Who knows what she's seeing there. "She rejected it, the Church, everything, but she's come back. She says it's a great comfort."

I wonder at how Catholicism fits in with the mismatched laughing eyes and the craziness of her youth. It doesn't work for me. Maybe I'm too young to understand that.

Sophie's already scrambling down the cliff to the beach, and I follow her, down to the sand and the water and the sense of coming home that's always part of being there. We flop down together on the sand, waiting for everything to settle down in our hearts and minds, waiting for the peace of the place to overcome us again.

I think about the beast out there, lurking, watching, and I am afraid that some day I'll come here and the peace will be gone.

But not today.

It happens every time; like magic. The dunes are like the ocean: they don't let you worry about anything for too long, if you let them.

I breathe deeply, consciously, filling my lungs with the salt air, holding it in before releasing it and breathing more in. The sea-monster I'm imagining, Helen, my parents, Anna, even Sophie: everything recedes, becomes trivial, unimportant. There is no end to the beach: it's always changing and never changing, and timeless and yet filled with life. I think you could stay here for a hundred years and not run out of things to see. The land is ancient; the back-shores are glacial outlands, the first settled, the last understood. When I tell Sophie what I'm thinking, she laughs.

"If you can call it settled," she says.

I point back behind us, in the direction of the Pilgrim Monument, invisible behind the first dune cliff, unseen from the beach. I've read my history. "The pilgrims," I recite primly, "came to Provincetown before they ever went to Plymouth." I've seen Plymouth Rock, too, and it's nothing to get excited about. Especially not when compared to the monument.

"And who," says Sophie lazily, taking off her sandals and digging her toes into the wet sand at the water's edge, "was here before the pilgrims?"

I see where she's going. "The Indians never *built* anything," I object. "It didn't matter to them."

She laughs then, lying down and flipping over so that she's on her stomach in the sand, looking up at me. "And they told you that?"

I shake my head, befuddled. It all sounded a lot clearer in the history book I read at school. Was it only last year? It seems a lifetime away.

"They were called the Wampanoag," Sophie says. "Still are, for that matter, they're still around. But they don't own much of anything, now." She pauses and thinks about this for a moment. "If you ask people," she says, finally, "they'll tell you that the English and the Wampanoag got on well. For some reason, people seem t' need t' believe that." She shivers, as at an old memory or a sharp wind. But there is no wind. "But I didn't trust the books at school, and I was right. I *know things*," she says, the words emphasized to reveal deeper meanings. Yes, you do, I think almost irrelevantly, looking at her, her sudden witchiness perfectly natural. I wonder why I hadn't noticed it before.

Sophie is still talking. "The truth is, the English didn't bring enough food with them t' last them out the winter, and they weren't very good at fending for themselves. Have you visited the museum at the Pilgrim Monument yet?"

I shake my head, wordless, fascinated, still enthralled by my vision of Sophie as wise-woman, as witch.

"It says there that the pilgrims would have died," Sophie says, and sarcasm starts to lick at the corners of her voice, "except they found a supply of corn put away by the Wampanoag f'r *their* winter.

They took it back t' the ship and everyone was saved." She looks at me, a quick bright glimmer of tears in her eyes, and I wonder at the intensity of her feelings. "How does someone just find corn, Jessica? Did they think it just grew there, stacked and ready for them? Did their God make it magically appear? Or was it the fairies?"

"They stole it," I say slowly, stating the obvious, the dark thing that was moving about the Cape in another age, another time. For them, the ships arriving from Europe must have been a very bad sea serpent indeed. "From the Wampanoag."

"Of course they stole it," she says impatiently. "How the museum can keep that display there and not be ashamed of themselves, that's more than I can understand." She considers. "We have the dunes, though, because of them."

I'm startled. "How so?" I'd been thinking about touching her, but now I pull back, interested.

"This whole area was forest when the English came. That's why there're still rabbits and fox and deer here, they've all stayed, all managed t' change along with the land. They're the ones that it really belongs t', at the end of the day, and they'll be here long after we're gone." She takes a deep breath.

I frown. "There are dunes for miles and miles, Sophie," I say. "They couldn't possibly have used it all up. It's not—it's not mathematically possible." Jessica Stanfield, Academic Girl.

She laughs, but there is no merriment in her voice; I've never heard a laugh that sounded so little like a laugh. "Who do you think *paid* for them t' come? For their ships, their provisions? Sending ministers with them, doctors?" She flips over on her back and looks up at the sky, a cloudless blue, the kind of sky you see in paintings and don't believe it could actually exist; out here, those skies exist. "Companies did. And the people they sent weren't just supposed t' take care of themselves, they were supposed t' make a profit. And the profit was in the timber."

"They cut it and shipped it back to England?" I was trying to picture it, the sound of trees being felled in the still summer air, the creatures of the forest scurrying for safety. It had to have taken them years, I think, to clear all this land. My land; my dunes.

Sophie doesn't answer right away; she doesn't have to. "They built their port over t' the other side, they founded Provincetown," she says, her voice taking on a dreamy note. "It was safer there, secluded. Protected. They'd learned what a nor'easter can do to the backshore. Ship's captain's logs always said to beware the southern exposures, because in England, that's where the storms come from. It took them a while t' figure out that it works opposite, here."

"And sent the forest back to England," I say. I'm stuck on that point. I still can't quite assimilate it, the ridges and valleys and hills of sand, my place, my dunes, once covered with forest.

"It's what people do," she says. She is, again, the brave one, the cynical one, the knowledgeable one. The tears might have belonged to someone else, such is her detachment now.

And then she becomes the daring one, speaking the words that are scary to bring into reality, into the open, into our lives. "Jess, what do you think happened t' my father?"

The world holds its breath. Even the tide whispers a softer susurration at our feet, gentle, as though it too is waiting for an answer. So that was what all this history lesson had been about:

avoidance. "Was there a storm out on the Banks?" I ask at last, my knowledge of things nautical being limited, but her need reaching me, immediate and real and intense.

She blinks, but keeps her eyes fixed on the sky. "No," she says, and her voice is a whisper containing a world of pain. She rolls onto her side, propping her head up on one hand, her elbow settling into the sand. The beach is like that: it molds to your form, perfectly, allowing you comfort no matter how you turn, what you do. Sometimes I want to sleep on the sand all night, watch the stars wheel overhead, hear the roar of the surf echoing off the canyon side of the dune ridge.

Sophie still isn't looking at me. "There was no storm," she says, her voice careful, as though relating facts. *The pilgrims came and stole the Wampanoag's corn. My father was lost at sea on a clear day.* "The boat was fine, too, Dad's always careful about that. Him and his partner, they spend half their money on her, making sure she can run, get them out, get them back. So many safety considerations, and you can't cut corners, Dad says… Dad said." A deep shuddering breath. "And there are federal regulations, and… and… everything."

There's a break in her voice, now, and I reach over and touch her arm. I remember the note she wrote me, her detachment: *These things happen–these things are supposed to happen. Is it me? Am I wrong? Am I really cold? I just feel–removed–as if it had all happened to somebody else. Fishing boats go down, fishermen die, it's been that way since the first person put bait on a line. She knew it would probably happen back when she married my father. It's a tragedy, but it shouldn't be a surprise.* So she didn't really believe that. Or if she did, it was what Daddy would have called a coping mechanism. I know something about those.

She doesn't seem to believe it anymore.

I take a deep breath. "I'm so sorry, Sophie." Inadequate words, useless words. I try to imagine how I'd feel if Daddy died, and I can't. I can't think of the world existing, of time marching on and life going forward, without him being part of it. His death would end everything.

"The strangest thing," Sophie says, reading my mind, "is how everything's changed, and nothing's changed, all at the same time." She slants a look at me. "Fishing people—they're in competition out there, you know? They won't tell each other where the fish are biting. And they're the worst enemies when they come in with their catches and the train's waiting on the pier and they weigh the catch—then they're sworn enemies for sure." She looks at me again, perhaps to see whether I understand. "But when it's real, when it's festival time or there's a bad storm or the fish aren't biting, then we're family. 'Cause there's no one else in the world that lives like we do, that understands our lives, whose troubles are the same as our troubles."

"Finest kind," I say softly.

She nods and sniffs. "Finest kind," she echoes. She sits up and my hand slides off her shoulders; I don't know if I move it or if she wants it gone. The distance is there between us, the distance of our births, the distance of our experiences. "So the town knows," Sophie says. "The other fishermen and their families, and the folk that work the docks, they all know. They're all real quiet, real respectful. They know it's Dad today and it'll be them tomorrow." She draws up her knees and encircles them with her arms, sniffing. "But the rest of the town–the rich people, and the artists, the people who go about and sit in the bars and write things, they're all acting as though nothing's different. As though nothing's changed."

I say, helplessly, "But it's not their fault." That's the amazing thing about life: its individualism. Things that happen–good or bad–may seem like they happen to everybody; but all we can do is experience them individually: they only really happen to us as individuals. We're not able to comprehend events as they touch other people, not really. Even greater events, catastrophes that touch the world, are always experienced differently by everyone experiencing them. It continues to baffle me. "For them, it hasn't." And my guilt at my own reaction to her letter–pleasure that she still loved me, not a thought for her pain and grief–washes over me as I say it.

"They think they know so much," she says viciously. "They sit around an' they watch us an' they write their plays and paint their pictures and all the while they don't care that they're killing us! They don't think we know, but I know! They store up all these clever witty anecdotes they can tell their friends when they get back t' Boston or New York or wherever it is that they're from, and they stare at us, all the time they're staring at us, and the worst is that they look and look and they never see. There's a boat gone missing and they still want t' pretend that nothing bad could happen out there on a pretty summer day."

The parallel is too obvious to resist. "Like the people who stole the corn," I say, softly, and I wonder suddenly if there isn't a part of Sophie that sees me that way, too, like an interloper, a foreigner, not belonging.

I don't have time to pursue the thought: she rounds on me and I see that there are tears coursing down her face. "Yes, yes," she sobs, and I think I say something, and then she's in my arms, both of us kneeling in the sand with the ocean whispering off to the side, and Sophie is crying, hard deep sobs that leave her gasping for breath before they resume again. I hold her and stroke her hair and she is crying and crying, first incoherently, then in gasps that become words. "I want him back," she sobs, "I want him back!"

"I know," I say, words too inadequate for the tidal wave of grief that has engulfed her. "I know. Sophie, love, I know, honey."

It is minutes, hours, years before her crying slows, becomes intermittent, turns into hiccups and long wavering breaths. I want to say something important, something of substance, but I don't know what it is—Morning Prayer and Holy Eucharist in the dappled stained-glass colors of Trinity Church have not given me the words, perhaps not even the assurance that something this forceful demands. I am left with nothing to give her, no magical phrase, no talisman that she can hold and take to her heart, nothing that might comfort her.

At last I sense rather than feel her pulling away, and I loosen my grip and let her go. She stands up, stiffly, slowly, like an old woman, and stays still for a few moments, staring at the sea.

I wonder if she hates it now, this mad violent gorgeous sea, for taking her family from her. It's achingly beautiful, the ocean, and it beguiles you, it seduces you, so that you believe its beckoning and its promises. But it will turn on you in an instant, stealing boats and coughing wrecks back on shore, breaking back and shattering dreams in seconds, as though to show simply that it can.

She reads my mind. "It wasn't anything normal," she says. Her voice is still shaky, tremulous. "Storms and bad weather, leaking boats, rough seas, you can deal with all of that. People who fish hate the sea as much as they love it," she adds for my benefit, with a little bit of a snort. There is a long pause before she speaks again. "But this was different, Jess. Something happened out there."

The words are dark, ominous, and as if in response to them a cloud moves in front of the sun, the beach is suddenly enveloped in shadow. I shiver. I know what she's talking about: I've been feeling it too, the sense of something dark and dreadful, glimpsed only in passing, out of the corner of one's eye, waiting, biding its time. "What? What is it?"

She shrugs. "I don't know, Jess. But there's something bad out there, I can feel it, something bad and moving and horrible, and it's what got my dad and his boat and my brothers, may they all rest in peace." She says it like it is one word, may-they-all-rest-in-peace. "Something got them. Something that shouldn't have been there."

I shiver again and train my eyes on the horizon, expecting to see a sea monster rearing its head out of the waves, the flash of light on scales, a slithering movement as it goes under again. But nothing happens.

"Something's out there," Sophie says again.

And I have the horrible feeling that it's coming for us, soon.

Later, at night, we lie on the sand and look at the stars, a million of them, each with its own secret, each with its own story. I trace what Daddy has taught me is the summer triangle–Deneb, Vega, Altair–and Sophie laughs. "It's not a triangle, silly," she says. "It's the Northern Cross. See? There... and there..." She takes my hand in hers and traces the invisible lines in the night sky, and then she brings my hand down to her face and kisses it, sucking gently on my fingertips, and I am hers again. But worry is heaped on worry, now; if we can disagree on the names of the constellations, God only knows what other disagreements lie in wait, hovering just beyond the horizon, ready to tear us apart?

And that's without thinking about what is really waiting, what is... out there.

Later I awaken in the night, and that's all I can think of, that monster living in the deep, surfacing to destroy hapless vessels, drawing them down under the waves without leaving a trace behind. I fall asleep again and dream that I am on a bigger boat, an ocean liner, and I am sitting on a deck chair when the shadow looms over me, the sea-monster, and I scream and try to fight it off, flailing my arms and my legs and begging it to let me go... only when I open my eyes it is Anna who is holding my wrists and telling me to wake up. "You had a bad dream, *liebchen*," she says to me, her voice betraying the fear she felt when my cries awakened her. "It's only a dream," she reassures me again, and repeats it one more time like a talisman, like a promise.

But I wonder, as I watch her rearranging the mosquito netting over my bed, if that's really all it was.

At dawn, I walk on the beach. Every morning, now, I leave the dune shack before breakfast, before coffee, and run down the cliff as fast as I can, as fast as I dare, and strip my nightclothes off as I do. I don't slow down; if you hesitate in these chilly dawns, if you pause, you will lose your nerve. Clothes off, keep running, run into the ocean. The frigid water wakes me completely and instantly, and I strike out, long strong strokes, I swim as far as I dare before turning back and heading back to shore.

I've only been doing it a short time, and already I cannot imagine any other way of entering the day. I know from my studies that different cultures have various ways of greeting the dawn, and this is mine, my ritual, my religious experience, this freezing cold water, this sense of being reborn.

This morning after the storm, as I pull my shirt up over my head, I am shocked to see the beach is alive, shimmering, moving in waves of flashing light. I stop, staring, amazed. They are fish: small, silver fish, all of them beached and twisting and moving on the sand, flipping over and over in a desperate bid for escape.

I step among them carefully, amazed and appalled. What new tragedy is this—how can this have happened? The beach is inviting, personal, my private space, a space of beauty and peace. What is this mass suicide I'm seeing?

I look into the waves and there it is, the giant bluefish, swimming back and forth, trapping the shining prey, snapping its jaws again and again as it seizes the hapless ones that have not been able to elude it. The sand is alive with their bodies, where it will soon be covered with their deaths.

Predators and prey. The closer I get to nature, the more I understand it to be uncaring. Nature doesn't reward or punish: it supplies consequences, that's all. Life goes on, but on a grand scale. As people, we are accustomed to looking at life from an individual perspective, to prizing the individual. Nature does no such thing: survival is on a species level only.

I look at the fish on the beach, and I mourn.

***

My parents arrive via train and the dune taxi picks them up at the depot over on Standish Street and now they are here, looking at me as though not quite sure of what they are seeing. The sun has darkened my skin and lightened my hair, while the sand has strengthened my body; I'm not the girl who left Boston two months ago.

In many, many ways I am no longer that girl.

And while I cannot in truth say that I am impervious to the insects that swarm around—mosquitoes, nasty little black flies, greenheads—I have at least become accustomed to them. Mother swats at them desperately with a fan that looks like something her grandmother would have used, and swears at them in language her grandmother would never have dreamed of using.

"How was your trip?" asks Anna, hungry for conversation, any conversation, railway timetables and club car menus will do very nicely indeed, thank you very much. My father grunts. "Slow after Hyannis," he observes.

"It's always slow from Hyannis on," Mother points out. "Do you have enough to eat out here?" she asks Anna.

"*Ja*, the dune taxi, he come every other week, more if we want him to." As if to demonstrate the largesse with which we live, Anna brings out dishes: cold applecake, lemonade, black bread and ersatz butter, slices of apple topped with sugar and cinnamon. "Oh, I couldn't," Mother says, even as she does.

My father is restless. He won't sit at the table, won't eat anything, keeps looking out at the ocean. "They're out there," he says suddenly. "The Germans. It seems more real, imagining them from here, the distance plays tricks on your eyes. Maybe this isn't the best place for you to be after all."

The conversation is taking a dangerous turn: I don't want them getting any ideas of having me anywhere but near Sophie. "We're fine, Daddy," I say reassuringly.

"You don't know what's out there," he says dangerously, turning from the window, so that I see him only in silhouette. He's lost weight, I think irrelevantly, and I wonder, for the first time, whether it's all hard for him, back there in Boston with the screaming headlines and the passionate emotional late nights. And that's when he tells me, interrupting my sympathetic thoughts. "There are German U-boats out there."

I must look blank, because he starts to say something else, some long erudite explanation, no doubt. But this is Anna's domain, and she gets there first. "U-boats," she says, pronouncing the word very differently than my father did, "are submarines. The name, in German, it means *Unterwasserboot*. That is, in English, underwater boat."

"Yes," he agrees, looking at her strangely.

Anna flushes. "I know about them. They were used in the Great War," she says. "We studied about it at school, in Osnabrück."

"Well, they're all over the North Atlantic now," Daddy says, resuming his lecture. "And they've perfected their techniques. Appear just out of nowhere, disrupting shipping, any shipping. They surround a ship and it doesn't know where to fire. They've torpedoed freighters." He takes a deep breath. "They're trying to cut off the supply lines. They're trying to starve Britain."

"Freighters and a fishing-boat," I add under my breath. Anna shoots me a quick scathing look, and I don't say anything else.

"People are calling them wolf-packs," my father says. "They hunt that way, too. Scaring the living daylights out of everybody. They're talking now about organizing convoys, so that there's some protection, running destroyers along with the freighters."

My mother clears her throat. She's had enough. If she can't add something to a conversation, then the conversation isn't worth having. "There's no need to talk about war," she says, brightly. My mother is of the ignore-it-and-it-will-go-away school of thought. "Especially on a day like this! Jessica, tell me, darling, is it always this beautiful out here?"

"A lot of the time," I admit, drawn into her orbit in spite of myself. "When it's not foggy or stormy. The dunes have all sorts of different moods, and the ocean does, too. You should come out and stay with us," I suggest, secure in the knowledge that she wouldn't last a night in the dune shack.

She must be desperate to turn the conversation away from the war, because she says, "I might just do that sometime."

I look at her speculatively. "Mother, what's the matter? You don't want to come out here, you just want to talk about something else. What's changed? Back in Boston, you were convinced we were going to be invaded. You were counting cans; I saw you."

She gives me a reproachful look. "One can be prepared, Jessica," she says, her voice tuned to the *icy* setting, "without needing to *talk* about it. It's simply not done." She fusses unnecessarily with her light summer gloves, with her belt, smoothes her wide elegant skirt. Mother is nothing if not a fashion plate. "Men talk about the war all the time, and I suppose they have their reasons for doing that, though I don't understand, they do what they think is best." She shakes out her fan and addresses her next remarks to it. "Men do not necessarily listen to advice about such things. But there are *some* things, in any case, that ladies simply *don't do*."

The remark wasn't meant for me, I realize belatedly, as I wonder how many nights Daddy's been holding court in his study, missing dinner, climbing into bed after the last of them has left—or, worse still, leaving one or two happily snoring in the rich leather sofa and armchairs. That's happened before, and without the provocation of war as a topic for discussion; I suspect that it's happening more frequently now. My mother hated it then; she must hate it even more these days, more passion, more arguments, more people falling asleep drunk or exhausted in her house.

Daddy is exasperated. "Don't you think that before we make the decision to send thousands of young men over there to lose their lives we ought to give them the courtesy of having given the decision just a little thoughtful consideration?"

"What nonsense," says Mother roundly. "Patriotic young men will trust their country, their government, their president. It's not time to be questioning. It's unpatriotic to ask questions." She snaps the fan decisively, as though the last word on the matter has been spoken.

Daddy and I exchange glances; my mouth must have been open. Mother, however, has not finished. "Besides, no one in this room is going to be involved in making that decision. Our opinions on the matter are moot, and this discussion is frightening Jessica."

"No, it's not," I say.

Out of curiosity rather than a need to irritate my mother (which is often, sad to say, my real motivation: I'm not stupid, I know what I'm doing... most of the time), I ask a question. "But why are they torpedoing freighters and fishing boats? Aren't they supposed to be attacking military targets?"

God only knows where I got that bit of wisdom; I must have read it somewhere. "Or is it to force the United States into getting more involved, sending troops over to Europe? That would be really stupid on their part, wouldn't it?" All the authority and superiority of my sixteen years is in my voice. The German High Command certainly did not check with me before sending orders to their submarine captains; I would have set them straight.

Daddy sits down at last; he's been prowling around the shack a little like a wolf, himself. "America is providing a great deal of material assistance to Europe," he says. "Ships are built up in Maine, at Bath Ironworks and in New Hampshire at the Portsmouth naval yard—and down in Connecticut and even Philadelphia, too—and sent over so the British can use them. Iron, weaponry, all sorts of military materiel. Not to mention sustenance: food, provisions, clothing. Cutting that off means cutting off the lifeline of occupied Europe."

I am fascinated. I feel as though I have a front-row seat for something Important, something Significant.

"What about fishing-boats?" I ask. "We're not sending fish to England, are we? But a boat from Provincetown was torpedoed." I bite my tongue: Mother will surely jump on that one. Strangely, she doesn't.

"I think they shoot first and ask questions later," says Daddy grimly, and suddenly my mother has had enough. "Anna," she says, loudly and energetically, "how are you coming with that tablecloth? The blue one?" And they fall to talking about cross-stitching and thread colors. I make a face when I'm pretty sure that neither of them can see it, and Daddy catches the look. "Walk on the beach?" he suggests.

"Sure," I say, and we're out the door before Mother can muster an argument.

He slips a couple of times on the steep path down the dune cliff—calling it a path is really an exaggeration, after all, its just that it's where we've gone down to the ocean enough times that it's slightly easier to use it than to attempt any other place on the cliff of sand that faces the ocean—but he ends up on his feet. Not bad. Anna's tumbled twice on her way down. Well, twice that I *know* about.

"Your mother is frightened," Daddy says. We start walking along the high-tide mark and his eyes are down, searching. He sees something and picks it up, a flat stone, suitable for skipping. He sends it skittering across the water, once, twice, three times. "Humph," says my father, or something very close to it. He puts his hands in his pockets; his trousers have become very loose on him. We continue to stroll—east, down toward the other dune shacks. "That's why she sounds like that," he finishes, finally.

"You don't have to be an analyst to see that she's scared," I say. Honestly, sometimes Daddy takes this Freudian stuff a little too seriously.

"I know," he says, unexpectedly. "I just worry about her."

I squint at him. He seems less solid, somehow, than he had felt back in Boston, and it's not just the weight loss. "Why? If we get more involved in the war in Europe and they send troops there, you won't have to go, will you?" He must be too old, surely.

He laughs. "No, pumpkin. I won't have to go." He pauses. "But I might go, anyway."

I stoop and pick up a shell, examine it, discard it. Anna has issued a decree: No More Stones Or Shells. Even my sandbox by the dune shack is full. "Why would you want to go?" My voice is carefully casual. There's something here that I'm not understanding. Let's see... you don't *have* to go stand in front of a firing squad, but you'd *like* to?

Daddy says, "In the last war, a lot of soldiers got hurt without getting hurt physically. They couldn't deal with what the war made them see, what it made them do." He shrugs, lightly, as though not taking himself very seriously. "A lot of walking wounded came out of that war, men who lost everything, their homes, their marriages, sometimes even committed suicide. A lot more than people know; they said it was unpatriotic to talk about it. And that's the root of all problems, pumpkin: not talking about them. Ignore something that big, and it only gets bigger." He's searching for another stone to skip: examines one, discards it, selects another, straightens. "Seems unfair to treat them poorly. Seems that someone like me could be useful over there."

He's already there, I realize. Neither of us mentions how he said, so easily and naturally, "the last war."

Why is it that even when you say something is the last, you know that there's going to be another?

***

"Are you lonely out here?" Daddy's voice cuts through my reveries.

We've been walking in silence for a while; we've just drawn even with the shack up on the ridge that's inhabited by the woman with all the newspapers. Or so Sophie tells me. "Piles and piles of them, there's just a path to go through to get to the bed or table." Sophie knows about everything out here, and I spare the woman and her newspapers a passing thought, wondering if I should tell Daddy about her. It must be some kind of syndrome or mental illness, collecting piles of newspapers.

I decide against saying anything. In his current mood, he'd probably want to climb up and help her.

"I'm fine," I say, instead. "I've got Anna, and Sebastian is nice, he brings us gossip from Provincetown. We know whenever Norman Mailer's gotten thrown out of another bar."

"Good God, he's still at that?" My father is amused. He knows the author; he knows everyone. Tennessee Williams had dinner at our brownstone, more than once. So, for that matter, did Irving Berlin.

I want to tell him more, but am not sure how to do it—or how much to tell. I smile tentatively. "And I met someone," I add, wondering what exactly I can say.

Probably not much: *that's* a mental illness, too.

"Yes, you mentioned her before," he says easily, and there's nothing in his voice. I tremble when I mention her, I'm convinced that anyone listening must know, must be able to tell what's between us. Apparently I'm wrong. Daddy's a professional at this sort of thing, after all, and he hasn't guessed the truth. "I'm glad that you found yourself a friend."

His innocence makes me bold. "She wants to go to college and be a writer," I say eagerly. "She's read me some of her poems, some of her stories. She's really good." I do not add that I am the inspiration for her writing of late, or that at least one of those poems would shock him if he read it, much less realized that it was about his daughter.

"That's great, pumpkin. She lives in Provincetown? Are her parents writers, too?"

I laugh; I can't help it, given the tension between the art community and the Portuguese in town, personified in Mailer's swaggering into fishing bars and picking fights. "No, nothing like that. She'll be the first one in her family to go to college. Her father is– he was–he was a fisherman." I pause. "His boat was lost a few weeks ago."

He frowns, his attention clicking back to the war in a second. "Close by here?"

Quickly, I say, "No, of course not. It's quite safe here. The fleet goes out to the Banks–Stellwagen or Georges Bank, miles and miles out there." I fling my arm to the horizon by way of demonstration. "They stay there for days, weeks even." I pause, the reality of it sinking in anew, imagining losing Daddy somewhere out there. "They found some of the wreckage," I say more quietly. "Two of her brothers were on it, too."

"I'm sorry, pumpkin." For someone who spends his life talking about ideas, my father has a very practical side to him. "Is her mother all right? Will her family get by? We can help them if they need anything. I can write a check."

I turn and hug him. "Daddy, you're wonderful. They'd never take help from people like us, not in a million years, but you're the best for thinking of it." To be fair, Mother would have, too: she'd have had the Ladies' Auxiliary of Trinity Church putting on teas and bake sales for the next six months if she thought it would help. My parents are pretty nice people, when you come right down to it.

My father is frowning. "What do you mean, people like us?" he asks. Not defensively; his curiosity has been piqued. I recognize the signs.

"Provincetown," I explain, "is two towns, really, except that they're both in the same space. There's the Portuguese who do the fishing and the construction and the shops and so on, and then there's the artists and writers and musicians, and the only time they talk to each other is when they get in fights in the bars."

"Norman Mailer," he says, enlightened.

I nod. There's more to it than that, of course. I can almost see it happening, the story that Sophie weaves, the pictures her language paints. The poverty of the Azores, starting in the seventeenth century, the hunger, the longing for something better. And the war—it's always about war, at some level—and the conscription, boys taken from their mothers, widows walking the narrow sweltering streets wearing black, the insatiable demand of the war machine for more boys, more men, more widows, more cries of bereavement in the night… and it is in the night that they leave, slipping down narrow mountain paths to harbors where the ships awaited them. New England whaling ships, they are, and they too have an insatiable hunger for men: but if one can survive the gales and the nor'easters, the scurvy and the plague, the injuries and the pain, then one is paid for one's work, and paid well.

But they don't send their money back to the Azores. The go instead to the whalers' home ports—Provincetown, New Bedford, Gloucester—and they buy their own fishing-boats, mortgaging their lives to the sea that has already saved them once. They build houses, send for their families. They've snatched life out of death's jaws, against all odds, against the signs under which they were born.

These are the men and women who formed the backbone of Provincetown, who made it home up until the beginning of my own century. Until some socialite from New York—Mabel Dodge, or maybe it was Mary Heaton Vorse, I think, remembering the photographs and journals in Helen's cottage—came to Provincetown. So beautiful, she thinks. So perfect. So unspoiled. She puts money into the town, invites her bohemian friends from Greenwich Village to summer with her here. They come, and put on plays out on Lewis Wharf, writing novels in longhand late at night in rented rooms, painting the fishing boats chugging out of the harbor, get sunburn attempting to walk out to the Long Point lighthouse… and so by loving Provincetown as an unspoiled fishing village, Mrs. Dodge turns it into something else altogether.

The artists stay, most of them for the summer, some of them year-round, and now they make up a substantial part of the town, the East End being theirs for the duration. The fishermen resent them—who wouldn't? But, as I tell Daddy, such things are generally resolved in the bars, and it's usually the Portuguese who win.

Daddy listens, not interrupting, nodding in understanding from time to time. It's one of his professional tricks, that nod: so is the listening. Psychologists aren't afraid of silences. Most people usually rush to fill pauses, breaks in conversation, and by doing so, they say things that they wouldn't have said otherwise. Or so Daddy tells me; I wouldn't know, myself, I'm one of the ones who talk too much.

"Does your friend—Sophie, that's her name?—resent you for being here?" he asks at length, the good trick-cyclist bringing the general back to the particular. I could kiss him: all I want to do when I'm not with her is talk about her, think about her, hear her name. Still, I know I'm right to be careful around Daddy, right to talk about history and the echo of old grudges, about modern paintings and bohemian lifestyles. He's too quick, too good at what he does, and I don't want him thinking about my own bohemian lifestyle choices.

Still, he's the one who brought her up.

"Sophie's not like that," I say, choosing my words carefully. "She wants something more." I hesitate. "That's not right, it sounds condescending, and she's not like that at all, either. She loves Provincetown, it's her home, but she wants to live between the two communities."

"A difficult place to be," comments Daddy. "Liminality, that's what we call it: living on the threshold. It's hard to drop that kind of past, but still live in the middle of it."

"But that's the point!" I exclaim, passionate despite my efforts at detachment. "She doesn't want to lose her past, her heritage. She's proud of it, proud of what her grandfather and her great-grandfather were able to do. Her mother came from the Azores. They speak Portuguese at home."

Belatedly, I realize that I may be giving him too much infor-mation; but I don't like the pity I heard in his voice. "Why can't you have both, Daddy? The past and the future? Why can't you stay true to your heritage and still become what you want to be? The boys who left the Azores were following a dream, too!"

"Yes, they were, pumpkin, but they had to leave their pasts be-hind to live it," Daddy says quietly, studying me. There's a faint frown creasing his brow that I don't like. I shrug, pretending indif-ference. "Well, maybe it'll work out for her, maybe it won't," I say casually as though I don't really care one way or the other, my mind racing ahead for another subject, any other subject. For once, I come up with nothing.

He has decided not to pursue it, for reasons of his own, and he turns. "Best we get back soon, your mother will be worrying," he says. We walk along for some time in silence, until he finds another stone to skip. Twice: not one of his better efforts. I laugh. "What is it about you and skipping stones?" I ask, and I know full well that this is a conversation that will last us easily the rest of the walk to the dune shack.

I'm right, of course.

***

Mother is consulting her watch every few seconds and sighing loudly. Anna's eyes meet mine, and she raises her eyebrows; I shrug. "We're going to miss the bus," Mother says fretfully to Daddy. Passenger service to Provincetown has gotten complicated lately; if there aren't enough people to fill the trains, they send buses from Hyannis instead. Trains still run for the fish, of course. "The dune taxi's on its way. Where on earth did the two of you go?"

Daddy still has that look in his eyes when he glances at me, a sense of his thoughts being elsewhere—or as if he were doing sums in his head. He rouses himself from wherever it is he's gone and says to Mother, his voice hearty, "I can go for a walk with my girl sometimes, can't I?" And this time when he looks at me, there's no mistaking the twinkle.

Does he know?

I'm still working on that one when Sebastian pulls up in his battered old Suburban. "You see?" Daddy says calmly. "Plenty of time."

Mother makes some sort of noise and takes my chin in her hand. "Good-bye, darling," she says, her lips almost—but not quite—touching my cheeks. "Are you remembering to brush your teeth?"

Anna answers for me. "Every day," she says grimly.

"And your prayers?"

"Those, too," I say. Anna looks like she's finding it hard not to laugh.

"Well, then," says my mother.

"The taxi's waiting," Daddy says mildly.

"So now for a change you're the one in the hurry!"

Daddy just smiles. He never argues unless it's about something sufficiently abstract to command his attention. It's one of his more infuriating traits. "'Bye, pumpkin."

"Bye, Daddy." Kiss, hug, and I'm still wondering what is going on with him. Something happened here, but I can't quite put my finger on it.

Anna watches them go and then turns to me. "So you say your prayers every day?" she asks; but she is smiling.

"I don't share them with you," I say loftily. "You're not an Episcopalian."

"Thank *Gott*," mutters Anna.

I shake my head and leave her then, walking back to the bluff, not following the path down to the water this time, just looking out to the endless horizon. The monster is out there, its sleek, slithering body just under the surface, and as I watch it turns, the water sparkling and flashing as it rolls off its skin. It's coming closer every day.

Chapter Fifteen

I am down on the beach as the day starts closing in, unready to leave, prowling the shoreline, uneasy. Sophie has gone back to town; there is to be a memorial service at Saint Peter's for her father and brothers, her father's partners. No funeral: you need a body for a funeral. She does not ask me to come and I do not offer. We seem to both understand that the two worlds are separate and need to remain that way.

And yet I feel as if a part of me is missing. Is that wrong?

I watch the sun set and look at the horizon and think about Saint Peter, patron saint of all those "who go down to the sea in ships" (for the Episcopal lectionary teaches us the psalms, whether we wish it to or not) and how he has failed, this time. No storm, Sophie said, and I begrudgingly give Saint Peter his due for that one.

But if it is not his fault, who can I blame?

The point where sky and ocean touch is brilliant now with light, and I wonder what it would be like, to move into that golden water, to pass the first horizon and see the land disappearing from sight. Sophie is full of disdain for the colonists, but I wonder what it would be like to get on a ship—no matter how indentured—and sail off into this golden sunset, sail off into the unknown, into a future that could hold anything… but very certainly holds death. Passing that first horizon and not knowing what lies beyond it…

I look instinctively toward my own horizon. The sun moves imperceptibly toward the water, and as soon as it touches, the light stretching and dissolving into the liquid, it seems to remember a prior commitment. I don't understand what visual distortion makes it seem that the sun travels slowly through the sky when it's overhead, but then seems to suddenly change gear and move briskly and purposefully as it actually rises or sets; it's one of the earth's mysteries.

Perhaps Daddy knows; I'll ask him about it in my next letter home.

For now I watch as it quickens, spilling orange gold in a broad sweeping swath through the ocean, the waves sparkling gold and glittering as they chase each other in its path. Gulls stand placidly on the sand at the water's edge: terns and herring gulls, laughing gulls and black skimmers, all of them waiting for the darkness when they'll go back into the dunes. A good few of them ride the waves, moving smoothly up and down with each swell. They are suddenly disturbed by movement and take flight nearly in unison, rising like a black cloud against the orange and red brilliance of the sun; they wheel, cry, and settle again. False alarm.

I wait until at last the topmost curved edge of the sun dips into the water, now black ebony liquid, a magician whose tricks have just been exposed, and I turn eastward: I've unconsciously followed the sunset, and am on an unfamiliar patch of beach. It doesn't matter; it's all the same, the same creatures living under the sand on which I walk, in the air that I breathe, beneath the waves that I could reach and touch if I were so inclined. There is a strong smell in the air tonight, a smell of seaweed and salt and kelp, a smell of dead things.

Twilight is the time when the imagination runs amuck, where shapes lose their significance and take on other, more frightening meanings. I once stayed in the Concord woods too long, and I remember the eyes that watched me as I went by, the natural designs on the tree trunks transformed into twisted, malevolent beings, the sounds and sighs of the woods as some prepare to be predators – and others, prey.

Why am I thinking of that now? Is it because there is something in this air besides the smell of the dead seaweed and the salt, something I can sense beyond the rhythm of the waves, in the wind that is picking up again as it does every night at dusk?

The creature that is out there, under the sea, is stirring.

I shake myself mentally: that's nonsense, a fantasy born of my own bad dreams, my missing Sophie, my guilt over her pain. There is nothing here that I need fear. I am in the dunes; I am safe.

And yet, insofar as it's possible when walking in sand, I find myself quickening my pace.

It's easier to walk at the water's edge, in the hard-packed wet sand, and so – still half making fun of myself for being afraid of nothing–I cut across the beach, down to water's edge. I have to be more careful as I go here, of course; there are broken shells and stones to cut your feet, and once when I was walking with Anna in very shallow water, a crab closed its pincers on my toe. Still, these suddenly seem like trivial concerns, and I'm glad for their triviality. If I can just concentrate on these things, I tell myself, I will be home soon, and Anna chiding me for being out after dark. Anna is convinced that the dune foxes will eat humans, given half a chance; and the dune foxes are only hunting at night: ergo, I must not go out at night. Or so runs her logic. I smile as I think of it, imagining thinking of a small fox as a threat…

...when I lift my eyes from the sand and let them rest in the shallows, the water that stretches between the beach and the Peaked Hill bars, and a dark shape starting to emerge from the water.

My heart does several somersaults before my mind finally kicks in. A seal, a wonderful, beautiful seal, that's all it is, its head emerging from the swell of the waves just as it does in the daytime when Sophie laughs and talks back to it, and why shouldn't they surface just as much in the night as they do in the day?

My relief is overwhelming.

More dark shapes emerging now, and they are not seals, they are human, black shapes against the gray dusk, they are men, not seals, and I stifle a scream. Quickly, instinctively, I sink to the sand, flattening myself down, trying to become immobile and unnoticeable, another piece of wreckage the ocean has washed ashore.

There are three of them, I can see that now, larger than seals, dark shapes emerging terrifyingly from the waves, pulling themselves from the water, walking upright. They are all in black, with rubber hoods over their heads and tight black suits below. One pauses, leaning on another, taking something from his feet. Flippers. No, I think silently: no, no, no. It's not happening. They're not here.

My sea monster is real, after all.

***

I wait a long time. I wait until the three human shadows have blended with the shadow of the dune bluff. I wait until my heart has hammered one thousand, two hundred, and eighty wild frightened beats, although I cannot swear to the accuracy of that count, because I am also very, very scared, which takes a lot out of a person.

I wait until I know that Anna will be going out and looking for me within her limited comfort range; and, thinking of those three dark shapes rising up out of the sea, I am afraid for her, too, the lights of the dune shack behind her, the lights that, dim as they are, can still be seen for miles.

I scramble up the dune cliff. There is no path here, and I slip back nearly as much as I go forward and upward; but there is panic at my back and I manage it at last, my breath coming uncomfortably—and loudly—fast. A moment to get my bearings at the top. There is a dune shack near me, not a hundred yards off, a dim light shining from an uncurtained window. It is raised on stilts, as are some of the cottages out here, Sophie says that it's so the wind will go under the shack instead of slamming into it, which is what happens at Louis'—and I know that I've seen it before, passed this way, although I do not know who lives here. I creep by, holding my breath, but as I approach the shack I can hear someone singing inside and I move more quickly, thinking both that no one would sing if they were being held hostage by three men in frog-suits, and that the sound of the singing will drown any sound my bare feet might make in the sand.

I do not, of course, have a flashlight with me. Just as well, perhaps; this isn't a time to attract anybody's attention.

There is a moon rising, flattened against the sky, as big and orange as a ripe pumpkin. It looks close enough to touch. Around me, a sudden scurrying, then silence: the creatures of the night going about their business. I step on something that moves and am just able to refrain from crying out.

Some are predators, some are prey…

I quicken my steps and find myself in familiar territory: the curve of the dune, leading down into a windswept basin; I know where I am. The rising moon is brighter as it becomes less orange, more yellow: by the time it is fully risen it will be cold, white, unattainable. But for now I am grateful for what light it gives. I too am one of the creatures of the night, I am a shadow flitting swiftly across the sand.

Louis' shack appears more quickly than I thought it would, all the same. I am still looking around, still waiting for the frogmen to materialize at my side, still afraid of walking into a trap they may have set (for whom? An adolescent girl they hadn't even seen? How could I possibly be important to anybody? But still, darkness and solitude and shock assure me that it is true…).

I approach the hut stealthily. The kerosene lamps are lit, and there is backwash from the lamplight spilling out onto the sand and the beach-rose bushes surrounding the shack, as though encircling it protectively with a magical healing circle. I creep up cautiously and peer inside; Anna is alone, darning a sock in the lamplight. Her hair is in disarray. Everything is normal.

Did I imagine what I saw down on the beach? Could I have?

I look around me some more, but there seems little point in staying outside now, and in addition I am providing a feast for hungry mosquitoes. Predator and prey. I push open the shack door.

"Ach, and it's a heart attack you're giving me!" But her comment is good-natured, reassuringly ordinary. "You stay out too long, *liebchen*, and supper now is cold. Now it is you'll have to wait while I heat some for you."

I close the door and latch it behind my back. Anna doesn't notice, she is still talking. "It is the ham salad, the one your *mutti* and papa like to have on a hot day, but there is a roasted potato, too. Wash up before you sit at my table, *liebchen, Gott* only knows where you've been. And, another thing, no argument: tomorrow, it's a proper bath you are having…"

She turns from the stove, her hot pad grasping a potato wrapped in tinfoil, when she really looks at me for the first time. "Miss Jessica! What is it? Are you feeling poorly again? You look as if it's a ghost you've been seeing!"

She puts the potato on a plate and slides it over to my place at the table before coming to stand next to me, pulling off her oven mitt as she does. Hand to forehead: Anna's first line of defense. "Are you all right, *liebchen*? It is not a fever I am feeling."

I grasp her wrist and pull her closer to me. I find my mouth absurdly dry and I have to wet my lips before I can manage even a whisper. "There were some men down on the beach, Anna, I saw them."

"*Ach*," she says, unnecessarily loudly so close to my ear. "What is it—"

"Shh!" It comes out as a hiss and I tighten my hold on her wrist. I put my lips next to her ear and whisper. "Listen, for once. Three men came out of the ocean. They came from a boat, they had swum underwater in diving suits. They're here, somewhere, in the dunes."

At least that got her to lower her voice. Why this seems important to me, I cannot say; if indeed the three men who had come were watching us from the shadows beyond the lamplight, whispering no doubt will give them more evidence of guilt than speaking normally would have done.

I'm beginning to wonder if I'm any good in a crisis at all. My brain works like a spy novel. A bad spy novel.

Anna is trying to decide whether or not to take me seriously. "Where are they?" she asks, *sotto voce.*

"I don't know," I admit. I make an all-encompassing gesture. "Somewhere out there."

She doesn't say anything. We know all that needs to be said: that we are surrounded by miles and miles of dunes, inhabited and uninhabited shacks, with a town just over two miles away.

I feel the futility of it all as a weight on my shoulders, and I sit down at the table, feeling suddenly heavy and exhausted. Anna continues to serve me, her motions mechanical, her movement stiff, like the gait of toy soldiers.

I wait until lemonade, ham salad, and potato are assembled in front of me and Anna has lowered herself gingerly into her own chair. "What should we do?" I ask. It is automatic, that question. I've asked her the same question countless times, we share years and years of my asking the same question; and Anna has always answered it. Clear. Definitive. Crisp. She likes to tell people what to do. She likes order, clear directions, an unequivocal path to take. I wait.

Anna is white, pale, her face suddenly older and frightened. "*Weiss ich nicht*: I do not know," whispers Anna, and that is perhaps what frightens me the most.

***

They haunt my sleep, those three figures. Over and over again I see them rising out of the water, over and over again, like the monster I had imagined out there, a monster that's now taken human form, become real, defined.

Monsters under the bed, in the closet, around the corner, up in the attic. Dragons have always haunted my sleep, the way they do with most children; but now that I'm faced with real danger, the danger of life outside of fairytales, I find I'd rather go back to the dragon. Nice dragon.

I'm reliving that stark cold fear I felt, seizing my insides the way a cold drink does, when you drink it down it too fast on a hot day, only deeper, colder. All through my dreams I weave in the new terror, the dark shapes that should have been seals, but weren't; and every time the fear I felt in the dream wakes me up, and then I remember that the fear is real.

In the morning, Anna tells me that I must set out for town. "Someone must be told," she asserts, conveniently not saying who that should be.

I'm all for it. "Who should I tell?"

She looks at me, nonplussed. I was right: she hadn't thought it through that far. "I don't know, me, do I?" she asks rhetorically.

"*Weiss ich nicht!* The police? The mayor?" And then her expression lightens. "Your father! *Ja!* He will know what to do!"

"My father's in Boston, Anna. And what does he know about Provincetown? What does he know about anything that happens down here?" I can feel a headache building behind my eyes, squeezing my brain. It's Sophie I want to see, Sophie I want to tell.

About the sea monster.

Anna bristles. "There are telephones, *ja?* Telegraphs? There are ways to get through to him. And he will know what to do." She says it with a childlike confidence, her voice trusting and assured: of course he will know what to do. He always knows what to do. She trusts him as I trust her, and I don't know how to tell her that all this is beyond any of our abilities to fix.

The one unfixable problem. The monster from the sea.

"I don't know, Anna…" My voice trails off as I examine options, the possibilities of someone thinking it's a made-up story, the fear that someone will have to come back out to the dune shack with me, will see Anna, will react badly to her. People in official positions change, become different people, that is the inherited wisdom from the discussions in Daddy's study. They could pose a deeper problem than my sea monster does.

She slaps coffee down on the table, oatmeal, her irritation obvious. "I will go to town, then, me," she announces. "I will discover what to do."

"We both know that you can't do that," I say wearily. All I want to do is sleep: my troubled dreams have left me exhausted, the creatures of the night have spooked me more than I can say. A part of me spent the long hours of darkness tensing, waiting for an attack that never came, listening for footsteps outside the dune shack. "I'll go," I say finally, in response to her glare. Jessica Stanfield, Girl Hero.

She relaxes a little. "That's good, *ja*."

It's seems a longer walk than usual, walking into Provincetown today; and the walk is made even longer – or at least so it seems – by my need to jump at every small sound, explore every imagined shadow glimpsed from the corner of my eye. The sand spreads out around me, pocketed and dimpled, in hills and valleys, with the scrub trees and sparse dune vegetation covering it lightly. There is no place to hide out here, and yet I imagine a hundred hiding places, I visualize an army of men following the three I had seen, all of them crouching somewhere in the dunes, waiting.

It doesn't occur to me to wonder what it is they may be waiting for.

Chapter Sixteen

It's hot, too; even with my straw hat and sunglasses, both forced on me by Anna, it's mercilessly hot. I move through the last copse of stunted Cape trees and am crossing Route Six, heading down Snail Road, the tarmac is too hot and hard on feet conditioned by sand and water for so long, and I keep to the sides of the road, looking longingly (and still with some fear) into the woods with their stunted grotesque trees that surround me on both sides of the road. I do this all the way to where Snail Road joins the harbor and there is, finally, a breeze, a smell of the water, of dead seaweed and decaying shellfish. Morbid thoughts, I know. I entertain them anyway.

Walking along Commercial Street at last, through the calm and creative east end, shaded by the elm trees, with the harbor glinting peaceful and teal-blue and perfect in the sunlight. The fishing boats clustered around the piers look like child's toys, scrubbed and painted and pure, and I tick off the piers as I go past them, counting rather than naming, for I don't know all their names.

The train from Boston is already waiting for fish out on the pier when I reach MacMillan Wharf, and I'm seized with a sudden desire to get on it, go back home, see Daddy.

I am determined. I am not calling my father. I have decided this on the long walk in from the dunes. I have been charged with the responsibilities of adulthood, of caring for Anna and keeping her safe, and I am not going running to my parents the first time that something difficult happens.

I am *not*.

The police station, it transpires, is located in the cellar of Town Hall, which I ascertain by asking at Nelson's, he who fills Sebastian's dune taxi for us every week. Mr. Nelson himself gives me the directions, his eyes curious. "So, Miss Stanfield," he says, "how're you and the old lady doin' out there in the dunes?"

I have to smile. The "old lady" is Anna, somewhere in her thirties. I remember the myth of the elderly aunt and nod. "She's doing well," I say. "But she worries, you know what old people are like. She just wants me to introduce myself to the police."

He smiles a little condescendingly. All right, a lot condescendingly. "I'm sure they'll be glad to hear from you."

I'm quite sure that they won't. I shrug. "It's a little silly, really, but I said I would …" my voice trails off. "Thanks for the directions, Mr. Nelson."

"Sure there's nothing I can get you today, Miss Stanfield? If you have coupons, we have some nice ham today."

"No, thanks, Mr. Nelson," I say, automatically, and he smiles. "Our lady of the dunes," he says. "That's what my wife calls you."

I like the name. "Thanks, Mr. Nelson. I'll just be off."

Town Hall sits majestically in the midst of trees and emerald lawn. I glance around me before going down the stairs into blessed coolness and questionable shadows. I shiver, feeling like a prisoner, being taken here against my will, down these stairs… I shake off the feeling quickly. I am in control. I will be all right.

The desk sergeant—I presume it is he, the Agatha Christie detective novels that I used to read surreptitiously at night under the covers all have sergeants manning the desk in police stations, though now that I think of it, most of these books take place in

England—puts down his newspaper and smiles. "Hello, there, young lady, what can I do for you?"

He probably thinks I'm here to report a missing cat, I think, and there's a part of me (the smallest part, the part that's not afraid of what I saw last night) that is delighted to surprise him, that basks in the importance of what I have come to say. I clear my throat. "May I please speak to someone in private?" I ask. There are two men sitting on a bench by the door, neither of them smells any too good, and they're both looking at me in a way I don't like. Predators, I find myself thinking, and I have a sudden vision of Sophie, dark and beautiful and open. As I look at them I wonder why any woman lets any man touch her.

Not Mother, of course; Daddy's different. And, anyway, I can't think of my parents like that—doing *it*, as they say at school. Not *my* parents. The thought is disquieting and vaguely revolting: not *my* parents. They couldn't possibly have done that, not ever, yuck. I am undoubtedly the product of an immaculate conception, the kind the Catholics believe in, the kind that involves beatific smiles and *no touching at all.*

He's not happy with me, the policeman at the desk. "Well, now, missy, why don't you just tell me what the problem is, and I'll decide where we need to go, and who we need to see." So he's clever, I think, understanding intuitively that my request for privacy also inferred a request to see someone with more superiority. Usually I'm guilty of overestimating people's intelligence and intuition; not today.

I've worn my best dress, the one that doesn't need ironing, and I let Anna put ribbons in my hair; I take off the straw hat so he can see them, see how well groomed and civilized I look. I still have some cards to play–Daddy's name, among them. It always startles me to find that he is famous, that people outside of our circle have heard of him; today, I'm grateful for it. Extra ammunition, as it were.

I, too, can think in wartime terms.

But not yet. I'd very much like to sort this without his help, literal or otherwise.

I'm conscious of all of that and of the deliberateness with which I give him my best smile. "Please, sir–" God, now I sound like someone out of a Dickens novel "–please, it's awfully important." I glance pointedly at the men on the bench. "You see, I'd be *embarrassed…*"

"Oh. I see." His voice is hurried now: I've scared him. Something female, he is thinking. Something female that he doesn't want to know about. He is already calculating how quickly he can hand me off to someone else. "This way, miss, I'll just buzz you through."

He presses a button, and the gate (which only comes up to my hips, really, is this supposed to keep anybody out?) swings open. I give him what I hope is another dazzling smile. "Thank you, sir."

Mother always drills it into me, that I have to always always be polite, but it's Daddy who told me the truth of the thing. "Always be more polite than the other person, pumpkin," he says. "It puts them at a disadvantage."

I walk between rows of desks to an office at the back. "Go on, knock on the door," the man from the front desk urges me; and I do. I'm not feeling as shaky as I was, back in the wilds of the dunes; there's nothing, here, to be afraid of. Surely not.

"Come in!"

I am in an office that looks disappointingly like that of the headmistress of my school, an office I know rather too well and in which I've spent rather too much time. It's not Miss Harrington, however, behind the desk; this is a youngish man with sandy hair and tanned skin and a suit that looks a little too big for him, as though he recently lost a lot of weight or is wearing his older brother's clothes. He stands up as I come in and waits while I shut the door, carefully, behind me; but I see the quick look he directs through it first, Apparently young ladies in distress are to be dealt with at the front desk, not here.

I'm beginning to enjoy myself.

He comes round the desk and eases me gently into a chair. "My name's Lieutenant Foster, miss. Are you comfortable? Can I get you a glass of water? No? Well, then." He resumes his place behind the desk. I can see that it's covered with forms, and there is another one in the big Royal typewriter off to the side, the one he caught his sleeve on when he came round to offer me a seat. "How can I help you this morning?"

"I came to report something that happened last night. Over on the back shore," I say, and at once his body relaxes. The backshore, the dunes, is a place where anything can happen, he is implying, without ever saying a word. A bad place. Still, his expression is polite. "And what would that be, miss?"

"I was on the beach," I begin, but he holds up a hand. "Wait a moment, let's start at the beginning. Your name, miss, and why you were all the way out there last night?" He draws a pad of paper to him, uncaps his fountain pen, writes the date carefully at the top of the page. He looks at me expectantly.

"Jessica Stanfield," I reply obediently. "And I live out there, in my uncle's cottage." I think that Louis is in fact my second cousin, being Daddy's cousin, but am not sure; "uncle" seems to cover all eventualities.

He writes, but his head comes up again. "Living out there, are you, miss, in the dunes?"

I raise my chin instinctively and look at him. "That's right." Every ounce of Boston Brahmin that I can muster is in my voice.

He is not mollified. Perhaps he's just a nice man. "Miss, you want to be careful out there. The dunes, now, they're not safe places. You're isolated out there. Anything can happen."

It's my moment for high drama. "Something *has* happened," I say. "That's why I'm here."

He looks horrified and I can imagine what he's thinking, though what I have to tell him is, at least to my mind, far worse. He *is* being nice; perhaps he has children, even daughters. "Miss, are you living out there alone?"

"Of course not," I snap. He may well be being nice, but I'd like to get to the point. I'd like to get out of this stuffy little office and back to the dunes. I'd like to tell Anna that I've done my duty. I'd like to see Sophie. "My aunt—she's elderly—is staying with me."

He writes that down. "So you're here on a summer holiday," he says. He's relieved to be able to situate me, place me in a neat box, explain my presence. "So what is it that you wanted to tell us, miss?"

"I was walking on the beach," I begin again. "It was after sunset last night, but not long after: I'd gone down to the beach to watch it. The sunset, I mean." I am being less articulate than I'd hoped to be, and am frustrated. "So it was starting to get dark," I clarify.

He isn't writing this part down. He says nothing, just looks at me. He's probably wondering how much of his time I intend to waste.

I moisten my lips. The image is still there, the sight of the shapes rising out of the ocean, the three figures rising from the sea, the monster I've been fearing. I force myself to take a deep breath because even remembering is making me feel like I can't breathe, like the walls are closing in on me. "I was looking at the ocean, the way one does, and I thought I saw a seal. One first, then two others."

My heart races again at the memory. Something of what I'm feeling must be showing in my face, because he leans forward; but still he says nothing. "But they weren't seals. That's what I'm here to tell you; they weren't seals, they were men. All dressed in black. In rubber suits, even over their heads. They came up out of the ocean and took off their flippers and then they started up the bluff, up into the dunes." There.

He frowns. "And where were you, meanwhile, miss?"

"As soon as I saw them, I hid," I confess frankly. "There was some detritus just there, seaweed caught on some old planking, right at the high-water mark. I stayed there. I didn't move."

"Hmm." He looks at me, appraisingly. "Convenient it was just there."

"If it hadn't been," I say dryly, "*I* might not be *here*."

There is a silence as we each think our own thoughts. He doesn't believe me, I think, and part of me doesn't care, and the other part of me is scared of going back to the dunes, scared that more shadowy figures will arrive at sunset tonight, and tomorrow night, and…

"Perhaps I should talk to your aunt," he suggests suddenly, tearing me away from one set of fears and replacing it with another, and now I really panic. The last thing I want is for the police to question Anna. That was the whole point of living in the dunes, so Anna can be safe.

"She didn't see them," I say quickly. Then, to distract him, and giving up my last shreds of independence, I add, "If you'd like to call my father and see if he thinks I have a fanciful imagination, please go ahead. He's Dr. Robert Stanfield. He has a practice on Beacon Hill. He teaches at Mount Auburn Hospital and at Harvard University. I'm sure he'll be glad to interrupt his work to assure you that his daughter isn't prone to having visions." I straighten up, making myself as tall in my chair as I possibly can. "My education has taught me to be an excellent observer, Lieutenant Foster. Three men came out of the ocean on the backshore last night. I assume that they swam in from a boat of some kind. I thought I should go to the coast guard instead of the police; I guess I was right."

If you attack someone, Daddy told me once, it distracts them. They forget what you were talking about before they were attacked: it's a natural human response, the respond to defend oneself. He always smiles when he says the next part. If you need to, attack a man's professional vanity. There's not a one out there that can have it pass him by.

Lieutenant Foster is not one to let it pass him by, and I breathe a silent prayer of thanks to my father. He clears his throat. "I'm sure that you saw what you saw, miss," he says, scrawling on the paper. "You were right to bring it to us, and not to the coast guard. We can take care of it right here." He looks up at me and I see a thought forming. "From a boat, you say?"

I shrug. "I didn't see anything like that, no, but it stands to reason, doesn't it? The next land mass is Portugal, isn't it? Or is it Britain?"

"I think," he says, standing up, "that I need to pass a message along, Miss Stanfield."

I stand up on cue. "To whom?"

"Pardon me?"

"To whom will you pass this message along?" Our eyes meet, and mine widen in sudden belated comprehension. "Oh, my God. They were Germans," I say, slowly. How stupid could I have been?

"We don't know that yet, do we?" he asks neutrally, briskly. He walks around me and opens the door. "Spencer? Will you see Miss Stanfield out, please?"

The man in uniform abandons his post and threads his way through the outer office desks to stand next to me. There's respect in his face, now; I'm important enough to be escorted out, which either means that I'm very irritating or very important. He must read the latter from the lieutenant's face. "That's it?" I ask.

"If we need you, we'll be in touch," Lieutenant Foster informs me. "Sebastian brings your groceries out to you? Yes, I thought so, that's how most of them arrange it." His use of "them" was a slip, but his mind is clearly on other things and he is eager to get rid of me so he can get on with things.

The morning air is tinged, now, with a sense of urgency.

I can relax; he believes me, he takes me seriously, he will take care of the situation. There is nothing for it but to leave. I shake his hand, politely, and the man he called Spencer sees me out. There is no one on the front bench, now, and I have the disoriented feeling one gets when one has been reading for too long, when coming back out of that fictional place to the real world is a struggle.

It's bright, blindingly bright, even beneath the trees that grow around the building, and I shield my eyes from the light. Odd how it's bright out in the dunes, too, but there it feels natural, part of the life, of the wildness that lives in wild places. Here the sun seems out of place, painful, reminding me of appointments missed and people waiting.

I retrace my steps down Commercial Street, disappointed. What had I expected? To be included in the investigation? To receive assurances that I am perfectly safe, that nothing like this will happen again? To see the horror that is wrapping around me like suffocation reflected in their eyes?

I stop at a café before I get back to the East End and buy myself an ersatz coffee, sitting facing the street, scanning every face that passes in the hope that one of them might be Sophie. I need to tell her; I need to warn her. What if they have discovered that Helen's shack is empty? What if they are already sharing its cramped quarters while they do whatever it is they are here to do?

I sip the chicory, scalding hot and black. What *are* they here to do, anyway? There is nothing in Provincetown but fishermen and artists, each cocooned in their own little world, interacting with each other but living in parallel worlds ... neither of which having anything to do with the war.

Nobody important comes to Provincetown—no heads of state, no government officials. Well, not for a long time, anyway. There was a president who came to dedicate the monument—I should remember which one it was, it was back when the *Rose Dorothea* won the Fishermen's Cup—but I think he only stayed an hour or two. And that's completely irrelevant to the situation at hand.

Are they lost, or are they mad?

I finish the coffee and, my questions unanswered, set myself on the long walk back to the dune shack that I have, unconsciously but naturally, started to think of as home.

Chapter Seventeen

Out in the dunes, there are no blackout shades, and the dune shacks shine dim rectangles of light on the sand around them.

It never bothered me until I saw the frogmen coming ashore on the beach–my beach–but now I wish there were curtains, shutters, anything to make our little world feel safer.

There aren't any shades in town, either, and nor were there in Boston when I left; the city must light the sky for miles around. I remember Daddy saying that we're fools not to do what they're doing in England and Europe and even some places here in the States, and Mother being shocked. "The war won't ever come here!" she exclaimed, looking at him as if he's made an off-color joke, said something obscene. "How can you even think of such a thing? America will never be attacked!"

Mother likes to believe that the United States is some benevolent giant, policeman to the world, a kind authority figure helping out lesser nations that don't share our standards—of what, she never quite articulates, but I always suspect that it has something to do with morality. We're morally good, so we're rich: God rewards the holy. Anyone with the misfortune of being attacked–well, just look at the French, Mother says when pressed. We all hear about them, and it's no wonder that they're occupied. They didn't even put up much of a fight, now, did they?

Daddy finally intervenes when Mother starts talking like that, usually with a long-suffering look on his face and something behind it, something that might be sadness. I suspect that people like Mother are why some men feel that women shouldn't be allowed to speak at all, and it really angers me that she does that, because there are so many other women with terrific minds, women like Helen and Sophie and maybe even me, who are belittled by women like my mother.

Daddy always tries to educate her, an uphill battle at best. "It's a great deal more complex than that, my dear. Having one's home invaded is a very different proposition from having an ocean between oneself and the most recent aggressor."

"Well, that's it, isn't it?" counters Mother. "Once upon a time, the French were the aggressors. I'd say the tables have been turned on *them* now, wouldn't you?" She sounds almost pleased about the occupation.

Daddy sighs. "The United States," he says mildly, "has been aggressive enough in its time, my dear." She looks disbelieving; Mother has never let facts stand in the way of her opinions. Daddy goes on, undaunted, in full lecture mode now. "American expansionism, not to mention imperialism, has been well documented. Hawaii–we pretty much stole that one, dear. And Cuba in 1897–we declared war on Spain, then. The Philippines a year or so later."

"Well," says Mother huffily, "obviously, those weren't civilized nations. We have an obligation to take care of–"

I may have grown up a lot lately, but I haven't outgrown wanting to be cheeky toward Mother. "Spain wasn't civilized?" I interrupt sweetly.

Daddy shoots me a warning glance, but Mother takes it in her stride. "Spain and the United States both wanted to control Cuba," she says surprisingly; she knows more than we give her credit for. "It was a matter of deciding who should take care of them."

"Bet they thought they could take care of themselves," I say, ignoring Daddy.

"Just like you, dear," says Mother, and the subject is closed.

***

"I've read in the newspaper," reports Sophie, "that Portsmouth looks Edwardian. That's what the article said: 'positively Edwardian.' No lights at all! There's the naval yard there an' all, don't you know. Only a few cracks in the windows, where the shades aren't pulled tightly."

"There should be no cracks," pronounces Anna. "It's very dangerous. We could get bombed."

When we first came to the dunes, I used to laugh at Anna for all her fears; now I don't say anything, the memory of those figures emerging from the sea still vivid and real. They came ashore and went I don't know where, but they came, I saw them, I know the monster is here.

If that can happen, anything can happen.

Provincetown is observing dim-out regulations, which include hoods on the streetlights and cars using their parking lights for navigation. There have been blackout drills, too, Sophie tells us. "They're using the whistles from down the cold-storage places—Consolidated's got the loudest one—down the wharfs," she says. "Then the police cars go up an' down Commercial Street with their sirens on. Same for air-raid drills. Not sure too many of us knows the difference between the two, truth be told."

There are starting to be serious shortages, too. Sebastian, on his biweekly visits, rarely these days brings everything that Anna's requested. "Out of fresh fruit this week down t' Nelson's," he tells me, taking off his cap to scratch his head. "Not much sugar on the shelves over t' grocer's, so I brought you some extra, seein' as you had the right rationing cards," he says another time.

And the heat has set in with a vengeance. The sand is burning under our feet, and I have taken to wearing woolen socks when I go out. One night of agony with heat blisters on the soles of my feet was more than enough.

Lassitude prevails. Only the insects seem to love the weather, the bees droning over the beach roses, the bits and pieces of vegetation that, against all odds, have made a home in this place that looks like a desert but which in reality is anything but. I come across a dune fox one morning and, instead of running from me, it gives me a baleful stare—as though the heat were somehow my fault—before slipping slowly and casually away. The pump needs priming all the time, now, not just once a day, and we're using more and more water as it gets hotter and hotter.

The dunes sigh and undulate in the heat; they are a being, alive and somnolent beneath the sun.

Anna doesn't bake anymore: the thought of filling that small room with even more heat is unthinkable to both of us. The sky has lost its brilliance, and is now a uniform slate blue; even the tides seem to be moving sluggishly under that sky, and there is always haze on the horizon. I can hear the foghorn issuing its warning to Provincetown Harbor in the still air, once every ten seconds, and I wonder how the fishermen are faring, out at sea under this oppressive mantle of heat.

Perhaps it is cooler offshore: I would ask Sophie, but it seems cruel to remind her, needlessly, of her recent loss.

The trek over the dunes is difficult, these days, with the heat; but Sophie comes out two or three times a week, and I go into town sometimes, too, to break the monotony.

Sometimes Sophie walks out; she seems impervious to the heat. Usually, though, she begs a ride from the dune taxi and Sebastian obliges, seeing as her father was so recently lost. The whole town seems to share her bereavement, share her pain.

When I go into town, as I've been doing lately, more and more often, to reassure myself that the dark slithering creature I'm seeing in my dreams isn't the real world, that the real world is filled with bustle and laughter and the honking of an occasional car horn – when I go into town, I hear people talking about it. "You're little Sophie's friend, aren't you? Manny's girl?" And they shake their heads sorrowfully, the community mourning his loss as it mourns all the losses, all the finest kind who don't come home from the sea. "Poor little thing."

Somehow, I don't notice the heat as much when Sophie is out here.

Helen's shack has become stifling-hot, nestled as it is into a hollow in the dune: no breath of air reaches it, and there's no cross-breeze as there is at our dune shack; it bakes steadily under a sun that never seems to move. We spend most of our time together down on the beach, where the icy cold water gives respite from the heat. Sophie once laughed at me, saying she wouldn't swim on the backshore; she does it now, daily, with me, the water shockingly, wonderfully cold. We strip off all our clothes and charge into the cold water, joyously, splashing shining crystals of liquid all around us. Waist-deep in the ocean, we kiss, our naked bodies moving tentatively together, our hands and fingers and tongues exploring each other.

Sophie's body is my body: I know intuitively how to touch her, and where; how to give pleasure, and I gasp in delight when she touches me. Anna suspects nothing; why should she? We are the best of friends. That much, at least, is true.

And it is on an afternoon of such heat, wet and salty from the sea and from each other, that Sophie tells me. "They know what happened t' Dad's boat," she says suddenly, soberly.

I am lying on the sand beside her, my fingers interlaced with hers. "What?" I sit upright, scattering sand. "What happened?"

Her eyes are closed against the glare of the sun and she does not open them as she speaks. Perhaps if she does not look, she doesn't have to believe. "They were torpedoed," she says, her voice too calm, too matter-of-fact.

My eyes widen. Frogmen on the beach is one thing; torpedoed fishing boats is another. The war is closer; the war is here. "Why? I mean, why would they want to?"

Her shoulders move slightly in a shrug; if I didn't know her, I would swear that she's indifferent to the situation. "Why do people do all the horrible things that they do?" she counters. "Maybe they thought it wasn't just a fishing boat. Maybe they needed target practice."

I flinch. "Sophie, it isn't–"

She cuts me off. "It doesn't matter why," she says. "Don't you see? It doesn't matter why they did it. It's all the same, in the end."

There's a long silence. I haven't asked who "they" are. We both know. I think of the frogmen emerging from the ocean, deadly and dark. "The war's coming," I say in a very small voice.

"It's here already," says Sophie.

Chapter Eighteen

Anna has forbidden me to walk on the beach at dusk.

She is afraid of who I may see... and, perhaps more to the point, whether someone there will see me. I pretend to be disappointed–I do, after all, have an image to preserve–but the truth is that I'm grateful for her limits, her rules, they make me feel safe. Safer, anyway.

I have no intention of ever going down to the beach at dusk again.

It's out there, they're out there, terrible things are out there, and if I don't go down, I can pretend that they'll never come any closer than the Peaked Hill Bars, that they'll never reach the sand, that they'll never reach me.

Pro forma, I protest anyway. "But it's so hot, Anna!"

"You," she says sternly, "will do as I say, or your parents will hear of it." That's the threat she always makes: Boston is four hours by train from Provincetown, she reminds me, and three by boat. "They can come at any moment, and what if I am not doing my best to take care of you?"

"I thought I was supposed to be taking care of you," I say sullenly, but she ignores me. "Do not talk nonsense."

The dunes listen to us talking back and forth, and then they whisper back their magic words of reassurance, I hear them every time I'm out there alone. The dunes touch me, caress me, keep me ensconced in their secrets. I am safe here. I know that I am.

But there's danger in the wind, for all of that.

The weather is changing on an almost daily basis. There are places even within the dunes where it changes, too, where something feels different, even the air, even the taste of salt on my lips. It's an unstable area, geologically speaking, and odd things, inexplicable things often happen in places where the land itself is in motion. I feel the pull of something beneath the sand, sometimes, when I'm walking; there are places where the wind seems to turn and come back at you, as though to wrap you and smother you and take away your breath to make it part of its own. I don't know how it happens, I only know that it does.

When we first came out here, I thought that there was something holy, something sacred about this place, holy not in the religious sense but in some way that predates religion, predates humanity, even. That this was a place set apart, special, filled with mystery and awe. Perhaps I was right; only now I've begun to believe that the mystery is a dark one.

Late summer is here, and the nights already have the hint of fall in them, clear and starting to get cold, wind every night, biting around the edges of things. I am tuned to all the moods of this place, and I wonder what it will be like six months from now, when we are here in the snow. I imagine the nor'easters that Sophie talks about, and I shiver in something not unlike anticipation.

A storm is coming, I can feel it. The sun is still bright, but the wind has whipped itself into a frenzy, rattling all the windows of the shack. Something is changing; I feel it in the air.

Anna is worried. She won't let me to walk the beach at dusk, but she's taken my place there these days; every day as the light starts waning after the sun has lit the sky in brilliant oranges and yellows and reds, there she is, then, pacing a length of beach about a quarter-mile long in each direction from the dune shack. I cannot blame her, with all the time she spends in the shack, she must be getting a little crazy, just staring at the walls. After a while, they start to close in: you feel as though you cannot breathe anymore.

She should be happy about the storm: I know that I am. I race outside as soon as the wind picks up, scanning eagerly to see which direction the weather is coming from. Anna orders me inside. "Now, I said, Miss Jessica!"

It is the voice with which you cannot argue; no more *liebchen* here, and I go back inside, meek. "Wanna play cards?"

"*Nein*," she snaps. "I do not want to play cards!"

I put on the wireless that, once in a while, picks up a station we can hear. Daddy keeps talking about bringing us a shortwave radio, but has yet to actually do it. There is nothing but static and, frustrated, I turn it off again. The animals all know: the tree swallows first, diving into their tiny houses on stilts at the first hint of wind, prepared to wait out whatever might be arriving. The wind has become fierce, whipping around the house and howling like some demented soul; we're able to close the windows only by working together, and even then with difficulty.

We've had storms here before, but nothing like what this one is going to be.

It hits at a dusk that is already turning dark, great rain lashing across the ridge and finding our shack, the first obstacle in its path on the top of the ridge. I wonder fitfully about hurricanes, but surely Sophie or Sebastian or somebody would have warned us if one was on the way? The rain is hitting hard now, hammering on the roof like a thousand mallets, louder than I could imagine; we have to shout to hear each other, and we move quickly to light the kerosene lamps, to try and fill the room with brightness that holds the shadows at bay. One of the lamps, touched even in its glass chimney by an errant gust of wind that has made its way through the uneven planks of the shack, flickers and goes out.

All right, I'll admit it: I am thoroughly scared.

"This house has withstood worse, child," says Anna grimly, as though reading my mind. "There is not nothing to fear here." She only calls me child when she is worried about something, though, so I am not reassured, and her usual double negative seems prescient.

Lightning forks off to the left, cutting the night in two, and thunder follows, nearly immediately, the noise deafening. We cling to each other, sitting on Anna's lower bunk, and I flinch each time it rumbles. At one point I am quite sure that the roof is going to peel right off and we'll follow it up into the wind, like Dorothy Gale in her tornado dream; Mother was most upset with Daddy for letting me see *that* movie, I can tell you.

It ends as it began, in gusts of wind; and by the time it is gone it's completely dark out, the dark of night rather than of storm, and the room is suddenly, blessedly, cool. "We'll sleep well tonight," I say to Anna before I notice that she's lowering the lamps, getting ready to go outside. We've gotten in the habit of using the chamber pot inside the dune shack at night, so I'm surprised to see her readying her flashlight, putting her arms into the sleeves of a cotton sweater. "Anna, where are you going?"

"You never you mind," she says, and then adds, "and go to sleep!"

"Where are you going?" I'm still unsettled by the storm, and frightened by Anna behaving out of character. Frankly, I don't want to be left alone. "What is it, Anna?"

"It is nothing," she says, more gently, and comes to kiss me on the forehead. "Go to sleep, *liebchen*. I'll be quiet when I come in."

Still unsettled, I make my preparations for bed, cleaning my teeth in the lamplight, brushing my hair the hundred strokes that Mother says are required of any proper young lady.

And, just for an instant, before I fall asleep, I consider the fact that one might think from her behavior that it is Anna, and not me, who has the illicit lover.

Chapter Nineteen

There are German submarines off the coast.

It's become official news now, even though the reality is that everyone already knew. I was probably the last to accept it, but Sophie's information–that it was a German submarine out on Stellwagen that torpedoed her father's boat, for reasons that still remain mysterious–put any lingering doubts to rest. And then there were the frogmen... yes, I knew, I've known for a long time, the slithering great monster out there has a name, I just haven't wanted to speak it, to give it the power of naming it, acknowledging it to the universe.

Acknowledging that I know it, and that, at some dark level, it knows me.

There are German submarines off the coast. Some had already blown up two freighters a week or so before we arrived, but that was out further, over the horizon, safely out to sea. There's closer in, now, and anyone caught taking pictures on the coast, by the beach, is arrested on sight, their camera confiscated.

There are German submarines off the coast.

Anna knows, in that odd way of somehow knowing everything that Anna has, that she has had since my childhood. My parents know, because it has been in the news, the subject of many of my father's soirees with eager young aspiring psychologists and philosophers, the subject no doubt of long arguments between them.

But I know it better than they do; I know it in my stomach, in some visceral part of me that responds before my brain or even my heart; I know that the monster has come, that it is staying, that it already has its great glassy eye on us all. Sophie's father's boat was just the beginning.

Or perhaps I'm taking it too personally, perhaps the monster has its eye on someone else, something else, I am not important enough to be in its sights. I hate being thought of as insignificant, though on my more rational days I realize the truth if it, and that we are all, at the end of the day, quite insignificant indeed. Like the herring I saw that morning, flopping and writhing in the sun.

The next tide carried their bodies away.

If the dunes have taught me nothing else, they have taught me that. I am nothing; we are nothing; the sands of the dunes and the water of the ocean and the stars in the sky were here long before we were, and they'll still be here long after we are gone. We're a sigh on the wind, a passing thought, a murmur in the dune grasses. The earth will go on without us, and no one will care that Jessica Stanfield or Sophie Costa lived and died.

And I am driving myself crazy with these thoughts.

Chapter Twenty

In the dunes, voices carry.

I've noticed that before, of course; Anna says that she can hear me and Sophie when there's still a dune or two, tall hillocks, between us and the dune shack. I don't think that Anna ever thought it might work the other way, though.

She is out alone more and more these days, finding reasons to wander off to the beach when Sophie comes to see me. When I leave to go into town—as I've taken to doing about once a week—she seems relieved in a way that I've not been able to explain.

There's only one possible reason for this change: Anna has a secret.

Sophie and I wonder about it, whisper about it. Sophie thinks that Anna is carrying on with one of the eccentrics from another one of the dune shacks, but I can't imagine it. Mostly because I cannot imagine Anna having any sort of romantic involvement with *anybody*. It's like thinking of my parents having sex. Well, maybe not that bad, but... people shouldn't fall in love when they get old. It just feels wrong.

Still, there's something going on. Sophie is enthused about trying to discover what it is. Perhaps it gets her mind off her own problems, which are many. Her mother wants to go back to the Azores, and is the only one who doesn't see it as folly. She no longer has any close family there; her cousin would be obligated to care for her, and that would put a strain on his resources. "Besides," Sophie says, a little explosively, "What's she thinking? Ships are getting blown up out there, and she wants t' cross the Atlantic *now*?"

I shrug. "Maybe that's the point," I say.

She looks at me, incredulous. "You think she'd suicide herself? Don't be ridiculous," she says with absolute certainty. "It's against our religion." A quick glance. "I *am* a practicing Catholic, you know."

"It's not suicide if someone else does it for you," I say. I don't really care, one way or the other: Sophie's mother is not real to me, a woman known only second-hand, through Sophie's stories. Once, in town, Sophie grabs my arm and pulls me into the marine supply store. "Shh! That's her!" she says.

I'm mystified. "Who?"

"My mother!"

She walks by, dressed completely in black, a kerchief on her head. It's impossible to differentiate her from all the other widows in town. "Why are we hiding?"

"I just don't want her t' see us!"

I don't understand it—it seems to me that one of the advantages of falling in love with someone of the same sex is that being seen together in public is less a problem. As long as you're not actually holding hands…

Sophie continues to tell her mother that it's best to not make any important decisions until the war's over. It's a pep talk that Mrs. Costa seems to require on a daily basis, and I tire of it quickly. It takes up hours of our time together, because Sophie has such a driving need to discuss it with me. Besides, the more Sophie has to reassure her mother, the less time she can spend with me.

I never claimed to be altruistic, did I?

But Anna is becoming a puzzle. I look at her face in the lamp-light and see that something has changed, but I don't know what it is. She shoos me out of the house so she can heat it up with her baking, once again.

She is singing, too, humming tunelessly under her breath as she does her chores, laughing when I say something that's only the slightest bit funny. "She *has* to have met someone," I tell Sophie, with all the scorn of someone who has been in love forever (or two months, take your pick) considering something that might be transient. "She never goes in to town! I don't see how it happened."

"She must," says Sophie. "She must go sometime."

"You're kidding, right? Walk all the way across the dunes? It's two miles... once you hit the road."

"Don't I know," says Sophie feelingly, and I bat at her.

We review the possible candidates. There's the woman who collects newspaper—"too messy," I say, thinking of Anna's obsessive tidiness. "She's a woman," objects Sophie.

"So what? *We*'re both women."

"We're different, Jess..."

There's the man who lives up on the ridge beyond our shack, the one with the clusters of birdhouses all around his shack. He is, Sophie tells me, a recluse.

"I spoke to him once," I say haughtily.

"I don't believe you," she says. "He's a total recluse, he doesn't even talk t' me. How did you think Sebastian got in the habit of bringing groceries out t' the dunes?" she asks. "It's because of Bernie. Bernie and his swallows. They come t' him when he calls, can you imagine that? They sit on his finger."

"I don't believe you." I try out her line.

She shrugs; she doesn't care if I believe her or not. She's very secure about herself, is Sophie. It's one of the things about her that's so attractive, and something that I hope will some day rub off on me, too. "I don't think that Bernie cares enough about people t' even notice Anna," Sophie concludes. "Now, if she were a *bird*, on the other hand…"

I giggle. "She'd be a pigeon."

"Not a chance! An owl!"

We give up picturing Anna with feathers and return to our dune tour. "There's the Mad Russian," Sophie says doubtfully. "He lives in the hollow the other side of the ridge. He's been there forever, too. But he only speaks Russian. He came here after the revolution; I think he was some sort of aristocrat. Lost his mind along with his fortune, Helen says, though t' tell you the truth, she always had a soft spot for him. Spoke a little French, too. I think they all did. The Russian nobles, I mean. The language of diplomacy," she says.

"The language of love," I respond, without thinking.

She wrinkles her nose. She looks adorable. "Does Anna speak French or Russian?"

"Not that I know of. Besides, can't you count? He must be ancient. She's not *that* old."

We speculate for a few minutes on Anna's possible age without reaching a conclusion.

"Well," says Sophie at last, gathering up the remnants of our lunch—we are sitting on the beach, the sun a hazy shape above us and the tide low, the waves hissing over the myriad tiny rocks as they withdraw. "What you can always do is ask her."

"If I start invading her privacy she'll feel she has the right to invade mine," I say, not sure why I'm saying it. I feel vaguely uncomfortable asking Anna if she is having an affair. She is an adult and unmarried, away from the strictures of Boston and the shock an affair would generate there. That's the nice thing about Provincetown: no one cares. That part of the bohemian lifestyle is very pleasant indeed. I cannot reasonably enjoy it and violate it at the same time.

I shall never tell Mother about it, of course.

Sophie is looking at me with frank amusement. "Invade your privacy?" she says. "Jessica, isn't that her job description?"

"Yeah, well, if it is, she isn't doing it very well, is she?" We giggle and I lean over and kiss her. "But I don't want her to start, you know?"

"Then just let her keep her secret," counsels Sophie, her fingertips lingering on my face. We look into each other's eyes, a moment that stretches taut and shining between us like the filament of a spider's web, and I almost imagine that...

And then the moment is gone. "Come on," says Sophie, scrambling to her feet. "Let's go swimming."

"Are you kidding? Those are icebergs floating by out there." My words are empty; it's almost a daily ritual. Sophie has changed her mind about the suitability of swimming on the backshore; I can remember her saying she never would. Now, we do it all the time, an excuse to be naked, an excuse to be outrageous. We run into the water, grasping each other's hand, gasping as the cold hits us, racing then to see who can put her head underneath first, coming up spluttering. "It's cold!"

And I don't think about Anna and her secret again for a long time.

Later, when I go to fetch the water for cooking, my mind is still on Sophie, smiling as my arms work the pump and water splashes onto my feet. I straighten up from the pump and turn to go, and as I do so, glance down at the shoreline, where a sleek black head is just emerging from the water.

"It's a seal, it's only a seal," Anna croons as she holds me, reassures me. "See, *liebchen*, there's another. Just a seal." She made it from the dune shack to where I was standing in a matter of seconds when she heard me screaming.

"I know," I gasp. "I know."

But I'm not sure I know anything, now.

Chapter Twenty-One

The subject doesn't stay far from my mind. "If Anna has a secret," I say to Sophie, "I want to know about it."

"If Anna has a secret," she responds, "it's none of your business."

We are sorting through books at Helen's shack: she has asked Sophie to bring some of them into town for her. "I think she's feeling ill again," says Sophie. "I think the books are her old friends, they remind her of better times."

"I'll come with you," I decide. Even ill, Helen has more personality than anyone I've ever met.

It's dusty and hot in Helen's shack. I am cross-legged on the floor, reading parts of the journals that continue to fascinate me; Sophie is sitting on the bed, sorting through books, practical and focused. "These are classics," she says sadly, a volume of Tolstoy in her hands. "How do I decide what t' bring and what t' leave?" She shuts her eyes, brings the book to her forehead, addresses it. "Does Helen want you in town?"

"It says here," I read out loud, my eyes on the stiff spidery writing in Helen's old journal, "that she got drunk one night and slept with John Reed!"

Sophie is unimpressed. "Everyone slept with John Reed," she says, her voice dismissive; clearly she would have been the exception. "I think everybody was sleeping with everybody then, actually," she adds, a little tentatively, because we don't usually talk abut that sort of thing, we just do it. "It was part of the way they all lived. Artists have t' have sexual freedom."

I look at her. "You didn't just make that up," I say accusingly. "Where'd you read it?"

Her eyes are innocent. "I did too make it up," she says, nodding vigorously. "Anyway, it stands t' reason, doesn't it? Look at all those people" – her gesture encompasses the journals, the pictures, the whole of the back shore – "They all came from families where being married was being trapped, especially for women. Look at my *mother*, for heaven's sake." A quick bright glance. "Or yours, come t' that. Anyway, the major token of possession is sexuality. If you can be sexually free, then the rest follows."

I'm not particularly liking the corollary I'm drawing. "So you believe in sexual freedom?"

"Of course I do," says Sophie, clearly astonished. "I'm with *you*, aren't I?"

"Yeah, but we're" – I use my fingers to surround the word with quotation marks – "monogamous. Isn't that contrary to having sexual freedom?" There is a pause, then I add, aware of a sinking feeling in my stomach. "Um, we *are* monogamous, aren't we?" I'm wishing that we hadn't started this conversation at all.

I want to hear her answer. I don't want to hear her answer.

She laughs, puts aside the Tolstoy volume, and slithers down onto the floor next to me. She smells like honeysuckle. "You think I'm sleeping with somebody else?" she asks, her tone irritatingly playful.

"I'm asking the question," I say.

She laughs and puts her arm around my shoulders. "I think," she says, "that what we're doing right now is bohemian enough for us, don't you? It works for me. Besides, where would I find the time?"

"You're not cheating on me because you don't have time for it?" I ask, astonished. The perspective is dazzlingly humbling.

"No, honey, of course not," says Sophie and nuzzles my neck, her hand warm on my thigh. "I can't imagine being with anybody but you. You inspire me. I write more, and better, since I've met you. I don't want t' change anything." She straightens and gestures toward Helen's journal, still open in my lap. "We don't have t' sleep with everyone on the Cape t' have sexual freedom, don't you see that? We're taking our own route, and that's freedom. We're not dating boys and planning white weddings, that's the main thing."

"My mother will be very disappointed," I say, and inside I'm cheering.

"I don't think that it matters so much how you reject convention," continues Sophie seriously, as though I haven't spoken at all. "Just so long as you do." She picks up the journal from my lap, glances at it, and tosses it away. "Besides, you haven't even gotten t' the good one yet," she says.

"What good one?"

"The one," says Sophie, settling herself astride me, and beginning to kiss me, "where Helen sleeps with John Reed's *wife*."

***

Helen is indeed unwell.

Sophie lets us in to the house on Pearl Street; she has a key, but the door is unlocked, and it creaks under her hand. I expect to see

Helen hobbling our way down the narrow corridor, leaning on her cane, the extraordinary mismatched eyes stormy or twinkling—depending on her mood—but instead we're met with silence, a leaden silence, filled with old whispers and unspoken words that hiss by without you being able to catch them. There's a sort of mustiness that hadn't been in the house the last time I was here, a smell of bad dreams and decay, and I shiver despite the heat.

Helen is going to die, and soon. I can feel it in the air. And all the dust motes are already shimmering with grief.

If Sophie is thinking along those lines, she doesn't show it. Her voice, when she calls out to Helen, is strong and young and confident. I don't hear a response; but she does, it seems, because she calls out again. "Jess is here with me; we brought you books!" and starts up the wooden stairway that separates the kitchen from the dining room.

Upstairs, we're under the eaves; the dormer windows let in some light, but not nearly enough—the thick lace curtains see to that. Charming, I think sourly, but so impractical. I wonder why I'm fretting about unwashed curtains. I wonder if maybe Daddy is right about people's avoidance of difficult topics.

Helen is propped up in bed, her gray hair loosened and spilling down her back. It's gorgeous; she is beautiful in ways I've never seen before, and Mother's attempts to always look younger than her age seem suddenly vain and foolish. This is beauty; Helen is beauty.

The eyes are as bright as before. "Well, bring them over, then. Let me see what you brought."

"Hello t' you, too," says Sophie cheerfully, humping her box over and dropping it by the bed.

"Are you making enough noise, do you think?" asks Helen with some asperity.

"I don't know, old woman; am I?" Their eyes meet and they share a secret moment, an intimate moment, and I feel suddenly ashamed to be there. Sophie's hand goes out to Helen's, and they clasp each other for a long time, long enough for me to feel rather than see the tears glinting in Sophie's eyes, long enough for me to realize I'll never feel anything as deep as what these two share.

I want to bolt from the room, but I stay there, scarcely daring to breathe. It's like being in the forest, I think, or in the dunes. Or maybe in church, when it's at its most holy, the celebration of the Eucharist, with magic and mystery shimmering in the air. Something transcendent is happening here.

Later, as we walk through Helen's neglected garden, we flush a mourning dove, and I wonder how it is that the universe always tells you what you need to know.

Chapter Twenty-Two

I lie on my upper bunk, making my breathing as slow and even as possible, trying not to twitch, trying to seem asleep. I think that's what Anna is waiting for; she's extinguished all the lights but one, and I know that you can't read by just one lamp–I've tried.

I don't want to move too much, but I figure that I'm pretty much in the shadows and she won't look too closely. I slit my eyes so I can watch her.

Call it prurient curiosity if you want, but I really, really want to know what Anna does when she sneaks away. It's become my most recent obsession. Sophie has suggested that she gets naked in the dunes and calls down the moon and casts other witchy spells. Sophie sounds interested in this when she talks about it, eager for it to be true; but I can't really see Anna as a witch. Oh, there are days, of course... but not a real one.

We don't even have a cat.

Besides, there's something else, something darker lurking there. I don't know if there's a connection between Anna's changes in behavior and the dark fear that's at my back whenever I stop and think about it, the darkness that started with the frogmen on the beach and has done nothing but build ever since... but I think that, somehow, there is. It's as if we all started out in some story somewhere, and the future was mapped out for us, with us having no choice but to follow it, and accelerating all the way. Or perhaps we're just all trapped in a giant snow globe, with some not-so-benevolent hand shaking us up for its pleasure.

Whatever the analogy, something has started that hasn't yet ended, and it's scaring me.

What part do Anna's secrets play in it all? I am determined to find out.

She moves to the door, the old floorboard is creaking under her. The door is already unbolted: it's the last thing that we do at night, in case one of us wants to go to the privy before going to sleep. I am still listening when the door closes behind her; she is already gone.

I'm out of the bed like a shot. Under my sheets I've slipped out of my nightdress and now I'm dressed for espionage, wearing a pair of black slacks I borrowed from Sophie—they're not quite long enough—and a dark sweater of my own. My flashlight is in my pocket, my feet are bare.

Jessica Stanfield, Girl Spy.

We're always careful with the flashlights, on account of the batteries and how hard replacements are to come by, so I can just barely make Anna's out, turning on and off as needed, although I feel that she's still close, moving carefully past the privy and on down the path toward the hollow where Helen's shack stands.

I falter and decide not to put on my own flashlight. I know the path; I don't want to give myself away. It is no use, though: she is quick and silent, and it is only moments before I lose her.

Not only that, but very soon thereafter I don't know where I am.

I don't know where I took a wrong turn, branched off from the path Anna was on, such as it was—there aren't real paths through the dunes, just tentative ones, used by human and animal alike–but I know that somewhere I did, and I don't know how to get back. I'm thoroughly turned about, and I curse myself for not having paid better attention, to watch the stars, to watch the shapes of the hills and occasional trees and shacks and dark shapes that tell their own stories. Perhaps if I'd paid better attention, I'd know where I am now.

Or perhaps not.

There is a rustling sound in the dunes behind me, sending a message of fear shooting up my spine, and I have to mentally step back from the feeling and remind myself that any creature out there is likely to be more afraid of me than I am of it. A deer, perhaps; or a fox. It doesn't matter. This whole enterprise is a bad idea: Sophie is right: all I want, now, is to get back home.

I walk toward the sea; that at least I can do, I can hear it, scent it on the night air, the odor of salt and of rotting seaweed and of mystery. I walk carefully, however, tentatively, lest I walk off the dune cliff by accident. I can always tell Anna, if she returns and finds me gone, that I couldn't sleep, that I went out to look at the stars.

Which is an easy lie to tell, as it wouldn't be the first time. Even now, even after all these weeks living in the dunes, the sky leaves me breathless. It's not so much the brightness of it all that is astonishing–although that's a tremendous part of it, I never knew that the night sky can be just as bright as the city–but it's rather the fact that you can turn in a circle and see the stars all the way down to the horizon, anywhere you look, that is so amazing to me.

Daddy brought me a book of star maps, once he'd seen it himself, and I've become skilled at identifying them all: the bright stars

Deneb and Vega, the constellations—Cassiopeia, Hercules, Aquila, Scorpius. Sophie knows most of the stories associated with them, but she is the storyteller; I just look for the shapes, astonished at this brilliant blanket of light that covers us each night. The Milky Way, cotton candy trailing off into the sky, the occasional shooting star, more magnificent in its dying than it ever was in life. "But it's all a little narcissistic," I say to Sophie as we shelter from the rain in Helen's shack. Sophie, for her part, is ready with yet another tale from ancient Greece.

That stops her. "Whatever do you mean?"

"Well, after all, what we're seeing is in relation to each other, but only when seen from here. From earth, I mean."

She is mystified. "So what?"

"So we presume to make up all these stories as though everything turned around us, as though we were the center of the universe. It's all so very egocentric, isn't it? Anyway, Copernicus pretty much took care of that theory."

She bristles. "But they're part of our history, our story as humans!"

"There you go again. You're assuming that humans are the center of the stories."

"Well, for us, they are," she says stubbornly.

Whereas I wonder if there's someone on some planet somewhere who is looking at our solar system—our sun, seen maybe as some not-so-bright star—and is connecting it to other suns to form part of their story. I am thinking of that person now, as I sit cautiously at the edge of the bluff, the ocean with its soft susurration below me, getting my bearings so I can find my way home. Maybe right at this moment, that person is sitting next to an ocean and wondering if there's someone out there, wondering about–

There is the sound of a voice, a quick exclamation, immediately hushed, right next to me. Or so it seems; as I said before, voices carry, in the dunes, even near the sea. There is a silence, while others sit in the darkness, no doubt, listening to me listening to them. I'm surprised they can't hear my heart, which is warming up to lead a band down Main Street.

There is a rustling, slithering sort of sound, and I think about snakes. I think about dark heads emerging from the water. I think about someone coming up behind me with a knife to slit my throat. I'm quite sure that whoever is out there knows of my presence, and wishes me harm. There is another sound–a footfall, perhaps? Someone coming closer, even now stepping behind me with a garrote in his hands, a wire perhaps, ready to murder me and then move on to do whatever it is he's tasked to do in these dunes tonight...

My breathing isn't just fast, now, it's irregular, too, as I hold it and then let it go, every fiber of my being tuned to my environment, listening for the next step that will no doubt lead to my death.

I think that perhaps it might be easier to just jump off the bluff and end all the suspense, and I think I even make a small useless gesture in that direction; then I remember that it's not high enough for me to die, the sand's too soft, so I'll probably just lie on the beach with a broken leg and whomever is out there will do whatever he's planning on doing anyway, except that this time I'll be able to see him coming, behind on my back. Maybe.

In any case, not a great idea.

What I'm not thinking about is Anna, but she is suddenly here anyway, her fresh soap smell in my nostrils before I can even consciously identify it. "What are you doing here?" Her voice, too, sounds like a snake; it comes out in a hiss.

I forget my story about not being able to sleep. I forget about telling her that I wanted to see Cassiopeia again. "I followed you," I say miserably. "But I lost you, and then I got lost, too."

She swears under her breath in German. I can tell it's a swear, because of the mixture of passion and disgust with which she says it. "Stay here," she orders, and even if I were so inclined, I wouldn't dream of disobeying. Not with Anna using *that* voice.

I feel rather than see her move away, and there's that scuffling sound again, and some whispering. I force myself not to think about it. Sophie was right: this is none of my damned business. I sit still, miserable and ashamed of myself. It is one of those moments that occur so rarely in life–mercifully, I suppose–when you can see yourself through other people's eyes and you realize what a perfect ass you are.

She is back. "This way, Miss Jessica. I'm taking you home." No *liebchen* tonight.

I respond soberly. "Thank you, Anna."

There is really nothing else I can say. I take her hand and stumble along at her side, feeling about five years old. There's a sliver of a moon and it doesn't do much to light our way; but my eyes have adjusted to the darkness and I can see the path through the dunes and the grasses, gleaming faintly. I'd only been about ten feet off it when I got lost.

I spend the rest of the journey trying to think of creative names to call myself. Idiot heads the list. Oh, and imbecile. "Full of yourself"—only that one's not mine, that's the first thing that Anna says to me when we're back at the dune shack, the flashlights restored to their shelves, the lamps turned up again. Anna never speaks to me like this: she must be exceedingly angry.

"I'm sorry." What else, at the end of the day, can you really say?

"You have to know everything, *ja*? You are in charge of the world now, yes?"

I shrug. "I'm sorry, Anna. I was curious. I was wrong."

She is slamming things around, never a good sign. Water on to boil. "You will now your pajamas on put."

"Yes, Anna."

"We will not talk of this now. I am too angry with you, *ja*? We will talk of this tomorrow." Her eyes dare me to object.

I don't.

Habits die hard, and she still goes through the motions of taking care of me, giving me herbal tea to drink—chamomile, which I hate and yet drink obediently under her sharp gaze; real tea hasn't been available for weeks, and there is someone in Provincetown who makes the herb concoctions—and tucking me in, perhaps a trifle more roughly than is absolutely necessary, arranging the mosquito netting over me. "*Guten nacht*, then."

"Goodnight, Anna."

She blows out the flames in the lamps, moves about, then I feel the bed move and creak as she gets into her lower bunk. Some heavy breathing as she arranges her sheets and blanket—it gets cold in the night in the dunes, it seems that the wind is always coming off the frigid water of the ocean–and the mosquito netting, before settling in with a small grunt of satisfaction.

I wait. I close my eyes. It's no use. "Anna?"

"What is it now?"

"Are you in love with somebody?" I have to know. I need her to be, so that I can tell her that I am. There is nothing so lonely as a lover who has no one – other than the beloved – with whom to discuss one's feelings. Be in love, Anna, I urge silently. We can exchange secrets. We can identify with each other's feelings. Be in love, please, oh please, be in love.

"*Guten nacht*, Miss Jessica."

I sigh in the darkness.

***

Anna has no intention of telling me anything.

If I have any fantasies to the contrary, they die swiftly over breakfast. Oatmeal, again. I think Anna's given up her famous wonderful fry-ups because they're just so hard to clean up with no running water. I'd gladly heat the water and scrub the pans, I tell her, if only I could eat her sausage and eggs and bacon and cheese blintzes...

The fry-ups, like Anna's good mood, are something of the past. "We have to live close together, Miss Jessica, because it is a sacrifice to make in a time of war," she says severely, not offering me a second coffee. "But it is still important–no, what do I say? It is more important–to respect each other's privacy in times such as these.

You may think I have no right to a private life because I am a serv-ant—*nein*, you will listen to me now!—but I have my life and my dig-nity, and if you cannot be respecting them, then I write to your *mutti* and I give her my resignation."

I am seized with panic. "No, Anna, please! Don't do that!" I am at the center of rapidly expanding ripples, touching off more than I had bargained for. "Please, please don't do that! I love you, Anna! We all do." I cannot picture life without her. Anna has been part of the household since I was born... before then, even. Cooks and drivers and housemaids have come and gone; but Anna is al-ways there. Always. I can't imagine a world without her. "I was wrong, Anna, I know I was," I say desperately, pleading my case before this awful sudden tribunal. "I won't do it again, I swear! I promise!"

"It is not about having done something wrong," she says tartly. "It is a matter of respect."

I don't know what to say, and so I say nothing. I suspect that she sees my silence as sullen, but I don't know what else to do.

In any case, Anna has enough to say for both of us. "You think perhaps that there are things I see, things I hear, that I could not talk about?" Anna's English gets worse the more excited she is. "But me, I respect you, Me, I do not go following you to see where you go, to know what you do, even though it would be in my rights to do it, as your mutti has asked me to take care of you. You be-come a wild child, and do I say something? I say nothing. You stop wearing dresses, and do I say something? No: I say nothing. This is respect, Miss Jessica."

She stops to take a breath, and I still have nothing to say. Is Anna more sensitive than I've given her credit for being? What does she know about Sophie and me? And if she knows, why did she decide not to tell my mother? "Anna–"

"You don't Anna me, missy. You listen. You do not think about what does not concern you, *ja?* You do not talk about what does not concern you, *ja?* You spend your summer here and you behave well, and I do not speak of things that do not concern me, neither!"

I meet her eyes. She is right about the respect, but if I understood what she is saying correctly… "This is blackmail," I announce.

She nods, unperturbed. "Those are my terms," she says. "You call it what you want to call it, Miss Jessica, but you do not follow me and you do not speak of me and you keep yourself to yourself. This is the only way it will be, from now on. There is no argument. There is no opinion." Her gaze is drilling through me. "You agree?"

"Of course I agree," I snap. "It's blackmail." Like I have a choice here. But there's more, and I have to say it, no matter how poorly reality reflects on me. "It's blackmail," I sigh, "but anyway you're right, even if you aren't blackmailing me, and what I did was really rude of me, and really wrong of me, and I'm genuinely sorry. I really am." I wonder how many times I can manage to force the word "really" into a single sentence. It keeps me from wondering what kind of person I am, to go following my housekeeper through the night.

She stands up, clearing our plates from the table. "Apology accepted," she says calmly.

"Anna?"

"Yes, *liebchen*?"

"Can I have another coffee now?"

"You know how to make it yourself." The proletariat has arisen; we are, it would seem, on more equal footing now. I grin and put the kettle on, lighting the burner with only one match. I'm getting better at this.

"Anna?"

"Yes, *liebchen*?"

"Tell me something good."

She is washing our bowls in the Bakelite dishpan; now she pours water over them to rinse them and props them up, ready to be dried. Without being asked, I pick up the dishtowel and start wiping them, Anna raises her eyebrows but doesn't comment. She is tidying the table, putting coffee into the French press, ready for the hot water when it boils.

When she answers, it's oblique. "This is a time of war," she says. "It is a time of sadness. It is a time for people to be hurt." She sighs, lifts her shoulders, and meets my eyes. "If in this time of war someone can find something good, someone can find love, then it is a good thing. That is what I think, and that is all I have to say."

Which is just as well, because I am throwing myself into her arms, hugging her more tightly than I've ever hugged anyone.

Behind me, the teakettle whistles on and on.

Chapter Twenty-Three

In the night, there is rain.

It wakes me, hammering on the roof of the shack, drumming into my dreams until they dissipate around me. There's a flare of lightning that flashes bright as day, and I count the seconds until the thunder crashes in response: one, two, three, four…

When the lightning and thunder become simultaneous I start visualizing our dune shack, standing solitary and exposed up on the ridge and my stomach turns, then settles. It's all right; everything is fine. Then another crash shakes the shack and, it seems, the very shore around us, and I give in to the fear. "Anna?"

Her voice is calm, matter-of-fact, clearly awake. "It's only a storm, *liebchen*. It's nothing to be afraid of."

"Then why are you awake?"

"Because nobody could sleep through dis racket!" She sighs heavily and when the next flash of lightning comes, she gets up. "That is it, can't take it no more," she mutters, and the floor creaks under her weight as she moves. The sulfur smell of a match and she lights one of the hurricane kerosene lamps. "There. Come on, *liebchen*, we'll make cocoa."

By the time the water has heated and the chocolate melted into it, the worst of the storm has moved on, leaving only a moaning wind in its wake. Anna is more nervous, not less so, and when I drop my cup with a clatter she jumps. "Be careful!"

"I'm sorry, Anna," I say contritely. I really don't mean to make her angry; it feels like second nature, some days, annoying adults.

If I ever write a book about my life, that's what I'll title it, I think: Annoying Adults. A neat *double entendre*.

But there's something still wrong, it's in the air between us, shimmering and sad. It's like a crème brulée with just a sliver of glass in it, beautiful and deadly and delicious. Whatever happened with Anna and me isn't reversible, and saying one is sorry does not necessarily heal all wounds. It's a thought that makes me feel like I'm on the very edge of wisdom, not quite there, glimpsing something deep and meaningful and eternal that I may, just may, understand one day. Clearly not today, however.

I sleep again at last and dream of seals emerging from the ocean, dark and lustrous and mysterious, and when I wake I have a headache.

Sophie comes by, bringing fresh fruit. "Enjoy it, there won't be any much longer, they're sending it all to the servicemen," she says. "I used the last of your ration coupons for this month, Anna, I hope you don't mind?" But there is something else; she removes it from her string bag with a smile. "The tomatoes are from my mother's garden." Anna touches them reverently, as though they were some holy relic, as though they were gold.

Sophie's brought newspapers, too, and news from town. "The trains are stopping," she says. "Well, not stopping, exactly, they still need them for the fish; but they won't come twice a day anymore. They have to conserve fuel, they say, and they're also a target." She wrinkles her nose, adorably to my mind. "Transport always is."

Anna is back in a good mood today; there's a twinkle in her eye that I haven't seen there for ages. "It is correct," she affirms, nodding vigorously. "In Germany, in the Great War, my mother told me that they disabled the railways. The enemy, that is." She seems to realize which enemy she is speaking of, and stops her thought before it, too, can rattle off the tracks like a runaway train. There is a moment of awkward silence.

Sophie breaks it. "Well," she says cheerfully, "it's not like the trains are bringing all that much, anyway." She rummages through her rucksack, industriously, and comes up with a can of something brown. "Coffee," she announces.

"That's not coffee," I say, taking the can from her, and reading the label. "Oh, yuck! It's cracked wheat and soybeans!"

"Coffee," confirms Sophie, nodding vigorously, but with an evil glint in her eye that tells me she's already hooked in to some caffeinated black market. There's no way that the Portuguese were going to accept surviving without coffee. Real coffee.

Anna takes the can from me and shakes her head. "What will it be next?" she moans. "First no chocolate, no butter, now no coffee!"

"Meatless Tuesdays," Sophie chimes in. "On the radio, they're asking everyone to have meatless Tuesdays."

"That should be tough," I say. Anna and I haven't even had potted meat for weeks—who needs to, with the ocean right at our doorway? We've both gathered clams there, and Anna's been getting small silvery fish whose name I don't know but which roast up quite nicely when wrapped and placed on the outdoor fireplace we've constructed of stone and a metal grill. Mother would be appalled. I think that's why I enjoy it so much.

Besides, you'll never starve, if you live beside the ocean.

Sophie is full of news, from the papers, from the wireless, from the Provincetown gossip-line. "The OPA is at it again," she announces. "There are new posters all over at Nelson's. Use it up, wear it out, make it do, or do without." She recites this seriously, like a little girl saying a prayer at her First Communion, like it's the word of God.

As, in a way, it is.

Anna snorts. She is of a class and generation that doesn't require the OPA to tell her to be frugal.

Sophie has contraband, too, these days. I don't know where it comes from, and even Anna never asks, but from time to time she appears with something for which we didn't exchange rationing tickets. Catsup. Butter. Sugar.

"Expensive," I comment as she pulls out a container of canned corn from her bag. "You shouldn't use your tickets on us, Sophie, or your money. We can pay."

"Didn't hear me sayin' I used either," she responds.

I raise my eyebrows. I've led a sheltered life.

"We take care of each other," she says crossly. "The finest kind. No one wants."

"But," I protest anyway, because if I'm grasping anything from my parents' visits, it's the necessity of being patriotic, "when you do that, you're not helping the war effort."

She has me on the rough cabin floor in a second, knocking the breath out of me. "Don't you ever say that!" she hisses. "Them Germans, they killed my dad, and you're sayin' I'm not patriotic?" She loses her careful enunciation and grammar when she's emotional, does Sophie.

I can't breathe so I don't even try to respond.

She says something in Portuguese I don't understand, and rolls off me with a sigh of disgust. Getting up, dusting off her shorts, she doesn't even look at me. "You don't hafta take the corn."

I'm finally breathing again, grabbing great breaths of dust-laden air, it tastes like nectar, it tastes like life. "I'll keep the corn," I manage to croak. "Thanks, Sophie."

"You don't have cause t' say I'm cheating," she points out. Her voice has recovered its carefully cultivated consonants, though "to" still sounds like "tuh" to me. "I'm just trying t' help you."

"And we appreciate it," I say carefully.

She's looking nervous, and she's holding her hand awkwardly, in front of her shorts, and I know I felt something heavy there when we were on the floor. Glancing up at me, there's a cloud that passes over her expression, and I feel suddenly that something could be very wrong indeed. "Honey," I say, and my mouth has gone dry. "What's in your pocket?"

"Nothing," she says defensively, automatically, and I recognize the lie in her voice. It's the same voice I use when I'm lying, too: takes one to know one. "What is it?"

She looks around for Anna and, apparently satisfied that we are alone, puts her hand in her pocket.

This time, I recoil. "That's a gun!"

"Of course it's a gun," she says scornfully. "It's not going t' bite you."

"It's a gun, Sophie! What are you doing carrying a gun?" My sweet love has transformed into an outlaw in front of my very eyes, and I find myself panicking. It's not what she's about. It's not what we're about. Unseen hands are tugging at me, pulling me away from her, pulling us apart. She has no right to show me that, to carry it, to introduce something that wrong into the sheltered little world that is Jessica-and-Sophie.

She is unfazed. "It was Dad's," she says, easily, as if she were referring to a sweater or photograph.

"And that's a good reason to carry it?"

Her eyes meet mine with a snap that is nearly audible. "Who are you t' say what I should do?" she demands. "You're the one who saw those men coming ashore, and you think somehow that reporting it t' the police will take care of everything? You think it's safe t' go around now without protection?"

I'm speechless, stung as much by the raw anger in her voice as I am by the words themselves. I'd told Sophie about what I'd seen, of course; but she is right: I did think that reporting it was enough, and I certainly *do* think that it's better to go about without a gun than with one. Add that to wanting nothing more than to forget what I had seen, the nightmares that still plagued me.

I finally find my voice. "Why do you think a gun will help you?"

"Because," she says, and there's a scary undercurrent in her voice, "I want t' find them, and I want t' kill them, and it's the best way. I've been practicing. I'm getting good."

I am relatively uninterested in her acquired prowess with her weaponry of choice. "Why do you want to kill them?"

"They killed my father!" The undercurrent is stronger than ever, and I was right to be afraid of it: it's not even Sophie's voice, not the way I know it and love it. There's hatred there. It's another person talking, not my Sophie, who is holding and caressing this—

to my eyes—tremendously large gun as if it's the most normal thing in the world. "So what are you going to do?" I ask. "Kill every German you meet? Kill Anna?"

"Of course not!"

"It's not that easy," I say, really scared by now. "Once you start killing, how do you know where to stop? How do you know where to draw the line? How do you know you'll even be able to stop?" I touch her arm, wanting to reconnect with her somehow, wanting her to listen, to come back to me. "It's a line you'll cross that you can never come back over," I say, pleading now. "You can't go there, Sophie. It's not who you are."

"How do you know who I am?"

"Because," I say softly and sadly, "I love you."

We look at each other and she smiles, suddenly, impulsively, and reaches out to move a strand of hair from my face. She half-turns and thrusts the gun into her pocket again, invisible, away from discussion.

It seems that the internal storm has passed; but as we move outside together, Sophie laughing about something, I wonder if it has. It's like a party that's gone on too long, or a child up past its bedtime: there's a threat of more stormy weather ahead, and the air is heavy with fearful anticipation.

***

It rains again, and Anna is beside herself with worry. "It is too much, this rain," she frets, looking out the shack window toward the blurred line where gray water meets gray sky.

I am bored, sitting on my chair and trying to read. It's dark in the shack, and the lamplight fitful; and even though I've gotten used to the smell of kerosene by now, it still makes my hair and nostrils feel slick; I long to run down the crumbling sand cliff and leap into the sea and get clean again.

But not in the rain.

She has scoured everything in the shack to within an inch of its life and has sent me out for water three times already; but even with that activity, she cannot stay away from the window. "When will it stop?"

"Sophie says it's going to turn cold." I'm just making conversation, but she rounds on me. "Where did she hear that? How cold?"

I shrug. "On the radio, where else?" I am indifferent: every weather brings its own personality to the dunes, but it is always their own personality that prevails. I am coming to love watching the changing faces of the undulating seas – the one of water on one side, of the sand on the other, and how even in the midst of change, they really don't change at all. "I don't know how cold. It can't snow, or anything, Anna, it's still August, for heaven's sake."

"The nights are chilly," she says pensively, turning back to the water, to the flat sky and the flatter ocean. A solitary gull screams overhead; it seems prophetic.

"It will change again," I predict, scarcely interested. "There's still a lot of summer to go yet." And then? What will happen in the fall? I don't want to think about it. Wild ideas about running off with Sophie to some Provincetown writer's studio flit through my mind. We'll be like Helen's bohemian friends, always creating something exciting, always engaged in life. A renaissance of the artist's colony, and us in the midst of it, in love and secure and happy.

Anna is focused in the moment. She draws her shawl more closely around her shoulders as though a draft is passing through the shack; but there is no wind. Not inside, anyway.

Maybe it's just inside her.

She paces until she makes me crazy, and I run out into the rain, hard pellets on my head and face and shoulders. I go down to the beach regardless and walk quickly along the shoreline, watching for birds or seals or boats. Nothing shows up; everyone else has the sense to have sought shelter. While I'm out the rain lessens–softens, really–and becomes more of a summer rain, filled with relief rather than fury. I turn my face to it and open my mouth, just like I did when I was a little girl, and let it fill me. Wind and sand and water and girl all becoming one on that desolate beach.

By the time I get back to the dune shack, Anna has her nerves under control. She is baking, her solution to every crisis. "Running out of sugar coupons," she comments, and I manage to refrain from saying that I'll get some from my black-market girlfriend.

On the other hand, once Sophie hears that the famous and beloved applecake might be in jeopardy, she'll probably take care of supplying Anna on her own. I find a clean towel and start drying my hair.

"I will go out for a walk later," Anna announces, her back to me as she checks the kerosene oven. It's always a little temperamental. Her voice is carefully casual, and I match it. "It's getting better out there; the rain is lighter," I say, and then, just to goad her, "Do you want company?"

"*Nein*," she says, quickly, as I know she will. "You have reading to do. There is summer homework, to which you do not pay no attention. What your father will say when he comes, I do not know. You have become a wild child."

I recognize the technique–attack when feeling defensive–and so I manage not to rise to it. "All right," I say instead, earning a sharp look.

"There will be cake," she says, stating the obvious as further enticement, even though I haven't yet argued with her. "That's good," I say in agreement, and go back to drying my hair.

What I'm not going to do is follow her again, though I know it's what she's thinking about. I still want to know what's going on–who wouldn't?–but I'm not willing to risk Anna losing patience with me altogether and shipping me back to Boston, which she's quite capable of doing.

Boston: no Provincetown, no dunes, no Sophie. No tree swallows swooping around the dune shack in search of sustenance, no seals lazing on the water's surface, no sightings of fishing boats on the horizon. No Sophie.

It is unthinkable.

Whatever Anna's secret is, if that's the price I have to pay to learn it, I'm quite content being left in the dark.

Sophie is prickly these days. She arrives at the dune shack a while after Anna leaves for her walk, with the rain holding back but the clouds still threatening. "You should come into town more," she complains.

"You always want to come here." Mother left some of her nail varnish at the shack and I'm lying on the lower bunk with my feet propped up against the upper one, contemplating painting my toe-nails. I wish the red were not quite so bright.

"Well, I don't right now," she says, petulantly, and I sit up, nearly hitting my head. "What's the matter?"

"Nothing," she says, and sits beside me, though with a gener-ous distance separating us. I slide closer and put my hand on her knee; she swats at it like an inopportune fly. "Don't."

"What's the matter?" I ask again. This is starting to get tire-some: first Anna, now Sophie. Am I the only one in the dunes who isn't particularly moody these days?

Sophie's troubles are more easily diagnosed, though; she presses a hand against her abdomen and her expression tells me everything. I've already been through one of Sophie's periods, and I remember the dance. She is irritable until she has my full atten-tion, and then irritated by it. She wants me closer while she pushes me away. She is filled with a strange energy that is dark and erotic, a longing that cannot be satisfied, and I suddenly find myself step-ping back, seeing us sitting on the bed as if from a distance, as if I were not part of the scene at all, and I wonder who that girl is sitting there with Sophie, where she came from, why she is there.

There is fear gnawing at the edge of that thought, and I turn my mind away from it.

I don't suggest a walk; probably we'd end up running into Anna somewhere and she'll think I followed her again… but I'm drawn to the dunes anyway. With the cessation of the rain a wind has come up, moaning softly around the shack and flattening the dune-grass that I watch from the back window. I want to be here, feeling it razor-sharp against my feet and legs, my toes (with or without polish) sinking into the still-damp sand… But I turn my attention to Sophie and wonder how it is that I've ended up like this, reciting my lines listlessly, playacting with the two women who are closest to me in the world.

Chapter Twenty-Four

Sophie leaves at dusk, and Anna still isn't home when I get back from walking Sophie to the first ridge. Don't come tomorrow, I want to say to her, but I don't, and I wonder at the impulse. It's the first time since the moment I met her that I do not actively wish to be with Sophie twenty-four hours a day, and I cannot even understand why I feel that way.

She is not the only one who feels irritated, it would seem.

The wood of the shack and the porch and even the Adirondack chair perched there, they've all absorbed the wet, and even though an errant ray of dying sunlight briefly lights up the sky, lighting the heavy dark clouds of fire in a glorious pyrotechnic display, it still feels damp and dreary. Like Ishmael in Moby-Dick, I feel the drizzle internally, though whether in my soul as he did, or in my heart, is still unclear to me. I haven't yet figured out where the one ends and the other begins.

I stay outside until I cannot stand the mosquitoes anymore, and secure the screen door before lighting the lamps. There are herring for supper—I know this only because Sophie, fisherman's daughter, has informed me of their provenance—and I fry them up carefully, measuring out the smallest amount of rationed butter and filling the rest of the pan with water (which, come to think of it, is nearly as precious a commodity when you consider the energy it takes to pump and fetch it) and flipping them when it seems time. I heat up the famous corn from the purloined can as well, and slice some of

the sweet oatmeal bread that I baked last week under Anna's su-
pervision. She is still not sure that it's a good thing for me to learn
to cook.

"And what will your mother say?" she wails, wringing her
hands. I swear that's what she does: wring her hands. "A young
lady isn't supposed to do all that."

What neither Anna nor my mother know yet is that I have no
intention of becoming the proper young lady they still aspire for
me to become. If I ever did, it's a notion that disappeared sound-
lessly and completely three days after arriving at the dune shack.
No matter what else happens, I am not going back to that. No
coming-out party for me, thank you very much. I'd rather wear
dungarees and have a career, though I'm still a bit foggy on what
that career should be. It will come to me, I expect.

So I cook the fish and heat the corn and wait as the night settles
over the dunes.

It comes in gradually, the whine of the insects buzzing around
the screens fading first, and the last desperate orange reflections on
the clouds to the west fading to pink and then to purple. Then the
night sounds begin: the mysterious snuffling that often emanates
from under the shack, and the flutter of something else just beyond
the window. I've drawn the new blackout shades, so I am now like
an animal in the night, curled up in my cave, seeing nothing, only
hearing the life that pulses in the darkness beyond. Tonight some
creatures will die and others will eat, and in the morning there will
be no sign of the struggle that ended that way.

It's all very mysterious, somewhat exciting, and more than a
little scary.

There is a foreign sound in the night, then, a tread of human feet, and in a moment the door is unlatched and opens and Anna slips inside. Her face is flushed and her eyes bright, and she's wearing a brooch that I haven't seen her wear since we've been out at the dune shack, though she takes it out and looks at it often enough. It was a gift from her grandmother in Osnabrück.

"You're late," I tell her, more for something to say than out of any real need to chide. Honestly, I don't care where she is or what she does—I just want to *know!* It's a terrible thing, this curiosity; but I know better than to let it show. Best to cover it up by being curt instead. "Dinner will be dry," I say hopefully. "Maybe even inedible."

"It is all right," Anna says, oblivious to the sharpness in my voice. "It will be very good, *liebchen*, you'll see. You have progressed as a cook."

"That's not saying much," I say, automatically. "Anything would have been a move in the right direction." I give up trying to make her feel bad. "I'll set the table."

Nothing, now, notice, about a young lady not cooking.

What I'm really doing is looking at her for clues about where she's been, but aside from the predictable moisture clinging to her salt-and-pepper hair and colorful shawl – and it did, after all, rain for most of the day – there is nothing.

Dinner is oddly delicious, and the herring aren't even dry. Some things just don't work out the way you want them to.

***

There is sun when I awaken, streaming straight into my eyes, but by the time I've gone out to pump water for breakfast a fog has moved in, magically, and the ocean beyond has disappeared, we are encased in a cocoon of white.

But I have other concerns: Anna is unwell.

She hasn't gotten out of bed by the time I'm back with the water, the first time in my life I can recall that happening: Anna is no slugabed. She seems to be wakening slowly, and when I touch her face with the back of my hand I pull it away instantly, as though burned. She is feverish.

I've never had to make decisions about sick people: I've either been sick, in which case Mother and Anna care for me; or someone else is sick, and Anna cares for them. That's clearly not an option here.

I rummage in the cupboard and find the white tablets that she makes me take when I feel ill, and get a glass of water from the bucket I just hauled up the hill, and I sit on the edge of her bed and make her take the pills. I don't think she is even aware of me being there. She is shivering despite the heat on her skin, mumbling things I cannot understand.

I pull the blanket off my bunk and tuck it around her, and she pulls at it greedily, her body still shaking under the covers. I tuck them around her as best I can, and fetch some more water, but she's not cooperating about drinking it.

I'm starting to get scared. It is occurring to me that being raised to be a proper young lady doesn't leave you with a lot of useful skills.

The word soup floats into my consciousness, and I scrabble around in the cupboard, but there isn't anything of the canned variety there. Naturally; Anna makes soups from scratch. But there's some broth and I heat it over the stove, opening one of Sophie's illicit cans of vegetables–peas–and throwing them in. There should be chicken, I know; but we have no chicken, and there are no herring left from last night. I chop up the three carrots I find in the vegetable bin, instead, but it still look watery and unappetizing.

It's irrelevant, anyway; Anna won't eat any of it.

The fog isn't lifting, and it feels oppressive, isolating us still more in a malevolent cocoon. It's no good: I can't help her. All I do is put cold cloths on her forehead, which she immediately pushes off, and try and make her eat my awful soup. She is cold, and then she is suddenly hot, throwing the covers off with some sort of wild desperation I haven't seen in her before.

She is scaring me, and that's the truth.

The fog starts lifting around midday, teasingly at first, the sun boring a gradual hole through it until it looks like a snow sun; but it perseveres and I start noticing landmarks, the bluff, the low stunted Cape trees, warped shadows off behind the shack. The fog still covers the ocean, though, and for once the gulls are quiet.

And there things stay, irresolute, not clearing, not darkening, as though the world were holding its breath, waiting…

Waiting for me, I decide. Better to do something, anything, rather than stay here and feel useless, doing useless things when perhaps there is something more useful that I can do. I walk back into the cabin and squat next to her. "Anna," I whisper, "I'm going to get help."

She doesn't hear me. Her eyes are open, but they are wild, they see things that aren't here, people from her past, perhaps, or from her future.

I tuck her in yet again. "Stay warm," I say, though I don't know why I say it; and then I lace on my shoes and put the door on the latch and take a long drink of water and set off.

The dunes are wreathed in fog as I walk, though my feet know the way without my eyes' contribution. The bits of green here and there, the scrub pine and the curious mosses that live out here in the desert, appear as if by magic, and distances are odd, shortened and then lengthened until I'm confused and stop trusting my senses. The fog lifts suddenly as I dip down into a depression, then I am out of it and enveloped again in mist. It's a curious, unreal journey, one that seems to last forever, I have been wandering in this sand and following these wretched paths for hours, it seems; days, even; and then the trees move in and I am on a path through jeering branches and finally out on Route Six.

From there it is a straight shot down Snail Road to the harbor, and I follow Commercial Street all the way into town.

I don't know where Sophie is, and the only people I know are in the shops and over at the dune taxi; so I go to the general store first. Mr. Nelson is serving someone else, and I wait impatiently, standing first on one foot and then on the other (truth be told, they both hurt by now) and looking at the signs posted around the store, the ones Sophie told me about. "Food Fights for Freedom," reads one, with a dour-looking young woman raising her hand as though being sworn in court. "Produce and Conserve, Share and Play Square!" exhorts another.

Mr. Nelson knows me, by now. "Our lady of the dunes!" he exclaims, cheerfully. "What brings you into town. Miss Stanfield?"

"I need to see a doctor," I say. I've had time to think about what I'm going to say without giving away Anna's secret. "I'm fine, don't be worried, I just need to ask some questions."

His expression assures me that he doesn't need to hear more; God only knows what questions an adolescent girl might wish to ask of a physician – he certainly doesn't want to. "Well, there's Doc Barrow," he says, scratching the back of his neck. "He's where the missus and me, we always go."

"Where is his office?"

He smiles again. "I forget you don't really know your way around town," he observes. "Everyone knows where Doc Barrow is. Just go on down Commercial Street, miss, and turn right onto Atlantic Avenue, he's right up there on the right. After the Atlantic House."

"Thanks, Mr. Nelson." I have my hand on the doorknob when he calls me back. "Just you wait a minute, missy!"

I turn, apprehensive; but all he has in his hand is a bar of the ersatz chocolate that passes as candy these days. "Here you are. It's a long walk from out there in the dunes, you need something!"

He is beaming and I smile at his generosity. Ersatz or not, these bars aren't cheap. "Thanks, Mr. Nelson."

This time I really do leave. The doctor himself is in the waiting room, writing in a large ledger he holds on his knees; he looks just like my own doctor back in Boston, ancient and wise. I have my work cut out for me.

Deep breath. "Hello, my name is Jessica Stanfield."

He looks up. A twinkle. Maybe this won't be so bad, after all. "Yes, young lady? I'm Dr. Barrow."

"I live–I'm staying–out at my uncle's house. On the back shore." Sounds better than dune shack.

He isn't fooled. "Louis' old place? Thought I heard something about that. Young lady from Boston."

"That's me," I agree. Young lady twice in a row. "I want to know what to do about a fever."

He puts the ledger on the chair next to him. "You feeling poorly?"

I clear my throat. "Not now. But sometimes I am, and I'm all alone out there–well, with just my old aunt–I just want to know what to do if I get sick."

He smiles. "That's easy. You just put out the white cloth on the porch. When the dune taxi goes by, he'll stop off, bring you on into town."

I'm ready for this. "He doesn't come out very often," I point out, "and even when he does, he only comes out to our shack when he's scheduled to, or when my parents are coming to see me." I hear the automatic "our" in that sentence and hope that he doesn't. "I want to be able to take care of myself."

He thinks about it for a moment. "Come with me," he says, deciding, and leads the way back to his office. An examination table with a discreet screen around it is surrounded by pictures: a human body, apparently with the skin all removed; an eye; teeth. The rest of the room resembles my father's study at home: polished wood, leather chairs, bookcases filled with leather-bound volumes.

Dr. Barrow is already sitting behind his desk. "Very farsighted of you," he comments. "Very sensible." He is writing something on a small pad of paper. "Here's what to do. And I'll make you up something you can take, if you can wait a few minutes. But the best thing is to get yourself in to town. Being sick is one thing, but you can't diagnose yourself, young lady, and there are things you can die of."

I look at him startled. "Die? Of what?"

"Appendicitis, for one." He is at a table near the charts, measuring and mixing liquids.

"How will I know if I have appendicitis?"

He laughs. "Oh, you'll know. The pain is unbearable. You'll need the taxi then."

I am thinking, Anna doesn't seem to be in unbearable pain. But who knows? Who can tell, with another person?

"Here you go." He's put a label on it. "If you get a cold or influenza, this should help. Follow the directions. And this"—he hands me the paper—"will tell you what else you can do if you must. But try not to treat yourself, Miss Stanfield. I'd rather you left that to us doctors. We do go to medical school for a reason."

"Yes, sir." I don't care: he can lecture me all he likes, I have something to give Anna, Anna will be all right.

Leaving his office I think about going over to the dune taxi and talking Sebastian into coming out to the shack with me to take Anna back into town, but I feel the reassuring weight of the bottle in my pocket and decide not to. We'll see how this works, first, I promise myself. Then we'll see. It's important to keep Anna's presence in the dunes a secret, yes, but surely not at the cost of her life?

Provincetown is bustling today—well, it is every day, isn't it?—and seems loud, too loud to my ears. I walk slowly back through the cooler East End, trees sheltering the street, gardens to look at and sigh after. This is where the artists all live, I know, and I always hope that I'll see somebody at work. There are half-finished canvases out on porches, from time to time, abandoned as though the painter had just that moment left to get a glass of lemonade; on other days, I might wait and see if they return.

But not today. I force myself to walk briskly along, past the houses of all the luminaries who posed so many years ago for the pictures in Helen's shack, many of them long gone, some still around: John Dos Passos, Susan Glaspell, even Tennessee Williams, who might even be there today... Sophie's taken me down this route before, pointing out with casual satisfaction all the houses, naming the writers. I have no idea how she knows where they lived; probably Helen was able to walk this route with her before. She has no time for or interest in any other kind of artist; for her, it's all about writing.

One could say that Sophie is focused.

Helen's house itself is here, too, and I slow as I look at it, searching its windows for a glimpse of her again. I wish I had time to stop... I picture Helen in there, her infectious energy, her love for Sophie, her memories. I wonder what she thinks about, if she remembers the days when there was a playhouse on Lewis Wharf, if she thinks about her bohemian years.

Not for the first time, I conclude that I was born thirty years too late.

The dunes feel like home when I get back; their sounds familiar after the artificial noises of the town. Even the heat of the sand is a welcome feeling. I don't think I'll ever be able to go back to Boston, the city, the people. Better to stay here with the hawks and the seals and the scrabbling of the mouse in the night.

Anna is no better—but no worse, my anxious eyes diagnose, and I make her take some of the medicine Dr. Barrow mixed for me, along with two glasses of water (his instructions said to drink—and keep drinking—liquids), none of which she was any too thrilled about, but all of which went down and stayed down.

I gave up a few of our precious red coupons back at the store to get some tinned chicken, and I chop it and throw it into the concoction on the stove with some pepper and parsley, and it starts smelling like real soup. Sometime around midday (for who knows what time it ever is; the sun is high, suspended and motionless as it seems to be when it gets that high in the sky, I don't understand the physics of it, but I've observed the reality) she eats some of that, and then I wrap her up again and leave her to sleep. That was in the instructions, too.

The afternoon reflects my unsettled mood.

The fog has all but disappeared, a few tendrils still slithering around the scrub brush and along the horizon; but the sky is dark, cloudy, threatening. There is a stillness in the air and I wonder if there will be a storm soon. Staying here listening to Anna is making me crazy. I put water within her reach and slip back into my everyday sandals and go out to see what the dunes have for me today.

Helen's shack is, as always, my first visit on this little tour, and I'm aware of something different even as I approach it. The old floats are still leaning negligently against the side of the shack; the small circle of stones, miniature megaliths, that was Helen's last project before she had to move into town is untouched. But there is something, disturbed air, that has nothing to do with the tree swallows grabbing insects in sharp fast darts across to the bird-houses Helen left here for them, that has nothing to do with the frog tracks all around, still undisturbed from last night's revels. I don't know what is different, but something is.

And it isn't Sophie. I know, now, the signs that my love is here, the door off the latch, her rucksack leaning against the wall, her footprints approaching the shack from behind and rounding it, the windows opened to catch the sea air.

Sophie isn't here, but someone is.

I stop and consider the situation. I'm not frightened, not really; it's daytime, even if the air is threatening; and my trip into town and conversations there have made me impervious to my usual reticence about human interactions, so few and unusual out here.

But there's still something a little… disquieting… about approaching that door. I reach out and my hand encounters the wood, cracked and old after many summers in the sun, and I stay there, holding my breath, listening, waiting for God only knows what cue might come from within… But there is nothing, and, my heart hammering, I fling the door open and enter the room.

It is empty.

It is empty, but has not been for long. The bed has been slept in, the bedclothes ruffled and then smoothed down, but they're not as they had been, heaped with cushions, the last time that Sophie and I were here, making love … Someone has used the woodstove, too, and that may be what alerted my unconscious to the intruder, a faint smell of woodsmoke in the air, only recognizable once I knew what to look for, but which had registered in my senses as I moved toward the shack nonetheless.

I approach the bed, slowly, stretching my hand to touch it. An image flashes in my mind, us together on the bed, giggling and moaning and talking, and I am wishing, now, that I'd taken the time this morning to see Sophie. To try and heal whatever this thing is that's coming between us; the bed with its reminders of passion and giggles seems a reproach. It doesn't matter; someone else has been here, the fairytale has dissolved, the images already fading in front of my eyes. I have a sudden premonition, the desperately unhappy sure knowledge that we'll never make love together in this bed again.

After all, if everything isn't perfect, what is it? And everything had been perfect between us, no storms, and now that they're there I don't know what it means. Can two people heal something bad that's happened between them, even if they don't understand what it is? Even if they don't *know* what it is? Or is it over, is there nothing more there once that magical sense of togetherness, of perfection, is gone?

I don't know, and I feel small and cold thinking about it.

It's a relief to instead wonder who might have been here, a relief to turn from that premonition, that overwhelming sudden sense of loss, that sure knowledge that whatever Sophie and I shared is over.

I put my hand out to the stove, gingerly; but whatever burned here went out hours ago, and the stove is only slightly warm to the touch. I look around for any more clues, but I'd make a terrible detective; as far as I can tell, there's nothing else out of the ordinary here. Probably during yesterday's rainstorms, I find myself thinking; when the morning dawned clear, the visitor probably doused the fire and left.

To go where? And why?

I leave the shack and look around for clues, as if I'd recognize a clue if it hit me in the face. There are footprints all around, of course; but there always are, and I'm not able to differentiate ones from the others. There is dune grass that's been trampled and possibly even laid upon heading east, though, and I follow it, impervious to the sharp grass cutting at my legs. There it is, again, a place where the grass is flattened down. So perhaps I'm good at this, after all.

There are any number of tracks crossing and crisscrossing the dune ridge as I follow it, the grass sharp and painful, and I watch everything carefully, more aware of my surroundings now after three months in the dunes than I'd ever been in Boston. The beetles whose corpses littered the paths in June are gone now; but I can still see the other traces of life and death here: the tracks of a frog, a scattering of wings tinged with blood, a dead mouse. Death is not upsetting in the dunes, it is part of the natural rhythm, and I no longer shudder when I see a dead thing.

Once I was walking over in the beech forest, over where there are real trees—red and black oaks, and pitch pines, and hemlock, beeches, sugar maples – and lots of them, not just the small stunted ones you see in the dunes proper. The pitch pines have thick, fire-resistant bark; but many of the other trees' wood is bleached white, even here in this protected area; in the Province Lands, all wood is eventually bleached by the sun and the wind.

There are some marshlands there, and steep paths among the trees, places where you could swear you were anywhere in an ordinary New England forest until you look down and realize that it's all sand underneath, the roots thrusting down past the top layer of soil down into sand, ever-present on the sandbar that is the Cape.

And death, it seems, is everywhere. I'm suddenly remembering a walk in the woods near Concord, out at Walden Pond, a solitary walk though I can't remember why, as Mother's always been fearful of the Bad Things That Can Happen To Girls Alone.

I came upon a place in the woods where a bird had died. It had died violently, that much was clear: black crow feathers were scattered all around a certain area on the ground, some of them in clumps still held together by dark globules of dried blood. Sunlight slanted in through the tall pine trees, and where it fell on the feathers, they glimmered darkly with a light that was almost blue.

I don't know what had happened in that place. Perhaps there had been a fight, high above, in the trees—a hawk, possibly, trying to steal the crow's eggs: they do that, or so Sophie has told me. Or perhaps the encounter had happened on the ground, with some anonymous animal taking the body off to feed on it in a hole or hollowed tree at leisure. Whatever had happened was over now, and there was so little left there to say that the bird had lived and died: only that brilliant scattering of dark healthy feathers amid the pine needles and the moss.

Life and death; out here, it is all the same.

I walk along the ridge until the path dips into a hollow again and I follow it, unsure of what I'm doing, walking by instinct rather than tracking anything or anyone. The wind has picked up and it blows my hair around my face, I have to keep brushing it away so I can see. There is something pulling me forward and for another sudden moment I feel the cold claw of premonition in my stomach, as if going forward means making a decision, setting something in motion, awakening something that I do not want to awaken.

It's all silly, of course, and I push the thought from my head. My actions don't have that much importance, that is one thing the dunes have taught me. Every act out here is potentially life or death for the creature so acting; but the sun will rise the next day and the waves will pound the Peaked Hill bars and the seals will sun themselves on the ocean surface. And none of it will care.

Still, a creature's life, no matter how small in the great scheme of things, is all that it has. So perhaps there is something in the premonition, after all.

I can't shake the darkness, the fear I'm feeling over my shoulder, and I consider turning back, going to Louis' shack, tending to Anna and minding my own business.

And then the moment passes and I move on.

There's a cluster of shacks in the hollow, disused and in ruins. Sometimes tramps from the town come out here to sleep, light fires with the weathered shipwrecked wood that the shacks were built of, find a place to be left alone for a time. I've never seen any of them, but Sophie says they mostly stay in town now, and there are fewer of them anyway.

The war's done that, too.

I approach the ruined shacks slowly but without fear; surely nothing dangerous could be here. You can see the sky through the ceilings of two of them; another ten years of backshore storms and they'll be gone. Already other shack owners are pulling wood from them to perform maintenance on their own shacks.

There is a sudden clatter from within one of the shacks, a sound immediately silenced. I can almost feel the person within holding his breath, waiting to see my reaction.

And I don't even notice that I've already accepted the presence of a person in the shack as a given.

I've always hated in books when a character hears something amiss, usually in a dark creepy place, and immediately calls out, "Is anybody there?" As if anyone lurking about would suddenly come out and say, "Yes, here I am, you caught me." I understand the impulse, now, though; I have to bite my lip to keep from saying the same stupid thing. Instead, I step carefully up onto the rickety porch of the most substantial of the three shacks and, silently, push the door open.

There's an immediate whoosh and something hits me in the head. It hurts, but not blindingly so, and I grab the doorjamb for support. It moves under my hand and I stumble into the room beyond, flailing my arms to keep my balance. There is a scrambling sound beside me but I'm paying more attention to where I'm landing.

When the shack stops spinning around me I look in the direction of the sound. The moving shadows resolve themselves: a rickety bed with no sheets on it, a large figure wrapped in a dirty blanket.

I have found Anna's secret.

Chapter Twenty-Five

I don't know which of us is more frightened in that moment, the man on the bed, or me. We are staring at each other, eyes wide, I'm sure his heart is beating as obviously and painfully as mine. My senses seem heightened; suddenly I'm aware of everything around me, of the whistle of wind through the cracks in the walls, of the slash of a mouse racing for cover on the floor; of the man's heavy breathing.

And of the man himself, of course. As my eyes adjust to the shadows of the room I can see that he is less threatening than I'd thought, probably of medium height, with dark dirty hair and a streak of dried blood across one cheek. He's wrapped in a blanket so I can't see his clothes; but he's wearing scuffed boots, drawn up under him so that he is squatting on the bed. In another person it would be a dangerous stance, someone ready to spring. But in him I sense only lassitude and pain, drawing himself into a corner of the bed. He is frightened of me, I realize in some surprise. The dirt and smell belong to a tramp; this fear does not.

"It's okay," I say at last; someone has to say something. "I'm not going to hurt you."

The eyes don't believe me. I stand up slowly, smoothing down my skirt, and smile. Well, I try to smile. He looked like a cornered animal, a trapped thing, and my heart goes out to him. "You must be hungry," I say, the first reassuring words that I can find. "I can go and bring you something to–"

"No!" The word is explosive. His entire body is tensed, as though to fight or flee; but there is no room here for him to flee. "All right," I say. "I won't go get anything."

"Thank you." It is an odd response, and odd, too, is the accent I hear behind the words. He sounds, I find myself thinking, like Anna, only worse, the accent stronger.

"It's okay," I say. I have no idea what is going on. "You can sit down, if you want. I'm not going to take your blanket from you."

"Thank you." He repeats the phrase with dignity, sliding down into a sitting position, and now that I can see him better I see what else he has in common with Anna: this man is sick. The eyes are bright with suspicion, perhaps, but brighter still with fever, and I can almost feel the heat coming off him from where I stand across the room. He is shivering violently now and huddles down into himself for warmth.

More likely a thief than a tramp, I decide. Or some other kind of criminal, hiding out in the dunes until they stop looking for him. Only he got sick and now he can't fend for himself.

I take a deep breath. "Listen, I don't know who you are, and it's none of my business anyway, or why you're here; but you're sick, and you need some things: food, for a start, and heat—"

"No!" His voice is sharper this time. "No fire!"

"Okay," I say, trying to sound reassuring. "No fire, don't worry, I won't light a fire. No one needs to know you're here." He relaxes slightly at those words; I was right about him, then. But it only made sense: no one hides out in a derelict shack when they're sick unless they don't want to be found.

This is, I decide, a little exciting.

I clear my throat. "But you still need help. More blankets, for one thing. And food. And water." I remember Dr. Barrow's words: fluids, lots of fluids. I look around. There isn't so much as a flask in the shack, though there's an empty tin cup; Anna must have left him something.

He is shaking even harder, now, and doesn't react when I walk over to the bed. I touch his shoulder and feel the flesh tense under my hand. "Look," I say, loudly, "you have no reason to trust me. I know that. But I really don't care what you've done, or who's after you. You're safe here, but you won't be if you don't get warm and have something to drink."

No response. The eyes, now, are looking inward, to the pain. "I'm going to go and get some supplies. You don't have to worry, I promise. No one will see me: it's pretty wild out here, and I'll be careful. But you have to stay here so I can find you again. I promise, I really promise, I won't bring anybody with me. I *promise*."

I think he's beyond caring; dealing with my arrival must have taken his last strength. He doesn't say anything as I tuck the blanket around him as best I can. There isn't anything around to patch the cracks in the two walls the bed is jammed up against, so I make sure that the door is shut and take off. The path down to the cluster of shacks seems obvious now that I know he's there, and I take another route through the sand and dune grass, my energy level high. I'm excited, to tell the truth, excited about being in an illicit mission, excited about doing something to help someone. As I go, I wonder who he is. I should have looked at the newspaper when I was at the store this morning, I realize; perhaps I would have seen him there.

It doesn't matter, of course; I am committed now.

The wind has picked up again without me really noticing it, and it's in my face as I make my way back up to the ridge and Louis' shack. I have no idea what I'm going to tell Anna, and am already running some scenarios around in my mind.

It hasn't escaped me that Anna already knows. She is sick; he is sick. She has been secretive; he is in hiding. How he ever convinced her to help him is going to be a story worth hearing; but best to wait and see. With Anna, one never knows.

I'm both disappointed and relieved to find everything at the dune shack as I left it. Everything is in its place; Anna is sleeping. I put a hand to her forehead, and it's still warm, though not burning. She murmurs and moves in her sleep, but doesn't wake up.

I rouse her enough the take the medicine and drink a glass of water, but she's back in her own twilight world by the time I lower her head back down to the pillow, dreaming perhaps of her beloved Osnabrück, or of her even more beloved Boston.

Which is just as well, for my purposes.

I am quick. I put some of the chicken soup on the kerosene stove to heat it, and when it's warm enough I pour it into a flask; I fill another one with water and look around for more receptacles. I pull out my rucksack and start filling it: Anna's medicine. The blanket from my bunk. Two apples. The soup. Half a loaf of pumpernickel bread. A big piece of applecake. I grab my pillow and a jacket and am latching the door silently and on my way before my mind starts moving again, analyzing what I am doing, asking myself what I am thinking.

Jeannette de Beauvoir

I don't know what I'm thinking. I don't know what I'm doing. But if the dunes have taught me anything, it's the sacredness of life, it's the quickness of death, it's the imperative to help others survive.

Twice the wind blows me over. We live isolated from the wireless and its weather forecasts, and deal with it as the animals do: by adapting to what is, instead of anticipating what will be. There was no hint of anything happening, other than the unnatural stillness I'd noticed on the way back from town; but a storm is on its way now.

I open the shack door, half-expecting him to be gone.

He isn't. He's sleeping lightly, in and out of consciousness, and he mumbles something I don't understand when I approach him again. I don't try to strip off the old dirty blanket, much as I'd like to; instead, I wrap mine around him, and ease him down to my pillow. "I've brought you some things," I say, more so he can hear the reassurance in my voice, and less to impart actual information. I'm babbling, actually. "There's soup, and you should have that, but some water, first. I know it's cold, and you're cold, but you have to drink, that's how you'll feel better. Then there's soup, and bread, and fruit. Oh, and applecake."

That got a reaction. He twitched and opened his eyes, and they met mine. "You've had it before," I say, sure of it now. "Anna's applecake. It's quite good."

He can only manage a croak. "Anna?"

"She's fine; don't worry. Well, she's not exactly fine, she's sick, too, but she's safe and I brought her soup and medicine, too, so you both have to eat it if you want to get well." I don't know how much of that he hears; he slumps against me and swallows the water and soup and medicine alike that I hold to his lips, obediently, like a child. And perhaps I am childish in return, but I can almost see the change in him as the water hydrates him and the soup warms him. It is magic.

It is life.

By the time he's finished, he's exhausted, and the cabin is quite dark. I use the flashlight I brought from Louis' with me to gather my gear together and replace it in the rucksack. The wind is higher now, screeching around the building — or what's left of it — and rattling the wood. I fear for the window, for the glass in it, and go outside with the flashlight to find a board to put over it; there are plenty in the other two wrecks. There's that odd phosphorescence on the ocean again; it's the only way I can distinguish the ocean from the air around it. That, and the sound, the sound of the waves, the smell of the sea.

I am relieved when I can shut the door behind me again.

Inside, only the sound of snuffling and an occasional cough. I light the lamp I brought—far dimmer than the flashlight, but more peaceful—and settle in. There's no way I can get back to Louis' shack now, not in this darkness, not in this weather. Already the rain has started drumming against the roof, and I have to move several times before I can find a comfortable place to sit where I'm not getting leaked on.

I think I have nodded off, because there are eyes watching me in the lamplight, clear eyes; the fever must have broken.

I take a deep breath. "How do you feel?"

"I am better." The voice is deep but with an oddly light inflection. "Who are you?"

A man who does not waste time, apparently. "Someone who just saved you," I say, a little tartly. Part of me thinks I should be the one asking the questions.

"I know this. I am grateful." Clipped speech, like Anna's, though the accent is different, thicker, harder to parse. "Who are you?"

A one-track mind. I take a deep breath. "My name is Jessica Stanfield," I say. "I live here, in the dunes, with Anna Walker."

I'm watching his face carefully, and there it is, a flicker of recognition, of concern, moving across his face. Dust from a comet's tail. I dampen my lips. "I think you know her."

"It is possible."

There's a moment of silence, awkward, sitting between us. I clear my throat again. "Now it's your turn," I say carefully. "Who are you?"

"It is not your concern."

I raise my eyebrows. "Really? Maybe it shouldn't have been my concern to look after you, either! For someone who owes me your life, you're not showing a lot of gratitude. Not to mention courtesy."

To my surprise, a smile lightens his face. He begins to laugh, but it quickly turns into a cough and he doubles over until it passes. It's not a reaction I'd have anticipated.

He is still smiling when the coughing subsides, and I cross over to him and help him drink from the water flask. He nods when he's had enough, and I withdraw again. "I have never been accused," he says, a little stiffly, but still with that smile glimmering in the shadows of the room, "of lacking in courtesy. My name–" a slight cough, again "–is Aicelin Hauptmann."

I am fascinated. "You're German," I say, pointing out the obvious.

A nod. "I am–" he seems to struggle with the information for a moment before making me a gift of it "–Lieutenant Aicelin Hauptmann."

"The U-boats," I breathe. "The wolf packs."

He smiles grimly. "I was on U-boat, yes," he says, pronouncing it the way that Anna did, that afternoon with my parents at the dune shack. "*Unterseeboot* 116."

"I saw you," I say in recognition. "Weeks ago, I saw you. Three of you."

He frowns, shakes his head. "I think not," he says. "I have only been here a short time. But there are–" He gestures tiredly.

"Others," I supply. "Other wolfpacks, other U-boats." The monster out in the deep, the darkness I feared, it is his home, his milieu.

He says nothing; there is nothing to say. I picture them, prowling the coast, the sea-monster of my night terrors, boats filled with men like this one. Ordinary men. "Why did you come ashore?" I demand suddenly. "What are you supposed to be doing here?" A thought seizes me. "Was there an accident? Did your submarine…" My voice trails off. Sink doesn't seem to be the appropriate word.

He looks even more tired, and doesn't answer about the U-boat. "I cannot speak of my mission," he says.

That seems to be that. I sigh and turn away from him, wrapping my jacket more closely around me. There is something in the pocket. I reach in; it's the fake-chocolate bar that Mr. Nelson gave me this morning.

"Here," I say, handing it to him and feeling oddly grownup as I do. "It's not very good, but it's better than nothing."

He bites into it ravenously. "I do not remember," he says, simply, "when I ate last."

I try to image that, and cannot; I don't go for very long between meals, snacks, and the moments my mother refers to as "a little something" when she is "peckish." Anglophile that she is, we often take tea and something else called "elevenses." Hunger isn't something I understand, and I realize again, with that thought, how incredibly privileged I am.

I wait politely until he's finished with the candy bar. "When did you see Anna last?"

"She is all right, Anna, *ja*?"

I nod. "I'm taking care of her."

"It is seeming to me," he says carefully, "that you are of us all taking care."

I move restlessly. I'm not being nice because I'm nice–I'm not–but because I'm flat-out curious about what's going on; the compliment is unsettling. And I'm still more than a little scared of being the one suddenly in charge. How doomed are we all, if *I'm* the one at the helm? "How are you feeling?" I ask again.

He considers his answer. "Better, I think."

I lean back, take my knee in my hands, most unladylike. "So what do I call you? Lieutenant?" He pronounces it far differently than I do.

A glimmer of a smile in the shadows. "I think Aicelin is acceptable," he says. "And shall I call you Jessica?"

"I don't see why not." No one has ever asked me for the privilege of my first name before; it's an adult thing, and I find myself liking it. I give him the gift of my name, and there's a glimmer in his eye as though he understands, though he's much, much older than I am and probably doesn't remember what it was like to be sixteen.

Probably not much older than Anna, and attractive in an older-person sort of way, I find myself thinking. Darkish hair, though it could well be blond and streaked, as Anna's is; it's so dirty now it's hard to tell, the way it lays in lank strips across his head. He's not big–I know that from tucking him in, and wouldn't Mother swoon at *that* thought?–but there are muscles there, too. If one were to fall for a man, he might be the man to fall for.

There is another awkward silence. This conversation is simply not going to take off on its own. And I'm still curious about the shadowy sea monster I've been living with–in my mind, at least–for the past months. "What happened to your–um–boat? Submarine?"

He's not saying; as soon as I ask it, I realize it's a stupid question. Isn't that treason, revealing secrets like that in a time of war? I bite my lip and try to think of something else to say, to talk about. "Anna's been taking care of you, hasn't she?"

A nod. "Yes. She is very kind."

"She's from Osnabrück." Oh, nice one. What a brilliant thing to say. "I've known her most of my life."

A considering look. "Yes. You are very young."

"I'm not! I'm sixteen!"

He laughs again at that one, a fresh bout of coughing. "Ah, yes," he finally manages to say. "You are of an age considerable."

I don't say anything. I agree: I do think that I'm of an age considerable. I think about adding that I'm old enough to be in love, but I'm not trusting our secret to someone I just met, no matter how vulnerable. "It's not real chocolate," I point out instead.

"Yes, I know."

I eye him. "Where are you from?"

"You speak of in Germany? My city is Dresden called."

It's meaningless to me, but I don't want him to know that. "You must be homesick."

He looks up sharply, as though to see whether or not I'm being sincere. "Yes, I am," he says at length, taking my words at face value. "My city is with beauty filled. I–miss–my family, and my work." He pronounces it "vork."

"What *is* your work, when you're not on a submarine?"

"I am lawyer," he says. He shifts his weight slightly, and grimaces. "I the law like: it clarity to things brings."

It's a new thought, but one I'll have to examine later. "How long have you been–here? In the dunes–the sand, that is? Out here?"

He looks uncomfortable, and I think that perhaps he won't answer. Maybe I'm treading too close to state secrets again. "I do not know," he confesses at length. "I was hurt, and then I became ill.

We–I had to stay in the ocean for a long time, and my suit for the water, it was damaged. The water was very cold."

"It is," I agree. "It's the Labrador Current that goes by this side of the Cape."

"I believe that I was to the cold overexposed," he says quietly and exactly. The name of the current that has hurt him is irrelevant. "I was sick for a long time after that."

"And Anna found you."

This time, he doesn't hesitate. "And Anna found me," he repeats in agreement.

There's something in his voice when he says her name, there, and I suddenly *know*, the sure knowledge coming over me all at once, like a flash, clear and true: Aicelin and Anna are in love. I have never thought of her as the object of anyone's romantic affection, but I can see his eyes in the murkiness, and I see there her reflection as I have never seen her. I see love shimmering in the dark shadows, and I feel humbled.

Then I remember his words and I look at him sharply. "But… you have a family back home," I say. "A wife? Children?"

He nods. "I have both of those," he says gravely.

"And it doesn't matter?"

"They to me matter, yes, very much," he says. "The one does not the other eliminate." He shifts his position again with another grimace of pain. "Is it that there is more water?"

I pass the flask over. "Here."

"*Danke.*" He drinks deeply, then screws the top back on tightly. His eyes are watching me, and he sees that I know. "You think it is—how do you say, unlikely—that two people so different can feel for each other so quickly?"

No: I think it's unlikely that two people so *old* can feel for each other so quickly; but I don't say it. And falling in love at first sight seems to be what is happening, this summer. I look at Aicelin and say, "It's different, out here. In the dunes, I mean." I gesture around us, trying to encompass the sand and the water as well. "We're in our own little world here. Magical things can happen."

He likes that; I can tell. "*Ja*," he says, gently, in agreement, and I can hear Anna's voice in that small word. I stop feeling superior. It is the sound I hear in Sophie's voice when we are together, the light that courses through my voice and my life since I've known her, and I find myself surprised that others feel it, others hear it, others share it. I feel stopped in the moment, in the realization of shared feelings and experiences, another confirmation of the magic of life here in the dunes, the sense of everyone as part of one whole.

Of course, the fact that the two countries we live in are at war with each other provides something of a damper on those particular flights of fancy.

I must have sighed aloud, because he nods again, as if we were still in conversation. "War cannot well end," he says. "It never does."

"It's pointless," I say, but even as I say it, I know I'm wrong: there is a point, there is always a point. I know this from the discussions in my father's study, from the passionate monologues I've listened to there, from the heated arguments. There is always a point, and it usually has to do with money. Oh, there's national pride—there's a lot of national pride. But that's usually what's being manipulated in order to get to the money. The money is what matters.

The money is always what matters.

Aicelin is leaning back now, his eyes closed, and I decide that it's probably not a good time to discuss the philosophy and economics of war. Especially with someone from the other side.

But I still wonder how it can all seem so simple, here.

Chapter Twenty-Six

I go out at some point; with no outhouse, I find what shelter I can from a low scrub pine and relieve myself. The wind and rain are harder than ever and I decide not to drink any more water. Which shouldn't be difficult: Aicelin needs as much as he can manage. I'm trying not to think about what happens when he needs to go outside …

I think I'm half-asleep; I must be, because I'm dreaming, though with part of me very aware of the ruined dune shack, the German officer slumped across from me, the wind whistling through the cracks in the shelter.

But I'm seeing other things: I'm falling down a long tunnel, and I cannot scream, I cannot move, I can only feel. And then Sophie is there with me, and we're both helpless, falling, though then it is more like being drawn into something, that's it, something sucking us toward it, into it, and there's nothing that we can do. And then we are on the beach, on the sand, and I am running after her, but the sand is sucking at my feet, pulling me down, pulling me back. I gasp and find myself, again, fully present in the shack with the German; but part of me stays with the fear, and I know that it is, somehow, not a dream, that it is real and threatening and present.

I just don't know what it means.

Aicelin is watching me again. The cabin has gotten, imperceptibly, lighter; there won't be a sunrise to watch this morning with the clouds and rain, but it is there, somewhere, lifting the world from darkness into a murky gray, making the day and the events it will bring more real, more immediate, more frightening. I've missed the liminality of the first false dawn, and am suddenly plunged into the real one.

I'm not sure that I'm ready to face this day.

I clear my throat. "How do you feel?"

He moves slightly and grimaces. "I will be all right." There's a stiffness in his voice that wasn't there in the night, and I wonder if he, too, is taking stock of the situation, is bracing himself for—or against—what the day will bring.

He faces it squarely, though. "What do you intend to do about me?"

I come from a family where no one ever says what they think, unless it's about an abstract concept. Or maybe they do and I just haven't listened closely enough. Daddy's given up trying to make us a model psychologically healthy family; Mother defeated him on that count long ago. I've learned to be more forthcoming since I've been in the dunes, but even Sophie might have been taken aback by this kind of directness. "I don't know," I answer honestly. "You can't stay here. There's not enough shelter, and you're right on one of the paths down to the beach. People come this way. Not often, but they do, and once would be enough."

"That is not what I mean." He's in pain, I can see that now. People in pain share that same ugliness, that drawn expression with the eyes somehow looking inward, that attempt to transcend something that can't be transcended. I am thinking that he said something, in the night, about having gotten hurt, and I wonder if there's more to what's wrong with him than simply being sick.

"I know," I say contritely. "You mean you want to know if I'm going to turn you in."

His eyes are watching me steadily. "Yes," he says.

"Well, I'm not, for what it's worth," I say. It never occurred to me to even consider turning him in, to be honest, though Mother would have been appalled to hear it. We're at war with Germany; but not, I think, with Aicelin. I don't know how to be at war with a person.

He isn't letting it go. "Why not?"

I'm surprised. "Do I look like the sort of person who gives a wounded bird back to a cat?" I ask, without thinking; the analogy isn't all that felicitous. I shake my head impatiently. "Anyway. That's not the point. I'm not fighting the war."

"Your country is. My country is." He's *really* not letting it go.

"So what? Just because they're wrong doesn't mean we have to be." I'm thinking of the posters I saw before I left Boston, the ones I've seen all over Provincetown, too. Next to the banners that proclaim "Food is a Weapon: Follow the National Wartime Nutrition Program," and "Where Coupons Go," are others less innocuous: "He's Watching You," the one whose demonic eyes follow you all over, wherever you move; and "They're Closer Than You Think."

I swallow. They sure are.

Aicelin is somewhere dark, I see it in his face. "We are all wrong," he says softly. "We are wrong to do that which is wrong, and wrong to say nothing." He looks up at me, and the despair is tangible, a presence in the room with us. "But what can one to do? If you say somessing, you are sent to the Eastern Front to die. I do not want to die. So we say nothing. The war has made cowards of us all. We say nothing, and we go where they tell us to go, and do what they tell us to do, and it is our lives that wear out."

I can't touch that remark; I can't fathom that pain. I can't even begin to understand it. I glance around the shack and address practical matters instead. "I know you don't want to hear this," I say, "but you need to move."

"I know it," he says. "Do you know of a place that will be safe? Is there such a place?"

I grimace. "I could take you to *our* place," I say. "No one comes in, because of Anna. She's sort of in hiding here, too." But even as I say it, I'm discarding the dune shack as an option. Sophie comes there; the dune taxi comes there. It's exposed up on the ridge, with no place to hide, nowhere to go.

Aicelin has already discarded it. "It would not be proper," he says, stiffly. "I will not Anna into any danger put."

No mention of me, but I let it pass. I'm scanning the ridge in my mind, seeing nothing but occupied dune shacks, exposed dune hills, trees that hide nothing but their own secrets. "There's an old coast guard station," I say, slowly. "It's very isolated. It's not considered very safe, but it's tucked away, no one goes there. The road disappeared years ago." I feel like an old resident now. As, in a way, I am; the dunes are more my home than Boston ever was.

"How wide?"

I stare at him, stupidly. "How–wide? Is that what you said? How wide is the station? I don't know; it's got a cement base, I never measured..."

"No, no!" Impatience showing, hardly a surprise, with the pain he's in. I'd have been impatient a long time ago if I felt like he does. Downright petulant, probably. "How wide from here?"

"Oh." Realization dawns. "How far? Um, I don't know. I was never good at figuring distances." It's an obvious question and an obvious concern. I think about it for a moment. "It's around the bluff, the other way from here, up closer to Race Point." I look at him consideringly. "At least half a day to get there."

"I will do it," he says matter-of-factly.

"Rest some first," I say. "I have to go check on Anna before we do anything. And maybe the rain will ease off a little. I'm going to leave you for a while, but I'll be back and we'll move you then." I stand up, zip up my lightweight jacket; it's still oddly cool, though that's better than the heat that will burn sand and skin once the sun comes out. "I'm leaving everything here. Finish the soup–finish everything, come to that. You'll need your strength." I slip Anna's medicine back into my pocket; time to administer it to my other patient. "And don't move. You're safe as long as it's still raining, no one comes out to the dunes in bad weather."

"You are kind." He's taking me seriously; he's leaning his head back, and his eyes are already closed.

I hesitate. "Tell me something?"

"*Ja?*" He doesn't open his eyes.

"You were in the other shack before, weren't you? The small one, with the bed and all the books?"

"*Ja.*"

I shake my head; Anna was foolish to let him stay in Helen's hut. It was the first place Sophie heads for anytime she comes out to the dunes.

I don't like that thought and put it out of my head... for at least the first two minutes. But it comes back, insistent. Why am I so afraid of Sophie seeing Aicelin? She is my friend, my love, my soul-mate: surely she will devote herself to his well-being the same way that I do?

But I know the answer to that question is no. And I don't know why.

Jeannette de Beauvoir

Chapter Twenty-Seven

Anna is awake and restless, sitting up, her streaked blonde hair loose and tangled down her back. "Where is my soup?" she demands as soon as I reach the porch. "There was chicken soup, I know this. Where have you put it?"

If she's strong enough to scold me, she's strong enough for the truth. "Hello, Anna," I say, closing the screen door behind me. "I gave the soup to Aicelin."

She's too restrained to allow herself a reaction; her impassivity has been her hallmark for too many years. "So you know," is all she says.

"I know," I say. "Why didn't you tell me?"

"It was a secret," she says. "My secret, not yours."

I raise my eyebrows. "What did you think was going to happen? He was going to get well and signal his submarine to come and get him?"

She's staring at me in something that looks a lot like terror. "He is sick?"

"Worse than you," I say. "Same flu, I should think, but he's worse. He was in the water for a long time, he says, and he's injured, isn't he? He wouldn't tell me, but it's clear he's in pain. And he has to move."

She nods. "I know. Come sit here, *liebchen*, and tell me what happened." She pats the bunkbed next to her, and I obey, my reaction automatic out of a lifetime of obedience to her.

"You had him at Helen's shack, didn't you? The little one with all the books in it?" I ask, then continue without waiting for a response. "I didn't know you knew where it was."

"There are many things I know," she says obscurely.

I don't have time to pursue it. "He left it and set off somewhere. Or maybe you helped him." I look up and meet her eyes; the glimmer there answers for her. "The storm didn't help. It's cold in there, and everything is damp or worse." I shrug. "So I took your medicine—"

"I have medicine?"

"I went into town yesterday. No, don't worry, I didn't say anything about you, and of course I didn't say anything about Aicelin, I didn't even know about him then. I just said I was scared of being isolated and what if I got sick. And I got some medicine for colds and flus, and I gave it to you, and I gave it to him, and it's working on you."

She takes my hand. "You have done well, *mein Schätzchen*. I am proud of you."

I squeeze hers. "I am, too," I say, surprised. Now that I can share my burden of secrecy, of responsibility, with someone, it feels lighter. "I didn't think I had it in me."

"You have made good decisions," she says. "But now there are others to make."

I take a deep breath. "He has to move," I say. "As soon as the weather clears there'll be people going down to the beach there. Not many, but it only takes one. Or even a tramp looking for a place to sleep. He's far too vulnerable there."

She nods. "I know. I myself could get him no further than the ruined buildings."

"You were already feeling ill," I point out, a little too heartily. She's still not in great shape, if you ask me; not for what lies ahead of us, and I'm starting to get seriously worried. "Listen, Anna. I'm thinking the old coast guard station. It's the other end of the Bars, and no one goes there, really. There's a decent foundation and the old building is pretty much intact, and we can keep him hidden there. You can't see it from anywhere until you're practically on top of it, and you can see it from the ocean…" I let my voice trail off, suggestively.

She doesn't pick up on the unspoken question. "I do not know of this place," she says. "How far is it?"

I giggle despite my worry. "That's what the lieutenant wanted to know. Only he asked how wide it is."

"His English is good?"

I gape at her; of course, they wouldn't have spoken English together. "It's good," I acknowledge. "Is that typical?" I've never really thought about Anna's English, any more than I've ever really thought about Anna as a person other than being my housekeeper.

Maybe it's time for all that to change.

She shrugs. "Schools in Germany teach English," she says, but she's not interested in pursuing the thought. For once, I'm not in for a lecture about how German schools are better than American ones; she has other things on her mind.

I take the moment to study her: I'm trying to imagine her falling in love with the wounded Aicelin. There isn't that revulsion that you feel when you think about your parents being romantic to-gether; it's more a matter of something more detached, a kind of clinical curiosity. Insofar as I can imagine any adults being physical, I can just about manage it. But it still feels odd, like considering space-alien sex. Or mermaid sex. Something like that.

Anna comes to a decision. "We will move Lieutenant Haupt-mann to this coast guard place," she says, briskly. "We will start now."

It's my turn to act like an adult. "Not so fast," I say. "You're not in any state to help. You probably can hardly stand." I pause. "Maybe I could get Sophie –"

"*Nein!*" It flies out of her mouth and starts her coughing. I pat her back and wait, and when it's over I reassure her. "It's okay, Anna, I won't involve anybody, I promise."

"Not even Sophie!"

"Not even Sophie," I agree. I'm not even all that sure it was such a good idea, myself. I look at Anna speculatively. "But you can't help."

"I can," she says, her voice determined. She stands up and walks over to the sink, where she sways for a moment before lean-ing against it. Great. I'm going to end up carrying two invalids over the sand.

What is worse is that there's clearing out on the horizon, I can see the line between sea and sky, and it's light. There's no time to lose.

"All right," I say briskly, taking the decision away from her. Time to get moving. "You're staying here. I'll get him over there, and then later if you want I'll take you out there to see him." Oh, for a dune taxi of my very own!

Anna isn't used to having me tell her what to do; but her face is pale and she's not stupid, she knows that she'd just get in the way. "*Ja*," she concedes. "This is a good plan. And you will make sure that no one can see where you have been?"

"I'll cover our tracks," I assure her distractedly. I'm rooting in the cupboards. Hot chocolate would be best, but there isn't any. I pick up an orange and push it into one pocket, get some dried codfish in the other. It isn't much, but there isn't much time. "I'll be back as soon as I can," I tell Anna as I kiss her cheek.

"Go with *Gott*," she says, and there is a worried crease between her eyes.

I'm pretty worried myself, but I force a cheerful smile. "It'll be fine, Anna," I say heartily, and then I'm out the door and heading along the top of the ridge, the rain suddenly sweet and welcome in my face. Let it rain, let it rain, no one will see us in the rain. Please let it rain.

The sand here never turns to mud, not like one always expects it to. It gets wet and clings, but it's easier to walk in when it's wet. It's wetter down on the shoreline, of course, and for a moment I toy with the idea of taking Aicelin down the bluff and walking him around the coast, walking on the wet sand by water's edge. It's an absurd thought: we'll still have a bluff to climb at journey's end, and it will be a far longer way to go, as the shoreline sweeps around to the west. No: there's no getting around it, we will have to go through the dunes.

It's a daunting thought.

Aicelin has been sensible in my absence; he's alternated resting with walking about; I can see his footsteps in the damp sand around the ruined huts. I call out, for some reason oddly hesitant about just walking in on him, now that he's up and about. "It's me. Jessica. May I come in?"

The door opens in response, falling back as the wind grabs it and slamming against the side of the shack. "It is good weather not," Aicelin observes grimly by way of greeting.

"It's perfect weather," I assure him. "No one in their right mind will be out here. No one will see us."

He grimaces in response. Seen in the light of day, he's both older than I thought... and in more pain. There is dark stubble on his chin and his hair is unkempt; but it's the lines etched deeply into his face that speak eloquently of both age and pain. "Thank you for this doing for me," he says stiffly, as if we had just met, as if we hadn't spent the better part of the night together.

I wonder if he tried to leave, so that I would not find him here when I returned. I wonder if he tried, and found that he could not.

"Breakfast first," I say, cheerily. "I have fish and fruit, and you have to eat them both, whether you want to or not."

He knows; he has survived something awful before, I can see that in his face, too. Perhaps worse than this. There is a special courage in one who sits down with such determination and eats what is patently inedible, forcing the orange sections into his mouth with the dried cod, swallowing with difficulty, doing it over again. It's a courage I've never seen before and I find myself strangely in awe of it.

While Aicelin eats, I set myself the task of eliminating or disguising all traces of his occupancy. I've brought rope, and I roll up the blanket and pillow, attaching them none too elegantly but effectively to my rucksack. The flasks that once held soup and water go into it, and the thin smelly blanket I found him in — no doubt purloined from Helen's shack — gets rolled up and stuffed in too. I go outside and bury the orange peel a small distance from the shacks; some enterprising animal will dig it up in due time, or it will decompose into the sand. Either way, it will not stand out, will not scream of recent human passage there.

He is ready, standing stiffly outside the shack by the time I return. I go in and sweep debris as I can into random piles. I pull the boards down from the windows and leave everything open: within a half-hour, I reckon, the wind will do the rest.

"Onward," I say heartily. "Do you want to lean on me, or try going under you own steam?"

He says nothing, just sets off determinedly in the direction I'm facing. I hoist the rucksack to my back and follow. "Over there… where you see the boulder showing? That way."

It is hell. I knew it would be hell, but I didn't know just how bad it would be. Aicelin stumbles on the first downhill and I'm unable to reach him in time to catch him; I think he got a nasty twist to his ankle, or perhaps he just underestimated his own injury and weakness. In any case, from the first ridge, he is leaning against me, more and more heavily as we progress.

And progress is slow. Excruciatingly, maddeningly slow. My dunes, my beloved dunes are the enemy now, fighting us every step of the way.

After a while I lose track of time. Aicelin falls, we get him up, we stagger off again. One step. Two steps. I focus on my feet, putting one in front of the other. He is limping horribly; I consider telling him to take off his shiny uniform shoes, which must be constricting; but he must know that better than I do, so I say nothing. I need my breath for propulsion, not conversation, anyway.

One step. Another step. He falls, and this time it takes longer to get up. I straighten and look around us, worriedly. The sky hasn't cleared, but it has brightened, there is light behind the clouds; and the rain has stopped. The tiniest inhabitants of the dunes have appeared now that it's not raining anymore, and they buzz and cluster around us, little black gnats, flies, mosquitoes.

Aicelin is oblivious to them. He seems to be passing in and out of consciousness even as I urge him forward. We've passed Helen's hut, and are in the low hollow two ridges from my own dune shack; halfway there. "Come on," I mumble, my own muscles screaming in protest. I cannot imagine what he feels, if I'm in this much pain, if I'm this exhausted. "Wake up, Aicelin. We have to move on."

I pull him up and he stumbles forward. I guide him off the path; the sand here is deeper, not good for walking, but we're leaving traces behind us, and I don't know when I can come out and remove them. I don't want to leave a track running right to the old coast guard station.

Years pass, or so it seems, and the journey is a blur. He falls; we stumble together; we push on. Twice he goes down for so long that I'm afraid he won't get up again. Once I go down and he falls on top of me and I burst into tears from the tiredness and the fear and the sense of futility.

I'm still sobbing as we resume the journey.

The weapon threatening us is the sun, which finally breaks through the clouds when we're still far–excruciatingly far–from the coast guard station. As happens in the dunes, it is suddenly as though the storm, the bleak weather, had never happened at all. Heat begins to shimmer off the sand; the insects become more insistent; the sun begins to burn my shoulders.

We stumble on. I am breathing hard, now, through my mouth, pausing more and more frequently to gasp more air into my lungs; I'm aware of them, as I am of my whole body–the blisters on my feet, the aching of my calves, the cramp in my side I am trying to ignore, the headache that increases with time. Water is our ally; we both drink greedily from the flasks I brought from the dune shack.

And then, when it feels as though we'll be stumbling through this desert forever, we crest the ridge and see the stunted trees I've already recc'ed, and within moments we've made it past them and into the shelter of the old station.

And this is when I pass out.

Chapter Twenty-Eight

I feel nauseated, and it's with some difficulty that I orient my-self, aware of little besides the feeling of sickness. I stir, and there is an exclamation, and in a moment there is Anna, pressing a cool cloth against my forehead. I am in bed in my room on Common-wealth Avenue, and I must be getting over a flu.

Flu. The word jars my brain and reality comes washing back over me. I sit up, fast. "Anna!"

"Shh, shh, *mein Engel*, it is all right," she says. "Here, you must drink water now."

I take a sip and then it is as if I cannot get enough into me fast enough. I end up coughing and spluttering. "Thanks, Anna, where's—"

"Shh," she says again. I begin to form consciousness of my surroundings. There are shadows, deep ones: it is twilight, the long lingering twilight of midsummer; the sun must have only now set. I am on a bunk, but not the one in our dune shack; I've never been here before.

And then someone else moves nearby and I see that it is Aicelin, lying like me on a makeshift bed, and I realize that we're in one of the rooms of the old coast guard station. "We made it," I whisper.

"*Ja, liebchen*, you did," says Anna, and I've never heard her voice so warm. "You did beautifully, little one."

"Not so little," I protest, but the words are mechanical. How did Anna find us? But I push the thought away; I've had a good look at the German and his pallor is scary. "Is he alive, Anna?"

"Yes, thanks to you, *mein Engel*," she responds. "Shh, rest now."

"He looks awful."

"*Ja,*" she agrees, and I hear the fear in her voice. "He is not so good."

I struggle to get up, but my muscles aren't having any of it. "Anna—he's going to be all right, isn't he?" I am back to the magical thinking of my childhood: If I say something is so, that makes it so.

Anna doesn't live in that magical land. "I do not know," she says, and her voice breaks on the words.

I look at her, really frightened now. "He's not going to die!" I exclaim. "He can't die now!"

"Hush," she replies, another word from my childhood. "Hush, now, and let him rest. We will see."

"You don't understand," I say, my words coming fast; I have to persuade her. I grab both her hands and make her look at me. "Listen, Anna. I've been thinking. They can't hurt him. There's a law about it, I've heard Daddy talk about it, about enemy combatants. He's in uniform—sort of—he's clearly in the navy, they can't hurt him. They'll put him in a camp, a prisoner-of-war camp. There are doctors there, Anna. They'll take care of him." She says nothing, and my voice goes up a notch on the hysteria scale. "We can't just let him die!"

"Do you not think I know that?" she hisses back. "You listen to me, Miss-I-Know-All-About-The-War! You don't know, I didn't know, we are isolated from everything in these damned dunes! There was a *Rudeltaktik*, a wolfpack, three weeks ago."

"I don't understand," I say slowly. I remember Daddy talking about wolfpacks, and I imagine the submarines prowling the ocean like wolves. But isn't that their job? What makes this so horrible?

"No, you do not," she agrees. "These wolfpacks, they are not permanent, *ja*? Only for a few weeks are they together, they hunt the convoy, then surround it and draw in. All convoys are being lost. Hundreds of men on them all, and supplies–supplies for Europe." She gestures toward Aicelin. "His U-boat, *Unterseeboot* 116 it is, it was part of wolfpack three weeks ago."

I close my eyes. Real blood on his hands, then. I saw the newspaper in Provincetown, read the *Advocate*'s screaming headlines. Out in the north Atlantic; they got the whole convoy. A convoy heading out from Boston, heading out past the Cape, bringing food to Great Britain. Nonmilitary, with destroyers to guard them.

People from around here might have been on those ships.

I look at Aicelin. In sleep, his tense muscles have relaxed, he looks younger, more innocent. "I still don't know why he's–"

She cuts me off. "It does not matter why he is here," she snaps, the old Anna back again, impatient. "It matters that we cannot tell of him being here. No doctor."

"He might die," I point out.

"I know this. It is his choice, it is what he wants." Her grief is obvious; her whole being is fear, is grief.

I touch the back of her hand, lightly, with just one finger. "You love him, don't you, Anna?"

"*Gott* help me, *ja*, I do," she agrees softly, not taking her eyes off him. "I think never will it to me happen, this love. It is for other people, this is what I think. But now it has come to me too late."

"Maybe it's not too late," I protest, though I know that she is right.

She snorts and looks at me now. "You forget, perhaps? I am Jewish, me. Through my mother only, but it counts, it counts for everything. In my country, this is not a good thing to be, not anymore. We have all changed now. German has turned against German. Everything has changed."

I stare at her, transfixed, and in my mind I hear the echo of Aicelin's words: "We are all cowards now."

I begin to cry; it's impossible not to. I want a happy ending; for Germany, for the United States; for Anna and Aicelin; for Sophie and me. And even as I think that, I have another of my dark shudders, my premonitions of doom, as the sudden certainty washes over me that there cannot be a happy ending here, that we have all been set like automatons on this path and we cannot turn from it, but only move forward and play out our assigned roles. And I know, I know with utter certainty, that there is nothing but tragedy in our path.

Cats torture their prey before killing it. Sometimes the gods just like to pin us down and watch us struggle.

Evening is falling when Anna rouses me again. "You have to go back to our shack," she tells me. "Someone may come by; we cannot both be missing if that happens." People don't come by for weeks on end, but her fear is infectious, and, wide-eyed, I agree. "What about Aicelin?" I whisper miserably.

"I will watch him," she says simply.

I nod, but I'm not ready to go yet. "Is there a plan, Anna? What's going to happen to him?"

She shrugs, but there is no indifference in her. "I understand," she said carefully, her voice low, "that if we can get him to Portsmouth–"

"Portsmouth?" My interruption is involuntary; Portsmouth is in New Hampshire, nearly two hundred miles away. It took us every bit of strength we had–and a lot I hadn't known we possessed–to move less than a mile.

"Shh!" She looks around warily. "In Portsmouth, there is someone who can get word out, who can have him picked up and taken home. It is the only thing we can do. Nothing is safe here."

She's right about that. I take a deep breath that is more of a sigh of despair, kiss her dutifully on the cheek, and head back. The flashlight marks a path—a new one, I'm still being careful—among the dune grasses and through the sand, skirting the small stunted wind-gnarled trees and what small vegetation has taken root there.

Our dune shack, when at length I arrive, feels luxurious by comparison. I light the kerosene lamps–all five of them!–and heat water for tea. There is food in the refrigerator, and I start to gorge myself, until thoughts of Aicelin sick, possibly dying, fling themselves unbidden into my mind, and I find that suddenly I have no more appetite. I drink the tea, though, and take the cup on a walk across to the bluff over the ocean. It's a clear night and I watch the sky as I sip the hot liquid, feeling small and inconsequential under the dazzling blanket of stars. The Milky Way is like a gauze ribbon of light stretching across the sky, and the stars seem closer than they've ever seemed before.

As I stand there, one of them suddenly streaks across the sky, brighter than the others, a brief explosion of light, so fleeting that I don't even have time to wish on it.

It is an omen, however. Tomorrow, like it or not, I will have to act.

***

It's another clear day and I'm awake as soon as the sun hits the shack—5:30 by my calculations on my makeshift sundial. My body feels stiff, but I'm oddly rested... and determined.

The chicory actually tastes like coffee today, for the first time, so that's progress of sorts.

I leave a note for Sophie in case she comes by, which has to be wishful thinking, as she hasn't been out to see Anna in over a week. But I tack it to the front door anyway, just in case she comes by and then goes looking for us. "I'm in town; Anna's gone for a walk toward Truro." Truro is in the opposite direction from Race Point and the old coast guard station; it's the best I can improvise. Let her think that perhaps Anna has befriended another shack resident; they're all eccentric enough out here that no one would think to abuse her the way she was abused in Boston before we came.

And then, just for good measure, I write another note, more intimate, more special, but still revealing little, and pull up the loose board on the porch and slip it in there. Our secret hiding-place, our illicit post-box, used to transmit an untruth. I love you, Sophie, I'm thinking. Please understand.

She might look there first. She might assume that I have nothing but good things to say to her. I feel a stab of guilt at my perfidy.

As I step out of the shack, a tremendous flock of birds–some sort of plover, I think–suddenly takes flight from the beach below, thousands of them, startled no doubt by some predator; a detached part of my brain remembers hearing that there's been an eagle sighted. The sound of their wings fills the air as they fill the sky, their migratory paths encoded in their bloodstream, and for a brief moment they blot out the sun.

I try not to see it as a sign.

Today the walk into town seems to take forever, and once I reach Snail Road I stick my thumb out for a ride. I'm being optimistic: no one drives much anymore, not with the big campaigns about wasting fuel that our boys need overseas; but eventually an old wheezing pickup truck stops and I hop in. He's a Wellfleet farmer, come to sell what produce he has in Provincetown, and he drops me off by MacMillan Wharf and adds a bonus to the ride: a big, beautiful, illegal carrot that I devour instantly and hungrily.

I tell myself that my luck is turning. Perhaps the plovers were a good omen, after all.

The train from Boston is in, as it happens, and I walk out the pier along the tracks, curious to see who and what has arrived. Fewer people than ever; vacations are unpatriotic, these days, and anyway a lot of people are away at the war. But the refrigerated cars are ready for the fish: war or no war, everybody has to eat, and I stand off to the side and watch the loads coming out of the fishing boats' holds and into the train. The catches are weighed, first, and then paid for, men in shiny aprons and slide rules making calculations, passing money over to the fishermen. I hear Sophie's voice in my mind and find myself thinking that the bars will do well tonight, anyway.

But that's not why I'm here. I'm here for the draggers, the herring trawlers.

I leave the main pier and venture down onto the side docks that sprout off it like a Christmas tree, where the fishing boats are tethered. Some of them have been ambitious and have replaced their gay blue and red paint with dazzle designs, and I find myself thinking that Sophie's father had had dazzle paint, too, and he'd disappeared anyway. In the wheelhouses I see the fetishes, the good-luck trinkets, the evocations against the evil eye, and I can feel my heart beating faster. These are the people I have to talk to. Many of them don't speak English, and my private-school French and Latin won't serve me well. Sophie, the one person who might have been able to help me, is also the one person to whom I cannot appeal.

Sophie…

There are tears in my eyes, and I dash them away with my hand. I have to focus, I cannot think about her. There are bigger things at stake here, more important things at stake here, than my lovesick yearnings, my bafflement at what is happening inside her. If she had only come out to the dunes to live with us! We could have shared Helen's tiny shack, cooked our breakfast out in front of the hut, overlooking the sea, with the sun and the gulls wheeling overhead. It would be a good life.

What it was, was a dream.

The draggers are easy to recognize: they don't have the big up-right "birds" of the longline boats, but rather a tremendous spool at the back of the boat to haul in the nets. All the boats are theoretically options: they all go out to the Grand Banks, I often see them from the back shore, heading out … and then, sometimes days later, heading back. No one hugs the coast, no one goes near Portsmouth, which has its own fleet, and all the fleets are seriously jealous of other boats.

I've chosen the herring captains, though, because I know that the catch is down. They stay in one place longer, dragging the ocean bottom, and they've had to curtail trips due to the U-boats. They're poor. They're hungry.

And I have money.

I'm not telling them who he is, of course; that would be suicidal. "Hello, I know that you can't make a living because of the U-boats, but hey, if you'll just help me rescue this one U-boat survivor, well, I'll make it worth your while." No; I don't suppose that's the right approach.

I haven't quite figured out exactly what the right approach will be, of course; but I'm hoping that it will come to me. Aicelin doesn't have time for me to figure everything out.

I've narrowed it down to two: the *Brenda S.* and the *Ellie*, when I hear a voice behind me. "Well, if it isn't our lady of the dunes!"

Damn, damn, damn. I turn, and there is Mr. Nelson. "Good morning," I say, politely. I think it's still morning, but who knows? Once I'm away from my sundial…

"Good morning, Miss Stanfield," he says. "Taking the train back to Boston?"

Jeannette de Beauvoir

"Oh!" The train also stops in town, so this is a roundabout way of finding out what I'm doing down on the wharf. "No, not today, Mr. Nelson. Just... feeling a little lonely for people. It gets quiet out on the back shore."

He raises his eyebrows. "That's a lot of lonely, Miss Stanfield."

He couldn't know what I'm about, but I'm seized with an irrational fear. After all, most of the anti-German posters I've seen are in his store. *Loose Lips Sink Ships.* I clear my throat. "I'm used to the city. I want to spend more time in town," I say. It sounds lame, even to my ears. "And—maybe do my part for the war effort, too. Just a little."

He smiles. "And how are you doing that, Miss Stanfield?"

My hand closes around the money in my pocket. "I want to make a contribution," I say, "to the families of fishermen who've been lost. You know, to the Germans."

His smile turns into a beam of delight. "Well, now, Miss Stanfield, I can't think of a nicer thing for you to do. Very generous, I'm sure."

I smile self-deprecatingly. "I was going to ask the harbormaster how to get them the money," I rush on, stronger now in my story. "But I wanted to look at the boats first."

"Then I'll leave you to it, Miss Stanfield," he says, tipping his hat. "Stop by the store if you need anything before heading back out."

"Thanks awfully, Mr. Nelson." I smile my prettiest smile, but I'm gritting my teeth. Go *away*, Mr. Nelson.

He goes away. Maybe magical thinking does work, after all. I cross my fingers that it will make Aicelin well, then turn back to the

- 310 -

boats. It's time I did my part, all right, but I have a more immediate task to hand.

The trouble is, there's no one around. I peer into wheelhouse after wheelhouse. Maybe when the boats are docked no one stays with them.

At the end of the pier someone is stacking lobster pots. I approach him timidly. "Say, can you help me? I'm trying to see… if there's anyone who can take me to Portsmouth."

He looks as me as if I'm speaking a foreign language. "Portsmouth?"

I nod. "In New Hampshire."

He continues to stare at me, and I make a gesture of frustration. "Thanks, anyway."

It occurs to me that I probably do look like a madwoman. Most people wishing to go anywhere do so by the most obvious route: train to Boston, change lines, train to Portsmouth. It's not that difficult. They must think I'm a loony, trying to hire a boat.

I don't have the option of doing it the "right" way. In fact, I'm running out of options, period.

I trudge back up the pier, people bustling about me. A fisherman jostles me and turns away, exclaiming. "You all right?"

"Yes, thanks."

He narrows his eyes. "You sure, miss? Yer oughts get outta the sun. Yer don't look so well, 'scuse me for sayin.'"

I smiled tiredly. It's true that the sun feels hot now, different somehow from out in the dunes, everything brighter and louder and more threatening. "Thank you," I say again.

He isn't having any of it. "Yer come here, miss." He pulls me over to the lee of the train, which is still being unloaded, and sits me on a crate. "Yer jus' sit here for a minute in the shade, miss. Yer'll feel right as rain in a minute." He removes his cap and scratches his head under it. "What yer doin' down here anyway, 'scuse the question, miss? Ain't no place fer a lady, yer'll 'scuse me sayin.'"

I smile again. I don't feel much like a lady. Our lady of the dunes, Mr. Nelson calls me. "I'm trying to hire a boat," I say, without much hope in my voice.

"Fer what you wan' a boat? Them's expensive things. There's petrol rationin', miss, wha' with the war on an' everthin.'"

"I know." I sigh. "It's hopeless, I know."

"Where you be wantin' to go, come to it you fine a boat?"

I give him a lopsided smile to show that I'm fully aware of the enormity of what I'm asking for. "Portsmouth. New Hampshire."

He whistles and shakes his head. "Yer got that right, miss, about it bein' hopeless an' all." Another scratch under the cap. He turns suddenly and stops two men striding down the pier, big rubber boots on their feet, fishermen. "Ho! Jake, there! You know anyone got a boat for rent?"

They stop, both gaping at me, and I squirm under their gaze. "Where for?"

"Portsmouth, the lady say."

"Not a chance," the one called Jake says, then takes in my clothes. They're worn, but still clearly good. "Mebbe I can ask around. Who's wantin' one?"

I slide off the crate. "My name is Jessica Stanfield," I say, the name sounding odd and stiff and formal. "I live–you can leave a message with the dune taxi."

That places me, all right. "You one of them loonies?" Jake inquires immediately. "Living out to the back shore?"

"Now, Jake, there's no call for that," remonstrates my benefactor.

"No call for no boat, neither," says the other, derisively. "You keeps your pennies, lady. No boat's gonna go anywhere as long as them fish is out there for the haul."

"I shouldn't have bothered you," I say. "I'm sorry; I'll be on my way now. Here," and I plunge my hand into my pocket, coming up with a dollar, heavy and substantial. "Here's for your trouble, for helping me. Good-bye."

As I walk away, I can feel him standing there, the dollar coin foreign and significant in his hand, staring after me. For someone who's supposed to be being discreet, I've made quite a fool of myself.

I'm weary far beyond my physical exertions–can despair make you tired?–and so I seek out the dune taxi. Sebastian is sitting outside the taxi office, whittling a piece of wood. He is unsurprised to see me. "You be wantin' to head back now, Miss Stanfield?"

"Yes, Sebastian, please." I sit down next to him on the warm stone wall. "How'd you know I was in town?"

He smiles without looking up from his handiwork. "Here in Provincetown, everyone knows everyone else's business," he observes. "An' I mek' it my business to listen. Penny to be turned, that way."

"So you knew to wait for me here?"

"Ah, don't be gettin' upset, there, Miss Stanfield. It's the same with everyone. I spend most o' my time waitin,' happen. Last night, I hear that there writer, Mr. Mailer, he be havin' too much to drink over to the Atlantic House, all I do is, I wait. Parked close, I am. When he comes out, I'm ready for 'im." He glances up from the figure he's whittling. "'S how business is done, Miss Stanfield. 'Specially in these perilous times. So I hear you be down the docks, and I know you be tired, so I thought, I'd just wait for you to come by."

"I suppose so," I say. I think about asking him about a boat for Portsmouth, but if he listens, chances are he chatters, too. I am hot and hungry and discouraged. We're going to have to find another way of getting Aicelin to New Hampshire; that's all there is to it. "What are you whittling?" I ask.

He holds it up. "Statue of Our Lady," he says, reverently. "To give to Father Brown, over to Saint Peter's."

I take it from him and run my finger over it. Our Lady...

Abruptly, I thrust it back into his hands and stand up. "Will you take me back to Louis' shack now, please?"

"Sure will, Miss Stanfield. Taxi's ready. You takes your seat there, and we'll be off."

I slid wearily into the front seat of the car. The upholstery is hot from the sun and burns my thighs.

All I want to do is cry.

Chapter Twenty-Nine

It feels like years since I've been in the dune shack; hard to believe it's only been hours. There's an old, musty smell to it, as though people haven't lived there for a very long time. Partly it's that horrible sickroom odor that hasn't aired out, even though Anna is better; part of it, no doubt, is my overtired imagination.

The little premonition voice is acting up again. It's telling me we won't come back to the dune shack, that nothing will be as it was before.

I tell the voice to shut up, and start packing food for Anna and Aicelin. I made Sebastian stop by the general store and picked up some fresh bread from Mr. Nelson, and I put this in the hamper, along with what we still have for cheese and dried fish. Cans of vegetables–I don't let myself think of Sophie, even as her image forces its way in front of me–and packets of crackers. Everything that's in the cupboard, in fact.

I eat the heel of the crusty bread on my very roundabout way to the old coast guard station.

At first I think the place is deserted. Nothing is stirring in the long rays of the late-afternoon sun; some tree swallows are darting in and out of the eaves with absolutely confidence, which they wouldn't be doing if people were moving about within. When they see me, they dart for cover.

I stop and listen. Nothing but the surf, closer here than it is at the dune shack, and the sudden scream of a gull overhead that nearly gives me a heart attack. No voices; no movement. I approach the door cautiously, standing to the side as I look in. There's been some effort to replace it on its hinges, but it's still half-open as I move toward it, and I am suddenly afraid of what I'm about to find. Which would be worse–to find them gone, or to find them dead?

They are neither. They are both asleep, rolled together on the hard concrete bunk, the blankets under them, their two heads on the one pillow. His arm is around her, protectively, and I stop and look at them in something approaching awe. If I ever doubted that this odd thing could be love, in this moment I know. I feel them as one organism, feel them together in a way that I've barely felt with Sophie–and never with my parents.

If I'd started out wanting to help Aicelin because it was the right thing to do, now I want to help them because of their love.

It is oddly exciting and energizing. They should be together; they should be allowed to live, to love. Anna and Aicelin's feelings somehow make mine for Sophie more real, more pure, more true. And I'm even more certain of hers for me.

I put down the string bags I've filled, and that tiny noise wakes Anna and tells me everything I need to know about her alertness. She says nothing, her eyes focusing on me with relief, and I can sense her body relaxing. She puts a finger to her lips and slides out, carefully, from under Aicelin's arm, her hair wild and messy and gorgeous. I'm still looking at her and seeing someone else, a younger woman, strong, with laughter in eyes that have not yet faded, with the expectation of joy ahead of her. I want to hold Anna, to tell her that everything is going to be all right, that I will do everything that I can to make it so; but I know that she will not understand. Instead, I gesture to the bags. "I've brought food."

She nods, still silent, and draws me outside. "Shh! He must sleep."

I turn to her. "How is he?"

She shakes her head; the lines of tiredness and worry and fear are etched again on her face. "Not good. I think there is blood poisoning."

"Blood poisoning!"

"Shh!" Her voice is a hiss. "Be quiet!"

I am panicking. "People die of blood poisoning, Anna! What happened? How did it happen? Are you sure?"

She shakes her head impatiently. "I look like a doctor, me? I do not know that for sure, *nein*. It is what I think, this is all." She sighs. "But I know he needs a doctor. He will go nowhere until then." Thus reminded, she looks at me with some hope. "What has happened in Provincetown?"

She sees it in my eyes even as I'm drawing breath to respond. "It was a long shot, Anna."

"It was the only hope we have," she says, flatly, and her eyes have filled with tears. "He will surely die, *liebchen*, and there is nothing that we can do." The emptiness I see in her fills the world, stretches out to the horizon, encompasses the sky and the sand and the ocean; it is deeper than anything I have ever felt, anything I have ever imagined. I am crying again as I stand on the edge of her grief, on the edge of something bigger than the earth.

I put my arms around her and hug her close. "Don't give up, Anna!" I whisper fiercely. "It doesn't have to happen."

She is sobbing in my arms and I cry with her, because in truth I don't see how it won't happen. He is injured, ill, exhausted, marooned among people who wish him harm, far from his home and his people. All he has is Anna.

And all she has, I realize, is him.

I don't know how long we stay there, as wave after wave of despair washes over her and she erupts into tears afresh, and I hold her tightly through them all, saying nothing, just the way that she held me when I was a child and some childish event had made me feel that my life, too, was over. She held me when the cause of grief was inconsequential, and I pour all my gratitude for that kind of love into my arms and my embrace, staying strong, letting the storm pass.

It does, eventually, and I let go when she starts to move out of my arms. She finds a handkerchief in her pocket and blows her nose into it, wiping her tears. "So," she says finally.

"So," I say.

She takes a deep, shuddering breath. "So," she says again, and there is some finality in her voice. "We will see if he can eat, *ja*?"

"Yes," I agree. It cannot hurt, and better for her to feel she's doing something.

Aicelin is difficult to rouse, and still more difficult to feed. He starts to take the water but swallows it too quickly and chokes; after that, he seems to lose interest in it. Anna meets my eyes. "I do not know what to do," she says, and her voice breaks on the words, her grief is palatable, shimmering in the air between us.

"We can't let him die," I say, desperately.

"There is nothing we can do," she says and turns back to him, smoothing the cloth on his forehead, tucking the blanket better around him. It is a hot summer day and he is in here, freezing.

She is murmuring to him in German, now, and their intimacy, the intimacy of her gestures, of her voice, becomes too much for me to handle.

I go and sit outside and look at the ocean for a long time.

It's a quiet day today, with just a small breeze moving the dune grasses and ruffling the surface of the ocean. It's a different view from what I'm accustomed to, but it's really just a matter of the same players being on a different stage. Gulls glide overhead on the wind currents and cry with voices that are almost human, almost meaningful. The surf makes its rhythmic sound, in and out, in and out, the sound of the ages. Out further, I think that I can see a whale's spray. If I investigate the shoreline, I will find it teeming with both life and death.

I'm the one who always says that death is natural in the cycle of life. Ever since I've come to the dunes, I've been a philosopher, though perhaps of random things. I've given deep thought to dead beetles and mice, to fish pulled from the ocean by cormorants, to the sudden death-cries of anonymous creatures in the night. Life ends; life goes on.

But now that death is approaching my own species, I find myself at odds with the process. Or—perhaps it's not about my own species at all. I live in a time of war and am strangely unaffected by the violence that must be an intrinsic part of it. I think that some of the young men who have sat in my father's study and poured out their ideas and opinions have, in all probability, taken those ideas and opinions with the rest of their kit as they pack to go to war; and I expect that many of them will not return to Boston, but will stay in France and Italy and North Africa, and fiancées and mothers and sisters and daughters will flood their worlds with grief–but the death of those we do not know cannot touch us, not really, not in the heart.

No; it's not about my own species, I am not guilty of prizing it above others. My heart is touched by those who have touched my life, and it is them I wish to keep safe, to keep close to me, to keep from harm. And it is them who, apparently, I can do nothing to save.

I stir restlessly, pull my knees up to my chin, encircle my legs with my arms. Is there anything else I can do? The question is the only one that matters, spinning around and around with the memory of this morning, the heat on the docks, the derision of the fishermen, the condescension of Mr. Nelson. What should I have done? I search my memory for the wisdom I can find there, for the thought of those who have brought it to me. In Daddy's study…

Daddy.

The answer comes at last, relief pouring into me, pure and simple and echoing with all the confidence and trust of my childhood: Daddy. Tell Daddy, and he'll make everything all right. Tell Daddy, and he'll fix things for me. Tell Daddy, and you don't have to worry about things anymore.

Tell Daddy.

I scramble to my feet, suddenly energized and ready for action. "Anna!"

She doesn't move, doesn't even shush me, her whole being is focused on the man lying next to her. I'm beside them in a moment. "Anna! I know! We'll tell Daddy! He'll help us, I know he will! He figures out stuff like this all the time, he'll know what to do."

She tears her attention away from Aicelin for a moment as she considers the question. She has years of experience with my father; and no one can make a better judgment of a person than those who work for him. That's one of Daddy's sayings, too, slipping unbidden into my thoughts, and my relief is flooding my whole being. I must be bursting with light, I feel so suffused with sudden wisdom.

Anna knows. Her eyes meet mine, and I finally see a flicker of hope in them. "*Ja,*" she says, and there's an inflection in her voice that makes me want to cry. "*Ja,* he is very smart, your father."

"He'll know what to do," I say again, with absolute certainty. We've gotten too independent, out here in the dunes. We don't remember the fundamentals of life. We don't remember the primary lesson of my childhood: that my father is omnipresent, all-knowing, all-loving. What the Christians attribute to their god, I know is in my father.

He will save the day.

***

Anna is energized by the new plan as well. "Go back to Provincetown," she instructs, her mind clearly moving quickly, making one decision, discarding another. "You send him a telegram, *ja?* Or perhaps you go to Boston?"

"I'll send him a telegram," I say quickly. I don't want to leave the Cape; what if my parents decide that it's better, safer, for me to stay with them on Commonwealth Avenue now? "It will get there faster than I would," I say, quickly, to Anna, before she has any other ideas. "I'll send it from the general store, there's Western Union there."

"*Ja*," agrees Anna. "Tell Mr. Stanfield to come urgently, yes? It is better he is here, this cannot be talked about in public, not on the telephone neither."

"No," I agree fervently. "Not on the telephone."

Third time into town in two days, after weeks of staying out in the dunes. This time I don't even notice the distance – or, rather, I do, with an impatience that makes me stumble in my haste. I run where I can, when I'm not in deep sand, when the dune mosses allow my feet some grip. I emerge from the trees on the edge of Route Six and sprint across it and down Snail Road. Luck is with me again: a boy about my own age on a motorbike that was probably older than either of us slowed down next to me. "Goin' into town?"

"Yes!" I shout breathlessly over the sound of his engine. "Can I ride with you?"

He indicates the seat behind him with a jerk of his chin and I don't hesitate, never mind that my skirt is pushed up on my thighs, never mind that I have to put my arms around him to steady myself. Daddy will know what to do. Daddy will make everything all right again.

My benefactor drops me off in front of the store and I smooth my skirt and hair as best I can before running up the steps, across the porch, through the screen door that always slams behind me. "Mr. Nelson!"

He looks surprised this time. "Miss Stanfield! What's the matter?"

I didn't know my face is that transparent. Not a good thing. There's nothing I can do about it, now; especially when I need Western Union. People only use Western Union, my mother told me once, when there's bad news. Good news never comes via a telegram.

This is no exception.

"I have to send a telegram to my father," I say, as seriously and soberly as I can. "Can you help me, please?"

"That I can," he assures me, and leaves the pickle barrel whose contents he'd been stirring when I arrived. "Over here, then, miss. Not a problem." We proceed over to a small counter in the back of the shop where he actually puts on another hat, a visor that says Western Union on it.

We are commencing a religious ritual, it would seem.

He pulls a form ponderously from a drawer and licks the end of a pencil. "What you be wantin' it to say?"

I clear my throat. The truth is, I have no idea. "Dear Daddy, please come down to Provincetown—"

He cuts me off. "'S'not the way telegrams are phrased, Miss Stanfield." Now that I am doing something official and formal, he addresses me formally. "None of this dear sir sort of thing, not even full sentences. You pay per word, you see," he adds anxiously.

I wave the concern away. "It doesn't matter what it costs," I say.

He frowns; wrong answer, in a time of war. Nothing is to be wasted these days. "There is still an etiquette," he says stiffly.

"Okay," I say desperately; the voice inside me is screaming to get on with things. "Phrase it however is proper, please, Mr. Nelson. You know what to do; I don't."

That satisfies him; he dismisses my *faux pas* for the ignorance he's willing to believe it to be. "We could say, 'Important you come Provincetown,'" he suggests.

"That will be fine," I agree. His eyes are filled with questions, and I have a sudden flash of inspiration. I lean closer to the screen that separates us. "My father is a doctor," I say quietly. "And I have some—female problems—that I cannot discuss with anyone outside of the family."

That gets him, all right. He doesn't want to know any more; hell, he doesn't want to know that much. I don't add that my father's doctorate is in philosophy, not medicine; I haven't lied, not technically. Anyway, I'd lie a thousand times to Thursday if it would save Aicelin.

He is all business now. "How about if I ask for a response?" he queries. "That way, you can stay here and wait, see when he'll be coming." A thought occurs to him. "Perhaps you should just take the next train up to Boston yourself, miss. Or the boat. You can just make the afternoon boat."

I place a hand flat over my abdomen and grimace. "I don't think I can," I say, and, caught up in the moment, he fortunately doesn't question how I can walk four miles, two of them over sand dunes, but cannot face a train or a boat ride. "Of course not," he agrees quickly. "I'll send it at once, Miss Stanfield."

I nod and retreat to the bench that runs down one wall of the store, under the posters urging us to conserve. He does whatever it is one does to send a telegram, bustling importantly about behind his screen; and when he's finished, he brings me a lemonade. "Sweetened with honey from Mrs. Nelson's own bees," he tells me proudly. "It'll make you feel better, you'll see. Better than sugar, and no coupons to waste!"

I thank him and drink the lemonade gratefully; the honey in it is wonderful. "How long until there's a response?"

He frowns. "It all depends, that's the thing. Sometimes if it gets delivered first off, and the person answers right away, well, it can be within an hour. Other times..."

I put the glass down on the bench beside me with a bang. "An hour!"

"Well, yes, miss." He is unhappy about delivering bad news. "The messenger, see, he has to deliver 'em all, so even if there's an answer, sometimes he has to go somewhere else with another message, see? On a bicycle, he does it. But maybe there won't be other messages today."

"What about the telephone?"

He considers it. "Mebbe, yeh, mebbe they'll do it with the telephone," he acknowledges at length. He clearly doesn't have a clue what he's talking about. "Anyways, miss, you just make yourself comfortable, and I'll wait here with ya."

Charming thought.

I drink another lemonade and watch the clock. A very large woman comes in and haggles about the price of eggs. Ten minutes go by. Two children come in and carefully take rationing coupons from their books, conferring together *sotto voce* before concluding the correct number and color to use, handing them over grimly with the money that is equally carefully counted out, and receive bread and cheese in return. Another fourteen minutes. Another woman comes in and purchases some shredded cheese, milk, and flour. She leaves and there is almost a half-hour gap before the next customer. A Portuguese man comes in and finds his lack of English no hindrance in purchasing a cigar (Mr. Nelson takes this out from a hidden drawer in the sideboard, giving me a glance as he does), some milk, and some cheese.

Cheese, I reflect, is clearly making a comeback in the American diet.

I'm on my third lemonade-and-honey when Sophie walks in.

If I have any thoughts that she, too, might be merely a customer and our encounter accidental, she dispels it at once. She walks over and knocks the lemonade onto the floor.

"Excuse me, miss!" That's Mr. Nelson, distressed at the waste.

We both ignore him, staring at each other. She's furious, I can see, and I'm not sure exactly why. I mean, there are a lot of reasons why she might be angry, and I'm unsure about taking the lead in case I guess incorrectly and make things worse.

"What do you think you're doing?" She hisses the words, her voice sibilant, like a snake. The question is not helpful; I'm no further ahead than I was in terms of understanding the source of her anger.

"I'm waiting for a telegram," I say, stalling for time.

"What is wrong with you? Everyone's talking about you, all over town!" Her voice is rising and she glances at Mr. Nelson, avidly drinking it all in. She grabs my elbow. "Come on, let's go outside."

I say, loudly, "I'll just be outside, Mr. Nelson, if the telegram arrives, please come get me?"

"Right you are, Miss Stanfield."

Sophie is glowering, and even though I'm anxious about—well, about more things than I can begin to list, actually—I'm happier than I imagined possible seeing her. I haven't liked the distance that's come between us, that preceded even the business with Aicelin, and seeing her again, no matter how angry, makes my heart sing.

That she clearly does not feel the same, however, is what's causing my stomach to clench and unclench painfully.

Outside, she throws a hand up against the sun and squints at me. "What's going on?" she demands.

"Anna's been sick," I say. Smile, just once, smile for me, Sophie. "I want Daddy to come down and see her. I wanted to get her medicine without anyone knowing that it's for her. It's not that difficult. Where have you been all this time?"

"Everyone in town is saying you're crazy," she says, ignoring the question. "Everybody's talking about you."

"So you mentioned," I snarl. "You might know more if you'd been around more recently." It's an unfair remark; there is no way in the world I wanted her around, lately. But it's what I'm expected to say—and, besides, it's true. I've been missing her horribly.

She makes some obscure gesture and turns away, kicking a pebble with far more violence than is absolutely necessary. She turns back to me, thumbs hooked into the waistband. "Maybe you should tell me the truth," she says.

I turn cold inside. The little claw of fear that's been scrabbling at the base of my spine starts up again, and I feel as if I can't speak, I can't think, I can't breathe. I don't want to lie to Sophie. She is my love, my best friend, my world. I have to tell her…

It's not my secret to tell.

I'm just staring at her, and she must be feeling uncomfortable, too, because she's the one to break the silence. "Don't you love me anymore, Jessica?" There's fear in her eyes, and her voice breaks on the words.

It's the last thing in the world that I expect. I don't care that we're on Commercial Street; I reach out and grab her hand. "Of course I do!" I say, fiercely. "I love you with all my heart!"

"Then what's wrong?" she cries. "Is it us? Is it… is it that you'd rather be with a boy?"

This conversation has turned surreal. "Oh course not!" I exclaim, astonished. "Why on earth would you think that? I never want to be with anybody but you, honey! You're–" Words fail me. She's watching me; here, at least, I have no one I need to protect; here, at least, I can say what's in my heart. "You're everything to me, Sophie. I love you, and I'll love you forever!"

There's a noise in the doorway and we glance up; Mr. Nelson is standing there, his straw hat back on his glistening forehead, his expression disapproving. He doesn't say anything and this time I take the lead, drawing Sophie away from the doorway, across the street where the cars used to park when people still could afford gasoline, the lot sloping down to the harbor. A gull swoops low and caws as it passes us. I don't care what anyone sees, what anyone hears; I just care, now, that we make things right between us.

There are tears in her eyes that I'm not understanding. "Why did you think I don't love you?"

She jabs at her eyes, impatiently and ineffectually, with the heel of her hand. "I just wondered."

No one just wonders. "Who told you that?"

"What? Was it something they knew?" She is back on the attack, and the little claw of fear is starting up again at the base of my spine. Why won't she look at me like she used to? Why won't she talk to me like she used to? What's happened between us that's made this chasm open up, this distance that I can't overcome?

I remember, sometime in the remote past, in Boston, hearing the word "heartsick." I'd never understood it. I wish that I didn't, now.

I grab Sophie's shoulders and make her face me. "No one knows anything," I say, fiercely. "I fell in love with you the first moment I met you and I haven't fallen out of love with you since. I don't want a boy. I don't want another girl. I don't want anybody—anybody!—but you. Not now, and not ever." I take a deep breath that, to my distress, is far from calm. "I don't know what you want me to do to prove this to you, but I'll do it, Sophie, I will!"

She's looking at me, finally. "I was so sure," she says, slowly, "that there was someone else. That you were avoiding me because you'd met somebody else."

"I wasn't avoiding you!"

It's the wrong thing to say. She pulls away, sharply, and walks down to the water's edge. The harbor is calm and the waves are hardly more than the water's placid movement; they make little lapping sounds at our feet.

"Sophie!" I try and touch her but she jerks her arm away from me.

"Look, I know I've been in a bad mood lately," she says, not looking at me, but over toward MacMillan Wharf. "And I guess I should say I'm sorry. But it—it was hard t' come back, after the last argument. I thought that maybe things would get better magically, but they haven't. And my mother's been pushing me t' see Peter Silva—"

"Sophie!" It's my turn to feel a stab of jealousy, dazzlingly painful.

She shrugs. "It doesn't mean anything, it's just Ma, but it got me thinking. About maybe whether you'd like t' be with a boy, instead."

"Why, do you want to be with him?" This conversation is getting seriously out of hand, becoming seriously absurd, and I don't know how to change it. It's like a runaway train, tearing faster and faster down some disused rail line and there's bound to be a crash at the end, and I can't see how to stop it. Hell, I can't even make myself stop, the absurdities keep coming out of my mouth, out of my heart, I'm being struck at a more visceral level than I'd ever imagined existed. I know that I'm only making things worse, and I can't stop saying even more things to make the situation worse still. "If you want to be with this boy, go ahead!"

"Is that what you want?"

We face each other, angry and hurting, at the water's edge; and it's as though the shimmering heat of the day, the town, the harbor, everything has retreated into the background. There is just Sophie and me and our pain.

And I don't know how to get rid of the pain.

Then she shows me why I love her: the anger dissolves from her face, a light goes on somewhere inside, and suddenly she has burst out laughing, the laughter mixed with hiccups, tears still in her eyes, but it doesn't matter, she has smiled, the world is right-side up again. Nothing else matters, but her smile and that look in her eyes.

"Why are you laughing?" There I am again, still stuck in that stubborn angry place even as waves of relief wash over me, still testing her, still prodding the wound, still wanting her to prove herself to me. "What's so funny?"

"Us!" She doesn't stop, but reaches out and clasps my hand in hers. "Look at us!"

I take a step closer, allow my fingers to enlace hers. "What about us?"

"You are the silliest girl in the world, Jessica Stanfield. And I love you!" With a whoop that may have been of joy, she lets go of my hand and throws her arms around me, a spontaneous, generous gesture full of delight and promise, and I dissolve, hugging her back. "Sophie–"

"Shh. Don't talk." And there in front of Mr. Nelson and the whole of Provincetown we kiss, the taste of salt, the taste of her, the world is spinning around us and I don't care, it's just found its way back on its axis.

Jeannette de Beauvoir

And in that moment I find hope again.

Chapter Thirty

Summer days are long, but this one is sliding by at an alarming rate.

Sophie and I sit outside the store, holding hands, not caring. She's more daring than I: these are her people, in every sense of the word: the Portuguese community, the fishing community, the commercial community. Provincetown is her home, her only home, and she's willing to risk it to be with me, to reassure me. I'm in awe at the grandeur of the gift.

Then again, girls can hold hands and it doesn't mean anything, right?

Now that the immediate danger — the danger of losing her — is past, I'm back to worrying. Daddy has not responded, and Mr. Nelson is looking askance at us. I'm going to have to go back out to the dunes, and I don't see how I can persuade Sophie not to come with me.

Or even if I should.

Surely she, who loves me more than anyone in the world, will share my feelings about what's happening? Surely she, too, will be able to see the love between Anna and Aicelin, not so very different from what we share, and want to help them? Why is it that I even hesitate? What is it that's keeping me silent, that's forcing me to withdraw from this woman I adore even as she holds my hand and chatters on about where we'll live when her mother asks her to leave because she won't marry Peter Silva? What is it that tells me that this secret is not mine to share?

And what am I going to do about it?

I am smiling and giggling and snuggling with her, and all the while my brain is whirling, fretting, frightened. I can't risk losing her again; I feel like we just pulled back from the edge of some sort of precipice, that one more step would have spelled disaster and despair. I can't go back there; I can't lose Sophie. When I clear my mind of everything else and just focus on me, that's the most compelling truth that I won: that Sophie is my life, and that without her, I don't have anything. A future without her in it is unthinkable.

I'd rather die.

And now: how to get my girl to stand up and walk home with that same sparkle in her eye and a promise to see her soon? That's not the emotional space we're in, and the day is coming to a close more rapidly than any other summer day ever has. I need to make sure that what's happening between us is real, that it's not as fragile as it feels, that we'll be able to pick up from here sometime–I don't stop to define when that time will be–and move forward. I need to do all that, and still manage to persuade her not to come back with me to the shack, something she seems perfectly inclined to do.

Meanwhile, out on the backshore, in the dunes, a man lies dying.

She is talking about it now. "So Anna is sick? I know what we'll do. Ma has a recipe for Portuguese soup; it's what she always gives us when we're sick. Oh, and there's a liniment, too–" she wrinkles her nose at this "–that you rub on the person's chest. It smells terrible, really, really awful, Jessica, you have no idea, but it works, and I can get some of that…" Her own relief is reflected in her chatter, in her babbling; she would talk about anything, like this, right now.

Unfortunately, this is not a good topic. An image flashes into my mind: Us trudging up to Louis' shack, food and medications in hand, only to find Anna gone. "I can't imagine where she might be…" No; not a good image. I put it out of my mind quickly lest the magical thinking take over again and I create a reality I don't want.

Sophie is going on about some of the cures handed down from her grandmother. "She's from the Azores, you know, so she picked up all this stuff, who knows where. A lot of it has some kind of magic mixed in. Spells, and whatnot." She pauses, laughs. "And the evil eye! Oh, if someone's sick, that's the reason, not germs or anything like that. Someone's cursed you, it means, someone's given you the evil eye. She has all these spells against it, all these—gestures—she makes, t' ward it off." She brightens as an idea occurs to her. "Oh, Jessica, I know what we'll do! We'll go out with the dune taxi and bring Anna in town! T' my house! My mother can take care of her–she's dying t' take care of someone–and they're about the same age, anyway, and she won't tell anyone, they'll get along fine and Anna will get better."

I've painted myself into a corner and have no idea how to get out of it. "Your mother is the worst gossip in Provincetown," I say. It may or may not be true, but I have a feeling it is. "She'll talk about Anna, you know she will. So don't even consider that."

It's a quick save, but not a permanent one. "You're right," Sophie acknowledges with a sigh. "Well, then, I'll just go home and get what we need. She knows about you, I'll say it's you that's sick. She won't offer t' come with me, she thinks the back shores are haunted." My lovely twentieth-century Sophie makes the sign against the evil eye, herself, quickly, at the thought.

I have other things on my mind. "Anna has her own cures," I say. I'm still stuck somewhere back in the conversation when Sophie said that Anna and her grandmother are the same age. Impossible: the Anna I left was growing younger by the minute, immersed in love. Sophie's grandmother, Sophie has told me, has a moustache. Sophie's clearly wrong. Anna's in her forties. Could her grandmother be in her forties? "She won't want anybody else's."

She considers it, and I relax when I see her nod. "You have a point," she concedes. "But what's your father going t' do?"

"She asked me to call him," I say, seized by sudden inspiration. "You know how it is, my father and Anna have been together for years and years and years. She sees him almost as *her* father, too. She thinks he can solve anything, take care of anything." Well, one of us does, anyway.

Sophie has her head tilted to one side, like a bird. I think she's adorable. "Is that the way it is, with people working for you?" she asks, then answers her own question. "Yeah, of course it is. The men who worked on my father's boat, they were like that with my father. It was like he was their father, too. But I always thought that's 'cause we're all related here, sort of, all the Portuguese in Provincetown."

"My father could probably explain it better," I say, thinking of the study and the brown leather and the tobacco smoke and the discussions. "But I do know that it happens, is all. I mean, it's probably a little different when it's servants…" My voice trails off uncertainly. I might as well have "child of privilege" tattooed on my forehead, when I talk like that.

Sophie doesn't care; she's immersed in the idea. "Some people must become teachers, you know, or leaders, that sort of thing, because they bring out that feeling in others," she says. She's clearly thinking about how to use the concept in her writing.

I'm thinking about taking advantage of her distraction to try and work my way out of my metaphoric corner when the corner disappears altogether. The shop screen-door slams and a short, dark woman, wearing what look like carpet slippers and a kerchief, comes shooting out of it. I look up to see her bearing down on us. "So this is where I find you!" she cries triumphantly, then launches into a torrent of conversation in a language I don't understand.

I understand the punctuation, however, with perfect ease.

I'm beginning to wonder if she's confused me with someone else when Sophie sighs. "I been here for a while, Ma," she says. "Speak English."

"I dunno why I should speak English when you don't listen t' me none anyways," she snaps.

"Because we're in America, Ma," Sophie says. I have the impression it's a conversation that they've had before. I realize that we're still holding hands, facing each other, like it's a wedding ceremony or something, and I disengage my hand quickly and step back. Sophie looks amused.

"You have told me many times that you are taking care of the washing and you are not there taking care of the washing," she says.

She appears to notice me. "And you are not now telling me who you are with."

I clear my throat. "How do you do?" I say politely, putting out my hand to shake hers. "I'm—"

"So you come looking for me just 'cause I haven't done the laundry?" demands Sophie.

"I come lookin' for you 'cause you're never home no more and I need the help. I come lookin' for you 'cause I never know where you are, and your papa isn't here no more t' come lookin' for you." She adds something in Portuguese that I don't understand but which definitely sounds rude. I look at Sophie, alarmed.

She is unruffled. "Go on home, Ma," she says. "I'll be there in a few minutes."

"But you said—"

"In a few minutes, Ma!" Sophie sounds exasperated, and turns back to me as though her mother has magically disappeared. "I'm gonna have t' go do this or she's going t' follow me around all day naggin' me," she says.

I'm too busy thanking all the stars in the sky for this sudden and unexpected solution to my problem that I can't even pretend disappointment. "Never mind," I say. "We'll catch up later." I glance at her mother. "Very nice meeting you, Mrs.–um–"

"Costa," says Sophie with an elfin smile.

"–Costa," I finish. I turn back to Sophie. "I'm going to go see– um–I'm going back out to the back shore. I'll let you know." I've belatedly remember that not only can I not mention Aicelin in front of Sophie, I cannot mention Anna in front of her mother. Lies aren't just uncomfortable, they're damned difficult to maintain.

She's glaring at her mother, who is saying something else in Portuguese. "All *right*, Ma! I'm coming!" She turns to me, distracted. "I'll see you later, honey," she says, and gives me a chaste kiss in the lips. "All right, Ma, let's go!"

I watch them walk down Commercial Street, my body going weak with relief. One down. I square my shoulders and march up the steps into the shop. "Mr. Nelson!"

No matter what speculations he's been nurturing after watching us together, there's a knee-jerk response to my imperious tone. I hate myself for using it, but I need all the help I can get. "Dr. Stanfield must be occupied," I say. "When the response comes, will you please be so kind as to have the dune taxi deliver it to me?"

Brahmin Boston at its best. I am cringing inside. Mr. Nelson does everything but doff his cap. "I'll do that, Miss Stanfield."

I can't stand leaving it like this. I lean across and touch his forearm, gently. "Thank you for all your help. You're a very good person."

Before he has time to respond, I'm out of there, hurrying now. I want to rush, I want to run, to outrun the sadness and despair I'm feeling lurking just over my shoulder, the final certitude that we're on our own. On our own, and running out of options.

I don't take the dune taxi back; I don't even follow my usual route down snail road and into the dune through the copse of trees that promises much and delivers so little. I'm heading somewhere else. I walk briskly up Conwell Street, cross Route Six, and follow Race Point Road, moving off it and through the beech forest and the Province Lands with their hardscrabble vegetation, scrub trees, and from there into the dunes themselves. A hawk is circling above me, not one of the low-flying marsh hawks I see so often at the dune shack, but a red-tailed hawk, peering down to catch the movement of its prey, its vast wings using the lift of the air current to move effortlessly, circling round and round, and I feel like the prey, waiting in fear for the hawk to dive, knowing with grim inevitability that it shall, my heart hammering in anticipation of my own death.

I scramble across unknown dunes, their hills and dimples unknown and yet somehow familiar; the dunes, I know, no matter how random they feel, are mostly formed of the same curved parabolic ridges; Daddy told me this once, I don't know why it's coming to my mind now, perhaps so that I can think of anything, anything other than what lies ahead of me at the old coast guard station.

It's because of the wind. The identical parabolic shape of the dunes, I mean.

I scramble along the ridges and leave the wind and the hawk and everything else behind, and finally it is there, suddenly, as happens; it's actually very well hidden indeed. I chose the spot well.

I will not allow myself to think that I may have chosen an appropriate spot for death.

Aicelin is still alive; I can see it in Anna's face when she meets me at the door, alerted to my presence by my stumbling down the last dune and running into the structure. "*Liebchen*! So what?"

I shake my head. I'm a little breathless; I'd hurried as though driven. As, perhaps, I was. "No answer," I say. "I told them to send it with the dune taxi, but who knows, they may not even be home." I don't have to say any more; Anna knows as well as I do how often my father travels, sometimes taking my mother with him, to lecture or present a paper at a conference or teach a class for a colleague. It's a crapshoot, really, finding him at home at any given time.

She knows it; she knew it when I set off. She was desperate. I see in her face how much she was counting on this working. I want to say something, anything, to make her feel better; but there's nothing.

Maybe that's the definition of despair, then: that there are no words left to say.

We stand there for a moment, the time spinning out fine and pale between us, the silence weighing more heavily than all the sand in the dunes; and then, as though reaching a decision, she raises her shoulders, slightly, before they slump down again. "Come in, then," she whispers, and I follow her slowly and reluctantly down the rise and through the door.

There's an odor in the air, now, and I have to fight my instincts to keep from covering my nose. Was it there before, and I'd just grown accustomed to it? Or is it my journey into town and back through the dunes, with their scrubbed, washed appearance, their sharp tang of salt in the air, that has made it more obvious?

No; it is new. Before, I could smell that Aicelin's body was unwashed; now I can smell that it is dying.

Anna's eyes meet mine; she knows what I'm thinking. I'm shocked at her, too, to tell the truth: she has aged ten years in the past few days. While the first flush of love swept time away from her face, the heartache and worry has replaced it, and more. I wonder if she'll ever be the same.

I wonder if any of us will ever be the same.

I watch her as she bends over him, her hands gentle and caressing as they smooth the blanket, touch his shoulder, help him drink a little. I watch her, the tenderness in her movements, and feel my throat tightening again. To have found one's love and to lose it again seems supremely unfair.

"We need more water, *mein Engel*," she whispers to me. "Can you go to the pump at home for us? I don't want to leave him."

"Of course you shouldn't," I say, automatically. "Of course I'll go." I've been of precious little help in any other way, I think bitterly as I gather all the containers I can carry. I'll bring a bucket when I come back from the dune shack, it will be easier to carry.

It seems longer and longer every time I make it, this journey from the old coast guard station to Louis' shack. The shack seems musty. I take a few minutes to wash myself, brush my teeth, change into a fresh skirt and blouse, then I fasten my sandals and pin my hair up and head down the hill to the pump. It takes forever to prime it–we're nearing the end of the summer, and it hasn't been used every day–and my arms are aching with the effort by the time the water finally, blessedly, begins to flow.

I'm hot and wretched and unhappy. I don't think about talking with Sophie, the one source of light in my world; I feel guilty, suddenly, taking pleasure in our closeness, in the anticipation of a future together, in my delight that we really are all right, when meanwhile Aicelin is dying and Anna is in despair. My happiness seems obscene compared to what they are going through.

The buckets are heavy before they're filled and heavier after. It occurs to me, suddenly, that I'm exhausted; if I were to lie down, now, I would probably sleep for days. I take a deep breath, let it out slowly, and pick them up for the long difficult trek back to the coast guard station: spilling water now would rather negate all the effort I've just been through.

I take the regular path. It seems pointless, now, to try and disguise my route; and it's easier to stick to the ridge for as long as I can, for as far as I can.

I'm walking into the sun, lying low on the horizon now; straight ahead through the dunes is Race Point and one of the only places I've known where you can watch the sun set into the ocean. Sophie showed it to me; with her, I've sat on the beach in pleasurable anticipation, watching the sun lower slowly, imperceptibly, until it finally touches the water and sets it afire. The sunset always seems to speed up, once that happens.

But now it is in my eyes and makes my way even more difficult, even more uncomfortable. I want to be there; I don't want to be there. I've never seen anyone die, before.

I'm not sure that I want to start now.

Chapter Thirty-One

The shadows are longer by the time I'm back at the old Coast Guard station. The dunes themselves are casting shadows, the dimples and depressions in the sand dark. It is that liminal time, that time outside of time, when reality is blurred and you could swear that inanimate objects are watching you, that time when anything can happen.

I am being watched, I am quite sure; I feel the weight of a gaze on my spine; but when I turn and look, no one is there, only the dunes. They've watched me since I've come to live here, of course; but always I've felt their watching to be protective, sheltering, just as they shelter all the other creatures who come to live out here at the tip of the Cape, at the tip of the world: the eccentric, the wounded, those rejected by other, more refined society.

Today the watching has turned malevolent, and I feel the fear again, passing through my body with a force that is palpable and real.

I turn and slide down the last few steps to the old coast guard station, taking care, still, to balance my buckets of water. I have no choice but to go forward.

I wonder if any of us ever had any other choice.

It is hushed in the room where Aicelin lies dying. Anna has him propped up with what pillows she's found—I recognize mine, from the dune shack—and is sitting beside him, on the bed, holding his hand. He is conscious, awake; they have been talking together in hushed voices but stop when I arrive. There is no alarm, this time, at the sound of my arrival; they both know where this is going to end, and perhaps have already made their peace with it.

Perhaps.

I place the buckets on the floor and go over and kiss Anna on the cheek. She looks a little startled, then smiles. "*Danke, liebchen,*" she says softly. I look at Aicelin. "How do you feel?"

Amazingly, he, too, manages a smile. "There no pain is now," he says, with a touch of surprise in his voice. I glance quickly at Anna, but she is smiling, too. So they *have* made their peace with it. I envy them that: I'm still ready to scream at the impossibility of it all, the unfairness. Love in a time of war is the worst thing, it would seem, that can happen to anybody.

Except for me and Sophie, of course.

I turn away from their calm that I cannot fathom and busy myself filling flasks with water. I hand one immediately to Anna and she helps Aicelin drink. "Thank you," he says to me, and I want to cry. He says something to Anna, in a low, urgent voice, something in German; and she doesn't argue with him, though I see from her reaction that she's not happy with what he had to say. "Come here, *liebchen,*" she says to me, and I obey, looking around for a place to sit, and finally sinking cross-legged to the floor.

Aicelin is watching me. "So," he says, and it sounds like *zo*, "I thank you for what you have for me done. It is very much, Anna has told, and I am in your debt."

I'm embarrassed and don't know what to say. "I wish I could do more," I say, helplessly, feeling that I have somehow failed him, Anna, myself, the universe.

"It is much, what you done. No one else would have, for an enemy."

It's been a while since I've thought of Aicelin as an enemy. I have to stop and remind myself that a mere three days ago I hadn't even known of his existence.

He looks at Anna again, and she takes his hand and nods encouragingly. I see it again there, that spark of electricity between them, running strong and true, rippling along the skin of their arms, straight from their hearts to their fingertips. He interlaces his fingers with hers and then it is, amazingly, contentment that I sense. Contentment in the face of death. It's a new concept, and one I don't particularly want to think much about.

I clear my throat, uncomfortable with their intimacy. Aicelin looks at me, a quick bright look, and smiles again. "So I have thanked you," he says. "And now I will also you tell why I here am."

I look at Anna, alarmed, but she is still relaxed, still smiling.

Aicelin takes a deep breath before continuing. "I am from U-boat 116," he says. "We do not the submarines a name give, only a number. We left France—the submarine base at Nantes—in July for north Atlantic patrol. Are on patrol in north Atlantic." He glances at me, apparently assessing what my war knowledge really is. "It is war against trade we do," he explains. "We attack convoys, the ships who supplies to England carry. It is to England starve, so it surrenders."

I nod my understanding. I've already heard—or overheard—this and more from the late-night sessions in Daddy's study; but the information seems different here in the deepening shadows, recited as facts by someone who has lived them.

Satisfied that I understand, Aicelin goes on. "In time we are asked to join *Rudeltaktik*–wolfpack–for convoy. We in packs like this work, with radio contact, you see, so we can communicate. We have codebreakers, they–what is word?" He turns to Anna and says, "decipher?"

"It is the same word in English," says Anna in English.

"So. We have the British Merchant Marine codebook deciphering. So we know where to look for convoys, their messages tell us, yes?"

I nod.

"So. And the U-boats, they into a long patrol line in front of the convoy routes spread out." He pauses to take a drink of water. "So. Once in position, we use binoculars to look all around us, *ja*? At the horizon. We are looking for the masts of ships, or for smoke. Even at night, we this can see."

I'm thinking of the dazzle paint on the fishing boats. Not such a stupid precaution, after all.

"So. When we see something, we report it, and all the others in the wolfpack are told where is the convoy. We wait for night, and we attack. But there is not just one, we are all attacking at once. Like the wolves."

I shiver at the image, the eyes burning fiercely in the night, surrounding the prey, isolating it, moving in for the kill.

"So. This is what we do. But not so much good now. British are smart, they put out anti-submarine patrols. More and more U-boats are not coming back. It is very bad for us, bad for morale, you see?"

I nod. I'm thinking about a submarine getting hit, losing propulsion, sinking slowly to the bottom of the Atlantic, the crew alive and knowing full well what is going to happen to them, losing oxygen. It's a horrible thought.

Aicelin shrugs slightly. "So we go west, further and further vest, so we can get convoys before they reach British anti-submarine escorts. We come here," he says, the words stark and simple.

"But why come ashore?" I ask. "You're not the first one; I've see others in the dunes."

Aicelin shakes his head. "Is not always possible to do the right thing," he says with difficulty. He's getting tired now. He takes another deep breath, and this one ends in a cough. "So. Americans are not at first good about war," he says. "They do not about blackout know, so we wait until ships are standing against lights, lights from the shore, and we shoot. At first this is very effective. Then Americans start vith convoys and defend them with destroyers and airplanes, and many, many U-boats are lost. This summer, we are on last patrols off United States coast, all other U-boats are in North Atlantic, because between Greenland and Iceland there is a gap, there are no aircraft, we can still pick off convoys there."

I am wondering why I need all this information. He is clearly exhausted and getting more so. But there is a reason—no one squanders their energy like he's doing without a reason—so I say nothing.

"So. We know that in Boston is a man, he is the commander of North Atlantic aircraft. It is him who has plans for the fall."

I am staring at him. My mouth is probably open. I forget my resolution to not interrupt him. "You were sent to assassinate somebody?"

Anna makes a gesture of distress and Aicelin shakes his head. She's about to speak but, watching him, says nothing.

He looks at me. "It is crucial," he says. "We are losing all of our U-boats. So many not coming back to port. So many, too many, gone, we do not know where, we do not know how. Filled with men, good men, men with families, with dreams for better life. It is one life for many, do you see?"

"And you came ashore on the Cape because it's unguarded," I say, understanding. They could scarcely sail into Boston harbor, after all.

"Yes, it is so," Aicelin acknowledges. "It is so we can get to him. There are several of us—different groups, you see, so that if one does not make it through, others will."

The frogmen on the beach back in July, I think. And now Aicelin, and whoever was with him. "But you're alone," I point out.

"I was not to be alone," he agrees. "We are hurt. A boat, it sees us, it fires on us. My friend, he dead is right away."

"And you're hurt," I say, understanding. Aicelin didn't have Anna's 'flu; Aicelin's fever came from an injury, something internal, something awful.

"It is a miracle he did not die," says Anna, looking at him with that same odd light shining in her eyes. He squeezes her hand.

I have another objection. "If you were fired on, if somebody saw you, why didn't we hear about it? No one in Provincetown's been talking about that."

"In time of war," he says carefully, "people are told only what it is determined they need to know."

"Panic," Anna adds.

I am feeling immensely depressed. Perhaps the reality of the war is finally sinking in: that nice, good-hearted people on both sides are being told by their governments to kill each other. They pray to the same God to take their side. I remember Aicelin's earlier words: "We are all cowards now." And the waste of it is overwhelming me.

I understand less and less how Anna and Aicelin have made peace with their situation.

"So it's really bad?" I ask, desperate for a flicker of hope, a rag of good news. "You cannot move now? You cannot go–if we were able to find you transport, somehow–you cannot get back home?"

From the doorway comes the answer.

"No one's going anywhere," says Sophie.

Chapter Thirty-Two

It's as if a ghost has spoken.

Anna gasps. Aicelin doesn't move, but there is something new in his eyes, something I haven't seen there before: fear.

I'm in an awkward position on the floor. By the time I twist around and clamber up, she's advanced a few feet into the room. I start to say something and then I see what's in her hand.

Her father's gun.

"Stay still," Sophie says to me. She's looking straight at Aicelin.

Anna finds her voice. "Sophie–"

"Shut up!" It's a voice I don't recognize as my love's, and there's something cold clutching at my heart right now. Stupidly, because I don't know what else to say, I repeat her name. "Sophie–"

"Shut up, I said!" But her gaze shifts from him to me. "How could you, Jessica?"

"You don't understand," I say, urgently. "He's not–"

"I know exactly what he is," she says, and now I've identified what it is in her voice that seems so unfamiliar: it's hatred. It's so not part of who Sophie is, who I believe her to be–no, who I know her to be–that I'm sure I must be misunderstanding.

I must be misunderstanding.

Anna isn't trying to understand; she knows what she has to do. Slowly, she stands up. "Sophie, there is no threat here," she says in a clear, steady voice, devoid of all inflection: not Anna's voice at all.

"Shut up," says Sophie again, and her voice is as empty as the polar wastes, I want to cover my ears so I don't hear what she's saying, my darling, articulate girl, my writer, reduced to words of hatred, to words of fear. Please don't do this, I plead with her silently. Don't do this. Don't become one of them.

She takes another step into the room. "All this time," she says in that same, distant voice, "all this time, I thought you were my friends."

"We are your friends," says Anna.

"He's not!" She gestures with the gun, and we all jump a little. "He killed my father!"

I find my voice again. "That's ridiculous, Sophie! You can't think that–"

"Shut *up*, Jessica." She doesn't spare me a glance: I have become insignificant to her. She is cold now, focused, dismissing my interruption as if I were an importune child.

I'm not going to let this happen. I am not going to lose everything I care about in these lonely dunes, on this starlit night. I'm *not*. "Sophie, stop it! Look at me! This isn't going to help anything!" I take a step closer to her. "It won't bring your father back–"

"Don't call me that! Don't you *ever* call me that again!"

There's a sudden sharp pain in my chest, and I wonder, for a fleeting moment, if I've been shot. It's horrible pain, as if all my insides were involved, as if my heart were trying to push its way out of my chest. I haven't been shot; perhaps I wish I have. Perhaps that would be better than losing her this way. Because in that bleak moment I know that I've lost, I know that no matter what happens, now, in this room, it's over. I've lost her, I've lost my life. I've lost it all.

The stillness after that is oppressive. And then, into that horrible tense silence, Aicelin speaks.

"You are right to hate me," he says. "You are right. If I did not your father kill, I have others like him killed. I was on the boat. I have done these things."

She doesn't say anything, but her hands holding the gun are trembling infinitesimally. I find myself thinking, irrelevantly, how heavy it must be.

Anna doesn't like what Aicelin is doing, I can see that, she makes a small supplicant gesture toward him with her hands; but she doesn't take her eyes off Sophie, as if willing her to stop with her gaze, as if by not looking away she can keep the next page from turning.

He's the only one Sophie's allowing to speak, anyway.

"You hate me and that is what in a time of war happens," he continues. "You will probably kill me, and that is what happens, too. I cannot stop you from doing that—look at me! I am a poor excuse for an officer of the Third Reich! And who is to say which is worse? You will out of love and hatred kill. I killed because I was ordered to. Your way, perhaps, is the better one."

I gasp. Anna's eyes haven't left Sophie.

"But you cannot forever hate," Aicelin goes on. "The hatred only means that more people like me, people who never for anything but a quiet life asked, will be ordered to kill more. It cannot go on."

"My father," says Sophie steadily, "asked for a quiet life, too. And my brother."

"*Ja*," he agrees. "Your father, your brother, they are fishermen, *ja*? And me, I am lawyer. They should not die. I should not die."

"*You should die!*" she blazes. "You *should* die! You killed! You killed my family! You killed and you were going t' go on killing! My father never killed anyone!"

He lifts his shoulders in surrender. "You kill me now," he says, "and you may better feel. Perhaps for a moment, perhaps for a while, it will be good. You will better feel. You will feel justice is done. But it is not that easy." He looks exhausted, I cannot imagine what this speech is taking out of him. I wonder, too, why he's pleading for his life; surely he knows that he is dying? "I see what sort of person you are. I know from Jessica what sort of person you are. And when you kill, it will touch your soul."

"Like it touched yours?" Sarcasm, now.

He smiles, but there's no warmth in the smile, it's touched with an early and eerie frost. "Perhaps one day, if I myself to feel allowed," he acknowledges. "Perhaps then it would have to me happened. But I did not see the people I killed. I stayed in my U-boat. It takes a long time for that kind of killing to touch the soul."

"There's only one kind of killing," Sophie says.

I'm still looking at Aicelin, and I'm realizing why he's saying all this. It's Sophie he wants to save, not himself.

Anna's still watching Sophie, a reflection of some sort of sick fascination, revulsion, on her face. Maybe it's up to me to do something, I think, and cast my eyes around the room for inspiration. It is dark now, fully dark, and the one lamp Anna had burning when

I got here isn't casting enough light to read by, much less locate anything. And what would I be looking for, anyway? A weapon I'd know how to use? A weapon I could use against a gun?

A weapon I could use against *Sophie*?

Aicelin seems ready to concede her point. "You perhaps right are," he says. "And now it is I who shall be spared, spared the haunting of my soul that comes with killing." He stops and coughs, the cough going into a convulsion. He regains a little control, enough to finish his thought. "I will be spared. But you will not."

"No," agrees Sophie, and pulls the trigger.

As she does, Anna moves. Not far, but quickly, putting herself between Sophie and the figure on the bed, between life and death. The sound is deafening, echoing off the walls, I never imagined gunshot to be so loud.

And then the smoke clears slightly and Anna is lying on the floor, motionless, and my throat constricts. *No no no no no…* I am down next to her, touching her face, feeling for a pulse, for a breath, for anything. Not Anna. Not Anna.

She is dead and so, apparently, is Aicelin. A heart attack? A ricochet? Something that he knew was going to happen even as he engaged Sophie in conversation?

She is still standing there, the gun in her hand, a dazed look on her face. The room is filled with the acrid smell of gunpowder, ugly and heavy and bitter. There's smoke, too, actual smoke; I didn't know that guns did that, either.

I look at Sophie, and there really isn't that much between us. Just a few feet… and one small death.

***

I stumble out into the night. The moon has risen—it's full, or nearly so—and the dunes are bleached white and ghostly beneath it. I'm running without knowing where I'm running to, running down to the beach, the roar of the waves louder than I remember it. I am crying and screaming and running and not paying much attention to where I am going.

It's over. Everything is over. My life is over, too, and by the time I calm down and am walking more soberly, exhausted, I find myself by the water's edge, and the obvious thought floats unbidden into my mind. Just make sure everything is over; swim out and keep swimming until there's nothing left to do but die. You wouldn't really feel it then; you'd be so exhausted. The waves would just take you.

I keep running along the shoreline, I run until I'm too exhausted to think. I am gasping for breath; my side seizes up in pain. I want to run forever, to escape what I left behind there, not just Anna and Aicelin, but Sophie and what she has somehow become.

I slow my running to a walk, half bent over, crying and pulling in great gasps of air at the same time.

I've been making my way down from Race Point and I realize, soon, that despite my blind escape, I've in fact come home. Here is a stretch of sand that I recognize; there's where the piping plovers nest, their fast little legs taking them skimming over the sand as though on wheels. Here is where I've swum close enough—almost close enough—to touch the seals that come and regard me with such curiosity.

Here is where I first met Sophie…

Sophie! It's a strangled cry. Sophie, who will never again hold me or laugh with me or talk to me. The chasm between us is too great; even I understand that now. I draw in a long, shuddering, hiccupping breath.

I am wrapped in loss. The loss of Anna, my family, my childhood. The loss of life, which I've never before seen. The loss of Sophie, the only love I've ever known–the only one I will ever know, I tell myself as if it were obvious: we were made for each other, soulmates, and now there is no one, there is nothing ahead of me. It would be easier to die than to feel this loss, this howling, overwhelming loss. There's pain blazing like fire inside my chest; I am burning from the inside out.

I've come to our own stretch of beach now, and I still have no idea what to do. I fling myself down onto the sand and sob again, taking great handfuls of it up and throwing them uselessly toward the bluff. I think I'm screaming words–words like *why?* And *how could you?* And I want to die; but mostly I'm just aware of the fire inside me, the need for annihilation. The world is over. How can I go on? How can I wake up tomorrow morning and face a life without these people in it, a life where others will want to take their place, a world where others will never even have heard of them?

I turn and sit and sob some more, my hands on my face, sand everywhere, I don't care. The tide is high, the waves lapping at my feet, familiar as an old friend, comforting and ordinary and constant, yet tonight they have betrayed me, tonight I will not be comforted by them. The ocean, the dunes, it is all an artificial landscape, the background for an avant-garde and not very good play. The water is bright with the reflection of the moon; everything is clear.

Including the gunshot.

I have no strength left, but I find it somehow, magically, strength enough to scramble up the cliff of sand, up the bluff, flying fast past the well and up the path to Louis' shack, the dune shack, our shack. No, please no, not this, not her. There's a light on inside, I can see it now, dim by comparison with the moonlight flooding the dunes and making them into a lunar landscape, a reflection of itself, cold and uncaring. Up the stairs, quickly, *no*, across the porch, my heart hammering, *no, no, please no,* pulling open the screen door, stopping abruptly in the doorway.

I suppose it was the only thing she felt she had left to do. But still I sit and cradle her head in my arms and talk to her until dawn, not paying attention anything but her, not to the blood or the gun or even to the cold knowledge of finality, the ache at the end of things.

About the Author

Jeannette de Beauvoir is a writer by day and a reader by night. Her work has been translated into 12 languages and has appeared in 15 countries, and she's determined to eventually visit them all. In the meantime, she works to support her caffeine habit and the rigid entertainment schedule required by her cat. She ignores tweets but can be occasionally seen lurking on Facebook at www.facebook.com/Jeannette.de.Beauvoir.author.

Acknowledgments

My first thanks go to the Outer Cape Artist in Residence Consortium, which enabled me to live for two weeks at the Margo-Gelb dune shack, my model for Louis' shack in Our Lady of the Dunes. OCARC is made up of four non-profit organizations: three arts organizations [the Fine Arts Work Center in Provincetown (FAWC), the Provincetown Art Association and Museum (PAAM), Truro Center for the Arts at Castle Hill (Castle Hill)] and a dune shack advocacy group, the Peaked Hill Trust (PHT). I wrote the first 350 pages of this novel on a typewriter while living out there in the sand and the sky and the sea, and couldn't have found this story anywhere else. And also many thanks to the Museum of World War II (museumofworldwarii.org) in Boston.

Thanks also to my first readers, in particular Fred Biddle and Maria Nazos (the former Commercial Street Writers!), Dianne Kopser (who coined an unfortunate nickname for me after reading the book), and to Paul (Not The Painter) Cézanne. A special thank you to brilliant cover artist Kyre Song, designer extraordinaire, and the amazing Arthur Mahoney of HomePort Press, who made it real. And, finally, to Lukas Ortiz, who never gives up.

Did You Enjoy This Book?

If you did…

• please share your opinion on Goodreads, Amazon, BN.com, and Powell's.

• visit my Amazon page and read some of my other books.

• give the book a boost on by telling people about it on Facebook and Twitter.

• subscribe to The Novelist's Notebook at www.JeannetteDeBeauvoir.com (scroll to bottom of page) for book reviews, short stories, quizzes, free stuff, previews of upcoming work, and more.

• ask your local bookseller to stock *Our Lady of the Dunes.*

• make it your choice for our next book club meeting (I'll even join you by Skype if you'd like me to!)

• email me at jeannettedebeauvoir@gmail.com and tell me so!